MOOR

A MODERN RETELLING OF SHAKESPEARE OTHELLO

TWISTED BARD

GIOVANNA REAVES

TWISTED BARD

A retelling of Shakespeare's Othello

BLURB

Loyalty is sacred; betrayal is unforgivable.

Des, a young doctor who has always followed his parents' expectations, is inexperienced in love and life. That all changes the night he operates on a dangerously handsome patient. Des's growing attraction quickly turns into an irresistible desire.

Othello, bound by loyalty to his family's code, has just been named the successor to Verona Heights' most powerful underground organization, La Famiglia Romano. With immense responsibility weighing on him, he believes there's no room for love—until a certain doctor catches his eye.

As passion ignites between Des and Othello, a dark conspiracy against Othello threatens to tear them apart and endanger their lives, forcing them to confront their fears and desires.

Can they survive the treacherous forces working against them, or will their love be destroyed forever?

This modern-day retelling of Shakespeare's Othello is filled with betrayal, loyalty, romance, and a little love at first sight. Part of the Twisted Bard series, where multiple authors bring the Bard's timeless tales into the present.

"She loved me for the dangers I had passed, And I loved her that she did pity them."
Othello— (Act 1, Scene 3)

FIND ME ON SOCIAL MEDIA

I love hearing from you. Email me at <u>GotRomance@GiaReaves.com</u> or sign up for my newsletter to receive updates on what I'm doing next.

Check out my website for more deals and more: https://giareaves.com

Join my reader's group:

https://www.facebook.com/ groups/

 facebook.com/Giovanna.PM.Reaves

 instagram.com/giareaves

 tiktok.com/@giarwrites

 reamstories.com/giovannareaves

 youtube.com/@giovannareaves5712

BOOKS BY GIOVANNA REAVES

Goliath's Mate: G-Force Federation (Book Three)

ALSO BY GIOVANNA REAVES

Bewitching Love: A Valentine Romance (Vale Valley Series)

Love is in the air, and Vale Valley's magic is bringing lonely hearts together.

Love is in the air, and Vale Valley's magic is bringing lonely hearts together.

Sirius is a skilled doctor and a witch who has always been a loner.

Being a witch in the human world has been hard on him since he cannot use his magic for fear of revealing himself. After years of

hearing about Vale Valley, he packs up everything he has, hoping to have a new start and be his true self. But with a new life comes new experiences, information, and things he wasn't aware were possible. Will Sirius be able to handle the changes coming with his new life, especially when the bewitching take effect?

After the death of his grandfather Trenton Vale twenty years ago,

Alphonso and his parents left Vale Valley. Although he keeps in contact with his extended family, he can no longer ignore Vale

Valley's magic calling out to him. He returns home for what should have been a short visit. As a single father, his only goal was

to let his daughter experience the wonder of the small town he still holds close to his heart. A chance meeting with the cute

doctor makes him want to reconsider moving back to Vale Valley permanently.

Bewitching Love is the twelfth book in the second season of the

Vale Valley series. It is a heartwarming story of two men falling in love and building their new lives together.

Thank you, Shane, for the opportunity to write Moor. I had a lot of fun stretching my writing legs. You are the best.

ACT I

"She loved me for the dangers I had passed, / And I loved her that she did pity them."
Othello (Act 1, Scene 3)

Othello Romano-Moor looked appreciatively around the abandoned warehouse that was converted for the late-night meeting between the Falcon and the La Romano Famiglia clans. His men had done a good job making it amenable. The dimly lit room had a single table surrounded by stone-faced men as tension rose between the two factions, both part of Verona Heights' underworld.

As the newly appointed successor and underboss, Othello sat on the right of his adopted father, Alessandro Romano, the don of La Romano Famiglia, at one end of the table. On Alessandro's left side was his adopted brother and best friend, Iago Romano, the family's consigliere.

Don Alessandro was a robust man in his early sixties, with dark, wavy hair and slightly graying temples. He recently needed a cane due to a slowly healing injury to his left leg. Behind the three men stood their soldiers, watching their backs, not to mention the ones outside guarding the warehouse.

Across from the Romanos were the Falcons, led by the young and inexperienced Don Julian Falcon, who had just assumed leadership after his father's untimely death. His trusted advisors, seasoned but wary, stood behind him, their eyes scanning the room for any sign of danger. However, Julian's father's death was not the reason for their meeting.

Four weeks ago, Don Francesco Rizzo had been murdered under the combined efforts of the Falcon and the Romano factions, leaving no successors. Now,

Alessandro and Julian were both in a hostile takeover, vying for the most lucrative assets of Rizzo's properties and select clan members.

Since Central Verona was a neutral territory, they wanted the business in the surrounding areas. For years, Don Rizzo had accumulated a lot of prime real estate, taking out anyone who went up against him. He only trusted his consigliere, who'd also died in the shootout. One thing Othello appreciated about Rizzo was that he had a good eye for business and knew how to hide his criminal activities very well.

Othello knew Don Alessandro wanted to consolidate all the businesses in the East Bridge's financial district, Midtown, and River Front, which had a high concentration of tourists, shopping, gambling, and extortion operations, but most importantly, the ports that controlled what came and went from the city. He also wanted the Old Town; the South Shore was prime for real estate value. The don was willing to give up the East Side and West End properties, even though they were ripe and had more potential than Rizzo had been willing to put into them, which was why Falcon felt Alessandro was giving him scraps.

"I don't see why the fuck we should settle for crumbs," Julian growled, slamming his fist on the table. "What the fuck? We did most of the heavy lifting. The financial district should be ours."

"Watch your mouth, youngin," Iago snapped. "Know who you're talking to and show the don some respect, so mind your fucking language."

Othello hid his smirk behind his hand. He knew how much Iago hated it when others spoke to the don disrespectfully.

Alessandro leaned back in his chair, his expression a mask of calm, but Othello could see the anger in the don's gaze even from where he sat. "You and your men certainly played a part in offing Rizzo and his lieutenants, but let's not forget who provided the intelligence, most of the resources, and did the cleanup. If it weren't for us, the cops would be breathing down your necks right now!"

"Should I be fucking grateful?" Julian barked.

"You should be on your fucking knees begging the don not to kill you right here and now," Iago hissed.

Don Julian went to speak, but Othello interjected in a deep and steady voice: "One of our family mottos is never regretting your choices."

"Family motto," Julian scoffed. "I've heard you lot have a shitload of them. How the hell do you keep track of them all?"

Othello didn't respond and continued to speak as if the man hadn't said anything. "We agreed on the property division before we went into this." He steepled his fingers, looking Julian in the face. "Trying to change the terms now is not only unfair, it's dishonorable—something I knew
your father wouldn't have done."

"Don't you fucking bring my father into this," Julian snarled.

Othello felt Falcon's lieutenants' heated gazes, adding more tension to the room and conversation. He could have cut it with a knife, but didn't remove his eyes from Julian. However, Othello was unfazed by intimidating looks. He'd dealt with people like Falcon before. Even with his guards covering his back, Othello knew that Falcon was scared of the three of them.

"If you haven't noticed, I'm not my father," he sneered.

"Pity," Iago said. "He at least knew his place."

"Look who is talking about his place," Falcon countered, and the guard behind him sniggered. "Isn't your place to follow behind Othello's ass? Everyone knows how worthless you are."

Iago went to respond, but a commotion halted the words on his tongue. The entire room fell silent as the sound of gunfire echoed through the warehouse walls. The room descended into chaos as the men from both factions drew their weapons and pointed them at each other.

"What the fuck is going on?" Don Alessandro barked, rising to his feet with the aid of his cane. "Are you trying to stab us in the back, Falcon?"

Just then, the doors burst open, and a La Romano Famiglia guard staggered in with a gunshot wound to his side. "Ambush!" he managed to gasp before collapsing.

Othello sprang into action just as he saw the faction leaders exchanging quick, suspicious glances at each other, conveying the same thought.

You stabbed us in the back!

Before Othello or anyone had time to dwell on that thought, bullets flew into the room, and sounds of shattering and splintering wood filled the air. Thinking quickly, Othello shoved Don Alessandro behind him and then flipped the table over, using it as cover.

"Stay down," Othello yelled, but his voice was barely heard over the sound of gunfire.

In all the commotion, he'd lost sight of Iago, who he
was certain was next to him when it all happened. Putting
his worry for Iago aside, he focused on getting them out of
there alive. Using the table as cover, Othello remained standing, aiming his gun, and fired at any moving target. Bullets
were coming and going from all directions as both factions
took cover, unsure of who they were fighting against. Amid the
chaos, Othello felt a searing pain tear through him, causing
him to clutch his chest, stumbling back and struggling for a
second to stay on his feet.

"Boss, you're hit!" Tallen, one of his most loyal soldiers,
shouted, rushing over to him.

Gritting his teeth through the pain, he waved off Tallen's
worry. "Don't worry about me. I'm fine." He pushed Tallen next
to Alessandro. "Protect the don. No matter what happens to
me, get him out of here alive."

Tallen nodded, and Othello turned his focus back on the
shitstorm happening. He was no doctor, but he could tell his
wound was serious. The table had been a good cover for the
moment, but it wasn't foolproof. If whoever shot had perfect
aim, they would have hit his heart. He didn't want to think that
someone was gunning for him because that would make no
sense when everyone had bullets flying full speed at them.
Othello was just happy that the don hadn't gotten hurt. His
other worry was Iago. He prayed his friend was still alive.

Sweat drenched his body, mixing with his blood-soaked
shirt. He stumbled when he felt another burning sensation in
his side too close to his ribs, causing him to stagger a little and
hit his head on the table so hard his vision blurred, and he
could feel blood running down the side of his face. But it didn't
stop him from firing his gun until it ran out of bullets. He
hurriedly fumbled for a fresh magazine.

During the confusion, Othello couldn't help but wonder
what faction the attackers were from. *How come they have so*

many fucking expendable men? Just as the thought crossed his mind, there was a loud whistle that cut through the gunfire, and the attackers began to withdraw as if they had accomplished their objective, which was unclear to everyone, but their damage didn't go unnoticed. The warehouse looked like a war zone.

The warehouse suddenly fell into an eerie silence. The air was thick with smoke, and the stench of blood, along with the groans of the wounded, interrupted the stillness. Othello stumbled once more and knew he was going to hit the ground hard this time. But he was saved when an arm wrapped around his waist, allowing him to lean on someone.

"Hold on, Son," came Alessandro's deep voice next to his ear. "Someone come help us!"

Othello looked at the older man and smiled, hoping to ease the worry etched in the don's eyes. Othello wanted to say something, but his knees weakened and buckled, bringing him down despite the don holding him up.

"Boss!" Tallen rushed over, knelt next to him, and pulled his shirt open, hissing. "Fuck, boss, it's..."

"I know," Othello gasped. He didn't need to hear how bad it was. The bottom line was that he was fucked.

Tallen pulled off his jacket and pressed it to his injuries, making him wince.

"Hold on, Othello, we'll get you some help soon," Alessandro said, patting him on the shoulder.

Othello looked at Don Alessandro, feeling his strength waning, but he needed to know. "Who...were they?" he panted, gritting his teeth since it was hard to utter a word.

"I don't know yet," Alessandro replied grimly. "But we'll find out."

Othello tried to move, but Tallen stopped him. "Boss, don't move."

Just then, Don Falcon approached them with a slight limp.

"This wasn't us, Romano," Falcon said. "We were just as blindsided by everything as you guys."

Alessandro sighed, giving a slight nod. "We'll deal with that later. Right now, we need to get our men to safety."

Othello listened to both dons come to an uneasy truce, but he kept looking around for Iago. Grabbing Tallen's arm, he got his subordinate's attention.

"What is it, Boss?"

He was about to ask about Iago when the man's deep voice rang out in the room, putting Othello's worry to rest.

"Don, we need to go. The cops are coming!" Iago informed them, rushing to their side. His eyes widened when he saw Othello. "Fuck, O, what the hell, man? How did you get shot?"

Othello would have cracked a joke at the moment, like saying it was part of the job to protect the don, but he was in too much pain to speak. Seconds later, the don gave out a few orders just as they heard sirens wailing in the distance, letting them know they didn't have much time before they got there. Othello could only hope his injuries didn't slow their escape.

"Tallen and Iago, get Othello to the car. Marco, clean up his blood. Leave no trace that we were here," Don Alessandro commanded just as Othello started to go in and out of consciousness.

Iago and Tallen gently lifted Othello. He wanted to stop them and tell them to leave, because with every movement, he felt as if his chest was going to split open and he was going to bleed to death. In the background, he heard Don Falcon ordering his men to sweep the place and get the fuck out. Once outside, Iago and Tallen carefully loaded him into the car, but he could feel his condition worsening by the second. He knew his head was on Don Alessandro's lap and his legs on Tallen's thighs. Othello couldn't tell if it was his sweat or his blood, but his back was soaking wet.

"Papa," Iago said. "His injuries are too..." "I'm fine," he panted, cutting Iago off.

Othello knew he was about to die, but as long as his family was safe, it was all that mattered to him. Grunting, he held on to Iago, trying to sit up but being pushed back down.

"What the fuck do you think you're doing? Iago shouted. "And you're not fucking fine. You have a damn hole in your chest and no exit wound. How you're still awake and trying to move around is a mystery to me."

Othello gave a weak smile, closing his eyes and being comforted by Iago's ranting. He knew the day he died, he'd hear his friend cursing him to hell and back as he felt his consciousness slipping deep, and there was nothing else he could say as he heard Tallen shouting his name.

* * *

"QUIET," Alessandro said, his tone soft but speaking many volumes about why he was the Don of the Famiglia Romano. They had gotten away from the warehouse with a minute to spare before the cops arrived.

"Don, are you sure it's the right decision to take him to the hospital?" Iago said. "We could get our in-house doctor to patch him up while we find a doctor to take care of him. If we take him to the hospital, the cops will know we were at the warehouse tonight."

"Iago, shut the fuck up," Alessandro snarled. "Look at him and tell me if he can wait!"

"Papa, I…"

Alessandro held up a hand, stopping Iago's nattering. He sighed, pinching the bridge of his nose. He couldn't deny that Iago was right. Taking Othello to the hospital would put them in the bullseye of the cops—well, the ones that weren't on his payroll. As crazy as it might sound, for as long as he had been the leader of a criminal organization, having a member of his family getting fatally shot was on his bingo list for confirming the rumors of those he did legitimate business with. To those in certain parts of Verona Heights, the Romano family's wealth came from a prosperous construction company that had been in the family for years.

We have to have somewhere to hide the bodies.

But Alessandro didn't care if the family was found out to be a criminal syndicate. He couldn't lose his precious son. Othello wasn't his flesh and blood, but that was only semantics. He wasn't a doctor, but he could tell that Othello would die if they didn't get to the hospital soon.

"Marco, how far are we?" he asked.

"We'll be here in five seconds," came the answer, but Marco wasn't the one to respond. Looking at the passenger seat, Alessandro realized Julian Falcon was in the car with them. "I have someone working in the emergency room tonight. I let them know we're coming in hot, and he'll keep things on the hush-hush, but it looks like your guy will need surgery, and I don't know if he'll be able to help."

"Thank you." Alessandro nodded. "I'm grateful for any help right now."

"Think nothing of it. We're allies, after all," Julian said, looking down at Othello.

Alessandro looked at Othello, unable to hide his worry.

This kid has always been giving him trouble ever since the day he and Iago came up with the scheme to pick his pocket. He'd allowed them to do whatever they wanted and brought them into a world that most would warn their kids to stay away from. Othello was a curious child he'd guided to his adulthood. Othello was intelligent and tactical, took no prisoners, was loyal, and lived by the family and his own moral code, even in a criminal world, which was something Alessandro admired. Those were some of the reasons he chose Othello as his successor.

He knew which of his sons could handle the pressure of being the boss. Othello was decisive and never backed down from his mistakes; he only learned from them. He had once thought that he'd scared Othello with one of his actions, but instead, the boy wholeheartedly embraced his world. Many would question his parenting skills, but he knew how strong his boys were, just as he knew the risks of the world he brought them into. Alessandro didn't care if he lost all his material things. He could regain them again; he just couldn't survive without his sons and wife, who was going to kill him when she found out about her precious Othello. But he couldn't worry about that; now, he had to focus on keeping his son alive.

The car stopped abruptly, pulling Alessandro from his thoughts. He watched Tallen rush out of the car without anyone ordering him to and disappear into the hospital. Not even a minute later, he returned with hospital staff pushing a gurney. Without saying a word, the staff got to work whisking Othello away, leaving Alessandro and the rest to follow behind them.

While the staff worked on Othello, Alessandro stood aside, refusing to let them draw the hospital curtains blocking him from his son but not wanting to get in their way, while his instincts were telling him to take control of everything. Still, he would only make the situation worse. He didn't look away from the doctors working furiously when he felt a presence next to him, but he knew who it was.

"This changes everything," he muttered. "We might be rivals, but I have a lot of respect for Othello. Whoever did this knew when and where to strike."

Alessandro nodded as his admiration for the young don grew. "We'll find them and then make them pay," he said, his voice low.

"Yes," Julian responded, then groaned, causing Alessandro to take his eyes off his son. That's when he noticed that Julian was bleeding from his left shoulder.

"You should get that looked at." He looked around and saw two of Falcon's guards standing not far from him. "Get him looked at."

"Yes, Don Alessandro," they answered together.

One of the men stepped over to Julian and was about to lead him away when the young man held up a hand. "Let me say this before I go. I didn't lose any of my men tonight. Sure, we got a few scrapes here and there, but

nothing as severe as your son."

"What are you saying?" Alessandro asked, feeling as if he knew where Falcon was going, but he needed to hear the words.

"I know it was chaotic in there, but I'm certain all this was to take Othello out. Like I said, we came out with minor injuries. He's the only one on death's door."

If what he said was true, Alessandro couldn't let this matter go on for too long. He had to have his people look into it. They both nodded, coming to an understanding, and then Julian's men led him away. When they were out of sight and hearing distance, Alessandro turned to Iago.

"Contact our people at the police station and tell them

to collect everything the police might have found tonight at the warehouse. Then, Iago, I want you to do this discreetly. Investigate our people."

"Papa, you're not thinking that one of our people did this?"

"What am I supposed to think? If he dies, Maria will never forgive me," he said, looking at the hospital staff still working on Othello, whose blood now soaked their scrubs, bed, and floor. "Find out who set this up, Iago, and bring them to me."

"Yes, Papa."

Iago didn't leave right away, and Alessandro could feel his

reluctance. Alessandro knew Iago was worried about his brother. They had been close since childhood, sharing woes and joys.

"Go, I'll keep you in the loop," Alessandro told him.

Iago sighed, hugged him, then left. Minutes after Iago left, the doctor approached Alessandro.

"Doctor, how's my son?" Alessandro asked.

"He's stable for now. We got the bullet out, but it caused a lot of damage that will require surgery immediately."

"Do whatever it takes," Alessandro told him, his tone raw and emotional. "Just save my son."

"I'll make sure he gets the best on staff." He smiled and then turned to the nurse at his side. "Contact Doctor Ellington. Let him know he's needed in the ER."

"Yes, Doctor." The nurse left, but the doctor stayed.

"Is there something else?" Alessandro asked.

"Yes, I must warn you. The surgeon will have questions. Normally, we need to report a gunshot wound to the police."

"Then get someone else, or you do it," Alessandro said.

"I'm not as good as he is. He's our youngest and best surgeon on staff, and with him, your son will live; with me, you'd be taking too many risks. His heart stopped once already. I don't want to take the chance. Julian might be my brother, but I know even he wouldn't be able to protect me if your son dies by my hand."

Just as Alessandro was about to speak, the machines around Othello started beeping madly. The doctor cursed and ran to his side, barking out orders that Alessandro couldn't understand. "Fuck, we need to get him to the OR now. Tell them we're coming!"

Before Alessandro could ask any questions, they wheeled Othello away.

"Sir, I need you to follow me to the operating waiting room," a nurse told him. They could not move too fast because of his hurt leg, so the gurney with Othello was long gone. "We're about to have your son operated on, and I will need you to sign off on it."

"Get me the paperwork now," he ordered gently. As they walked, she handed him a clipboard. He scanned it, signed his name, and returned it to her. Once they got to the waiting room, Alessandro released a breath he hadn't realized he was holding. He looked around the room, spotting the rest of his men. "Tallen, spread the word until we know Othello is fine— no one tells Maria."

"Yes, Don." Tallen ran off to do his bidding.

Alessandro sat in a chair and dropped his head in his hands, sending prayers to every god in the universe, begging them not to take his son from him. He was going to kill whoever did this. Someone must have thought he had become soft and that they could strike at him by taking out his beloved son. They had another thing coming because he would wreak havoc on their lives when he found them.

"Marco, find out who the surgeon is and how we can ensure he doesn't talk. See who's on our payroll, who's a part of the hospital board," he said, looking up at his soldier. "Also, get me the name of everyone who died and got hurt."

"Yes, Don."

With everyone gone off to do the tasks he ordered, Alessandro leaned back in his chair and waited because that was all he could do.

SCENE II

DES

Desmond Ellington, or Des to those close to him, was the surgeon on call. He had just completed one surgery and was preparing for another. He'd gotten the report on Othello Romano-Moor, his patient, who was in critical condition. Doctor Moretti stabilized him before removing the bullet.

Still, there were fragments near major blood vessels, posing several risks to the patient's survival, which was why he needed to operate immediately. Des knew it was going to be a long and difficult surgery.

Once he was ready, Des entered the operating room and

greeted the staff. With their masks on, Des couldn't tell who they were, but he knew that he had never worked with this group of staff before. He wasn't sure why that thought came to him at such a moment, but he couldn't deny that he had questions and hoped to get the answers later.

"Alright, people, talk to me." He walked over to examine the X-ray again.

"His vitals are stable," Nurse Campos said.

Des nodded, then moved to Mister Moor's side. For a second, his brain stuttered. He had never taken notice of the people he operated on, or anyone else for that matter. But he couldn't take his eyes off the impressively built man lying on the operating table. He was far too good-looking to ignore, even in his dire state. Des's eyes traveled down Moor's body, taking in every aspect of his light bronze skin, his chest, and the tattoos on his arms, stopping at his fingers that were even inked with letters he couldn't quite read because of the position he was lying in.

Des was thankful that Moor's bottom half was covered, or he'd feel like a straight-up perv the way he was checking the man out. But still, he couldn't help but wonder if that thing was just as remarkable as the rest of his body. He felt his face heat up at what he was thinking.

"Doctor, are you okay?" Nurse Campos asked, snapping him out of his perverted thoughts.

"Y-yeah." Des cleared his throat, hoping no one noticed he was checking out the guy he was about to operate on. "Let's get to work. We have a life to save."

Someone turned on the music as the team began working in sync like a well-oiled machine. Des made the incision and got down to business, keeping his eyes and ears on the patient's vitals. He could see the damage from the bullets and was amazed the man was still alive. He kept searching for the first fragments that were near a very delicate spot near the pulmonary artery, and just as he got close to the fragment, the machines started beeping widely.

"Doctor, he's crashing," Nurse Campos announced.

"I know that, dammit," Des snapped.

Des worked furiously to retrieve the fragment, but he was having some difficulty due to all the bleeding. He barked orders, mentally blocking out the beeps and using his instincts to search for the fragment. Since becoming a surgeon, Des hadn't lost one patient, and he didn't plan on losing one now.

"Come on, come on," Des muttered to himself. "We're not losing you tonight, handsome, so stay the fuck away from the light."

In the next second, Des struck gold, clasping the fragment and slowly pulling it out. He quickly attended to the bleeding just as the machine slowed down, going back to normal, but Des couldn't breathe in relief yet; he still had to get the other fragment. His brows creased tighter when he realized the fragment was another bullet that, if it had gone any closer, would have pierced Moor's lungs.

Fuck, how did Doctor Morreti miss this?

Adding that to his list, Des focused on the matter at hand. His hands moved with expert grace and speed, every motion deliberate and precise, putting every bit of his energy into keeping the patient alive. The minutes flicked into hours before he could say the surgery was complete. Othello Moor was still in critical condition but no longer knocking on death's door. Des twisted his head from side to side, working out the kinks as he stretched his aching back, then stepped from the operating table, exhaustion etched on his face, but he was satisfied with his work.

"Well done, everyone. We saved another life." The operating staff clapped, relief evident in their eyes.

Des nodded to his team, leaving them to clean up and going to the waiting room to speak to the Moor family. Although he had saved another life, becoming a doctor hadn't been his dream since growing up. Truthfully, he'd wanted to be an artist, but trying to express those ideas to his parents, who were doctors and administrators of the hospital he worked for, was completely out of the question.

To them, he could never make it as an artist like the greats, and he should just give it up. He was their son, had a legacy to continue, and was groomed from early on to take up the mantle. And they made sure he did by setting the structure of his education and limiting who he could hang out with. He was the youngest graduate in his high school and medical school, and later, he was a hospital resident who was sometimes envied and sometimes liked by the hospital staff.

Des couldn't deny he was good at what he did. He was confident, with a very steady hand, but there were times he wished he could buck the parental system and do what he wanted. He would quit being a doctor and return to college, getting his fine arts degree and having the life he'd strived for. At twenty-six, Des had become so accustomed to them taking over his life that he wasn't sure if he was living their lives or his. While most medical students were just starting out, he was a third-year resident. It was only recently, after he had moved out of the family home, that he gained control of his bank accounts.

Hell, I'm still a virgin, for crying out fucking loud.

Des was born with the mark of a carrier that was on his upper right thigh, hidden by his testicles. It was shaped like an iris. Carriers were men able to bear children and were recognized at birth by a mark somewhere on their bodies. The mark could be a flower, an animal, or even something like a star. Other than being able to birth children, no one had been able to figure out if the marks meant anything more. They did not distinguish how many children a person might have; it was simply a symbol of another societal purpose. He would be a fool to say some carriers were not discriminated against once their status was known, whether out of jealousy or disgust.

But even if he weren't a carrier, Des had known he liked guys from an early age but had never even been on a date. Maybe it was because he never found anyone interesting enough for him to ask them out. He and his parents had never discussed the fact that he was a carrier; it was as if they were ashamed that he was one or they didn't care. Growing up, all he ever did was study. In high school, his parents never allowed him to play sports or spend time with other kids to gain a friend or two, even though he didn't have any to begin with. It wasn't until college that he met two people he'd come to care for as a family. His parents were strict about his doing anything that would ruin his hands because they knew he was destined to be a surgeon. But they had no problem with him learning to play the piano.

They knew the long hours of sitting in a proper posture would strengthen his back and the flexibility of his fingers, not to mention all the other benefits. It wasn't as if Des didn't try to do his own thing. He'd endured his parents' rules, believing that he would be free of them when he got to college, but he was dead wrong. Des had applied to the fine arts program. However, his parents put a wrench in his plans, making him realize just how far their money and influence stretched, and influenced the school administrator who rejected his program application. When Des found out, he was pissed as hell and confronted them.

"Did you think I would pay for some idiotic art degree?" his father yelled. "You will become a doctor, and that is the end of this conversation."

"You cannot keep running my life," Des shouted.

"Desmond, you will do as your father says. Can't you see we're thinking of your future?" his mother added softly.

"My future? Are you going to continue using that excuse for the rest of my life? I have done everything you ask me to do. I missed out on being a child, studying, and graduating early because you wanted me to. I'm a high school graduate with no friends to call on, no damn life whatsoever, and I want to be an artist. Is that so damn wrong!"

"I will not argue with you any longer, Desmond. Your father and I have already decided. You will stop this artist nonsense and do as we say."

Ignoring his mother, Des snarled, "I want the inheritance grandfather left me."

"This idiotic boy," his father snapped. "Then I suggest you go to medical school because you will never see one red cent of that money unless you graduate."

At that finality, his parents left him with no other options. He'd conceded like he always did. Des admitted he could have gotten a job and worked his way through school, but at sixteen, he wasn't sure how to sustain himself. He couldn't have gone to another family member; they would have taken his parents' side, no question. As for the inheritance from both his maternal and paternal grandfathers, the only way to get his hands on it was, believe it or not, if he became a doctor and stayed in the field for at least five years.

His maternal grandfather owned Branford Healthcare, one of the largest healthcare companies in Verona Heights, and until he died, Des wouldn't see a red cent of his inheritance. Since the man was still alive and kicking, Des didn't even think about that money. His paternal grandfather had also been a doctor, known as one of the best surgeons in his field, and he'd contributed many medical advances in his lifetime that were used today. Des figured he could hold out for that long. He was just happy there weren't any other stipulations like getting married and having a certain amount of children before they could get a divorce.

Des was two years away from fulfilling the stipulations, but he didn't know how much more he could take. He'd fast-tracked everything, from college and medical school to his residency, hoping the years would pass quickly. It felt like that for a while, but the last couple of years felt like they were dragging. He wasn't ungrateful that he was given the best in life; however, he felt trapped by his surroundings.

There were many times he felt like saying fuck it all to hell and walking away from it, but he had to wait. He needed his inheritance to accomplish his goals and get his parents off his back. He secretly did everything he could to prepare for the day he got his inheritance and walked away from his parents and medicine. Over the years, he'd been going to school online part-time and would be finishing his BA in fine arts by the end of the year. He would have loved to fast-track his art degree like he did his medical, but with his irregular work schedule, he had to make do with taking his time. He wished his heart was in the job because he was doing good by saving lives. But he felt like a robot going through the motions, waiting for someone to turn the off switch.

The only thing that brought him to life was his love for art. It wasn't that he wanted to be a world-famous artist but to open his own art studio, teaching others with his talent and dream. Most would think it was silly for him to want stardom for others rather than himself, but he wanted a simple life. When he had time, he would lose himself in his art or go to museums, wishing he had someone to appreciate the works of the many greats who came before him.

He would love to be in a relationship or have a family someday. As much as his parents had their faults, he knew they loved each other, and he envied that aspect of their lives. To be able to be honest with his feelings with someone. But he was afraid to open his heart. Des couldn't blame cautiousness on his parents. He wasn't sure if he could trust someone to take control when he needed it properly.

Although he had never been in a relationship or had sex unless it was his hands, Des knew he had a kinky or a fetish bone. If anyone ever tried to break the password on a certain folder on his computer, they would know exactly what he wanted in bed. He got off on images of being tied up, being spanked, being fucked in public, being blindfolded, and many other things. Des kept his proclivities to himself, afraid that if he said them aloud, others might look at him weirdly or with disgust. Maybe it was why he didn't have a lover.

For that to happen, he would need to trust the person completely, and he'd seen others go through way too much for love. Some would say being a surgeon was risky enough since he had control over a person's life, but he saw things differently. As much as he didn't want to be a doctor in the operating room, he knew what he was doing, and his patients and their family put all their trust in him to save their lives; outside of it, he was a lost fucking cause.

Des stopped just before he got to the waiting room and collected his thoughts. A few seconds later, he entered the room and saw a group of men of various statures dressed in dark suits, stopping whatever conversation or activity they were doing and staring at him. For a second, he thought they were the secret fucking service guarding the President of the United States. Amid the men sat a gentleman with graying temples, adding a certain elegance to his brown locks. He had a commanding presence, with his dark, intense eyes and thick eyebrows framing his masculine and handsome features. Des wouldn't lie. He was afraid of how intense all the men's eyes were on him.

He cleared his throat, hoping to remove any tremors from his tone. "I'm Doctor Desmond Ellington. I'm here

to speak to the Moor family."

"Doctor, how's my son?" the gentleman with graying temples asked as he stood with the aid of a cane and the man closest to him.

Truthfully, the man didn't look old enough to require a cane, but since Des didn't know the man, he kept that part to himself and answered the man's question. "Mister Moor is in stable condition. I got all the fragments, including the second bullet, which Doctor Morretti missed. I will be honest with you, the next twenty hours are critical, but I'm confident he will pull through."

There was a collective sigh from the other men, and the older gentleman nodded, and a soft expression passed through his eyes so quickly that if he wasn't looking, he was certain he would have missed it.

"Thank you," he said softly.

"You don't have to thank me," Des responded. "It's part of the job. He will be taken to the ICU shortly and watched for the next twenty-four hours. But I'd advise tonight that only two should go in at a time. Can you tell me what he was doing before he got shot? I didn't see it in his file. I need to put it in my report."

No one responded, and Des felt it wasn't a question he should have asked. *Well, that's not suspicious at all*, said no one ever.

If they weren't going to answer him, there wasn't anything he could do. He'd just have to let the proper authorities do their job. Des nodded respectfully because he felt that was what he had to do, then left them to their business, with too many questions but too afraid to ask. Besides, it was not for him to know. Going to the on-call room, he pulled out his cellphone, and saw five missed calls. Two were from his mother, one was from his good friend, Gray, and the last two were from his best friend Bianca, whom he'd known since college, who was probably calling him to brag about the new guy she'd met a couple of weeks ago but still wouldn't tell Des the guy's name or what he did for a living. She would say he was the sweetest guy she'd ever met or dated.

Deciding that he'd rather get some sleep and would deal with them all tomorrow, Des pushed his phone under his pillow and then grabbed a quick shower. He tried to be as quiet as possible; he didn't want to wake up the other doctor, who had probably just closed his eyes for a quick nap like himself, just in case he got called again. Des wasn't the only surgeon on call, but some nights, he felt as if he were. Opening his locker, he grabbed his towel and then stripped out of his scrubs before heading to the showers.

Standing under the steaming water, his mind drifted to the handsome man he'd just operated on. He'd never considered the reasons that brought a person to his operating table, but the wounds were too deep to ignore; if the bullets had been to the right, they would have torn his heart apart. It made him wonder what kind of job he did. Maybe he was a cop like Gray, who got hurt on the job. But as soon as the thought crossed his mind, he pushed it away; by the look of those guys in the waiting area, they all seemed as if they were part of the mafia.

But that's silly, right? Mobster shit is only in the movies. Turning off the water, he wrapped his towel around his waist as he walked out of the bathroom and dressed as his mind wandered. Des knew that there were criminal activities going on in Verona Heights, figuring it was like any other big city or state, but he thought there was still an active mobster element. Or maybe he was naïve in his thinking, and a deep, dark underworld ran through Verona Heights.

But then again, why would he care? He was a doctor and not a cop like Gray, whose job was to take down the bad guys.

Getting into bed, he set his alarm in case he got to sleep a bit longer before getting up for his rounds. Snuggling deep into the cover, he put thoughts of the mafia and everything else from his mind and drifted off to sleep.

* * *

IN THE HOSPITAL room lit by the moonlight, machines beeped rhythmically next to Othello, who lay unconscious. His chest rose and fell with the help of the ventilator. His wounds were hidden beneath layers of bandages as his life teetered on the scale of life and death.

A tall figure stood at the large windows of the private room, gazing out at the horizon as the sun slowly rose, waking up the world, completely unaware of the previous night's events. At times, he wished he could burn the world to ash, but he was certain there would be someone to ruin his well-thought-out plans like the night before.

He was sure a bullet to the heart would have taken the bastard out, but as always, Othello was one lucky fucker. The tall figure glanced at the sleeping man, tempted to take him out now, but he wasn't ready to show his hand. He was growing tired of sitting on the sidelines and watching everyone get what should have been his from the start. The figure scowled, thinking about how his loyalty to Alessandro Romano had given him nothing. It should have been him who got the position of underboss, not fucking Othello.

What the hell has he done to gain such a high position when I've been by the don's side through everything? The man scoffed. *Be prepared, because sooner or later, your time will run out.* He turned, forming his fingers into a gun, pointing at Othello's chest before moving it up to the man's head. *I'll have another chance, and I won't miss it next time.* A sardonic smile crossed his lips as he pulled the pretend trigger. Chuckling, he put his hands in his pockets, turning his back to his sleeping form, plotting Othello's demise. *Enjoy the time you have left, Othello.*

* * *

As IF SENSING AN ENEMY NEARBY, Othello stirred in his sleep. His fingers twitched slightly, showing signs of life but no other movements. It seemed to Othello that the battle was far from over—it was only the beginning.

SCENE III

OTHELLO

The sleeping figure in the hospital bed slowly became aware of the rhythmic beeping of machines. He pried his eyes open, squinting as they connected with an unfamiliar white ceiling. From the sound of the machines beeping in his ears, he was in the hospital.

So I didn't die.

The events of what happened last night came back to him. He recalled the ambush and being shot in the chest during the meeting with the Falcon clan. His chest felt tight, but it didn't hurt. He thanked all the gods in the universe for whatever drug he was on. In all his years being a part of the La Famiglia Romano, he never thought he'd see himself in the hospital, laid flat out on his back, staring up at the white ceiling because of a bullet wound to the chest. They had gone in unprepared. Usually, Othello would have worn a bulletproof vest when they met with other clans or worn one of his suits that was made out of Kevlar. The suits were not foolproof since they were made to handle low-caliber rounds, but he might not have ended up in the hospital. Some would say it was karma for all the shit he'd done to people over the years, but he wasn't above telling those same people to go fuck themselves.

Gritting his teeth, he tried to sit up but decided not to when he felt a slight twinge in his chest. Instead, Othello stayed in his position, vowing to find out what the fuck happened and who was behind it. He did not doubt that the don was already looking into things, but it didn't make him feel any better when what went down last night shouldn't have happened. He opened his eyes and allowed them to adjust to the brightness before turning his head and scanning his surroundings. He paused when he spotted Tallen and Marco sitting on the couch, passed out asleep.

He decided not to wake them, knowing they were tired from the night's events and keeping watch over him. Othello turned his gaze to the window and looked out at the beautiful blue sky. He was genuinely happy to see it, even though he had been prepared to die. Life and death in his world were nothing new. He'd known what could happen when he chose this route as a career. He and Iago, who was his brother of heart, not blood, were taken in by a crime organization when they were thirteen, and they didn't regret it at all.

Thinking of Iago, he was sure his brother was doing the job that Othello could not do at the moment, which was protecting the boss, their adopted father, while trying not to go ballistic on whoever ambushed them. The only clan that knew where they were meeting was Falcon. But Othello didn't want to think the Falcons had anything to do with the ambush. He just hoped Iago didn't act before he thought things through. Right now, their father needed a level-headed thinker. Iago was a fucking hothead. He'd been that way since they were children. He and Iago had been thick as thieves since they were kids and met in the group home where he had been placed after the death of his parents.

The memory of his parents' deaths was fragmented, like a shattered mirror, but a few images remained vivid. Even after becoming an adult, hiring a private investigator, and seeing their pictures, he still couldn't capture a memory of them. But he knew his father was a low-level member of a crime organization that had long since been taken out of the game. So, he was destined to be a part of a crime syndicate. He often wondered if he'd made his father proud that he followed in his footsteps. From the reports, the accident had nothing to do with what his father did for a living.

He was eight years old, sitting in the back seat of his parents' car; they were driving back from getting ice cream, a dessert Othello could not enjoy to this day because it brought back the pain of his parents' deaths. They had done something fun, like going to an amusement park or the playground, but Othello couldn't remember. He recalled the sound of rain pattering against the windows, his mother humming along to a song on the radio, and then the sudden, violent impact followed by darkness and silence. When he woke up, everything in his little life had changed. He was in a hospital bed, surrounded by strangers. His parents were nowhere to be seen. He had asked for his mother and father, and the strangers, who he later found out were child services, told him they were watching over him.

What kind of shit is that to tell a kid who just lost his parents?

He got a few scrapes and sore muscles from the accident, but that was it. Since no one told him how his parents died when he was a kid, when he got older, Othello did his research and found out they were hit by a drunk driver who tried to run away from the scene but was hit and killed by another car. Unfortunately for Othello, his parents had no other living relatives, so he became a ward of the state. He was instantly placed in the Willow-Brook group home, receiving millions in donations from wealthy people who wanted to make it look like they were contributing to something good in society.

Willow-Brook was well-equipped and maintained and surrounded by many trees, making it look like it was in the middle of a forest, or that's what he looked like to Othello when he was a kid. It wasn't posh, but it also wasn't rundown where they had to scramble for food and clothing even though they slept two or three to a room and wore hand-me-downs. It was livable, and he didn't have to be afraid, even if some of the kids thought it was haunted. As an adult, he now knew it was an old mansion given to the owners of Willow-Brook, where he'd met Iago, who was the same age as him.

Iago had arrived a few months before Othello. Iago's parents had died in a fire that had started in their home while they were sleeping. Firefighters had been able to rescue Iago, but not his parents. Iago and Othello instantly bonded, forming a friendship that stood the test of time. Including Iago and Othello, there were twelve children altogether, considering there was a rotation of kids coming in and getting adopted. Even with enough staff on hand, twenty-four-seven, Ms. Mooney expected them to help with the younger ones and do their daily chores.

Othello had been at the group home for two days before anyone spoke to him. He had never been one of those kids who rushed to make friends. The first person who spoke to him was Iago. Othello was sitting on the swing in the backyard, thinking and missing his parents, when Iago walked over to him.

"Hey, want to go somewhere really cool?" Iago whispered, looking

around to see if anyone was watching them. "I haven't shown it to the other kids, because I don't want to tell Ms. Mooney."

Othello looked at Iago skeptically, who had dark hair and eyes, before nodding. Hopping off the swing, he followed Iago to a small, hidden corner of the expansive backyard. Lifting one of the loose boards on the fence, Iago squeezed through it and motioned for Othello to follow. For a second, Othello wouldn't do so because he remembered the rules that they were not allowed to leave the property without one of the staff members.

He had never gone against an adult's word before, but he was bored and curious about where the other kid wanted to take him, so he squeezed his body through the fence. Iago took off running the second he was through, and Othello was right behind him. He wasn't sure how far they ran, but he could see signs of Willow-Brook if he glanced back. When they finally stopped, it was in front of a lake, and he had to admit it was freaking cool. Seconds later, there was a splash. Turning to the sound, he saw Iago splashing around in the water shirtless.

"Come on," Iago shouted. "Stop standing around." He went back to playing in the lake.

Not thinking about anything, he'd stripped down to his undies and followed Iago, who laughed and played for hours, forgetting about the time and everyone else. They had snuck back into the home without being caught, but it had only lasted a few more times until the staff found out about their escape route. They got in trouble, and he got grounded for the first time in his life.

After the staff fixed the broken fence, they found other ways to get into trouble. They were inseparable, from sneaking into the kitchen to steal cookies to playing pranks on the other kids. Whatever Iago wanted to do, Othello followed, since he was taller and seemed bigger. Until one day, Othello grew just as tall as Iago, becoming his equal. But Iago was still the one who came up with most of their plans. The weird thing was when they got into trouble, it always seemed like Othello was the one who got the pats on the back, while Iago received the stern looks.

"Why do they seem to like you more?" Iago once asked, with a hint of sadness in his voice. *"You do the same stuff I do, but I'm the one that gets into trouble."*

Othello shrugged. *"I don't know."* He smiled. *"Maybe it's because I look more innocent, and you always look guilty. Learn to hide your facial expressions better."*

"Yeah, right," he huffed. *"If only they knew you're the one who always drags me into things."*

"Only once," Othello defended.

"Twice," Iago said, then started laughing when Othello tackled him.

As they grew, their friendship grew tighter, and they started telling people they were brothers. Not many questioned them, even though he and Iago looked nothing alike, but Othello saw the looks they got whenever they said it. He could understand their confusion since Othello was a brown-skinned kid with a thick, curly afro that he learned to wear in twists or braids as he got older. He had a mix of Arabic, Spanish, and African features. Iago's olive complexion showed his Italian heritage, with wavy hair reaching his shirt collar.

They saw themselves as brothers in every way that mattered, sharing dreams, fears, joys, and sorrows. Each year, Iago talked about the death of his parents and how not having his parents in his life was affecting him. Othello recalled missing his parents, but over time he forgot them. One of their dreams was to leave Willow-Brook once they were old enough. Their chances of getting adopted were nil since they were no longer the cute and adorable babies that most people wanted. They were mischievous preteen boys who had other interests. It didn't matter that they got good grades. They still liked to get into shit they shouldn't have. As pretty as Willow-Brook was on the outside, on the inside, Ms. Mooney would constantly shake her head and tell them they'd be in jail before they turned eighteen.

Looking back, Othello couldn't blame her for saying shit like that. They had stopped playing silly pranks on the kids or the staff in the group home and turned their activities to outside, where they became headaches to teachers and people in the neighborhood. But truly, no one ever bothered lecturing them anymore because it seemed like things went in one ear and out the other. They became the local bullies. Since they thought Iago was the more vocal of the two and tended to rough the kids up, it was believed Othello was the leader. But the truth was there wasn't a leader or follower. They worked together, scamming and beating up kids, even adults, who might come at them the wrong way. But it didn't mean they didn't go out to find their own trouble.

As time passed, their petty crimes grew into pickpocketing little miscreants, perfecting the craft so well that they never got caught—except for that one time. The corner of Othello's lips curled into a smile as the day came to him when they met Don Alessandro Romano. At the time, they had no clue the man was the head of a criminal organization or the role he would later play in their lives. They'd heard talk of gang activity in certain neighborhoods since the group home staff had discouraged them from going there. That was the only time they listened since both had decided they weren't ready to play with the big boys yet and had to work on their street cred, and they figured instead of just beating and scamming people, they needed to do something more daring. That was when they spotted their guy.

Othello and Iago were crouched behind a parked car on a bustling city street, looking for an easy mark. That was when Othello spotted the well-dressed man striding confidently down the sidewalk. He could tell the man had money, from his suit and the gleaming gold watch on his wrist, not to mention he had the latest, most expensive cellphone that had just come out on the market. They perfected the plan they'd used a few times as they watched the guy.

"Okay, he's really distracted on the phone," Othello whispered. "Let's do it now before he gets to where there's not a lot of people. I'll distract him, and you go for his wallet. I'm sure he has a lot of money on him."

Iago didn't need any more prompting, and they split up, pretending to go in different directions. Othello kept his eyes on the mark as he got to the crowded pedestrian crossing, which was perfect for putting their plan into action. Othello weaved his way through the throng of people. When he got close, Othello accidentally collided with the man who had his back facing him.

"What the fuck?" the man exclaimed in rightful anger as he steadied himself, swirled around. "Watch where fuck you're going," he said in a much harsher tone.

Othello groaned, dramatically falling on his ass, which was not part of the plan. Forgetting about his pain for now, he raised his gaze and looked up at the guy who seemed much taller and much scarier up close and in person. For a second, he wondered if he had chosen the wrong man to steal from, especially from the intense look in his eyes.

His heart pounded so loud in his chest that he felt as if he was going to have a heart attack at a young age. His fingers twitched, wanting to clutch his chest, but he held himself back. He was so scared that he almost forgot to breathe, and the real purpose of bumping into the guy, until he saw Iago approaching them. He thought about giving Iago the signal to abort the mission, but he couldn't remember what they'd come up with. Out of everything they did, this was the first time he was scared as hell. But he also knew that even if he told Iago to back off, his brother wouldn't listen to him.

And although he didn't want to stay in the man's presence for much longer, he did what he could to keep the guy's eyes on him.

"I...I...I'm...I'm sorry," Othello stuttered and apologized profusely. He pulled on his energy, pushing his fear away. He stood, holding on

to the man's jacket, which only angered him more, but it was the perfect distraction for Iago to make his move.

"Get your dirty hands off," the guy growled, pushing Othello away just as Iago walked by them as if he hadn't seen what was happening and mixed into the crowd.

"I'm really sorry," Othello said, standing up. "I..."

"Fuck, kid, stop apologizing," the man yelled. "Just get the hell out of my face. I have somewhere to be. Dammit, why did I let Maria talk me into coming here? Fuck, I should have brought my guards. I wouldn't have to deal with this shit," the man rambled as he continued dusting off his jacket.

"Oh...oh, okay. But I'm really sorry," Othello said softly, but the man heard him and growled, glaring at him.

"Leave," he snapped.

"Yes, sir."

Getting the message, Othello walked off as calmly as he could, even though he wanted to run as fast as he could and catch up with Iago, who was already at their hiding place, an abandoned building that used to be an old pizza joint. That day was the biggest windfall for them. They ignored the credit cards and focused on the thick stack of hundred-dollar bills that amounted to one thousand dollars that were easily split fifty-fifty.

While Iago spent his half, Othello saved his, thinking of his goal of getting away from the Willow-Brook group home. That was the difference between them. Othello was always thinking of what came next, while Iago lived in the moment, which was something he envied about his brother. He wasn't reckless, but Iago was rash, while Othello was a thinker. The differences in their nature had served them well, but it had also made them come to blows and arguments over the years.

After they had stolen from the man, Iago wanted to find another mark, but Othello had to convince him it was better to take a break and stick close to home for a bit. Three weeks later, just as they were returning to their old tricks, the man they had stolen from walked through the door, changing Othello and Iago's lives and giving them a far better life than they could've hoped for.

"Boss, you're awake," hearing Tallen's voice caused Othello to step back into the present and look away from the window and over to the two men who had been

sleeping soundly. "I'll go get the doctor."

He hurried out of the room, leaving him with Marco, who moved closer to Othello while fixing his suit. "It's good to see you awake, Boss. It was touch and go for a little bit."

"The don?" he asked, his voice raspy, having not used it for a few hours.

"He's fine. He and Iago have been working around the clock for two days to find out who ambushed us. Speaking of which, I should call him. He'll want to know you're awake."

"Two days?" Othello said.

"I told you it was touch and go for a bit." Marco pulled out his phone and stepped away from the bed to make his call just as Tallen and a hospital staff member entered the room.

"Mister Moor, it's good to see you awake." The doctor smiled, walking over to him.

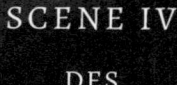

SCENE IV

DES

*D*es smiled and moved closer to Othello Moor, who was trying to sit up, but Des stopped him.

"Please remain in your position. I'd prefer you not rip open your stitches. I believe they were some of my most beautiful work," Des joked, looking into the handsome man's face, which remained impassive.

Okay, Des, don't quit your day job. You'll never make it as a comedian, he mentally chided himself.

Des was happy to see the patient fully awake. He had been watching over the patient for the past two days. He'd spiked a high fever, and Des was worried it would lead to an infection, but he was thankful it didn't happen. At one point, Mister Moor opened his glazed light amber eyes and stared at him for a few seconds. Moor had opened his dry lips and asked if he was an angel, before falling back to sleep as if nothing had happened.

Des was sure the man was delirious on the drugs he was on, or he thought he was dead. But it wasn't uncommon for that to happen with people who'd had major surgery. It wasn't the first time he was mistaken for a god or the devil, depending on the day or the patient. It was only the first time he'd wanted to answer.

Pushing past that thought, Des got serious about the examination. First, he adjusted the bed, positioning the patient upright and comfortably, and pulled out his penlight. He shone it in the man's eyes while asking him the normal questions, but truly, he was eager to hear what the guy's voice sounded like.

Never had he been fascinated by a patient, and honestly, he was feeling a little out of his depth. He was always a professional, but right now, he wanted to cater to the man's needs no matter what it was, when he knew next to nothing about Moor. Over the two days he'd done his due diligence as a doctor and checked on Mister Moor, he'd often wondered if the man was dreaming or walking to the light. Des could have turned the case over to another doctor, but he seriously didn't want to.

Many times, he'd muttered it would be a crying shame if such a handsome man were to die. Des knew next to nothing about the guy but understood that he was an important figure since he had guards watching him twentyfour hours a day. Des had also figured with the man's status, the cops would have been here to question the staff about the gunshot victim, but in the two days, no one had shown up. When he spoke to the head of his department, he was told to drop it and simply treat the patient and not dig too deep into things that weren't his concern.

But how could he not be concerned when he'd pulled a bullet out of his patient's chest? Des had pushed and threatened to call the police, but his boss had countered by writing him up, reporting him for insubordination, and informing his parents of his actions, which caused Des to back down. He'd had a good record so far and couldn't have it marred, not to mention reaching his parent's ear and having to deal with them putting Des in a corner he didn't want to be in.

His department head and a few of the higher-ups knew he had a strained relationship with his parents and sometimes used it to get Des to do what they wanted. He hated that he couldn't stand on his own yet, or he would have quit his job. He had money saved but not enough, and he didn't want to take out a loan. However, with how everyone pretended Moor wasn't a gunshot victim, Des couldn't help but be suspicious. What could he do about it?

Nothing but take care of his patient.

"Can you tell me your full name?" Des asked.

"Othello Romano-Moor," a deep, steady, and sultry voice responded, sending goosebumps all over him. Looking into the man's whiskey-brown eyes, which were staring back at him with such intensity, it was as if he were peering into his soul's depth. Clearing his throat, he turned off the penlight, holding it upright in his hand.

"Follow this with your eyes, please." He watched the man's eyes follow the penlight, counting it as a good sign.

"Are you in any pain, Mister Romano-Moor?"

"No, and call me Othello or Moor."

"Very well," Des said. "Are you having any trouble breathing?"

Mister Moor shook his head, and Des nodded. Pocketing

his penlight, he put his attraction aside and started checking his patient over. He continued to ask questions about how the man was feeling and could not believe Othello wasn't experiencing any discomfort after having had major chest surgery. Just to be sure, he checked the patient's pain meds to make sure he wasn't being overdosed.

"Is there a problem?"

At the question, Des looked up from the patient report. "Um...no, it's just a routine check-up. But I must say, most patients in your situation would be experiencing some discomfort right about now."

"Is that a bad thing?" Mister Moor asked.

"No, it's a good thing. If you continue like this, you'll recover quickly. Do you have questions for me?"

"When can I get out of here?"

"You just woke up, and already you're ready to leave," said a familiar voice, and one Des noticed brought a smile to Mister Moor's face.

Iago Romano entered the room and walked over to his brother, hugging him carefully as they passed a secret message between them, and Des could tell they were really close. He had met Iago the night before when he came to check on his patient and saw the man sitting at his friend's bedside having a one-sided conversation. He'd spent a couple of minutes talking to Iago, and it was revealed that both men had been friends since they were kids and were adopted by the older gentleman Des had met a couple of nights ago. They also worked for their father's construction company.

Des wanted to know more about the family and hoped Iago Romano could explain how Moor got shot. However, the other man would not provide any information that could help him, so Des took it as his cue not to ask more questions. It was pretty cool to know they had a deep connection.

Iago was just as good-looking as his friend, with an olive complexion, thick, short, wavy black hair, and dark green eyes. He was tall, and from what Des could glean in his suit, he was muscular but not like Moor, who seemed to be built like a tank, with a rich, bronze skin tone that was smooth to the touch. Des's gaze roamed over Othello's features, from his thick ink-black coiled hair that was long on the top and tapered on the sides to his well-defined eyebrows and prominent nose that went with his perfectly sculpted face.

On the other hand, looking at Moor and Iago really brought home how lonely he was most of his life. He'd spent all his high school years alone and didn't even find his real friends until he went to college. Des was an only child, with his parents always working when they weren't busy plotting out his life. He spent most of his time with the nanny, with strict instructions from his parents to monitor his daily activities. However, she taught him a lot, being a mother to him more than his own. Maybe that was why she was fired when his parents found out she'd allowed him to hang out at the local arcade after school.

"Doctor Ellington, did you hear my question?" Iago asked.

"Huh?" Des realized he had been staring off into space and hoped they hadn't noticed where he was looking. "Sorry, I wasn't listening to your conversation. I was busy reviewing his chart."

"How is Othello, really?"

"As far as I can tell, he's doing fine, but I'll know after a few more tests. I want to make sure he doesn't have any swelling or infections. His fever has gone down, but our goal is not to have it return."

"How long will I have to stay here?" Othello asked. "It depends. It could be three or four weeks." "Or less, right?" his patient interjected.

You are so eager to leave, and you just woke up. Does he think he's a superhero?

Des smiled, not showing his thoughts. "Let's see how your recovery goes before I answer that question. In the meantime, I'll order the additional tests, and we'll go from there." Putting the patient's chart down, Des left the men to their conversation to give the nurse his instructions. He then left to check on his other patients before meeting up with the other residents and doctors for a night of fun after the past couple of days he'd had.

* * *

OTHELLO'S EYES followed the doctor walking out of the room, wondering why it felt like he'd seen the man before. Shaking his head, he turned back to Iago, who was looking at him.

"Fill me in on what's been going on," he told his friend.

"Other than finding out what happened a couple of nights ago, nothing much."

"How did you guys handle the cops?"

"We had our guys fudge the records. The only report they had was a shooting at the abandoned warehouse, but they think it was a couple of local gangs. It was a miracle that none of your blood was found at the scene, but we still had our people take care of the cleanup. As of now, we're in the clear."

"What about the doctors?"

"Other than the surgeon, everyone has been taken care of. They've been paid off to keep their mouths shut."

Not liking the sound of that, Othello's brows furrowed. "Why is he left out of the loop? What could this mean for us?"

"His case is a little delicate, but we have someone working on him. He's more curious than the rest. We had his department head back off for now, but we have someone else making sure he doesn't talk. Don't worry."

Othello wasn't settled on that answer, but he trusted Iago to take care of things and eliminate any paper trail that might lead back to them. It wouldn't be good if the cops on their payroll learned about their activities.

"What about things with Falcon?"

"We've put that on hold for now," Iago told him.

"Why?"

"Do you need to ask?"

Othello sighed, sinking deep into his pillow. He didn't like what he was hearing. They needed that deal to go through. Othello had plans for the properties they would be gaining and didn't think letting the events of a couple of nights ago stop their progress was sensible. He needed to get out of here and take care of things, or at least convince Don Alessandro to go through with everything. He was awake now and wasn't at death's door, so they shouldn't wait any longer.

"What's got your brows so tight?" Iago asked.

"Nothing, just thinking." He looked Iago over, noticed the man had bags under his eyes, and wondered if he'd spent the past two days at his bedside. "How'd you know I was awake?"

"I didn't. I was coming to relieve Marco and Tallen. Everyone's been taking turns keeping watch over you." Looking around, Othello noticed the two men had slipped out while he was distracted by the doctor and Iago arriving.

"I appreciate it, but I didn't need twenty-four-hour guards."

"You're the successor of the clan, Othello. Did you expect the don to leave you unprotected? You know, since the day we ran our game on him, he hasn't gone anywhere without his guards. So, do you think he would let you be unprotected?"

Othello didn't respond to that statement when he had nothing to back it up; instead, he changed the subject. "Funny you should mention what we did. I was thinking about the first time we met Don Alessandro."

That brought a smile to Iago's lips. "How can I forget, but what brought that on?"

"I don't know. I woke up, and it was my first thought."

"Please don't tell me you're regretting things since you almost died." Iago sat in the chair beside the bed.

"Nah. I just recalled that it was the first time in my life I'd ever been scared."

"Lies," Iago said. "You almost pissed your pants when he walked in the front door of the group home."

"Maybe," Othello said through a yawn, feeling sleepy. "I'm going to take a nap. You should go home to Emilia. Did you forget she's pregnant? She might be a few weeks along, but she needs you more right now. So stay the fuck out of trouble while I'm in here."

"Why do you sound like the big brother instead of the little one? Don't worry, Emilia is fine. She yelled at me this morning and told me I was nagging the fuck out of her and to go do something with myself."

Othello smirked. "I knew there was a reason I liked her." Emilia Bellini, Iago's girlfriend of five years, was a junior partner for a well-named public relations firm. She'd stuck by his brother, who cheated on her a bunch of times when other women or men would have dropped his ass a long time ago.

Othello loved his brother and trusted him with his life, but the man was a bastard to the woman who loved him. Othello wasn't sure why Emilia had stayed with him for so long when he took her love for granted. Emilia had lost her parents a few years before she met Iago and wasn't close to her remaining family members, so Othello was always encouraging his brother to cherish the woman he claimed to love.

"If I leave, who's…"

"Go, Iago. I'm not dying anymore. It's creepy having someone watch me while I sleep."

Iago huffed and stood. "Stubborn bastard." He fixed his suit and walked to the door but stopped when Othello spoke.

"Do you regret it?"

"No," Iago answered, knowing what Othello was

talking about. "It's where I belong."

Othello smiled, feeling the same as the man he considered his brother. The day Don Alessandro showed up at their group home, he'd brought presents for all the kids, which had thrown him and Iago off guard. After looking at his driver's license, they knew his name was Alessandro Romano. But they'd had no clue how the man they had robbed would show up at their home with those intense eyes trained on them as if he knew everything from start to finish.

Twenty minutes into the visit, Othello and Iago were pulled into a room and berated for doing a shitty job of stealing from someone and getting caught. He wasn't angry that they had stolen from him, but how they went about it. Othello and Iago couldn't believe it, which took away most of the fear he had held onto since Alessandro showed up. He only complimented them that they didn't run out and run the same trick again.

"We didn't get caught if it took you three days to show up," Othello argued back, even though he was scared out of his wits. The man's intense eyes were boring into them.

"Five minutes after you guys stole from me, I knew. I just couldn't stop to deal with you two," Alessandro said, and to Othello, he didn't sound upset that a couple of kids had played a trick on him. *"I had to meet up with my wife and go out of town on business. So, I had my people watching this place to make sure it was legit and to keep an eye on you two. Whose idea was it?"*

"It was my idea," Othello answered.

"Next time, kid, don't look for your partner in the crowd. I realized what had happened after I had time to think things through." He sighed. *"What made me your mark?"*

"What are you, a cop?" Iago asked and was rewarded with a light smack on the side of his head.

"Cops don't dress as stylish as I do, kid," Alessandro said, fixing his expensive suit jacket, sitting back in the chair, and crossing one leg over the other. *"I own one of the largest construction companies in*

New York and another in New Jersey."

"Sorry," Iago said sheepishly, rubbing his head.

"Don't do that," Alessandro said, leaning forward and looking them both in the eyes. "Never apologize for anything you do. Simply correct things and move on." Both boys nodded as Alessandro stared at them. "You boys need to be taught properly. If you continue doing what you're doing, you'll get caught."

"Your clothes and the fact that you had the latest cellphone," Othello told him.

"You're the smart one, I see." Alessandro chuckled.

"How did you find us?" Othello asked.

"It wasn't that hard. I simply asked the right people. You brats are quite the troublesome pair. Be thankful no one has turned you both in for the shit you've been getting into." Tsking, Alessandro stood, and so did the two boys. "Be ready in three days."

"For what?" Othello was confused and curious.

"I'm taking you both home to meet my wife. Once she meets you two, she'll want to adopt you. And I have to admit, I kind of like you both."

"How come?" Iago asked, and Othello heard the curiosity in his voice that mirrored his own.

"I don't know," he responded. "But something in my gut tells me I should keep you two close. And I always follow my gut."

He'd walked out of the room, leaving them shocked by his declaration. Alessandro returned as promised three days later and signed them out of Willow-Brook for a day. Ms. Mooney was all too happy to let them go. When they reached their destination, Iago and Othello couldn't believe how massive the house was. Alessandro had money to live in one of Verona Heights' wealthiest neighborhoods, meaning he was influential. It was a gated area with guards that protected the neighborhood twenty-four-seven. Othello didn't know just how much power Alessandro wielded.

Before they exited the car, Alessandro instructed them not

to mention their stealing habits and to be on their best behavior. The minute they were introduced to Maria Romano, formerly Montemayor, she showered them with kisses and hugs. On their first visit, she tried to feed them so much food because she thought they were malnourished. Othello had to admit she sold him on her hugs and care, which made him realize just how starved for motherly affection he was.

Othello later found out that Maria was the daughter of the well-known actor turned director Enzo Montamayor. Maria was beautiful, with long, flowing dark hair and dark brown eyes that seemed like chocolate and complemented her smooth bronze skin.

Just as Alessandro wanted, they were perfect little boys, which warranted them visiting many times after that, even spending weekends. Both Alessandro and Maria were in their late thirties, and after many attempts to have children, they all resulted in miscarriages. Maria's body was too frail to carry a baby full-term. So they looked into the idea of adopting a baby or using a surrogate, but when Othello and Iago stole from Alessandro, they'd piqued his interest.

After a few months of being around the boys, they started the adoption process, with Iago and Othello's permission. Since the boys could be together and live in a large mansion, they were not against it in the least. However, until the adoption process was complete, they often stayed at the group home and visited the Romanos. That was Iago and Othello's idea. They wanted to get the younger kids used to them not being around rather than leaving them high and dry.

Each time they visited Romano's home, Othello grew curious about why they saw very little of Alessandro, why some people called him Don, why large men roamed around like guards, and what the man did for a living to afford such a large home. Othello, being who he was, would sneak around trying to get answers until one day, he walked into a part of the large house that Alessandro had told him never to enter and ended up spying on something he shouldn't have: the older Romano pointing a gun at a guy's head who was crying his eyes out, begging not to die. Othello's eyes widened in surprise because he had never seen this side of the man before. Sure, he was serious, but to hold a weapon to a man with a threatening stance was something new.

"*Do you understand that my wife and children are in the house?*" *Alessandro said, his voice calm, yet the look in his eyes spoke volumes more than Othello had ever seen.*

"*Don Alessandro, I'm sorry. I won't do it again. Please, don't kill me.*"

"*After what you did, do you really expect me to let you live?*" *Alessandro shouted.* "*You betrayed me, Lodovico, you know our family motto. Betrayal is unforgivable, so you know I cannot let you walk out of here alive.*"

Just as he said the words, the man's brains and blood were splattered all over, and his body tilted to the side, falling on the floor. Othello hadn't heard the gun go off, but he knew that his heart was beating so loud in his chest he was certain the man had heard it. Othello should have been terrified out of his mind. But he wasn't. He had never seen anyone get murdered before, but he was more excited to see what would happen next.

"*Clean this shit up,*" *Alessandro ordered.*

"*Yes, Don Alessandro.*"

"*You know where to bury the body. And take care of his wife.*"

"*Yes, sir.*"

When Alessandro made a move to walk towards the door, Othello ran away as quickly as his feet could carry him to the kitchen, where Maria and Iago were making cookies. He pretended that everything was fine and that he hadn't seen anything, but he couldn't get the image out of his thoughts for weeks. The good thing was that Alessandro didn't know he had seen the shooting, and Iago had never noticed his distraction. Even to this very day, Othello had never mentioned it. It was the one time he'd let his curiosity sit and fester. After being a part of the clan, Othello knew where they had buried the body. Owning a construction company came in handy in more ways than one.

On a particular Saturday during one of their weekend visits, they were all sitting at the table eating dinner like an official family when Othello blurted out his question.

"Why do they call you the don?"

Maria, Iago, and Alessandro's forks paused at their lips, and all eyes were on him.

"Where did you hear that from?"

"From one of the big guys that are always following you," Othello answered.

Alessandro didn't speak right away, but after a few minutes, he stood up, walked over, and kissed Maria. Maria nodded and gently squeezed Alessandro's right arm. Then, he looked at him and Iago and said, "You boys follow me."

That night, Othello and Iago learned what Alessandro truly did for a living and that the construction companies, although real, were a front. He pointed out the dangers of being Don Alessandro's sons. The La Famiglia Romano was about family and brotherhood, with a mix of Spanish, Portuguese, and, of course, Italian heritage. It was an underground organization that had been around for many years.

They were not the top dogs, but Alessandro's dream was to be the head of The Commission and to have his clan sit at the forefront of all the clans. They needed to take down the two main clans, who were the Ricci and Greco families, which made others shake in fear just at the mention of their names even now, which irritated the fuck out of Othello. In the past, the Ricci family cornered the market on prostitution and the Greco family on gambling and racketeering. Still, as influential as the Romano name was, they were considered a minor family. When Alessandro had explained everything to him and Iago, they'd had a long ladder to climb before they could reach the top.

Before the Ricci and Greco families took their place, there were seven families in total, each clan responsible for one economic factor that contributed to their pockets and society's growth. However, as time passed, the Ricci and Greco line cut down and consolidated with the other five families. While the Greco and Ricci families made no secret of their actions, none of the other clans opposed them.

Their bite and bark were loud and fatal. They were involved in more than prostitution and gambling. The steps of the two major families set off a chain reaction, and the other families wanted to dip their toes into every corner that would line their pockets, forgetting about the mafia organization's main purpose, which was economic growth.

But the Romano clan was close to accomplishing its goal. Slowly and quietly, it had shortened the ladder, removing the other families and merging their properties into the Romano family. Alessandro's father, who died young, had started the organization, leaving him in charge. Alessandro knew his wish would take a long time, but he had hoped his heir could complete it if he did not succeed himself.

Alessandro had always believed in telling them the truth and never sugarcoating things. He felt being honest with family was always the best. Other than their own family law, they lived by the omerta code of silence and secrecy. A blood vow made by even the lowest soldier never to cooperate with authorities or reveal what happens in the organization.

After laying everything out, he had given them the choice of being adopted by him and Maria, and neither he nor Iago batted an eye when they said yes.

"Good." He smiled. "One day, one of you will be my successor, and

the other will be his right-hand man. So show me your worth, and don't let me down."

Six months ago, Othello was chosen as Alessandro's right-hand man. Standing at the head of the family clan with his brother beside him meant everything to Othello. All that was left was to fulfill his promise to take the clan to the top of the underworld food chain.

SCENE V

OTHELLO

The next time Othello woke up, a wonderful smile broke on his face when he saw the most gorgeous and proper woman dressed in a name-brand pants suit sitting at his bedside.

"Mama," he croaked, his voice hoarse.

"Don't you Mama me, Othello Romano-Moor," she snapped without any real anger.

Although he was adopted and took the Romano name, he'd wanted to keep his birth parents' name, holding on to the last bit of connection to them, and Maria and Alessandro had agreed.

"Don't you have something to say to me?" Maria quirked a

perfectly arched dark eyebrow. "How did a simple meeting turn into bloodshed? Your father and Iago won't tell me, and from the look on your face, I guess you won't either."

As far as Othello knew, Alessandro had never kept the darkness of their world from Maria. She knew the inner workers and was respected in the organization and among the other clans. Sometimes, Maria had Alessandro's ear more than anyone else.

"Why didn't you wear one of those suits you paid so much money to have made to protect you?" she ranted. "Everyone else did. I'm disappointed in you, *meu pequeno*."

Over the years, Othello had made many changes to the organization, adding more security measures to the Romanos' home, outfitting the soldiers with better Kevlar vests or suits, and increasing their training. He bought out the two mansions on either side of the Romanos, turning them into living and training spaces for their soldiers. He built an extension connecting them to his parents' home.

"I'm sorry, Mama," Othello said softly, hoping to appeal to her tender heart. "I shouldn't have gotten hurt. I won't let it happen again."

"No, you shouldn't have, but what can we do?" She sighed and brushed his hair from his forehead. "How are you feeling, *meu pequeno*?"

"The drugs have worn off," he groaned.

"Do you want me to get the doctor?" She stood quickly and was about to leave.

Othello shook his head. "Not yet. I can deal with the discomfort for a bit. I want to spend some time with you."

"Even lying there in bed in pain, you try to sweet talk me.

Let's get your pain taken care of. I won't be going anywhere."

She pressed the call button, and the hospital staff arrived quicker than expected. Othello wasn't sure why he was expecting the doctor from earlier instead of a nurse show-ing up.

"Hello, Mister Moor, I'm Chloe. What can I do for you?"

"He's in pain," Maria rushed out before he could speak.

Not affected by Maria's words, Chole picked up his record and looked at it. "Okay, we'll take care of it. Also, Doctor Ellington left instructions for additional tests. You were sleeping when we came to get you, so we'll get that done."

"Is that his doctor? This Ellington?" Maria asked.

"Yes, he's the attending doctor and the one who operated on Mister Moor."

"Then where is he? Shouldn't he be here to take care of my son?" Maria had slipped completely into mamabear mode, and Othello felt sorry for the poor nurse.

"Doctor Ellington has gone home for the night, but other doctors are available if anything happens."

"Mama, I'm in pain," he said softly before Maria could utter another word. The nurse looked at him, and he saw the relief in her eyes.

"I'll get you those meds. I'll also have some broth sent up for you."

"Thank you," Othello said.

"She seems nice," Maria said when the nurse left them alone. "Very pretty, too."

"Mama," he groaned. "You remember I'm gay, right?"

Othello had come out to Alessandro and Maria when he was sixteen, and although he'd been scared out of his mind, he couldn't live in a box and was ready for them to kick him out if they were against it. Although they lived in an open society with male carriers, there were still some assholes who had issues with same-sex couples. But to his relief, they accepted him. Iago, on the other hand, had a hard time with him being gay, and it put a slight fracture in their relationship for a few months.

According to Iago, he felt betrayed by Othello's homosexuality and couldn't understand why everyone was so accepting of his lifestyle. He argued that Othello needed to find the right girl so he would know that he was straight. Othello grew insulted by Iago's words and got sick and tired of being unable to explain things to him so his friend would understand that he was born the way he was and it wouldn't change. It wasn't as if he found women disgusting. He could appreciate beauty when he saw it; he just wasn't attracted to them sexually. So, he simply stopped talking to him.

They'd argued and had drag-out fistfights for the first time in their friendship.

Othello had thought everything they had built was over, until one day, Iago apologized and told him that although he didn't understand the whole gay thing, he wouldn't lose his brother over it. He wouldn't lie and say that it hadn't taken a long time for them to build back the trust they have now.

"Of course I do. But if one day you find a lover who is not a carrier and you two decide to give me grandchildren, she's a choice for a surrogate."

Othello rolled his eyes. "Didn't you just find out you're about to be a grandmother? Don't give me that."

"I wished Iago had married the girl first," Maria pouted. "Maybe you should talk to him."

"Her name is Emilia, and they will when they are ready."

"I know what her name is," Maria huffed and agitatedly fixed his bed covers, grumbling about Emilia. "She's a sweet girl, and I hate what Iago has been doing to her, but I promise not to interfere in your love lives. As long as he is happy, I will support him."

At the beginning of the relationship, his mama disliked Emilia a little until she learned of Iago's cheating habits. As much as Maria tried to stay out of it, she couldn't stop herself from berating Iago and telling Emilia to break things off with him. Hearing those words must have done something to Iago because he promised to remain faithful to Emilia if she forgave him. However, Othello knew his brother and knew that he was keeping a mistress or two on the side, much to Othello's disappointment, and he'd told him to stop being an idiot. Othello thought Emilia was perfect for Iago. He could see how much she loved his friend and wished he had someone as devoted to him as Emilia was to Iago.

During her fussing, Nurse Chloe came in with his medication, and he was fucking thankful. Not long after, the broth came up, and as hungry as he was, he couldn't manage but a few spoonfuls.

Fuck, I need to get better quickly so that I can get the fuck out of here.

Othello had never told anyone, but he hated hospitals. He couldn't recall many details about his parents' deaths, but he vividly remembered the hospital's smell and the overwhelming emotions it brought. Even though he was an adult and Maria had been by his side the entire time, with each passing moment he was awake, he could feel those very emotions, and it was fucking with him far more than it should. A couple of hours later, he was taken for tests and then back to his room, where Alessandro had joined Maria.

"Don Alessandro, it's good to see you're in good health, sir."

Alessandro sighed and grumbled, "When are you going to start calling me Papa? You've been my son since you were thirteen."

Maria tapped Alessandro on his shoulder. "Stop complaining. Don't you know your son calls you that because he greatly respects you?"

"I get that, but he could say it just once," Alessandro pouted.

"Stop acting like a child," Maria said.

Maria was correct on one level. He had a tremendous amount of respect for Alessandro, but he'd never thought the man would care if he called him father or not. Maybe he had been wrong this entire time. Othello watched the two bicker lovingly, as they had since he met them. Alessandro was a fierce man, never to be trifled with, but the one person who could make him do anything they wanted was Maria, who had his heart completely.

It was sometime later that Maria had fallen asleep, giving Alessandro and Othello time to talk. "Are we sure the Falcons weren't the ones to set up the ambush? They take us out and get all the properties."

"Everyone is suspicious right now, but I hate to say it. Julian isn't that smart," Alessandro said. "The person who planned it was much smarter."

Othello sighed. "Since we agree that Falcon didn't set us up, I think it's important we continue with the negotiations."

"They'll want more than what we offered. If we don't play nice, we already suspect they are working with the Ricci and Greco families, and we don't want to cross Falcon bringing the fire down on us. That's something we're not ready to take them on yet."

"I know. Give them Liberty Heights and Greenfield. There's enough real estate for them to make a killing if they know what they're doing; we already have the financial district and most of the high-scale real estate. We'll take back the medical and art district. This way, we still have Bradford Healthcare in our pockets. Not to mention, the change of hands won't disrupt the art auction at the year's end. I wasn't keen on us giving up those properties, but I get you wanted them to see your good nature."

Alessandro asked, "What do you want to do with the slush fund we received from the auction?"

"The best way to look like a good businessman is to invest it. In the years we've started doing more business with the tech boys, we've been able to hide our business better."

"Damn." Alessandro tsked. "I knew Falcon wasn't as smart as his father, or else he would have seen all that he tried to give him."

"You should have known he didn't have what it took to be a part of this business when he turned down access to Rizzo's ports. We'll be able to control what comes in and out. His father would have seen an opportunity and taken it."

Unlike most families, the Romanos no longer dealt with drugs and human trafficking. They concentrated on buying and selling arms in other countries, prime real estate, and gambling, which brought in more money than they could spend in an hour. In the beginning, Iago was against the idea of them changing their business dealings but later saw how prosperous they were. Falcon, on the other hand, had no head for business or this world.

"Falcon wants to stay on petty shit that Iago and I used to do when we were kids. They can't play with the big boys. We planned on taking them out in the future anyway, but I say leave it to the cops. They'll fuck up their own bag by the end of the year. Then we can swoop in and take the bag that we gave them."

Alessandro sat silent for a few minutes before he spoke again. "I'll have the new agreement drawn up. Once everything is settled, we'll get started on the renovations of the old factories. Are you sure you want to turn them into condos?"

"Yeah." The construction companies were the perfect cover, as most of their illegal activities ran through them, but Othello felt they needed to expand and have a few legal businesses. Lately, the cops had been sniffing around their construction sites a bit too much—more than once, they'd had to deal with an undercover cop—Othello's plan was for their clan to appear completely legit on the surface, drawing smoke away from them. Alessandro wasn't a careless man by any means, but he was growing sloppy, drawing eyes on them, ones they didn't need.

"I'll follow your lead on this, Othello. It's why I made you my successor."

"Our other goal right now is finding out who set us up.

Are you sure we looked into everyone?"

"Do you doubt me?" Alessandro quirked a brow.

"Of course not. I want to make sure we covered all grounds," he said as another thought came to him. "What about the Ricci and Greco families? You know how much they hate me, not to mention Cassio; their underboss despises me."

"Even if they are the ones that put out the hit, we can't touch them. We can only speculate. I doubt they're ready to take out Falcon and his lot. But I also can't deny they would have a reason to want to take you or me out of the game. They find me disloyal for naming you as my heir."

Othello had never asked, but he'd always wondered why Alessandro hadn't chosen Iago when the two men were more alike than anything. As a matter of fact, he was certain Iago would have been the next in line. Othello had grown more laid-back the older he got, and he was enjoying his early thirties. Iago remained brash and unyielding but followed Alessandro's orders to the letter, while Othello did what felt right. When they were adopted, Iago didn't hyphenate his last name and immediately took the Romano name.

"Thank you for trusting me, Papa." Othello smiled. He saw a brightness engulf Alessandro's face for the first time, but he coughed, masking it quickly, and then changed the subject.

They talked more about dealing with the fallout of the ambush before he sent Alessandro and Maria home. Since he wasn't sleepy and thanked all the gods for his high pain threshold, he wasn't feeling pain that he couldn't handle. He grabbed his cellphone and responded to several emails. He would have continued if he hadn't felt sleepy and the nurse had come in to check on him. During the night, he was awakened by voices, but he remained still, kept his eyes closed, and listened to make sure he wasn't in danger. He hated feeling helpless. He guessed it might be the hospital staff since they were moving around his bed, fiddling with the covers as they talked.

"Did you hear Doctor Ellington turned down our Doctor Adonis when he asked him out on a date?" one person said.

"No way," a second voice interjected. "Who turns down Adonis? We call him that for a reason. Who does Doctor Ellington think he is? Did he give a reason?"

"Who knows, maybe he's seeing someone, or his parents already picked out his lover for him. You know he does nothing without their approval."

Fuck, why are they fucking gossiping in my room while I'm trying to sleep? Get the hell out so I can rest.

"I feel sorry for Doctor Ellington, though; he's kind, sexy, and pretty sweet," said the first voice with a giggle. "I fall in lust with him every time I look into his green eyes."

"He really is, and very good to the nursing staff."

Not wanting to hear anymore, Othello moaned and shifted in the bed as if he were waking up. He heard the two women gasp. Cracking his eyes open, he watched the two leave his hospital room. Not wanting to think about it anymore, he snuggled in the uncomfortable bed as he drifted back to sleep, recalling green gems that reminded him of an angel.

DES SLAMMED BACK his fifth or sixth shot of the night, before slumping down on the sofa. He was grinning like a fool as he felt the spirit run through his bloodstream, giving him the sweet buzz he wanted.

"You alright, man?"

Des turned his head, looking at Gray, who had stopped by unannounced with alcohol and Frango Assado com Piri-Piri from the local Portuguese restaurant not far from Des's house.

"Yeah. I'm good." His eyes felt droopy, but he knew he wasn't sleepy. "Are you going to tell me why you're here? And what reason do you have to get me drunk when you know I have work tomorrow?" He was slurring his words but didn't care.

Gray chuckled. "I didn't force you to drink. And can't I come and see my best friend?"

"Ha! Best friend, my ass." Des pouted. "You've been so busy I thought you forgot about me. It makes me wonder if you're seeing someone. You're starting to act like Bianca when she gets a new lover."

"Nah, I could never forget you. I'm just busy with work."

Gray, whose real name was Gratiano Marchetti, was quite handsome with his tall, muscular build, dark brown hair, and hazel eyes. Although they had been friends since college, they had never dated or done anything remotely intimate besides kissing each other on the cheek or falling asleep in the same bed. Des had seen the kind of men and women Gray liked to go out with, and Des could say he wasn't remotely Gray's type, which had never bothered him. Except for when they hung out together. Because men and women fawned over him, completely forgetting that Des was even around. It wasn't that he wasn't a looker. He'd been described as gorgeous with androgynous features.

He got his light green eyes from his dad and his jetblack hair from his mother. He kept his hair short and always appeared as if he'd just rolled out of bed, so whenever he wasn't working, he normally gelled it down to keep it in place. He kept in shape by swimming and doing calisthenics whenever he had time off. Thanks to his parents, he ate healthily but enjoyed a good hamburger and fries smothered in ketchup on a good day.

"How's work?" Gray asked.

Des shrugged his shoulders. "It's work. Nothing else for me to say. I saved a gunshot victim a couple of days ago." Sitting up, he poured himself another drink and took his shot, no chaser, since he wanted to feel the burn. "Want to know what's weird?"

"Yeah?"

"They don't want me to report it. I was practically threatened to tell my parents if I reported it to the police.

So I don't even know how he got shot."

"Do you want me to look into it?" Gray asked.

"No, I told you I can't tell the cops," Des snapped.

"Did you forget I'm a cop?"

"You're different," Des said, taking two more shots. "You won't do anything to draw attention to me. What if he's a part of the mafia..."

"Alright, that's enough." He took the shot glass away from him. "Sometimes I forget how you get when you drink too much."

"I need to drink so I don't have to think about how much I don't like my job."

"If you hate your job, Desi, quit," Gray said, rubbing his shoulder in comfort.

"You know I can't. I need my inheritance to open my gallery. And I don't dislike saving lives, Gray. I might not love it, but I am good at what I do," he said, then laughed. "Can you imagine it, though?" He turned to face Gray. "Better yet, picture me telling the folks that I'm giving up their dream for me because I want to follow my own."

Des had told everything to Gray about his enriched family

life back when they were in school, and he had been trying to convince him to walk his own path, but it was hard for Des because he was too fucking loyal to his parents. Not only that, he felt indebted to them, or that was how they had made it seem his entire life. They never failed to remind him they'd paid for him to attend the best private school, his college and medical school tuition, and even the apartment building he lived in was bought by his parents where he lived rent-free.

"Fuck, I hate this for you, Desi." Gray sighed.

"Don't call me that," he groaned, flopping over and resting his head on Gray's shoulder. "I want to meet someone. Hell, I want to lose my virginity before I die of old age."

"To do that, you have to step away from your parents' shackles."

"I know—two more years. I can do it, and then I won't have to deal with them," he said, snuggling into Gray's neck.

"I can give you the money you need, Desi," Gray said.

"No," Des told him. "I already have to rely on my parents and don't want to depend on you too. I need to do this on my own."

"If you say so." Gray kissed him on the forehead, and it felt good to have some affection.

"I got asked out by one of the doctors on my floor, but I turned him down." "Why?"

"I don't know. I never know why I turn them down. Maybe I'm waiting for someone special to sweep me off my feet."

Gray circled his waist, pulling him closer. "This isn't a fairy tale, Desi. Real life is a lot harder than that." "Can you not burst my bubble?" he groaned.

"I'm just being real with you," Gray said. "Don't give up on finding love," Des heard as he drifted off to sleep.

* * *

THE FOLLOWING MORNING, Des woke up to his phone buzzing, wishing he could ignore it. He peeked his head from the mounds of pillows, not even questioning how he got to bed after falling asleep on Gray last night; he knew his friend was the one to get him situated before he either went home or went to sleep on the couch. Des stretched for his still buzzing phone, squinting as he looked at who had interrupted his sweet dream.

He groaned, pressing the phone to his forehead when he saw Mom lighting up the screen. It was another temptation not to answer, but he knew Ava only called for a specific reason. His parents weren't bad people, and he didn't hate them—he really didn't; they just required so much from him.

"Good morning, Mother," he said, answering the call.

"I can't believe you're still sleeping," Ava's stern voice responded. "Don't you have to be at the hospital?"

He rolled on his back, staring up at the ceiling. "Not for another four hours."

"When your father and I were in your position, we would..."

"Mother, is there a reason why you called me at five in the morning?" he interrupted before she went on and on about how dedicated she and his father used to be at the hospital.

"No need to get snappy, Desmond," Ava said dryly. "Your father and I are having a small dinner party tonight, and we want you to join us after work. There are a couple of people we want you to meet."

This was how their conversations always went, like a business meeting where they told him where and when he needed to be. There were never any sweet family moments he could pull up in his memory that brought a smile to his face. Family gatherings were stoic and mind-numbing for Des. The good thing was his extended family wasn't so bad, but they hardly came around.

"Mother, you know I don't like parties." *Especially the ones you throw. I always have to pretend I'm having a good time.*

"It is a networking party, dear. Your father and I are preparing for your future. Plus, your father and I have a very important announcement."

Des knew he should be ecstatic that his parents were investing so much into him, yet he wasn't living his own life. *I don't want it! I don't want your future plans. I want my own.* Mentally, he was aware of how ungrateful he sounded, but he was very unhappy. "Mother, I don't..." He went to say he didn't want to work at the hospital anymore, but the words stalled on his tongue.

"What is it that you don't know, dear? Speak up, I have a lot to do."

"I don't know if I'll be able to make it. You know how unpredictable things at the hospital can be."

"That is true," Bianca said. "Very well. I will tell you the news we're announcing tonight. Your father has

decided to run for the New York Senate."

"What?" Des sat up in bed, surprised at his mother's declaration.

"Yes, isn't it exciting?" Des pulled the phone from his ear and looked at the name on the caller ID to make sure he was really talking to his mother since he'd never heard her sound so excited.

"Why? Why did he decide to go into politics?"

"Because it's something he'd always wanted to do."

"I thought being a doctor was his ultimate goal in life," he said sarcastically and was sure Ava hadn't caught on.

"He's accomplished that goal. Now, he's ready to move on to the next one. So with him running for senate, we'll both be retiring as administrators from the hospital. I'm sure that will make you happy not to have us looking over your shoulder."

"Since you're both quitting, can I do the same?"

"Whyever, for? Your career's just starting," she said as if he'd asked an insane question. "Anyway, you go and get ready for work. I'm off to prepare for tonight's dinner party. Please come if you can." She hung up before he could say anything else, but Des lay still with his phone still pressed to his ear.

Did my mother use the word, please? And with me? What the fuck is going on here?

SCENE VI

DES

es groaned, stretching and hearing his muscles pop in all the right places. The minute he'd stepped into the hospital, he'd been pulled into an emergency surgery for a construction worker who fell off a scaffold, breaking his spine in four places. That was five hours ago, and now he was aching and starving. After cleaning up and speaking with the family, he went to the lounge to grab something to eat and bumped into Doctor Fabian Castilian, or as the nurses liked to call him, Doctor Adonis.

"Oh, I'm sorry," Des said as he tried to step around the other doctor, but he was stopped with a hand on his waist.

"Nothing to apologize for. I was hoping to bump into you," the doctor told him.

"Oh really, why?" Des moved back, allowing the hand holding him to let go.

"I wanted to know if you've reconsidered my dinner date request. I was hoping for tonight."

I already turned you down. What is there to think about? What the fuck is wrong with this guy? Doctor Castilian was handsome, that was for sure, but the doctor set off his spidey senses whenever the man was near him. He knew the guy was a straight-up player and liked bragging about who he'd fucked. But other than that, Castilian was an exceptional surgeon. Or it could've been his imagination. "I don't think it will be possible. I promised my mom I'd have dinner with her and my dad tonight."

"Oh," Castilian said, seeming quite crestfallen, but Des didn't understand why when the man had plenty of others in the hospital to choose from. "Maybe some other time, then."

Des nodded and walked away, only to stop again when he noticed that the patient, Mister Moor, who was two doors down, had been watching their interaction. He was leaning against the doorframe with his arms crossed over his chest, and again, Des was surprised. Anyone who had just had a major surgery like Moor would be laid up in bed, not wanting to move for at least a week. It had only been a couple of days, and the man was already on his feet.

"Mister Moor, you should be in bed," Des said, walking over to him. "You've only been awake for a couple of days."

"I can't lie in bed all day, Doc; I'm not built like that," Moor said, his tone low and steady.

"Well, as your doctor, I'd advise you not to move too much. Your sutures cannot be disturbed." Des sighed, realizing he wouldn't be getting anything to eat anytime soon. "Let's get you back into bed so I can look you over."

Moor stared down at him since the man seemed significantly taller than Des had imagined, making him tilt his head back to look up at him. After a few seconds, he grunted and walked back into the room. Des wrapped a hand around his waist, giving him aid that proved to be a bit useless. Even injured, the man could still lift Des without breaking a sweat.

"You don't have to help me into bed. I can manage."

"Okay," Des agreed, not wanting to be bothered arguing with the man.

Once Moor was situated in bed, he began his exam, making notes on his file. He hadn't had time to review the test results from the day before, but Moor was healing well. However, it didn't mean the man could walk around at will.

"Are you really going to your folks' for dinner?"

Des paused and looked at the patient. "What business is it of yours?" he snapped.

"I'm bored." Moor shrugged his shoulders, then hissed at the action. "Call me curious."

"You know what they say happened to the cat, right?" Des said.

"Then I suppose I can rely on the other eight lives I have left," was Moor's snappy comeback, not taking his brown eyes off Des, still waiting for an answer.

"I don't discuss my private life with my patients, Mister Moor."

"Fair enough, but that guy won't give up. You've already rejected him twice. He'll try for a third and wear you down until you say yes."

Placing his stethoscope around his neck, Des tilted his head to the side. "How did you know he'll ask me again?"

"Guys like that don't give up." Moor laid back on his pillow, reached for his remote, and turned on the television. "I guess I can see why he won't. Too bad you're not my

type, or I'd ask you out myself."

"Who said I'd go out with you anyway?" Des growled, feeling quite annoyed with the man, especially when he smirked.

"So, you don't find me good-looking? Maybe I was mistaken, and you weren't checking me out yesterday."

"I'm your doctor, Mister Moor, nothing else. Please report me to the administrators if you feel I was doing something inappropriate or uncomfortable. Maybe they'll do me the favor of throwing me out on my ass. Now, if you'll excuse me, I have other things to do."

With that, Des walked out of the patient's room with a commanding air, but inside, he was so angry he could spit fire if he were a dragon. *How dare that asshole say I was checking him out?* But you were, came an annoying voice in the back of his head that he instantly shut off with a mental *fuck off*. Still, Des didn't like being called out on his shit. *What a cocky bastard. Dammit, and why do I find it so sexy?*

Pushing the encounter out of his mind, he went and got something to eat and finished out his day since he had to go home and get ready for his parents' dinner party. Des hated that he was far too loyal and honest with his parents, yet he wasn't honest with his feelings about his career. *One day. I'll tell them one day.*

* * *

OTHELLO CHUCKLED as he watched the doctor hurry out of his room with his back straight, trying to pretend he wasn't affected by Othello's words. He hadn't meant to upset the doctor, but truthfully, he was bored out of his skull. He'd contacted Tallen and told him to bring some paperwork to him to look over. But Tallen told him Don Alessandro ordered that if anyone brought work to Othello, he would chop their legs off. Tallen was loyal to Othello but was loyal and afraid of

Alessandro more than anything else. So, until then, Othello would have to find something or someone to occupy his time. And it seemed the little doctor was the right distraction.

* * *

DES STOOD on the balcony of his parents' home, enjoying the cool breeze. He'd only been there for thirty minutes and had not spoken with his parents. He'd seen them, but they were too busy chatting and laughing with their friends. Des was giving it another fifteen minutes before he made his escape.

"So this is where you're hiding," came a familiar voice behind him.

"I'm not hiding, Mother, just taking a breather." Des spun around and greeted her respectfully. They were not the touchy-feely type of people. He couldn't recall the last time she or his father had given him a hug. Maybe it was when he was in junior high school. He'd tried giving her a hug, and she rebuffed him. Ava Ellington didn't look a day over forty, and not a strand of hair was out of place, pulled back in a tight bun. She wore a designer hunter-green sequined strapless midi-length dress contoured to her thin frame.

"This is an important night for your father. Why did you wear jeans to the party?" she huffed, wrinkling her brows. "You could have at least worn a jacket. It won't look good with you standing next to your father when he

announces his senate bid."

"Mother, I came straight from work," he lied. He'd actually gone home, with enough time to shower, and got dressed in a dark blue suit and black shirt, no tie, and just as he was about to walk out the door, he decided to change and went with jeans and a black V-neck pullover sweater.

"You wanted me here, so here I am."

"Have you eaten?"

"Is that concern I hear coming from you?" he said, a bit taken aback.

"Why wouldn't I be concerned? You're my son."

"Mother..."

"When will you call me Mom?"

"What the hell is going on with you?" Des snapped. "I can't figure you out right now. You've never been concerned about anything pertaining to me. The only thing you and your father were concerned about was whether I got A's in school or came first. If it weren't for Nanny Cee, I wouldn't know what it felt like to be hugged by a mother figure..."

"Desmond, where is this coming from?" his mother said, sounding very surprised by his ranting.

Truthfully, he was as well. He hadn't meant for all that to come out, but in for a penny, in for a pound, as the saying went.

"You knew I never wanted to be a doctor. I only did because you and Dad forced me, and now you want me to stand here like a supportive son while he announces that he wants to run for senate when you both have never given me emotional support a day in my life. We are not a perfect family, Mother. What happened to 'we must carry on the family business?'"

"That is why we had you, Son," Ava said, smiling. "So you can take over where we left off."

Des chuckled, but it wasn't because he was happy. "So you two get to live out your dreams while I'm stuck doing something I hate?"

"Lower your tone," she said, looking around as if expecting others to pay attention to their conversation. "And what's wrong with saving people's lives? Art is a hobby, Desmond, not a steady career."

"There's nothing wrong with saving lives, but one has to have their heart and soul in it to feel that it is worthwhile to sacrifice everything for what they love."

"Have we been that terrible to you, Desmond?"

"Not in the way you might be thinking, but it's obvious you and Father don't believe in my dream, yet I'm supposed to smile and support you both while you accomplish yours. I can't do that or carry on with a mentally and physically draining career. So why don't you give me my inheritance, and let's cut ties with each other? Better yet, go and have the child you really want."

Ava gasped and clutched her diamond-encrusted necklace, staring at Des as if he'd said the world was ending. Seeing they had nothing else to say to each other, Des walked away, leaving his mother standing in the same spot, but if he was being completely honest with himself, he felt ten years lighter.

* * *

OVER THE NEXT FEW WEEKS, Des thought long and hard about what he wanted to do with his life. Now that he'd told his mother he never wanted to be a doctor, he thought of changing careers but would not immediately quit. He needed to speak with his grandfather's attorney to see his options. After his grandfather died, he'd only stayed at the will reading long enough to hear his grandfather's stipulations; if there was more to the will, Des didn't know what was said. He was too angry with his grandfather for siding with his parents. Growing up, his grandfather Sebastian had encouraged Des's love of art and told him never to give up on his dreams. So he felt it was a stab in the heart hearing the words he wrote.

When he was ready to read the will, his parents were completely against it. He'd contacted the lawyer who had read the will and found out he no longer worked for the firm his grandfather used. It seemed he'd quit a couple of days after the will reading. Des wouldn't deny that he'd grown suspicious of the whole thing. The new attorney who took over handling his grandfather's case was very close to his father, and Des didn't think he could trust the man to act in his best interest.

It may be time for me to get my own lawyer. Fuck, I should have done that a long time ago.

He knew he couldn't go on like this, waiting two years before being free. Des didn't know how much the inheritance was, but he knew it would be enough for him to put a down payment on a building to open his studio. He'd been on the east side, which had always been described as the artist and cultural hub of Verona Heights and where he originally wanted to live. From the art shows, the people, and the music to the theatre, Des came alive each time he went there to see if the building he'd had his eye on for years still sat empty. It was as if the property was waiting for him to claim it.

It was large enough and had two separate levels for him to have an art studio, where he could teach classes, hold exhibits, and do so much more, as well as an apartment. Des could only hope the building would be there in two years when he left this job. His parents would be angry with him, but Des didn't care.

It's time I stand up for myself.

He would quit his job if he knew his savings and small investments would sustain him for a long time. But truthfully, he was afraid of failing and proving his parents right when he wanted to succeed and rub it in their faces. Having his inheritance would give him a sense of security. He hadn't heard from his parents since the night of their party, and Des wasn't sure how to feel. Des had thought his mother would call to argue with him over his words, but it seemed they'd abandoned him like always.

"That better not be my medical record you're looking at, the way your face keeps changing."

Des looked up from the patient record and locked onto his patient Moor. His recovery had been going well, and Des was certain he'd be able to discharge the man in a day or two, which would be a relief. Since that day, Des had told him to mind his business; the man had done no such thing. Moor seemed to find it fascinating to delve into his private life each time he went to give the man a check-up. Of course, Des never answered his questions, but it only made Moor push more.

"As a matter of fact, I looked over your chart earlier. I have good news. You can be discharged in two days."

"Really?" Moor said, excitement brimming in his brown eyes.

"Yes. Your latest test results show no infections, and you can function without pain meds. Well done, Mister Moor."

"What about my diet?"

Since the man had chest surgery, he had been on a restricted diet while his injuries healed. "Don't go crazy, but slowly work more into your daily meals, and you should be fine."

"This is great news. To tell you the truth, I've been bored out of my skull."

"Well, you can get back to your normal life in a couple of days."

Moor looked as if he was about to say something when Tallen, if Des correctly remembered the man's name, got off the elevator and walked over to the nurses' station, where Des and Moor were standing.

"Boss, what are you doing out of bed?" Tallen said worriedly.

"What do you think will happen to me when the doctor and all these nurses are right here?"

Des listened to Moor's brash manner of speaking to his friend and didn't like it. "You could talk to him nicely. He's only concerned about you," he said haughtily.

"Oh, it's okay, Doc; boss doesn't mean anything by it. I'm used to the way he speaks."

"Why should I watch the way I speak to my people?"

"Is this your way of telling me to mind my business?" Des shot back.

Moor shrugged. "More or less."

"Oh, so it's okay to push your nose into my affairs, but I can't do the same with you. I never realized you were so hypocritical." Not wanting to bother the annoying man, Des grabbed his medical charts and left for a quiet place to work since he wasn't scheduled to perform any surgeries for the rest of the day.

* * *

"Boss, you're smiling," Tallen said, grabbing Othello's attention.

"What the fuck are you talking about?" he scowled. "I wasn't smiling."

"While watching the doctor walk away, your face had a weird grin. Do you like the doc?"

"He's not my type."

"Funny, I was sure he was," Tallen said, rubbing the back of his neck. "He's feisty and doesn't seem afraid to look you in the eye like some of the other guys you've fucked. Not to mention, he's pretty cute and has those dimples when he smiles."

"You were seeing things," Othello mumbled.

"Marco and I have a bet going that he's a carrier."

"What the hell difference does that make?" Othello's brows furrowed, looking at Tallen, who shrugged his shoulders.

"Well, if he is, then you can get with him and have kids, and Mrs. Maria could stop worrying that you'll die a lonely man. She doesn't show it when she's here, boss, but she's been really worried since you got shot."

Othello sighed. He really wished he could ease Maria's worry, but simply falling into bed with someone just to procreate wasn't his thing. Did he want children? Of course, he did, but it wasn't a dealbreaker for him. Sure, he'd had flings and even been in a committed relationship once, but things didn't work out. Othello desired too many things from his partner, one being their complete trust and loyalty. He wanted them to understand that he would never walk away from his family, not even for their love. He wanted them to be independent yet submissive to him, mainly in the bedroom. He enjoyed caring for and pampering his lovers, showing them they were the center of his world while needing them to be his safe space.

Truthfully, in the past few days, he had enjoyed watching the little doctor's green eyes burn with fire, and his cheeks turn pink as he got riled up before storming off to gods knew where. He would never admit that Tallen was right, and he had been checking out the doctor a little more each time they saw each other. Little Doctor Ellington was adorable and had some flavors Othello appreciated in a bed partner, from his petite stature to a nice-toned and svelte build. The doctor had beautiful eyes that reminded him of an angel from his dreams. He also had attractive lips, flawless skin, and a dimpled smile. His eyebrows were thick and perfectly arched, and his long lashes rested on his high cheekbones.

"Boss, you're still smiling. What are you thinking about?" Tallen said, breaking into his thoughts.

"About you going to school," he said, changing the subject. Othello had been trying to convince Tallen to attend college to further his advancement in the family.

"Boss, I'm not school material," Tallen said, scratching the back of his neck.

Othello shook his head—*this kid*. "I'm getting out of this place in two days," he said, dropping the subject for now.

"Really?" Tallen exclaimed. "About damn time. We've all missed you, boss."

Othello smiled. "Same here. I can't wait to sleep in my own damn bed. Why are you here, anyway?"

"Oh, I've got news. We caught one guy who was involved in the ambush."

"How? When?"

"Honestly, I don't know how it happened. Yesterday, Consig Iago got a call and rushed out of the morning meeting with the city bosses who were involved and came back five hours later with some dude that was all beat to shit but still breathing."

That's why he didn't come and see me yesterday. "Where is he? The guy?"

"Since he won't talk, we have him locked up in The Pen. The don figures a little more torture will get him to talk."

The Pen was a pit for illegal fights and gambling and a whole host of things that would have the cops knocking at his front door if they knew what really went down in the club. The Pen was only open twice a week, and the only way to get in was by invitation and a password that changed every week and never duplicated. The Pen had a jail cell built in the club's basement for hard-to-deal-with clientele. It was nothing like his other two establishments, Mirage and Starlight Haven. Othello had won the deed to Mirage in a poker match with Roderigo, an influential businessman with his hands in pockets they shouldn't have been in. Othello would admit that he and Roderigo were not and never would be best friends; in fact, he hated the man with every breath he took. But he kept the man at arm's length even though the businessman was Iago's close friend.

At that thought, he looked at Tallen. "Did anyone check into Roderigo's activities before and after the ambush?"

The Mirage was a strip club that offered more than just a couple of lap dances. Besides the expensive drinks and the talented strippers, clients were able to rent out highpriced escorts available to fulfill any man's or woman's dreams, whether for a day, night, months, or even a year. Othello conducted most of his illegal activities at The Pen and Mirage, which left Starlight Haven clean but offered many amenities to his clientele. The Starlight Haven kept the cops from looking too deep into the family's affairs. It was in the factory district and about ten or fifteen minutes walk from his apartment. He liked the Starlight Haven, but the Mirage padded his pockets, keeping his Smurfs busy, not just counting and distributing the large bills they took in within just one night but also keeping track of their gambling websites. When Othello took it over, the damn club was oozing money but getting nothing in return. Othello knew the man had an ax to grind with him and wanted his club back, but he didn't want to think Roderigo would be stupid enough to put Iago and Don Alessandro in danger trying to get to him.

"I think so," Tallen said. "Honestly, boss, the don looked into every one. I know we investigated if there were any Rizzo leftovers, but we took care of all of them. But we still don't know who did it. Until that fucker talks, we're back to square one."

Othello sighed and leaned against the window, feeling unsettled. He had hoped they would have more information by now. But there wasn't anything he could do until he left the hospital.

Two days later, Othello was wheeled out of the hospital by Tallen, with Iago by his side. He was finally leaving and couldn't be happier, but he had a shit ton of instructions about what he could and couldn't do for the next couple of months. Othello didn't care as long as he was heading home. He had hoped to see the cute doctor, maybe see him blush with frustration again, but the man was stuck in another surgery. Mentally shrugging, Othello looked at his friend.

"Make sure I never go through that shit again," he said.

Iago quirked a brow. "What, didn't like the accommodation?"

"Not the best way to spend my two-week vacation, that's

for sure," he grumbled, standing from the wheelchair. "Alright, let's head home. I have things to do."

"I'm glad you're alive." Iago smiled, clapping him on the shoulder.

"Me too, bro." They shared an understanding and then walked shoulder to shoulder to the car, their bond forever cemented.

ACT II

My noble Moor is true of mind, and made of no such baseness / As jealous creatures are.
Desdemona (Act 3, Scene 4)

*S*ix months later, Othello entered through the back door of Starlight Haven, entering the code on the keypad and waiting for the lock to sound. With Starlight Haven located in the former factory district, it brought him a lot of upscale clientele, since the old factories were bought and converted into coffee shops, bookstores, restaurants, gyms, offices, penthouse apartments, and clubs like his own. When the door opened, the scent of strong liquor, money, and machines invaded his senses.

Othello opened the club two years ago. Tonight, the club's second level hosted a party for a lawyer celebrating his wife's birthday. He spent almost half a million dollars on fifteen bottles of their priciest champagne and got to use their VIP lounges. The first floor was business as usual, with party and clubgoers enjoying themselves.

Entering his office, he sat at his desk and reviewed the previous night's receipts. Since returning from the hospital, Othello had been so busy that he couldn't explain it. The deal with the Falcons had been completed, and just as Othello had suggested, Julian Falcon went with what they offered. Othello would admit the Romano clan still got the better end of things, but the Falcons weren't at a loss, either. If Julian played it smart, they could make a killing out of the properties, but like he told his father, Julian didn't have the head or the heart for the business they were in. By the end of the year, they would be getting all of their properties back and more.

Othello and his family were still in the dark about who had ambushed them. The guy Iago brought back hung himself with his shirt a day later. They should have locked him up naked, because that's what Othello would have done. Othello couldn't shake the feeling that there was something off about the ambush. No one but the two clans knew when and where they were meeting, so they had a traitor in the mix. Dealing with traitors was easy, but that meant they were working with someone powerful to be able to get the drop on two clans. Othello secretly had one of his most trusted guys looking into things without telling Alessandro and Iago.

Thinking of Iago, Othello had hardly seen his friend in the past few months. Before he got shot, they'd have lunch at least once a week to catch up. But they'd both been busy dealing with restructuring the Rizzo properties. In between all of that, Othello had spent much of his time healing and building his body back, and Iago was probably worried about Emilia, who was seven months pregnant and seemed to be having some complications, but the doctors and the family were hopeful for a healthy baby. No one knew what she was having and wanted to be surprised. The door to his office opened, pulling him from his thoughts, and Iago walked in as if he'd known Othello was thinking about him.

"Hey, what are you doing here?" Iago asked.

Othello furrowed his brows. "Why wouldn't I be?"

"I thought you'd be at home resting." Iago entered, closed the door, and sat on the couch across from Othello's desk.

"Am I an old man that needs resting?" He chuckled.

"O, you were shot..."

"Six months ago. I'm fully healed and in better shape than I was before. I don't see what you're worried about." As he said the words, a thought came to him. "Do you

think I'm going to die on you or something?"

"Stop talking craziness," Iago said. "Nothing can kill you."

"I'm glad you're aware," he said, moving a few papers around. Just then, his door burst open, and Marco walked in.

"Boss, you need to come quick. We have trouble," he said.

"What kind of trouble?" Iago asked before Othello could say anything.

"Um..." Marco stuttered, looking between them both.

Othello mentally sighed. He noticed that had been happening a lot lately. It started the first week after he got out of the hospital. Subordinates seemed unsure who to call their boss, and the ones that usually came to report things to him would go to Iago as if he was the second-incommand. Othello had been ignoring the way Iago's eyes lit up each time it happened.

He knew Iago had run things for him while in the hospital, but he was only gone for two weeks. How the fuck did their loyalty shift so damn quickly? He would like to say that it didn't bother him; after all, he and Iago were not in any competition. He had never used his underboss authority since he had gained respect from his soldiers from the start. But it didn't mean he could let things continue any longer where they seemed to doubt who their boss was. He would have to address things with his subordinates and Iago. If he didn't, it made him look weak as fuck. But then again, Othello could've been imagining things. He knew Iago was under a lot of stress these past few months.

I should cut him some slack.

"What's happening, Marco?" Othello asked since the man had yet to answer.

"Members of the Rossetti clan came into the club. You said it would be cool if the other clans came to the party as long as they abided by the rules. Everything was okay until they started making trouble with a few of the customers at the bar. A couple of our guys tried to stop them, but things got out of hand."

"Fuck," Othello exclaimed, cursing even more, and shot out of his seat.

The Rossetti clan was not to be played with. They were a minor family, but had close ties to the Ricci clan. He wasn't trying to cross paths with the Rossetti or the Ricci family yet. More things needed to be put into place. Othello and Rossetti's underboss also had a very brief dating history. They were just as influential in the underworld as the Romano clan. He hurried to the dance floor, which was a disaster. People were running out of the entrance or hiding, while men of all sizes were throwing hard fists at each other. Through the loud punches and the crowd of people running, Othello heard a familiar voice and prayed that he was wrong.

"Don't you fucking touch me, you asshole!"

Othello followed the voice, and his breath caught in his throat when he saw angel-green eyes attached to a face he hadn't seen in six months. He had to admit time had done the man many justices, especially with his new look. The last time he saw Doctor Des, the man had a cute, boyish next-door look. Not the current, holding his own against a man twice his size.

He'd grown out his hair, which seemed to have done the job of taming it, and he got a couple of tattoos on his arms. Othello wouldn't deny that he liked and missed messing with the doctor.

"Hey, boss, isn't that the doctor?" Marco said.

"Looks like it," Othello said, watching the man fight, taking one guy down and jumping on the back of another.

"When did he get here?" Marco mumbled.

Othello felt compelled to intervene and stop the situation but couldn't tear his eyes away from the little doctor's impressive performance. The Beast screamed when the little doctor bit down on his ear. Meaty's hands reached for Doctor Des, and that was when Othello made his move. He sprinted across the dance floor and punched the Beast in the stomach. Doctor Des quickly got off his back when he hunched over, letting Othello kick the Beast in the knee. The Beast howled in pain as bones snapped, bringing him down and ending the fight for everyone.

Othello turned to Doctor Des, who was panting and staring at him wide-eyed. "What in the ever-loving fuck possessed you to fight someone bigger than you?" Othello yelled.

"He started it," Doctor Des shouted, pointing to the screaming man on the ground.

"I saw you jump on his back," Othello argued.

"It's not my fault," Doctor Des said through gritted teeth. Othello could tell the doctor was drunk off his ass, but he had a determined look in his eyes of a man who knew when he was in the right. "I was minding my damn business, having a drink at the bar, then he and his fucking friends came up to us and offered to buy us a drink. I declined, but he kept pushing no matter how many times I said no. Then he grabbed me as if I was his property. I pushed him, and things escalated. But he started it."

Othello sighed, pinching the bridge of his nose, collecting

his thoughts. "Will someone shut this asshole up?" he shouted, pointing at the man on the ground.

"We got it, boss," Tallen said, looking a bit banged up.

Othello turned to the doctor. "Are you alright? Did you get hit anywhere?"

"No, I'm fine, but he won't be if he doesn't get to the hospital soon."

"He'll be fine, but do you know how much trouble you just cost me?" Othello huffed, then he grabbed the little doctor and pulled him over to Marco, who was rolling down his shirt sleeve. Othello was glad the doctor didn't argue with him, since he wasn't in the mood to fight. He had a long night ahead of him already and needed his strength.

"Take him to my apartment. Stand guard, and don't let him leave until I deal with this shit."

"Yes, boss." Marco reached out for the doctor, who stepped behind Othello.

"What the fuck is going on here? I'm a grown-ass man. What room is he taking me to, and why? Are you trying to kidnap me in a room full of people? Wait, you own this club?"

Othello would have thought the man was acting scared since the fear in his voice didn't match the *I will kick your ass* expression on his face.

What a feisty little drunk!

"Yes, this is my club, and Marco is going to take you upstairs so you can rest," Othello simply explained.

"But I'm not..."

Othello didn't let him finish and nodded at Marco as he stepped aside.

"This way, sir," Marco said and began walking away.

The little doctor didn't protest this time and followed behind Othello's subordinate. He turned to the rest. "Clear out the club and close down for the night."

"Boss, the birthday party is still going on," one of his subordinates informed him.

"I guess the fight didn't ruin their fun," he mumbled. "Let them be. They paid for the entire night. But clean this shit up."

"Yes."

Just as he was done giving out orders, Iago pocketed his cellphone. "I've set up a parley for you and the Rossetti underboss."

Othello quirked a brow, feeling quite irritated at Iago's action, but didn't let it show in his words or expression. "I appreciate it, bro, but wait for my order before you jump the gun next time."

Iago nodded as an expression flashed too quickly in his eyes for Othello to register what it was, but he pocketed it for later and focused on the matter at hand.

"When and where will we be meeting?"

"East Street Diner, midnight," Iago answered. "It's the closest neutral spot."

Othello looked at his watch, noting that he had an hour and a half. "Alright, you head home."

"What? Why?" Iago asked, seeming taken aback.

"Iago, seriously, you should head home. Emilia is close to giving birth."

"But..." he started, but Othello stopped him with a gentle hand on his shoulder.

"I know you want to be there for me, but Emilia needs you there more than me right now."

Iago went to speak again but stopped as if seeing that Othello had made sense. "You're always looking out for me, aren't you? And especially Emilia. If I didn't know you bat for the same team, I'd suspect you're in love with her."

"We're brothers. Isn't that what we're supposed to do? You watch my back, and I'll watch yours," Othello told Iago as he pulled him into a hug, feeling how tense the other man was. "Honestly, I think Emilia is too good for

you, and I'm just trying to get you to see that." "I know she is." Iago sighed.

"Then stop fucking around on her," Othello told him. "Get rid of the mistresses."

Iago sighed, and his body relaxed, embracing Othello back. "You're right. I'll do better and be a good man and father to my family."

"I know you can do it, Iago."

"Okay, I'll head out. Take someone with you. Neutral or not, don't go alone."

"I won't," Othello assured him as they separated. Minutes later, Iago left, and Othello called Don Alessandro, explaining everything to his father and about his meeting with the Rossetti underboss. After he was done with his call, Othello trudged outside the club to the back entrance and took the short walk to his place, letting the cool air fill his lungs. Ten minutes later, he took the stairs of his apartment to check on the doctor. Othello liked his apartment's location. It was in a busy part of the city but gave him a beautiful view at any time of the day.

"Hey, Marco, go take a break."

Marco gave a curt nod, then walked away. Othello didn't bother knocking and entered the room. The lights were off, but it didn't matter to Othello; the industrial-size windows brought in enough light from the outside so that he could see his way perfectly. But he also installed electronic curtains to close some rooms if he needed privacy. This was his home away from the Romanos' home. No one was allowed to enter without his permission. He had it added on when the club was being built. Othello liked the area because it faced the water, and he liked to stand and drink his coffee at the window in the morning.

His apartment was once part of a chocolate factory with two levels, and Othello bought and remodeled it. The first floor had an open design concept from the living room, dining room, and kitchen. The same thick red drapes hanging on the windows also separated the bedroom, which had an ensuite bathroom and walk-in closet. Othello designed the first floor so that everything could be seen and reached with a few quick steps. On the second level was his in-home gym with a sauna and game room. A door led to the balcony where he grew a garden and had enough space for a pool and lounging.

The place was quiet, and there wasn't anyone in the kitchen. He didn't hear the shower on in the bathroom. He knew the doctor was still there since there was no exit except the front door, where his subordinate stood guard. Marco would have told him if the other man had left, which meant the guy was sleeping.

Moving over to the couch, Othello expected to see the little doctor sleeping, but it was empty. Furrowing his brows, Othello scanned the room and spotted a garment lying on the leather chair across from the sofa near the window leading to the large balcony.

He knew he hadn't left it there since he was a neat freak and always kept his place clean. Moving over to the chair, he saw another article of clothes on the floor, picked it up, and noticed it was the doctor's shirt. Othello tsked at the messiness as he followed the line of clothes that was dropped as the man had undressed. He finally stopped when he reached the bed, pulling back the thick red drapes and spotting the lump under the covers. Walking over to the bed, the only thing he could see sticking out of the cover was the little doctor's dark hair.

"How dare you crawl into someone's bed naked like you own it?" Othello mumbled, then smiled. He shook his head when he got a light snore in response. Othello wasn't sure why he'd allowed the man in his personal space when, after he broke up the fight, he simply could have thrown his drunk ass in a car and sent the little doctor on his merry way.

Not wanting to bother with the sleeping form, Othello left his apartment and headed to the meeting location. If he knew the Rossettis' underboss, the man would show up early at the diner. He left Tallen to stand guard and took Marco with him. As Othello had predicted, Rossetti was already there when they arrived at the diner. Since it was midnight, the restaurant was bustling with customers. Luca Rossetti was sitting at the counter when Othello walked in, and he simply joined the man. He ordered coffee and waited for Luca to start the conversation. Since it was his guys that had come into his territory unannounced and started shit, it was up to him to apologize.

"We will pay for the damage to your establishment," Luca stated. "I will also have my people come and apologize to you personally. They broke a rule, and it's unsatisfactory."

"What about the man he assaulted?" Othello asked, leisurely taking a sip of his coffee.

"Who cares about some easy ass?" Rossetti snapped.

Othello growled, not looking at the man. He didn't like the way Rossetti referred to the little doctor. "And what if that easy ass, as you called him, is one of my people?"

Despite fucking with the little doctor, Othello felt responsible for what happened in his club, even though it wasn't his fault; especially since the man had saved his life, he felt he owed the doctor protection.

"Fuck, then I supposed I owe you an apology," he said, even though Othello knew he didn't mean it. "But did you have to break his fucking leg? Beast is one of my best people."

Othello didn't respond, so he simply set his coffee cup down. Othello stood, ready to leave, but Rossetti stopped him. "That's it?" he asked.

"What more do you want me to say?" Othello looked at him.

"We haven't seen each other for more than a year, and the first time we met was to discuss something that could have been done over the phone."

Luca and Othello went back to their teenage years despite being from rival clans. After the Romanos had adopted him and Iago, they'd attended a prestigious middle and high school where they met Luca and disliked each other on sight, without knowing their family backgrounds. As they got older, their differences turned into a friendship, and later, he and Luca had a brief relationship that went no further than kissing, hand jobs, and rubbing their dicks together. They broke it off since neither was willing to bottom for the other. Their friendship wavered over the years, and the more intertwined they got into their perspective clans, the less they saw each other when situations like tonight happened, and whenever they did, there was an underlying tension between them.

"I heard you got shot a few months ago. I wanted to visit, but I didn't think you'd want to see me. Are you doing better?" Luca's eyes roved over him from head to toe.

"I'm good." Othello sat back on his stool and ordered another cup of coffee.

"Do you know who did it?"

"We're still looking into it," Othello told him.

"Let me know if I can help," Luca said to him.

"I will," Othello said softly.

"Look, there's another reason I agreed to meet with you. It's that our don wants to set up a meeting with Don Alessandro."

"Why?"

"We know what moves your side is making, and we want in."

"I need to know what you guys are offering before I can take it to the don."

Luca nodded. "I know, so here is what we propose." He explained what they were bringing to the table. The meeting went on a little longer than Othello wanted, and he left the diner at three in the morning. When he arrived home, he dismissed Tallen and Marco. He was so exhausted from the night's event he was moving on autopilot as he showered and moisturized his skin quickly. Before leaving the bathroom, he discarded his towel in the hamper. The second his head hit the pillow, he fell asleep immediately.

* * *

DES GROANED, slowly waking up, frowning. He rubbed his face on the pillow beneath him, hating that it was so hard. The last few times it happened, he and Gray had a heavy night of drinking, and not wanting his friend to drink and drive made him sleep over. Because Des was such a wild sleeper and always got cold at night, he'd sometimes roll over in his sleep, seeking warmth, and end up practically sleeping on top of Gray.

Feeling the sun bearing down on his face, Des moaned and burrowed deeper into Gray's chest. But then a thought came to his sleep-addled brain: If it was morning, that meant that they had to get up for work.

"Gray, we need to get up, or we'll be late for work," Des said sleepily as his arm wrapped around his friend's hard torso. He expected Gray to respond with his usual "five more minutes," only to be surprised by something new.

"Who the fuck is Gray?" a sleepy, deep voice said. "I don't appreciate you calling another man's name while you're draped all over me."

Des sat up quickly and blinked the sleep from his eyes as his gaze traveled up a naked torso. He stopped at the scar for a few seconds, before moving up the man's face.

His eyes widened when he saw who was in bed with him.

"You!" he shouted in surprise.

"Yeah, me," Moor said.

"What are you doing in my bed?" Des asked, still in shock. "And please tell me you're not naked."

The man smirked and went to push down the blankets, but Des shouted, "Don't you fucking dare!"

"Why not, Doc? It's not like you haven't seen me naked before."

He pulled his bottom lip between his teeth, eyeing Des's chest, and that was when he realized he was naked as well. He hurriedly grabbed the blankets and covered himself.

"Don't be shy now, baby. Last night, you were so fucking wild, I couldn't control myself," he said, sitting up on his elbows as the blankets moved down a little further, revealing more of the man's sexiness.

Des gasped, gaping at him. "We didn't—?" Before the other man could answer, Des clenched his ass and looked down at himself, sighing in relief when he felt no pain in his backside.

"Answer my question." Othello's brows creased together. "Who the fuck is Gray?"

"Why the hell do you need to know that? You sound like a jealous fucking lover, and the last I checked, we didn't sleep together," Des huffed, getting out of bed, but was pulled back down and groaned when the other man rolled over on top of him.

"Get the fuck off me, you asshole," he growled, pushing at the other man's chest, and thankfully, the sheet and blanket kept them from touching skin to skin.

"How do you know we didn't fuck last night?" Moor asked in a calm voice, and Des stopped struggling.

"Unless you have a pencil dick, my ass would be hurting right now."

"What if it was the other way around?" the man asked, quirking a brow.

Des stared at the other man for quite a few seconds, trying to recall his night's events. He'd broken his own rule, and instead of drinking at home like normal, he'd allowed Bianca to talk him into going to some club with her so she could meet her new boy toy, but she had disappeared the second she walked through the door. He'd deal with her later. There was a reason he drank at home alone or with his best friend; when he got too drunk, he'd black out and not remember anything he did the night before. So there was a possibility that he'd topped Moor.

"Did I..." He was about to ask Moor if he'd hurt him, but the man seemed intact, so he changed his question. Swallowing his saliva, he asked, "Was I good?"

Des felt his face flush when Moor burst out laughing and rolled off him and onto the bed.

"Oh, my fucking goodness." Moor laughed even harder, holding his stomach as if Des had said something so funny. But instead, his ego was bruised. He was that bad. The man thought he was a damn joke.

"You don't have to laugh at me," Des snapped. "You could simply tell me where I need to improve."

Des growled and kicked the man in the leg when he continued to laugh. Then Des crawled out of bed, grabbed the blanket, and wrapped it around himself. Spotting the bathroom, he hurried inside, slamming the door before he screamed, "Asshole!"

Othello didn't know when he'd laughed so hard that his stomach hurt. He really enjoyed fucking with the little doctor. He never knew a man smart enough to be a surgeon could be so naïve. Othello wiped his tears, got out of bed, and dressed in his robe. Last night, he had been so tired he had forgotten all about the doctor sleeping in his bed, or he would have slept on the couch. Othello pulled back the bedroom drapes and headed to the kitchen to make coffee. Meanwhile, the little doctor emerged from the bathroom wearing an over-sized shirt belonging to Othello.

"Why do you always like fucking with me?" the little doctor asked, yet his face reddened in the most adorableflush.

"Because it's fun," Othello said, unashamed. "You make it easy. You haven't changed in six months. For the record, if we had fucked last night, I'd be the one on top,

and Doc, you should know how big my dick is."

"How would I know? I didn't look when you were in the hospital," he said, crossing his arms.

"We can easily rectify that mistake." Othello waggled his eyebrows, smirking.

"Nope, that's okay," he said, as his eyes drifted down to Othello's crotch.

The corner of his lips curled in a pleasurable smile at how long the man's eyes stayed on the imprint of his sleeping beast covered by his robe.

"If you keep staring at it, you might wake up the beast, and then you'd have to put him back to sleep," he teased. "But I warn you now, he likes to go all day long." Othello dropped his voice and licked his lips, leaving no questions about what he meant, making the little doctor blush even more, turning as red as a tomato.

However, his embarrassment didn't stop him from glaring at Othello. "Will you stop with the teasing?" he said, pulling up the collar of his shirt and hiding his face.

"I'll try." He smiled. "You look good in my shirt, by the way."

"Um...I don't know where my clothes are and..." he explained shyly.

"I put them on the sofa," he said, cutting the doctor off and pointing to the large black-and-gray couch that was large enough to fit two big men of his build.

"Oh, thank you." He went over to grab them. "I should get changed."

"You don't have to, but do as you wish," Othello told him. "If you want to brush your teeth, there are extra toothbrushes in the second drawer of the bathroom counter."

The doctor nodded, turned, and went back into the bathroom while Othello went to see what he could make for breakfast. A few minutes later, he returned, dressed in his clothes from the night before.

"Since I know you were fucking with me, can you tell me how I ended up in your bed?"

Othello paused his search for breakfast ideas, turned, and observed the doctor with his rumpled hair, which seemed as if he didn't even try to tame its wildness, a stark difference from the night before. The doctor looked every bit confused, making it hard for Othello to fuck with him, so he told him the truth. "You got into a fight with someone you shouldn't have in my club, and I had one of my guys bring you up here to sleep it off."

The little doctor groaned, covering his face. "Fuck, this is why I drink at home. I'm sorry."

"It's all good. I smoothed things out with the other guy." Othello walked by him. "Sit tight while I get cleaned up."

"No, I should leave. I've already caused you enough trouble." He went to move, but Othello stopped him and sat him down.

What the holy fuck am I doing? his brain screamed at him, but still he ignored it. "It's no trouble. I'll be out in a bit and make you something to eat to help with your hangover."

"You..." the doctor started.

"Enough," Othello interrupted. "Think of this as payback for not letting me die on the operating table."

"I was only doing my job," Doc Des mumbled. "So you really don't have to do this."

Othello ignored the man and went into the bathroom. Truthfully, he wasn't sure why he was keeping the doctor around. If the man wanted to leave, he should let him. After freshening up, he walked back into the main room to see the doctor sitting at the large kitchen island. Othello took the time to observe the other man and noticed that besides his new look, there was something off with the doctor. Six months ago, when he met him, there'd been a confident air around him, but now he seemed defeated and sad. Othello wasn't the kind of guy to pry into business that wasn't his, but this time, he wanted to know for some odd reason.

"How do you take your coffee?" he asked, walking over to the cabinet and taking two coffee mugs from it.

"Black," the doctor responded, not even looking up at Othello.

"Do you like your coffee like you like your men, Doc?" He poured the coffee and handed it to the doctor, who took it but didn't bring the cup to his lips.

"I don't know. I've never had a man," he responded softly.

Othello quirked an interested brow. "Then women."

"Never had a woman either." He finally sipped his coffee, and Othello stared at the man in shock. Who in their right mind wouldn't want to have a taste of the little cutie?

"So you're one of those romantics, waiting for the right person to come along and sweep you off your feet. Make you feel all tingly, with butterflies flying around you."

"I wouldn't say that. More like I was focused on other things, and it's only recently that I've decided to live for myself and not others."

Ah, so that explains the makeover. But what's with the melancholy mood? Maybe I'm overthinking things, and he's hungover. Perhaps he's going through a late teenage rebellion?

Deciding to hold off on asking more questions, Othello set his coffee cup down, reached for the remote, and turned on the television. The cool thing about his place was that he could see the screen from any section of his apartment. He turned to the news to play in the background as he got ingredients to make a Spanish omelet. *"The New York Senate race is heating up for Doctor David Ellington, who has announced he is ready to debate his challenger, Benito Grant."*

Othello stopped when he heard a familiar name and looked

at the doctor, staring at the screen. Othello had been keeping up with the Senate race. After all, whoever won could affect his and the clan's business. If politicians couldn't be bribed to ignore or turn a blind eye to wrongdoing, they would have to find alternative ways to control them. Threatening their family was a good way—until he saw the doctor, who resembled David Ellington. It hadn't occurred to him that David and Des could be related.

"You know, Doc, you look like the guy running for senate," Othello stated, making small talk as he diced up the onions.

"That's what they call genetics," he said, facing Othello. "He's my father." Another air of sadness surrounded him.

"Oh, you don't sound happy that he's running for senate."

"It's not like that." He sighed. "It's hard to explain, and honestly, I don't want to talk about it, especially with someone I don't know."

"Come on, now, Doc, we slept together. I'd say you know me plenty," Othello teased, and it seemed to lighten the mood as the man gave him a smile that reached his eyes.

The doctor rolled his eyes. "All we did was sleep next to each other, so it doesn't afford me to tell you about my personal business."

Othello tutted. "You help a guy fight the Beast, and he keeps secrets from you."

"The Beast? What the fuck are you going on about?"

Othello was about to explain, but he was interrupted by his cellphone. Rinsing off his hands, he went to grab it off the nightstand. Seeing that it was Iago calling, he picked it up right away.

"What's up? Is everything okay?"

"Yeah," Iago answered. "Just checking to see how the meeting with the Rossetti underboss went."

"It went well. I'll update you on it when I get to the house."

"Why can't you do it now?" "I have company," Othello said.

Iago was silent for a few seconds. "Oh, oh," he said in surprise, which bothered Othello.

"Why do you sound like that?"

"How do I sound?"

"Like you're shocked by what I said."

Iago sighed. "Because truthfully, you haven't been with anyone since you broke things off with Philip."

Othello closed his eyes. He could understand what Iago meant. He didn't want to think about Philip Montano, the man he thought he'd spend his life with, only to discover the man was cheating on him. It hurt worse that Phillip was sleeping with Cassio Ricci, the brother of Dominico Ricci, the boss of the Ricci family. Othello was hurt and angry; honestly, he wanted to kill the man, but he disappeared before Othello could get the chance. Trust and loyalty were important to him, especially when he'd given his entire heart to someone, only to have it trampled on.

After Philip, he hadn't been in another relationship or even slept with anyone in the past two years since he broke it off, and his ex-lover left Verona Heights, never to be seen or heard from again. He stole a glance at the little doc, who had moved from sitting at the island and was now looking out the window with a troubled expression. He realized he should probably correct his friend's assumption that what he was thinking was far from the truth.

"Alright, I'll see you when you get here," Iago said and hung up before Othello could say anything.

Sighing, he looked at the dark screen, shaking his head, then set the device down. He focused on the doctor still standing at the window, staring out as if he had the world resting on his shoulders. Othello wasn't sure why or how he came to that conclusion, but he knew something was bothering the doctor. Standing, he went back to the kitchen and made breakfast as promised, with neither speaking, leaving the television to do the talking for them. When everything was done and plated, Othello got the doctor's attention.

"Hey, Doc, breakfast is ready." The man didn't move or make a sound to indicate that he had heard Othello. Furrowing his brows, he walked over to him and lightly tapped the doctor on the shoulder.

He wasn't shocked when the guy almost jumped out of his skin, and the empty coffee mug slipped from his hands. It was a good thing Othello caught it before it hit the ground. The doctor glanced at the cup in Othello's hand, then at his face. He seemed like he was going to cry, but he stopped himself by biting his lip. Othello was about to ask the doctor if he was okay, but held back. He'd already delved too far into the man's personal life. He'd promised to feed him and send him on his merry way.

"The food is ready," Othello said.

"Oh," the doctor responded, sounding a bit lost. "You really didn't have to make me anything."

"It's no bother." Othello shrugged. "I'm also hungry and was in the mood for a Spanish omelet. Besides, my mama would skin me alive if she knew I sent you off with an empty stomach. She's all about propriety and being a gracious host." He smiled, and the doctor smiled as well, and it seemed to pull the man out of his funk just a little.

"Come on. It won't be good if it gets cold."

Othello walked back to the kitchen area. He didn't look to see if the doctor was following him. He'd done far more than what was required of him. Before he sat down to eat, Othello poured them both another cup of coffee. Just as he sat the mugs down, the doctor joined him in the breakfast nook. They began to eat, and silence descended on them again, except for the television that had been switched from the local news. Neither seemed bothered by the noise as they ate their meal.

When Othello was halfway done with his omelet, a soft voice cut through the quiet atmosphere around them.

"Have you always wanted to do what you do?"

"What do you mean?" Othello glanced at the doctor, who still had more than half of his meal on his plate.

Should I feel offended that he's not eating?

"I mean, you work for your father's company. I think it was construction, right?"

"Yeah," Othello answered.

"What is it, your choice or your father's choice?"

"A bit of both." Don Alejandro had given him and Iago the choice to back out after graduating from college, to step away from the underworld, as he had when he asked them the first time. "I wanted to work with my father. I knew since I was about thirteen. But I also have my own side investments."

"Oh," he said and returned to pick up his food.

"Don't you like the omelet?" Othello asked.

"Oh no," he said, gaping at Othello with wide eyes. "It's great. There's just so much on my mind right now. I'm sorry. I feel bad for wasting the food you took the trouble to prepare for me."

Othello shook his head, more worried about the doctor than annoyed that he ate little of his meal. He pushed both their plates to the side. "I know we're not friends, but what the hell happened to you? You're not the same man I met six months ago, and I'm not talking about the new look."

"It's no..."

"Don't tell me it's nothing or none of my business," Othello said, cutting him off. "Come on, Doc, talk to me."

"I killed a patient," he cried out as tears streamed down his face.

Othello acted without thinking, grabbing the doctor by his neck and pulling him into his arms.

"I tried to save him. I really did, but there was so much blood, and I couldn't see and..." He wailed into Othello's chest.

"Shh...it's okay," he soothed, wondering what the fuck he was doing. When he'd asked the doctor what was bothering him, Othello hadn't expected it to be something on that level. "Hey, Doc, I don't normally do the grunt work, but if you need help hiding the body, I don't mind doing the lifting this once."

The doctor stopped crying briefly, and his shoulders began to shake lightly. Othello thought he'd started crying again until he heard snickers, and he pulled his head back, chuckling. Othello sat there staring at the gorgeous pink tear-stained cheeks, listening to the sweet laughter coming from the man's cherry lips.

Fuck, he's beautiful. He should smile more.

Blinking at his train of thought, Othello stood and gathered their dishes, moving over to drop them in the sink. He stole a glance at the doctor, who had stopped laughing but had a smile on his face. Shaking his head, he started cleaning up, but a gentle voice stopped him.

"Let me do that."

Othello turned to the sweet voice to see the doctor moving closer to him. "You don't have to."

"I know, but I want to. You've done so much for me in the past hour. It's the least I can do. It's not every day someone offers to get rid of a body for me. I appreciate the gesture, but it's not needed." He took the soapy sponge from Othello and eased him out of the way with his hip.

Seeing that he had no choice, Othello poured himself another cup of coffee and added a splash of milk and a sugar cube—the way he liked it—not too sweet and not too creamy. He sat at the breakfast nook, savoring his coffee, and watched the doctor skillfully clean up the kitchen, as if he had been there many times and knew exactly what needed to be done.

"So, how did the guy die?" Othello asked since his curiosity got the better of him.

The doctor's back stiffened. "Can I not talk about that?" he said, not looking at Othello.

"Up to you." He shrugged. "I just figured you might want to get it off your chest since whatever happened got you sulking."

* * *

DES GLANCED at the homeowner over his shoulder, realizing his attraction for the man hadn't waned even though he hadn't seen him in six months. Moor had put on more weight since the last time they saw each other and was more muscular in build. In the bright, sunlit apartment, the other man's honey-brown eyes seemed to sparkle, drawing attention to them, even if he tried to look away. The deep red robe he wore complemented his golden-brown skin tone. Des wondered if red was Moor's favorite color since it was a dominant feature in his home, accompanying the blacks, grays, and whites.

"I am not sulking, just contemplative," he said softly, recalling Moor had said something.

He was finishing up the last of the dishes. He grabbed the cloth and dried his hands, turning to look at Moor. Des wasn't sure why he'd stuck around for as long as he had. Maybe it was because he knew he had no one waiting for him at home or nothing really important to do. He should have left the second he'd changed into his clothes. The reason he'd drunk as much as he had the night before was because he didn't have to work that day, and maybe he knew he was going to spend the entire day sulking in his apartment.

Des couldn't say much had changed about him in the six months since he had left his parents' party. Sure, he'd grown his hair out, gotten a couple of tattoos, and maybe drank a bit too much on the days he didn't have to work. But he still had done nothing to change the status of his job. Honestly, he wasn't sure what he wanted to do. Des had become the kind of fickle person that he hated. It had become even more so since Mr. Alvarez died on his operating table.

Despite his feelings toward his job, Des was good at it. He had performed countless surgeries, including ones that most doctors thought were too difficult. Des was able to handle them. But how was it that he couldn't save Mr. Alvarez? He had done everything right. The operation was smooth, and just as he was closing up Mr. Alverez, his heart rhythm became erratic.

The monitors started beating frantically, and Mr. Alverez went into cardiac arrest, with blood filling his chest. Des and his team did everything they could to save him. It didn't take long for him to perform the procedures needed to get the man's heart beating again before he could stop the bleeding. But sadly, thirty minutes later, Mr. Alverez died.

Des had been so distraught about the patient's death that he'd all but lost his confidence. Despite the review confirming a blood clot in Mr. Alverez's left lung as the cause of death, Des couldn't shake the feeling of doubt. He questioned if he had followed the correct procedures and how he had overlooked the clot. Des had no one he could talk to about how he was feeling.

He tried to explain his feelings to Gray, but the cop didn't understand. He would have liked to call his parents, but they hadn't spoken to each other for the past few months. Des had contacted a few lawyers a couple of months ago, but none of them had gotten back to him. He was wondering if his parents had something to do with it.

"You're sulking...I mean, being contemplative again," Moor said, breaking into his thoughts. "You might as well tell me. I've been told I'm a good listener."

Des peered at the taller man, wondering if talking with a

stranger might help him get over what was bothering him. After a few minutes, he explained what happened with Mr. Alverez's death. True to Moor's word, he didn't interrupt Des once.

"Do you know your eyes don't sparkle when you talk about your job?" Moor said when he finished talking. "Tell me, Doc, do you like saving people's lives?"

"It's not like I want to kill people," he responded, furrowing his brows.

"But do you like saving them?"

Moor put his elbow on the breakfast nook, resting his jaw on his fist, and Des couldn't take his eyes off the man's good looks even with the seriousness of their conversation. "Let me rephrase the question. Do you like what you do?"

"Not particularly." Des didn't bat an eye or take a breath to think about the answer.

"Then why are you a doctor?"

"It's what my parents wanted me to do," he whispered. "It's hard to say no to them." *Especially when I'm dependent on them financially.*

"But what do you want to do?"

That question stumped Des. Other than his paternal grandfather, no one had ever asked him what he wanted. He was simply told what to do, no questions asked. "If I tell you, do you promise not to laugh?"

"It depends on what it is. But tell me anyway."

Des stared at Othello, wondering why it was he felt he could trust the man with his dream. "I want to open an art studio and help others fulfill their dreams of being an artist."

"That's not something to laugh at."

"Most people do or tell me it's foolish."

"Don't you want to be famous? Can you paint or draw?"

"I don't want to be in the spotlight," Des told him, shaking his head and screwing up his face. "And yes, I can do both and more."

"Then quit working at the hospital and go for your dreams," Moor said.

"I wish it were so easy," Des said.

"It's not a hard thing to do. People change jobs all the time."

Moor leaned back in his seat, and his robe parted open, showing his chest. Des knew that Moor's body was adorned with tattoos on his back, arms, fingers, and down to his legs, while his chest remained unmarked, save for a surgical scar. He had thought by now Moor would have covered it up with tattoos. But Des gave himself a mental pat on the back, knowing he did a good job stitching the wound, to the point the man wouldn't need plastic surgery to cover it up.

"What's holding you back, Doc?"

A lawyer, Des wanted to say, but he held back and shook his head. He needed to figure things out on his own. "You gave me a lot to think about," he said.

Moor smiled. "Good. As for the man dying, it sounds like you did everything you should have. His death was not your fault."

"That's what I keep telling myself."

"Then believe it. It was his time to go."

"How would you know that?" Des snapped when he didn't mean to. "It's not like you've killed a man before."

"And you have a hero complex if you think you can save every life that comes before you."

"I saved yours, right?" Des argued, noticing Moor didn't raise his voice once, but their conversation grew heated.

"Are you angry that I'm still alive?"

"Of course not," Des shouted. "I did what I was supposed to."

"So why are you fixated on Alvarez? He's dead, and you did

all you could. What more did you want to do? Pull his soul back from the brink."

"I..." Des stuttered, not sure what to say to that.

Moor leaned close and took one of his hands in his. "Does Alvarez's family blame you?" Des shook his head. "Then why are you beating yourself up?"

Again, Des couldn't respond, as he was finally realizing he wasn't the cause of the patient's death.

"You really are a good listener," he said after a few minutes. "Thank you."

Othello smiled. "I would say anytime, but I doubt we'll see each other again."

"Is this your way of telling me I've worn out my welcome?" Des smiled when the man didn't respond, and he took it as a yes. "I guess you're right. You've fed me and all, so I should go."

Des moved from around the counter and grabbed his cellphone, which had been sitting on the coffee table. Walking to the exit, he didn't look back to see if Moor was watching him. Just as his hand touched the lock on the door, he paused when the homeowner called out to him.

"Hey, Doc, let me see your phone."

Des turned and faced Moor. "Why?"

"How else will you call me?" Moor stood and moved over to Des, stretching out a hand.

Des stared at him for a couple of seconds, wondering if the man was being for real. He'd played so many games on him that Des couldn't help but wonder if he was doing the same thing now. Not wanting to think about it anymore, he unlocked his cellphone and handed it to Moor, who entered his number and gave it back.

"Don't waste it, Doc. I don't give out my private number to anyone." Des looked at the phone and then at Moor, trying to figure out if there was some kind of meaning behind his words.

In any event, he nodded and left the handsome man's apartment.

SCENE III

OTHELLO

*O*thello entered the Romano home and nodded to the house manager, Carlo, before heading straight for his father's office. Alessandro and Maria were getting older and needed more help at the house since he didn't stay home that much, and Iago lived with Emilia, his girlfriend, across town. Othello knocked and waited for Alessandro to respond before he entered.

"You finally showed up," Iago joked. "Looks like you wanted extra time with your new lover," but Othello didn't pay attention as he settled on the couch while Iago and Alessandro occupied the wingback chairs by the desk.

"Alright, Iago, don't start," Alessandro said. "Tell me what the Rossetti clan wants." Alessandro was the kind of man who liked to get to the point of the matter.

"We missed something in our intel when we planned on taking over the Rizzo clan territories. They had a deal with the Rossettis that they got to use the east side of the ports, and any business that crossed the lines had to go through Rizzo. Rossetti wants to keep the deal as is."

"No," Iago said instantly, just as Alessandro spoke up. "What are they offering? If I know Rizzo, he didn't do anything for free."

"Ten percent of the cargo."

Alessandro sat back in his chair, crossed his legs, and studied Othello before he spoke. "What did you tell him?"

"Fifteen percent, and it's not up for negotiation. We'll also have our guys police the cargo."

"I can't believe you," Iago shouted. "You know they deal with more than just imported art and cars. Their main supply is drugs, human trafficking, and whatever the fuck else they can get their hands on."

Neither Alessandro nor Othello could disagree with Iago. The Romano clan was known for their involvement in gambling, escort services, prostitution, and other unsavory deals, unlike other clans that focused on drugs and human trafficking.

"We have to step away from this deal," Iago said calmly.

"What do you think, Othello?" Alessandro asked.

"Why are you asking him?" Iago said, and they both looked at him.

"Other than the drugs and trafficking, why shouldn't we work with the Rossettis?" Othello questioned.

"Those are reasons enough," Iago argued.

"What if I told you the Rossetti clan no longer deal in drugs and all that shit."

Iago huffed. "Then I'd call you a fool for believing that your old flame's family has somehow grown a heart. You and I know how close they are to the Ricci family. How do you think they got so far up in just a few short years?"

"Good thing I'm not a fool then, Iago."

"What the hell does that mean?"

"Since Luca couldn't guarantee me that none of his cargo had drugs or human stock, I can't have him bring his shipment through our port. So they will need to find someone else, and since we now own the most effective borders, it will be pretty hard for them. Since we took over the docks, the cops have been patrolling them pretty heavily. I can't have the feds crawling around when we meet

with the Japanese in a few weeks."

"Why the fuck didn't you say that from the beginning?" Iago snapped.

"Because you blew up before I could get a chance." Othello tsked, shaking his head.

"Alright, boys, enough bickering," Alessandro said, then looked at Othello. "You did the right thing. We have our faults, but that shit will never be one of them."

Othello and Iago nodded in agreement. The subject was changed to other matters that took a couple of hours. They talked about the weapons deal they were making with the head of a Japanese yakuza and when the meeting would take place. At the thought, the little doctor came to mind, and he wondered just how good he was at the whole art thing, since it sounded as if his parents had forced him to be a doctor. Othello didn't think he could continue to do a job he hated, no matter how good he was at it.

He appreciated that Alessandro had given him an option for what he wanted. Once their meeting was over, Othello went to see Maria, spending a few minutes with her before setting off for the office. The construction company might have been a front, but it provided and took on legitimate businesses that Othello had to oversee.

"Hey, O, wait up," Iago called out to him just as he was about to open the front door.

"What's up?" He turned to see his friend coming down the hall.

"Let's grab dinner. It's too late for you to head to the office now," Iago said. "We haven't spent much time together since you got out of the hospital, and I miss my little bro."

Othello smiled and nodded. "Where do you want to go?"

"Let's go to La Casa Rosa. It's not far from the office."

"Alright, I'll meet you there."

They both walked out of the house, heading for their cars. Just as he started his car, Othello's cell phone vibrated. Instead of ignoring it, he glanced at the screen, seeing the unfamiliar number. He was about to delete the number but paused when he read the first few words of the message. Othello opened the message and read it fully.

"Thank you for breakfast. Let me buy you dinner sometime as repayment."

Othello grinned and sent off a quick reply. "Well done, Doc," he mumbled. Then, he texted Tallen to get all the information the organization had collected about the doctor to him. He really didn't investigate the doctor too much; he just went by word of mouth on what people knew about him. Putting his phone in the center console, he pulled out of the Romanos' driveway. The drive to Las Casa Rosa took about thirty minutes, and by the time he got there, Iago was already there, sitting at a table by the window. Othello ordered a light lunch since he had a big breakfast.

"So," Iago began. "Tell me about the new guy."

Othello chuckled and shook his head. "I should have known you were up to something. But there's nothing to

tell. I'm not dating anyone."

"But..."

Othello cut him off. "I don't have time for a relationship. I have too much going on right now."

"Please tell me you're not still hung up on that cheating bastard? Fuck, O, he was an asshole. And fucking, Luciano, the bastard of all bastards, makes me want to find the fucker and kill him."

"Calm the fuck down," Othello told him. He knew how much Iago hated Luciano for his backward thinking. "I'm not still in love with Philip. I haven't thought about him in years. Didn't you just hear me?" Othello sighed. "My life is too nuts right now for anything but a good fuck here and there to relieve my stress."

"You can't keep living like that, O. You should think about settling down and finding a man who understands our world and later have a couple of kids. It would be great if our children grow up together like we did."

"I'll leave the family life to you, Iago." He smiled. "Are you ready to be a father?"

"Hell no. I'm scared as hell." Iago gave a wry chuckle.

"You'll do fine. After all, you raised the kids in the group home."

"That's different. I had you to help me."

"And now, you have Emilia, who you should marry, by the way."

"I plan to after the baby is born."

"Have you asked her?" Othello shook his head.

"Not yet."

"I'd propose before the baby is born, so she knows you're not marrying her because of the baby. She's a good woman; don't make her feel more unworthy than you already have."

"You don't have to keep reminding me of how much I've fucked things up. I don't want to lose her," Iago said.

"You say that, but you started seeing a new mistress. And I

know you're using that shit again. Think of what it would do to Alessandro and Maria."

"It's not a regular thing, O, just occasionally," Iago shrugged his shoulders.

"I don't give a fuck if it's for a second. We got out of the drug business because of you and how fucked up you got." Othello sighed. "Look, I won't lecture you anymore, Iago. I can't and won't lose you, man. I need you to be by my side for life. But clean yourself up. Emilia and your child deserve better. She's gorgeous, smart, and has stuck by your side, even knowing what our world entails. If you love her, I say strongly committing to her would let her know she's not just an ornament on your arm. If you don't, walk the fuck away and let her find someone who will."

"People listening to us talk would think you're the older brother," Iago joked, but Othello didn't even crack a smile. He didn't know when it happened in their relationship, but it turned out that he was the one who became more responsible than Iago.

"You're the consigliere, Iago. I need you to be my advisor but more so my brother. Do what you need to do and stand beside me."

"You're right, and you make all good points," Iago said after a thought. "I'll work on myself."

Othello nodded. "Good man. I'm here for you, Iago.

Always. Brothers for life." Iago smiled. "Thanks."

They changed the subject and talked about the plans for Maria and Alessandro's surprise anniversary party they were putting together. They laughed about the past and present. Othello felt good sitting and talking with his best friend after so long.

* * *

DES CHEWED on his bottom lip, staring at the digits in his bank account. He'd gotten home, showered, and brought up the business plan he'd written up a few years ago and showed it to Sebastian, who was quite impressed with what he came up with, which was why he was so confused that Sebastian would side with his parents. The entire way home, he thought about his conversation with Moor. He'd been a coward for far too long. He leaned back in his chair, letting the decision he was about to make wash over him, just as his cellphone rang. Des furrowed his brows, not recognizing the number, but answered it anyway.

"Hello?"

"Hi, is this Desmond Ellington?"

"Yes, who is this?"

"Mister Ellington, my name is Erin Graham. I am an attorney at law for Casey and Nessar. I'm contacting you about your case and would like to know if you had time to meet with me today."

Des's brows got even tighter at hearing that. He'd reached out to the law firm a couple of months ago, and since he hadn't heard anything from them, he thought they'd turned him down without contacting him. "If you're planning on turning me down face to face, I don't see why we should meet."

"Turn you down?" Graham said. "You misunderstand. I plan on taking your case. After reading through the questions you provided to our paralegal, I find it strange that a big firm like Hamlin and Baxter would lie to a client."

"Wait, what do you mean?" Des sat up in his chair.

"Mister Ellington..."

"Please, call me Des," he said, cutting her off.

"Very well. Des, did you ever see your grandfather's will?"

"No," he sighed. "And every time I tried to get a copy, I've been rebuffed."

"I suspected as much," Ms. Graham said. "This is why I think it's important we meet."

"Where are you?"

"I'm at my office." She gave him the address, and Des noted she was in the art district, which was how he'd found the number in the first place.

Des looked at his watch and noted that it was still early in the morning, and around this time, there wouldn't be too much traffic getting there. "I can be there in twenty minutes. Is that okay?"

"That's perfectly fine." They hung up, and as he was about to get up, his phone went off again, and Bianca's name appeared on the screen. Des ignored the call. He didn't have time to hear her apologies about her ditching him the night before. He had other pressing matters to deal with.

Grabbing his motorcycle helmet, Des rushed out of his apartment to the parking garage, got on his bike, and entered the address into his GPS. Minutes later, he was zooming in and out of traffic with an elated smile. He'd bought the bike a few weeks ago and knew it was one of his best decisions. Des enjoyed the ride through the city. It had a mix of everything from towering skyscrapers to modest buildings. Each district had its own unique flavor and culture, the vibrant waterfront areas, scenic beaches, and more that Des hadn't explored, even though he'd lived in Verona Heights all his life.

Twenty minutes later, Des came to a stop in front of a small building with glass front windows that did not look out of place in the more eclectic district. After turning off his bike, he removed his helmet, walked up to the building, and entered the quaint office with neatly stacked bookshelves. However, what drew his eyes was the Vittore Caravaglia art hanging on the wall. Caravaglia was born in 1615 in Venice and liked to experiment by combining oil painting with textiles and textures, giving it a multi-dimensional appearance, not to mention adding dramatic flair to his work, making it unique. Many had tried to copy Caravaglia, including Des, but neither he nor they could quite get it right. Looking at the painting, Des knew it was a fake. Anyone who knew or studied art could tell what was genuine or a copycat.

"It's not real," came a voice behind him.

Turning, Des's eyes locked with a gorgeous statuesque brunette who was taller than him with deep brown eyes and honey-brown skin, dressed in blue jeans paired with a white shirt and black blazer. "I know," he said, looking back at the painting. "No one can recreate Caravaglia's work."

"I've heard that," she said.

Des glanced at her. "I'm looking for Erin Graham."

"That's me, I take it you're Mister Ellington?"

"Yes, and like I said over the phone, call me Des." "Then call me Erin." They shook hands quickly. "Come into my office, and we'll review your case."

"First," he said, stopping her before she got too far, "I need to know why you are taking me on as a client. I contacted a few offices, and they told me no flat out."

"Truthfully, I don't like bullies and fraud. I can assume other law firms wanted to take your case, but seeing the names Hamilin and Casey scared them off. But unlike them, I'm ready for whatever they might throw at me. I'm even more annoyed that someone lied to you. "

"What do you mean?"

"Come with me." She guided him to her office and moved to her desk. She picked up a stack of papers and handed them to Des. "These are only copies, but we hope to get the original soon."

Des furrowed his brows as he took the documents, setting his helmet down, and his eyes widened when he saw the title: Last Will and Testament. *It can't be!* Quickly scanning the paperwork, he saw his grandfather's name, and then it was as if his heart had stopped when he read more.

To my grandson, Desmond Ellington, I want you to follow your dreams, child. Go after what you desire, no matter who tries to step in your way. Des, I know you're scared, and you will listen to your parents because they are your parents, but do not give up. I believe in you, so to get started, I leave you thirty million dollars and the deed to the building at 134 Eastside Avenue. Des gasped when he saw the address.

His hands shook as he read the address at least three times. He felt like he couldn't breathe, and his eyes clouded with tears. *He didn't betray me.* His legs gave out, and he fell to his knees as tears streamed down his cheeks. *My grandfather didn't turn his back on me.* He thought back to the happiest moments with Sebastian and the regret that, for so long, he had blamed the man for not looking out for him in the end.

He knew his thinking sounded like a spoiled brat, but besides Nanny Cee, his grandfather was the only one who looked out for him while his parents ganged up on him. Des wasn't sure how long he knelt there and cried, but he knew it was also the first time he had shed tears since his grandfather's death. He was also grateful that Erin hadn't interrupted him. Taking a deep breath, he stood, took the tissue offered to him, and dried his eyes. *No more crying or wallowing in self-pity. It's time to fight, Des.*

"What's the plan?" he asked.

"I take it you're ready to fight? Fraud cases like yours are easy to win with the right amount of evidence."

"Yes," he growled. "Other than getting the original will, what else do we need as proof?"

She sighed. "I need to know a couple of things. Who was at the will reading?"

"My parents." He froze as he said the word, realizing the most pivotal thing. They knew what the will said all this fucking time. "Erin, thank you for this. I'll call you in a couple of days, but I need to take care of something. Trust me; I'm not backing out of this." Folding the documents, he stuffed them in his inner jacket pocket.

"Wait, Des. What are you going to do?" she stopped him, looking at him with worry.

"Something I should have done years ago." Des grabbed his helmet and hurried out the door. He was speeding across town in less than five minutes to his parents' place. He didn't know if they were home, but he didn't care. Des wasn't going to back down from this. Pulling up at the front of his family home, the main gate was open. Des noticed a few cars parked out front, which meant they were entertaining. He would have thought better of his actions if he hadn't been so angry, but he was too worked up to care.

After getting off his bike, Des pulled out his cellphone and fiddled with it for a few seconds before putting it back in his pocket. Then, he removed his helmet and barged into the house, scanning the place for his mother or father, ignoring the curious eyes on him. The second he saw Ava, he marched over to her.

"Desm—"

"You lied to me, Mother," he yelled before she could finish his name.

"What are you talking about?"

"Grandfather's will," he snapped.

Her eyes widened, and she turned to whoever she was talking to, making excuses before grabbing Des's arm and pulling him out of the crowded room. Des was seething, and he didn't hide his anger as they grew close to his father, who noticed the tension between the two of them. David apologized to his guests and joined Ava and Des as they took the stairs to David's office. When they were behind closed doors, Des let loose.

"I did every fucking thing you two wanted me to do. I grew up without friends and love, and all I wanted was to follow my dreams, and you two couldn't let that happen. How? How did you do it?"

"Desmond, I..." his mother began, but his father interrupted.

"How did you find out?" his father asked.

"Did you think I wouldn't suspect you two were up to something? I just needed the evidence to prove it." He reached into his jacket pocket, pulled out the documents, and threw them on the coffee table.

David picked them up, and Des watched his eyes scanning the paperwork. "My father was a fool like you. How dare he give you all that money to waste away? So I told Bradley Wade to change the will. I knew you wouldn't read it. You're usually smarter than this. I'm surprised it took

you all these years to figure things out."

"Do you think my life and dreams are some kind of joke?" He growled. "I will no longer be your puppet. Give me the original will."

"Why should I?" David said.

"Father, I get that in the past, I have let you walk all over me. Let you both keep me locked in a cage because I felt I had no other choice or lacked the confidence to fight back, but no more. I refuse to let you two hold me back any longer. If I'm not mistaken, I saw a few members of the press downstairs; I'm sure you don't want me to have a nice little conversation with them about how wonderful a father you've been. I'm sure your lead in the polls will dip really low once I'm done. You might never have abused me physically, but you two really fucked me up mentally."

"You little..." David went to speak, but Ava stopped him.

"David, give it to him," she said while her husband looked at her.

"You're not serious, Ava," David asked.

"I am," she responded, then looked at Des. "But in return, there is something we want from you."

"No," Des said, unwilling to listen to her offer. "I'm not playing games with you two any longer. Give me the original will, and I will be on my way."

When neither of them moved, Des pulled out his cellphone and dialed Erin's number, putting the call on speaker. He smiled when she answered instantly.

"Des, where did you go? We weren't done talking."

"Erin, I want to add two more names to the lawsuit against Hamlin and Casey." "Okay, who?" she asked.

His father growled. "We'll give it to you."

"Erin, it seems things might change. I'll call you later." Des hung up, quirking a brow at his parents.

David walked over to the far corner of his office and moved the fake Domenico di Medici painting, revealing a safe Des didn't know was there. Minutes later, it was open, and his father pulled out a box and then handed it to Des.

"What is this?" Des asked, inspecting the metal box.

"Everything your grandfather left you," Ava answered. "There were a few other things that weren't in the will. We never looked through the contents."

Des nodded and looked at them. "Thank you." He turned, ready to leave, but his mother grabbed his arm.

"Son, wait." He didn't look at her, but there was a tremor in her tone that he had never heard before. "We did what we thought was best. We didn't want you to waste your talent."

Des stood still, listening and hoping that she would apologize, something that would allow him to forgive her one day. Yet she remained silent. Pulling his arm away, Des tucked the box under his arm with his helmet and walked out of his parents' home. The crowd had thinned a little, but people were still milling around. No one dared to stop him or speak to him, which was completely fine with him.

Des wanted nothing to do with his parents. He safely put the box away, straddled his bike, and rode home feeling relieved yet sad at the same time. He'd been so angry at his grandfather and parents that he wasn't sure how to feel now. Once he got home, he didn't waste a moment. He drafted up a resignation letter and sent it off. He was done with that part of his life. Sometime during the week, he'd go to the hospital and collect his things. Now, all he had to do was look through the box with his grandfather's things.

Picking it up, Des moved over to the sofa and unlocked it with the key he found taped on the bottom of the box. His eyes clouded the second he saw the last picture he and his grandfather had taken. He'd just graduated from high school when his grandfather died. Setting the picture aside, Des noticed there were a couple of sealed envelopes on the bottom under a few knick-knacks that once belonged to his grandfather. Pulling out the envelopes, he noted his grandfather's scribbled handwriting that brought a smile to his face, and also noted they were still sealed.

Tearing them open, he spotted the deed to the building he had been gifted. He knew fate had intervened because it was the very one Des had his eye on for so long. Who knew it had belonged to him all this time? The other documents were the will and more deeds to properties he doubted even his parents knew his grandfather had owned. Setting it all back into the box, Des sent a quick text to Erin to schedule another meeting so that they could go through everything together.

After he had completed everything needed, Des sat back in his chair, feeling completely relaxed in his mind and body for the first time in forever. He was starting a new chapter in his life and wanted to celebrate. He couldn't believe how things had changed for him in a matter of hours. He chuckled excitedly, rocking back and forth on the couch. *I can't believe I threatened them with the press. When the fuck did I get so damn brave when it came to my parents?* The brevity of how he'd acted hit him like a ton of bricks, and he dragged his fingers through his hair. *Fuck, I need a drink. A very strong one. But I don't want to drink alone.* He was still holding his cellphone, so he pulled up his contacts and was about to call Gray and ask him if he wanted to hang out when he spotted the newly saved number in his contacts.

Don't waste it, Doc.

Des wasn't clueless as to what the man had meant. He'd found Othello Moor attractive from the first time he saw him on the operating table, and even though he seemed to like fucking with Des, Moor wasn't a bad guy. He listened with an open mind when he talked, and maybe Des was reading too much into things, but he felt a connection between him and Moor. It would be nice to get to know him more. Perhaps they could be friends.

"Oh hell, who am I kidding? I want the man to fuck me so good I'd be his willing slave." Des stared at his phone, chewing on his bottom lip, wondering if texting Moor was worth taking a chance. Would the man respond or ignore him? Before he could change his mind, Des typed up his message, and he hesitated only for a second before hitting send. He was waiting on pins and needles to see if Moor was going to reply. Not even five minutes later, he got his answer, which left him giddy.

Name the time and place.

Des got up and did a little dance. He had no idea what would be the perfect place, but he'd figure that out later since his stomach growled so loud it sounded like a wounded animal—humming while he went to make dinner.

Today didn't turn out so badly after all.

SCENE IV

DES

"Doc, when you said you would buy me dinner as repayment, this wasn't what I had in mind."

It took longer than expected, but the date came weeks after his initial text. He had been a little preoccupied with his grandfather's inheritance. Des was cleaning up, painting his new place, and taking his time redecorating it to his taste. It would be quite some time before his studio opened, but now he had time to dedicate his energy to finishing his art degree.

As for his case with Hamilin & Casey, it ended in Des's favor before it got too far. They settled by giving Des two million dollars and apologizing for their former employees' actions. Des couldn't say he wasn't happy that everything ended so quietly because he didn't want his life to be plastered on the front page of the news or some headline on the internet. Even with his father running for senate, he had been able to stay completely out of the spotlight.

Des wanted to give Erin the credit for the law firm's quick folding, but he knew it had something to do with his parents. They were trying to cover their asses to make sure the press didn't get a whiff of what happened. Des was sure this was another play on his parents' part, and they were getting ready to ask him for something and use giving him his inheritance as leverage. But Des had learned how to play the game just like them and had one more trick up his sleeve. Until then, he was going to live his life.

"I know," Des said. "But isn't it great? I haven't been here in a while. I used to sneak out sometimes without my parents knowing, and mostly, I would people-watch, wondering who was on a date or just out to have fun."

"I wouldn't say an amusement park is a good place for a date," Moor complained.

"You don't think so?" he mused.

"Look at my face and ask me that again."

Des looked at Moor and noticed he was far from happy. "Fine, if you don't want to do this, we'll leave. I've just been having a few good days and thought this would be good for us to hang out and have fun."

"Do I look like I'm dressed for fun?" he asked, moving his hand up and down his body.

Des's eyes roved over the taller man, in an expensive navy blue suit, a black shirt, no tie, and a pocket square. Des, on the other hand, had gone a bit more casual with a white V-neck sweater and dark blue jeans. Sighing, Des had known this was going to be a mistake, but he had listened to Bianca, who'd encouraged him to text Moor. Gray, on the other hand, was completely against it but wouldn't give a reason why. It was during one of their painting sessions when the conversation came up.

"So now that you're able to live the life you want, when are you going to start dating?" Bianca asked.

"For fuck's sake, Bianca, let the man breathe," Gray said, putting the paintbrush down.

"Stop being a hater, Gray. Just because he has time to get down and dirty with someone, and you don't." "Who says I don't?" Gray asked.

"All you do is work," Bianca added.

"And all you do is party. When in the hell are you going to grow up?" Gray growled, glaring at her.

"Alright, alright," Des butted in. "That's enough. You two were talking about me, remember?"

Back in college, Gray and Bianca had dated briefly, but they broke up, and neither would tell the reason. Des had the strange feeling that it wasn't Gray's idea and that his best friend still had feelings for Bianca. He grew increasingly jealous each time Bianca met a new guy, and it didn't help that Bianca was getting serious about her current boyfriend. Des wished Gray would find someone to love because Bianca only saw Gray as a good friend.

"You're right, Desi," Bianca said. "Sorry, he just makes me angry sometimes. Anyway, let's not get into all of that. How about I set you up with someone."

"No thanks, but I kind of like someone," he told her. "He's an old patient of mine and helped me out the night I got into the fight with that guy. His name is Othello."

"Oh my gods, you don't mean Othello Moor?" Bianca asked.

"Yeah, you know him?" Des asked.

"I don't know him, but I know of him. He's hot, right?" She smiled. "Tall, dark, and so fucking handsome and rich as hell "

"Don't you ever fucking quit?" Gray snapped at her and then

looked at Des. "Don't get involved with Othello Moor." "What? Why?" Des questioned.

"Yeah, why?" Bianca interjected.

"I don't have to give you a reason why. Just do as I say."

"You're not his father, and he didn't ask you to be," Bianca argued on his behalf, rolling her eyes. "Des, if you like Othello, call him and go on at least one date, see where it goes before you close the door on something that could be worth it. Don't listen to that idiot." She smiled. "I could get his number if you want. I've got connections. It might not be his personal number, though I hear he's pretty private."

"Nah, it's all good. I have his number already." "What?" Bianca said just as Gray spoke.

"How did you get it?"

"He gave it to me after we had breakfast."

He looked at the two of them staring at him with their mouths open in shock. "Why the hell are you two looking at me like that?"

Gray cleared his throat and moved to stand next to Des. "When did you and Moor have breakfast?"

"I ended up spending the night with him..." "You fucked him?" Gray said, aghast.

"When did I say that?" Des answered.

"You said you slept together," Bianca said. "Yeah, we slept in the same bed."

"Fuck, I feel like we're missing something, Desi," Gray told him. "Start from the beginning."

Des sighed and shook his head but did as his friend asked, explaining what had happened when she left him alone at the bar after they had a few drinks and not remembering anything else until he woke up in Moor's bed. He expressed that they didn't sleep together — and finding out that he'd gotten into a fight with someone named The Beast.

"The Beast?" Gray said.

"Yeah, I don't even know what the guy looks like, but Moor said he took care of it," Des told him. "Anyway, he cooked breakfast. We talked about a few things, one of which was that I should quit my job. And when I was getting ready to leave, he gave me his number."

"So that's why you were angry with me." Bianca smiled. "Tell me you called him at least?"

"I texted him, thanked him for breakfast, and told him I would take him out one day, but that was two weeks ago," he said sheepishly.

"Holy hell, what the hell are you doing?" Bianca shouted. "Go call him right now and set up a date."

"What if he deleted my number or forgot about me?"

"What if he didn't, and he's been waiting for you to call him?"

"He could call me too, you know? He has my number," Des said. They argued back and forth for a bit before Gray interjected.

"You two are driving me fucking crazy. Des, I don't think it's good for you to start dating or think about going out with anyone, especially Moor. I think you should take some time to focus on the things you've wanted to do now that you're free from your parents' stranglehold." "You talk as if you know the Moor guy," Bianca said.

"I know of him, and he has a type that he goes for. And if Des goes out with him, I'm afraid Moor will devour him on the first night."

"Maybe I want to be eaten up," Des said.

"Yeah," Bianca agreed happily. "Let him get eaten."

"Fuck it," Gray said, grabbing his paintbrush and going back to work. "I warned you."

Des sighed and walked over to Gray, hugging him from behind. "I don't want to sit on the sidelines anymore, Gray. I have done that for a long time, and now I want to experience the world as I should have.

It's just one date. Who knows if he'll respond?"

"Trust me, he will," Gray said softly. "Who can say no to you?" "That's debatable." He chuckled.

Gray turned and hugged him. "I want you to be happy, Des. You deserve it more than anyone."

"Thank you."

"Look at me," Gray said, leaning back. "Learn to have fun, okay?

Experience meeting people and never hold back from taking what you want."

"You sound like a daddy about to marry off his son," Bianca said, joining their hug.

"Fuck, I feel like one," Gray grumbled, and they all laughed before going back to work.

"Hey," Moor said, snapping his fingers in front of his eyes, getting Des's attention. "Why the hell did you just space the fuck out?"

"I was thinking about what you said, and you have a point. Let's go somewhere else." Des went to walk away, but his arm was grabbed, stopping him.

"Wait," Moor said, causing Des to look up. "Maybe it's not a bad idea." That brought a smile to Des's face. "I haven't been here in a while myself. But next time we hang out, I'm picking the place."

"Are you saying we'll go out again?" Des smiled, doing a little mental jig.

"Maybe," he shrugged a shoulder. "Let's see how the night goes," Othello said. "Come on, let's do what you came here to do."

Des grinned and grabbed Othello's hand, pulling him toward the large rollercoaster. The amusement park was a staple in Verona Heights. It shared residence with the Velora River and was separated by a long walking bridge leading to a botanical garden and a few shops and highclass restaurants built in the past couple of years. The city had spent a lot of money on the park's upkeep and improvement over the years, and it was looking to expand, which Des knew his parents had a hand in.

"Admit it, you're having fun," Des said one hour into their outing as they walked through the botanical gardens.

They had gone on a few rides and played a few games that Othello won, but declined to take the prizes. He especially won the shooting games, proving the man knew his way around a gun. During those times, Des studied Othello's expression. Try as he might to hide it, Des had caught the man smiling a few times but masked his expression when he realized Des was looking at him. Des wasn't the only one watching Othello. He'd also spotted a couple of men and women admiring the taller man's good looks. Des wanted to snap at them or excessively flirt with Othello to ward them off, but he knew the man wasn't his. Hell, he wasn't even sure if this was considered a date. It was more like they were two people hanging out.

"I'm still waiting for you to feed me," Othello said, cutting into his thoughts.

"What are you in the mood for?"

"How about Italian?" Othello said.

"Okay, do you know a place?"

"I do," he said, grabbing Des's hand and pulling him toward the other side of the botanical garden.

Des smiled, allowing Moor to lead him. He wasn't even watching where they were heading. His only focus was on Moor. He wasn't sure how long they walked but groaned when his face hit the larger man's hard-muscled back, realizing they had stopped.

"Ouch," he groaned softly, stepping back from Moor, rubbing his nose, and noticing they were standing in front of a classic Mediterranean-style building just as beautiful as the surrounding garden. From the elegantly decorated indoor and outdoor tables with white tablecloths, they were at the Italian restaurant Othello mentioned. The place looked very inviting, and the food smelled divine. However, there was a problem: all the tables were taken.

"It looks packed. I doubt we'll be able to get a table," Des commented.

"We will. Come on," he said, gently squeezing Des's hand. They walked into the restaurant and up to the hostess's desk.

"Good evening," Moor said to the handsome host. "Could you tell Signore Conti that Othello Moor is here to see him?"

It might've been Des's imagination, but he swore the young man's eyes widened, and then he nodded and ran off without saying a word. Not five minutes later, a portly olive-skinned man, Des, suspected to be Conti, came out to greet Moor.

"Signore Moor, I wasn't expecting to see you tonight. We don't have..."

"I need a table," Moor said, cutting off whatever Conti was trying to say.

"A table." To Des, Mister Conti seemed surprised at what Othello said.

"Will that be a problem?"

"Yes...I mean, no, right away," Conti said, snapping his fingers quickly at the young host.

"I prefer a private room," Moor told Conti, who nodded and rattled off orders in Italian.

Again, Des felt he was seeing things because Conti seemed to have beads of sweat on his forehead the second he saw Moor. Des stole a glance at the taller man, wondering what the relationship between Conti and Moor was. He put it aside to ask later because Conti returned in less than five minutes and guided them to a private room where a bottle of red wine was uncorked, breathing and waiting for them.

"With how quickly he got everything set up, it makes me think this guy owes you money because you're a part of the mafia," Des joked as he took his seat. When Moor didn't speak, Des looked up to see the man watching him. "Did I say something wrong?"

"No." He smiled, draping the napkin over his lap. Des got the feeling he'd missed something important.

* * *

OTHELLO SMIRKED, not responding to the doctor's curiosity. If only he knew how right he was. Conti owed him close to two million dollars plus interest. He'd needed money to open his restaurant, and since he couldn't get a loan from the bank, he turned to Othello, who practically owned half of the restaurant with how much Conti still needed to pay. Conti would pay him for the rest of his and his children's lives on the weekly interest alone. He had never forced Conti to take his money; the man practically begged him, and even Othello had told him to think things through. If anyone asked Othello for the shirt off his back, he'd give it to them, but that didn't mean it came for free.

Someone would have to pay.

"Thank you," the doc said, getting his attention.

"For what?" Des placed his menu down on the table.

"You could have said no to hanging out with me tonight after it seemed like I ghosted you. But honestly, I was getting my life together after I quit my job and dealing with some family shit. Also, I know going to an amusement park wasn't what you had in mind, but another truth, other than hanging out with my best friends, Gray and Bianca, I've never been on a date before. Wait, is this a date?"

"Do you want it to be?" Othello stared into the doctor's pretty green eyes. He watched the doc chew on his bottom lip as if he was nervous about saying what was on his mind, so he said it for him. "I don't put out on the first date."

That brought a smile to the green-eyed man's face, and not for the first time that night, Othello thought his eyes reminded him of the angel he saw the night he was shot. He hadn't thought about that in a while. Knowing that it was all a figment of his imagination, he pushed the thought aside and focused on enjoying the rest of the evening.

"You also don't have to thank me. Your text came at a good time."

"How so?"

"My mother was nagging me that I work too much. Since my brother's having a baby, she's hoping I'll see the light and find a guy to settle down with."

Doc shook his head. "Well, at least you know she cares."

Othello sighed. "I do." He smiled. "So, you quit your job?"

"Yeah, in a roundabout way, I took your advice," Doc said. "I didn't like being a surgeon. I'm following my dream to be an artist. I'll probably be in school for the rest of my life with all I want to do, but I don't care." "Good for you, Doc," Othello said.

"You shouldn't call me that anymore. I'm no longer a doctor."

"What would you prefer I call you, then?" he said in a low voice that surprised even him, but he didn't show it. The look in the other man's eyes flashed a few ideas in his mind.

"I..." the little doc started but stopped when the server came in with the antipasto, a tray filled with Italian cured meats, bruschetta, cheese, marinated vegetables, and basil paired with a dry sparkling wine.

"I hope you don't mind. This menu was already preselected for any time I come here," Othello told him.

"No, it's fine. I haven't been here before, so I'll let you take the lead for the rest of the night."

Othello paused for a second at the doctor's words. If the other man knew just how enticing those innocent words were to a carnivore like him, the little carrier would probably run for the exit. Instead, he opted to watch the doctor as he ate and sipped on the wine, savoring the crisp acid taste of the alcohol. Othello didn't need to see the man's mark to know the man could carry children; his instincts about people were never wrong, and usually, he'd stay far away from guys like that, but there was something about Des that called to him.

He couldn't tear his gaze away as the doctor licked his lips, relishing every bite he took. Othello felt the doctor didn't truly know how alluring he was. The man was pure in every sense of the word, and if he stuck around him, Othello would surely ruin him, whether it was as a friend or more.

One of his reasons for agreeing to go out with Doc Des was that he was hoping to find a fuck buddy for a bit. But he couldn't use the man sitting across from him, especially after reading the information Tallen sent him. Des was an only child forced into a career he didn't want, with parents who only cared about being in the spotlight. The man in front of him should be protected from all the wolves in society, he being one of them. If anyone knew his thoughts right now, they'd laugh at him. Othello had no qualms about fucking someone just to relieve stress, and he thought about doing the same with Doctor Desmond, but now it seemed he was having second thoughts.

"This is really good. Aren't you going to eat?" Doc Des asked, pulling him from his thoughts.

Othello set his glass down and started eating. "So you were saying before the server came in."

"Oh, I...I...forgot," he stuttered, cheeks and neck flushing red. Othello knew it was a lie, but didn't call him out on it.

"Hmmm...if it comes back to you, let me know."

Scooping up some marinated vegetables on a toasted slice of bread, Othello sprinkled some of the cheese on top and then brought it to Des's lips. "Open," he instructed, watching as the doctor followed his instructions without any objections.

"Oh, this is so good," Des moaned, licking his lips, with a little oil lingering on them. Othello grabbed his napkin to clean off his lips, but froze when he realized what he was about to do.

Fuck, he's not my baby boy. But it would be so easy to make him mine. No, I can't go down that road again. Giving himself a mental shake, Othello searched for something to talk about.

"So, when are you going to paint something for me?"

"Is there something particular you're looking for?"

An image of the little doctor naked in his bed and posing on all fours, chest pressed down and legs spread wide, popped into Othello's mind, but he quickly pushed it from his thoughts. "Anything you think would be good to hang on the empty wall in my office," he said instead.

"I can think of something." He smiled.

Othello saw a new light and confidence in his eyes that hadn't been there the last time they met. As the rest of the dishes were served, they kept talking, and Othello shared a little bit about himself, but nowhere near enough to give the doctor the full picture of who he was. Othello had already established that even though he found the man interesting, his innocence made Othello afraid to get too close to him. It wasn't as if he was looking for a relationship, but even friends with benefits wouldn't suit the doctor. He needed to be with someone who would love him for a lifetime.

* * *

DES WAS HAVING A GOOD TIME. The conversation, food, and wine were flowing. But suddenly, his dinner partner went silent, leaving Des to do most of the talking.

"Be honest with me," Des said, taking the bull by the horns. "There won't be a second date."

Moor furrowed his brows. "Why do you think that?"

"You've gone quiet on me."

"Maybe I like to hear your voice," Othello said with a smile.

Des tilted his head. "I don't believe you."

"What did you hope to happen between us tonight, Doc?"

Des sighed and leaned back in his seat. "I don't know. I told you I've never done this before."

"And that's why we can't see each other anymore. If you stay around me long enough, I will ruin you."

"What do you mean by that?" Des asked, honestly confused.

"The world I come from is not the same as the one you live in."

Des scoffed. "You make it sound like you come from outer space."

That thought brought a smile to the man's face. "Not quite."

"I feel like I'm being dumped, and we're not even going out."

"If you were mine, Doc, I wouldn't ever let you go," Moor said softly.

Then why don't you want me now?

Des leaned forward. "I like talking to you, so can we at least stay friends?"

Fuck, I hope I don't sound like I'm begging for a friend or a pickme?

Moor didn't respond immediately, and Des thought he wouldn't answer. "I allow my friends to call me Othello." Des smiled upon hearing that. "Then call me Des." He breathed a long sigh, grateful their date had ended on a good note. Who knows, maybe their friendship would blossom into something more.

A FEW DAYS LATER, Des sat in the 3C cafe, sipping on the most delicious coffee he'd tasted in a long time. The Cs stood for cups, canvas, and coffee. There was a separate room where patrons could sip on a cup of coffee while they painted. The walls were filled with the customer's paintings. Des loved the idea and couldn't wait for his studio to be fixed up so he could put his vision into action.

Even though he still had his apartment across town, he was spending a lot more time in his new one. Or maybe it was an excuse to visit the art district more. Because the building had been sitting empty for so long, it had collected more than just dust over the years. Des wondered why his parents had held onto the building. They had every opportunity to sell it. He still couldn't believe the shit they pulled. Des had trusted them so easily and didn't expect his parents to stab him in the back. He didn't think he'd ever forgive them.

Des was using up all his free time since he was going back to class in two days. Luck was on his side, and he was able to easily transfer to a classroom setting from online. Someone gasped, and it caught Des's attention. He looked to where the sound came from and noticed the young lady next to him seemed transfixed on something across from her.

His curiosity got the better of him, causing Des to turn his head slightly. His eyes widened when he saw Othello Moor walking down the stairs, but he stopped and spoke to his companions. Des hadn't seen or spoken to the man since the night they went out. He'd thought about reaching out to him but didn't want to seem too eager, since Othello placed them in the friends category when Des wanted more.

As always, Moor looked and acted like he owned the place, even though everyone was casually dressed in jeans, shorts, and t-shirts. Moor's hair was braided back from his handsome face. Des had never realized how long it was, touching his shoulders. He also had on an olive-green suit that complemented him in every damn way, paired with a beige shirt and no tie, looking every bit as sexy as the last time Des saw him. He was surrounded by a couple of guys that Des recognized from the hospital and another he'd seen on the news quite a few times: Jackson Durrant, the campaign manager of his father's opposition.

Des wouldn't deny his curiosity, but it was none of his business. He had been staying as far away from the senate race as possible. Realizing he had been staring too long, Des turned around and grabbed his coffee, gulping it down and thanking every god it wasn't that hot. He hoped Moor didn't see him. He wasn't sure why he was hiding. They'd agreed to be friends.

"Are you hoping I didn't see you, Doc?"

"I'm not sure what you're talking about," Des said, looking over his shoulder. His eyes connected with Moor's amber jewels.

"Always playing coy." Moor smiled. "Tallen." "Yes, boss," Tallen responded.

"Do we have time for a cup of coffee?"

Tallen looked at his watch and then nodded. "Your next appointment is not until four, so you have time."

"You and Marco, go find something to do. I'll call you guys when I'm ready to leave."

"Okay." Tallen didn't even bat an eye or look in Des's direction before he left and walked out of the cafe.

Moor, for his part, sat opposite Des and took the cup from his hand, and took a sip, screwing up his face. "Why did you let it get cold?"

"No one told you to drink my coffee, so why don't you get your own?" Des told him.

Moor licked his lips, staring intensely at Des. "I figured yours would taste better."

There he goes, flirting with me when he was the one who drew the line in the sand. What the hell is up with him and the mixed signals? And why the fuck is my face feeling flushed by what he said? Hell, he needs to either fuck me or leave me alone.

*O*thello smirked, watching the little doc squirm in his chair, trying to mask his blushing cheeks.

Although he'd drawn a line between them, he couldn't deny how adorable Des was when he was flustered. To spare the man some grace, he changed the subject.

"Do you know the man I was meeting with today?" "Why should I?"

"He's asked me to gather information about your father. Would you be opposed to me doing that?"

"I thought you worked in construction."

"I do far more than that." Othello smiled. "So, would you care?"

Des shook his head. "It has nothing to do with me."

Othello wasn't sure what he'd been expecting, but he was pretty sure that wasn't it. "Why? Aren't you curious about what I might find out?"

"My father knew what he was doing when he decided to run for senate. If he has secrets, he should have known they would get out. I only ask one thing."

"What's that?"

"Whatever you find, don't tell me."

"I didn't plan on it."

"Good."

"You keep surprising me, Doc."

"What do you mean?"

"Here, I thought you were the dutiful son and would tell me to leave dear old dad alone. Instead, you shrug it off."

"Like I said, my dad knew what he was doing, so I'm sure he's prepared for anything that comes out about him."

"I won't say I'm not curious about your relationship with your father, but I won't ask."

"Thanks."

"Don't thank me yet."

They changed the topic, and neither of them noticed the time ticking by slowly. Although he sponsored businesses in the art district, Othello didn't normally venture out this way. If it wasn't for Jackson Durrant wanting to meet, he was certain he wouldn't have seen the former doctor today. Othello had thought about the pretty doctor in the past few days but did not attempt to contact him because he wanted to stand firm in his decision. But the second he'd been going to leave the cafe, he felt the man's presence and knew he couldn't leave without speaking.

"So, this is what you do with all your free time?" Othello asked.

"Not really. I've been busy cleaning up my new place. My

grandfather bought it for me before he died. It's been sitting for a while and needs a lot of tender loving care."

"And you're just the right person to do it."

"Yes. It's where I plan to open my studio. Do you want to see it?"

"Are you inviting me to your place, Doc?" Othello leaned back in his seat

"So what if I am?" Des asked with a spark in his green eyes that drew Othello in.

You're playing with fire, little doc, Othello thought. "Sure," he said, seeing that he still had time.

"Cool." Des stood and grabbed his empty cup. "It's not far from here."

It took them fifteen minutes to get to the studio. Othello recognized it as a building once he put a bid on it, but the owner refused to sell it, no matter how much money he threw at them. Now he knew why. It was two levels large enough to convert into a club and hookah bar. The place had good lighting and would've set the mood for what he had in mind. Des showed him around and laid out his plans for what he was thinking, and just like the night they were at dinner, his eyes sparkled as he came to life. It made Othello want to see what they looked like when he was being fucked.

"My studio will be down here, and through there," Des said, pointing to the door on the far side of the room, "it leads to my apartment."

"Do I get a tour of that as well?" Othello's voice dipped as he walked closer to him, but not enough to touch.

"I...it's not ready." He looked down, and Othello couldn't deny his cock twitched at the submissive pose.

"Look at me," Othello softly ordered.

Des raised his head, and their gazes connected. Othello was truly questioning this whole "let's be friends" thing. The way he looked right now, Othello suspected he could simply pull him into his arms and do whatever he wanted to Des, and the man wouldn't stop him. Des's lips parted, and Othello couldn't help but lick his own at the thought of tasting the little doc. He moved closer to Des and was about to tell him to forget the whole friend thing. He didn't do one-night stands, but at that moment, the little doctor was far too tempting to ignore. But then his cellphone rang.

"You should answer that," Des whispered and stepped around him.

Othello sighed and pulled his cellphone from his pocket. "What?" he answered, turning to look at Des, who had his back to him.

"Boss, where are you? We have to go," Tallen said.

Fuck, being with Des, he'd quickly forgotten he had other business to attend to. "Alright, I'll meet you back at the cafe."

"Where—"

Othello hung up before Tallen could ask more questions. "I have to go."

"Do you want me to walk you back to the cafe?" "No." He moved over to Des and pinched his chin. "Don't be a stranger, Doc. You have my number. Text or call me anytime."

"You too."

Othello stood there for a few seconds, tempted to follow through with his plan to kiss Des, but he thought better of it. He had a feeling that getting one taste of Des wouldn't be enough for him, which was why he said they should be friends. It was safer that way. Releasing the man's face, Othello walked away, conflicted for the first time about whether he was doing the right thing.

* * *

DES WATCHED the taller man leave, feeling a little disappointed that their time together had been cut short. It wasn't planned, but he was having a good time with Othello, and if he hadn't been mistaken, he could have sworn the man would kiss him. But maybe that was all in his imagination. Des knew he wouldn't object to Othello's touch, especially his kiss. Hell, he was hoping the man would fuck the life out of him. With their status as it was, he didn't see that happening.

Maybe it's time I cut my losses and start dating other people like Gray suggested. Yet Des wasn't sure that would happen since his mind and body had been stuck on Othello Moor since the night he met him. *I guess the saying is true: the heart knows what it wants, and there's nothing I can do about it for now. Fuck, who knew having an infatuation would be like this?*

* * *

"I HEARD you were at Conti's a couple of weeks ago,"

Alessandro said to him.

"Yeah, I took a friend there for dinner," Othello responded, not looking up from the paperwork he was reviewing. "The books look good, but we should still get the accountant to review them. I..." His cellphone vibrated as he spoke. Reaching over, he picked it up, smiling when he saw it was Des. They had been texting back and forth since the night they had gone out, but they had both gotten extremely busy.

Doc Des: I'm free tonight. Do you want to get together? My friends seem to be busy. Othello: So I'm your second choice?

Doc Des: I can read the sarcasm; it's not a handsome look.

Othello: I'm always handsome.

Doc Des: Someone is so full of themselves.

So, can we get together tonight?

Othello thought about it for a minute before telling him to come by the club. He had a few errands to run, but he should be back by then. After getting a reply, Othello put his cellphone down and let his thoughts wander for a second. In the past couple of weeks, he and Des had been meeting quite often, whether it was for dinner, a cup of coffee, or to hang out, which was something Othello hadn't done in a very long time. During their time together, Othello could feel his body relaxing more, bringing on another problem: his growing attraction.

The best way to stop it from happening would be to distance himself from Des, but truthfully, he didn't want to. He enjoyed being in his presence and watching his eyes shine the more he learned about himself. Des was intelligent, but maybe it was not only his growing confidence but also his naivete that called to Othello, making him want to protect the little doctor from not only him but also the entire world. At his wayward thoughts, he shook his head.

I'm being foolish. He's better off with someone else.

Othello went back to work. They had a couple of stores in the diamond and gold district, but Othello wanted more. Yes, he was greedy, but it was a dog-eat-dog world, and he was like a lion wanting to be the king of said world.

"I think we need to stop looking into who shot you," Alessandro stated. "For now, at least."

"Are you giving up?" Othello asked, furrowing his brows.

Alessandro shook his head. "I can't believe we haven't found a fucking clue as to who did it. The one lead we had died."

"I find that just as suspicious," Othello told him.

Alessandro stared at him. "You think we have a spy on the inside, don't you?"

"It wouldn't be the first time another clan or the cops have tried to get something on us." Othello leaned back in his seat. "I have a plan you might not like." "Tell me anyway," Alessandro sighed.

"When was the last time you took Mama on a vacation?"

"What does that have to do with what we're talking about?"

"I have a feeling that the way things went down wasn't how

the person who set things up was expecting it to go. Either one of us or both was supposed to die."

"What about Iago?"

"I doubt they know we have it set up that he would be the don if something were to happen. Fuck, not even Iago knows that."

"So what's your plan?"

Othello leaned back in his chair. "Anything we do, we need to continue to keep our actions quiet from the two major families. I'm not counting them out as suspects. They hate me and are completely against me being the next don."

"I'd like to disagree with that, but I can't," Alessandro said sadly. "Although some things change, some things remain the same."

The two main families disliked the fact that Othello, a man they considered as other or an interloper, made waves and was liked and respected by the remaining clans, who were hoping Othello would one day take up the mantle of head of The Commission. They would rather have Alessandro name Iago the heir, and it was no secret why. His Italian heritage was more pronounced in appearance and color. On the other hand, Othello was one percent Italian, seventy percent African, and the rest Portuguese, Albanian, and Spanish. Mixed blood was what some whispered behind his back, but never to his face. Although The Commission had some say in what the minor families did, they had no right to choose the next in line.

"Anyway, the witness killed himself. No other way to explain that than if whoever ambushed us was working for the main families. He was more afraid of them than us. The question is, who in our family is working with them? I have a feeling they're waiting for one of us to get out of the way so they can really act. Most know you've named me your heir, but they don't know I've already taken up the mantle. But you still carry a lot of weight, Don. In the other dons' eyes, I'm not ready."

"So, with me completely out of the way, you get to see who the real players are?" Othello nodded. "Okay. I'll take Maria away for a bit, but it won't be until after Emilia gives birth. I've promised to take Maria to Spain, Portugal, and Italy. Shoot, we might even jet off to Africa." He stood and walked to the door, but stopped. "When we return, Othello, I hope you're ready to introduce the young man who put that grin on your face to me and your mother. Better yet, bring him to the anniversary party you and Iago are planning."

What the hell is the old man talking about? Scoffing at his father's silliness, Othello got back to work.

* * *

LATER THAT DAY, Othello pulled into the parking spot marked for the owner of the Mirage Club. Getting out of his car, his brows furrowed when he spotted Roderigo's car two spaces down. He wondered what the man was doing here. It wasn't time for the club to open, and he knew of no private parties happening. With the two clubs he owned, Othello kept a log of all that went on in his establishments. He was kind of anal when it came to things like that. Pocketing his keys, Othello entered the club, feeling annoyed that there wasn't a guard at the door that shouldn't have been unlocked.

Looking around, he tsked at not seeing any staff who should have been there preparing to open the club. "Where the fuck is everyone?" Just as he uttered the words, he heard a scream coming from the back room. Othello rushed in that direction and burst through the door, seeing Roderigo about to strike a female staff member.

"Where is it?" Roderigo yelled and swung his hand, only it didn't connect with the staff's face since Othello grabbed his arm and roughly pushed him to the ground. "Who the fuck—?"

He tried to get up, but Othello raised a foot and stomped him back down.

"Stay the fuck down," he growled, and he could see the fear of all the gods flashing through Roderigo's eyes when he noticed him. Othello looked at the female employee's face, remembering her name was Lucy, whose cheeks were red, evidence she'd been slapped around a couple of times before he arrived. Lucy was one of the high-paid girls who did more than strip for the club. Feeling rage burn in him, Othello's gaze flashed to Roderigo, who was still being held down by his foot. Reaching into his pockets, Othello pulled out some money and handed it to her. "Go home and rest for the night."

"What are you doing? I bought h—" He didn't get to finish the rest because Othello kicked him in the stomach, shutting Roderigo up.

"Go," Othello said, looking at Lucy. "Don't come back until your face is cleared up. And don't worry, this won't affect your pay." Not only that, he couldn't let Tallen see her like that. His soldier had a huge crush on Lucy.

"Yes," she said, running out of the room.

Once she was gone, Othello turned to Roderigo and spoke in an even tone that did not hide his anger. "What are the rules of my club?"

"It's not your club," Roderigo spat.

Stepping back, Othello removed his jacket and loosened the first couple of buttons on the top of his shirt. Never taking his eyes off Roderigo, who struggled to his feet, Othello unbuttoned his shirt cuffs and slowly rolled them up. Roderigo was a well-known businessman, or so he liked to tell people, but the truth was he lived off his daddy's money and made shitty investments, and that included the club Othello had won from him. It wasn't until he took control that the place saw a profit.

"I'm giving you leeway, Roderigo, by repeating the question. What are *my* club rules?"

Othello had a code of conduct for both his entertainment establishments that must be followed, especially for the Mirage where he had strippers and escorts of all genders employed. The patrons could spend as much money as they wanted on his people all night long, or hell, days, but one major rule was never to lay a harmful hand on one of his people. The rule Roderigo broke. Growing tired of waiting for the man to answer, Othello raised a hand and slapped the man so hard he howled in pain as he stumbled back, hitting the wall hard. Othello didn't let up.

He hit him a couple more times.

"Tell me," he snapped, slapping him even harder.

"Stop...please," Roderigo begged. "I won't do it again, please. I'm sorry."

Not feeling appeased, Othello kicked him in the crotch and watched as he doubled over in pain, feeling no sympathy. Othello was not a nice man, but abusing women, children, and those deemed weak did not sit well with him. He really hated people like Roderigo, who had power and abused it because he thought he could.

"You're banned from every one of my establishments. If I see you enter any one of them, I will kill you. Now get the fuck out!"

Roderigo struggled to his feet, glaring at Othello. "You won't get away with this!"

"Why the fuck are you still here?" Othello snapped.

"Just you wait, Othello. I'll make sure you pay for this."

"You sound like an idiotic television villain. Fuck, you're annoying." Othello grabbed him by the collar and dragged him to the entrance, and threw his ass out. When he returned to the club and saw that it was still empty, Othello decided that besides Lucy, he would have to rehire a whole new staff.

"Fuck, and today started out so well."

* * *

DES REMOVED HIS HELMET, stowed it away, pocketed his keys, and walked to the club entrance. Just as he was about to open the door, he was stopped.

"Hey, Doc."

Turning, he saw Tallen walking over to greet him. "Hey," he said, greeting him back. "I'm here to see Othello."

"I know," Tallen said. "It's why I'm here. He got caught up in a meeting and told me to meet you and take you to the apartment. He'll be up as soon as he's done."

"I don't have to wait for him there. I can just go to the bar."

"You can't," Tallen said hurriedly. "The boss forgot a private party was happening tonight, so the club is closed to the public."

"Oh, I'll go up then."

Tallen nodded and led him to the apartment, about a ten-minute walk or less from the club. Tallen let him in with his key and left him to take care of his own things. Since he was preoccupied the last time he was there, Des took in the entire apartment without invading Othello's space. His stomach growled, reminding him he hadn't eaten in a while and had hoped to catch a meal and drink with Othello. Going to the kitchen, he opened the fridge and looked for something to eat. Not seeing anything he liked, Des decided to go shopping. Maybe he could cook something for dinner. He stopped at his thoughts, wondering if Othello would think he was thinking too far with their friendship.

Des didn't know how to explain what they had going on. Over the past few weeks, they'd gotten together on and off and texted constantly. Their flirting became so distracting that lately, he couldn't concentrate on the painting project he was working on for Othello or sit through a lecture. He found his attraction to Othello growing rather than waning. He'd grown accustomed to Othello being a part of his circle, and he spoke with his two best friends less than normal. It didn't help that each time he felt them getting closer, Othello would pull away, putting distance between them.

"Fuck, I don't know if I'm coming or going with this guy." His stomach growled again. "Forget it, I'll just cook something. He can think whatever the hell he wants."

Opening the door, he was about to step out, but stopped when he saw Tallen standing outside.

"Hey, Doc, do you need something?"

"What are you still doing here?" he asked, instead of answering the other man's question.

"Oh, I'm waiting for the boss to get here, plus he wanted me to stick by your side in case you needed anything."

"O-okay." He went to leave, but once again, Tallen got in his way. "Um...is there a reason you're not letting me leave?"

"No, of course not," he said with a wry chuckle, scratching the back of his neck. "But if you need to go somewhere, I can take you."

Des stared at Tallen, wondering what his deal was, but put it aside for now. "I need to go to the store. I want to make something to eat."

"Did you check the garden and the freezer?"

"Um..."

"Boss's garden is on the roof, and the freezer has extra meat and stuff."

Well, that's efficient. "I didn't check, but still, I want to get fresh meat. I can get a few things and then look at the garden when we return."

"Alright, make a list, and I'll shop for you." "You don't have to. I don't mind doing it myself." "Then I'll go with you," Tallen insisted.

Des was getting ready to object again but felt Tallen wouldn't let up. "Okay, let's go."

"The store is a few minutes by car and much longer on foot. Plus, it's too hot for you to walk."

Des had to admit Tallen had a point. "Sounds good." As they walked to Tallen's car, the man talked nonstop, mostly about his boss. But Des had to admit it eased the weirdness he had felt around the guy a few minutes ago. During their shopping trip, he discovered Tallen had started working for Othello six years ago and sometimes acted as his assistant.

He wanted to ask more questions that he knew Othello wouldn't answer, but he didn't want to put Tallen in an awkward position. So, instead, he simply listened, hoping Tallen would let something slip. It didn't take them long to get what he needed. Soon, they were heading back to Othello's apartment, where Des had to drag Tallen inside, because, for some odd reason, he didn't want to enter. Des told him he had to show him that garden, and it ended up adding another reason to fall in lust with Othello.

The man is too damn perfect. Does he have any flaws?

OTHELLO

Othello entered his apartment and paused when a delicious scent hit him. He realized he hadn't seen Tallen standing guard at the door as he'd instructed, making him wonder where his subordinate was hiding.

"Oy, Doc, I think it's done."

"Are you sure? Let me check. And I told you to call me Des; I'm not a doctor anymore."

"I'm not used to it yet. Give me some time."

Othello's eyebrows furrowed, listening to the conversation. *What the fuck is Tallen doing in here?* It was against the rules for his subordinates to be in his apartment when he wasn't home. Othello wasn't in the mood to teach another person a lesson.

He'd had a hard day and would rather fuck the tightest ass until they couldn't walk straight. He'd spent most of the day hiring a new staff to run the Mirage. Not all the positions were filled, so he had to close the club for the rest of the week, which pissed him off royally because it was cutting into his profits.

"I don't think it's done yet. It needs more time," Des said.

"Are you sure?"

"Yup."

"Doc...I mean Des, I didn't know you could cook."

"I had a good teacher. Let's hope your boss likes it."

The uncertainty in the doctor's voice caught his attention, prompting him to go to the kitchen. He saw Tallen and Des facing away from him, fixated on whatever was on the stove. Othello was initially willing to overlook Tallen's mistake of being in his home. Still, he became annoyed when he saw Des and Tallen standing very close, with Des's arm around Tallen's shoulders, as if they were closer than Othello thought.

"You two better not be burning down my damn apartment," Othello said in an even voice. He watched Tallen's back stiffen just as Des turned to look at him with a grin on his face.

"You're home," Des said, but his smile slipped when he noticed Othello's serious expression.

Instead of saying anything to the doctor, Othello directed his gaze to Tallen, who still had his back facing Othello. "Leave," he ordered.

"I..." Des started, but Othello stopped him.

"I'm not talking to you, Doc," he said, his eyes still trained on Tallen.

"Why the hell are you being so damn scary right now?" Des snapped. "Can't you be nice? And especially to Tallen."

"Um, Doc, it's okay. I knew the rules," Tallen stammered, turning to look at Othello.

"Rules, what's this shit about rules?" Des cursed.

"You're a grown-ass man."

Othello quirked a brow at Tallen.

"I should get going," he said, making a mad dash to the door.

"Wait, where are you going? Didn't you want to see how I put everything together?" Des said after him.

"Um, no, I forgot I had plans."

Before Des could say any more, Tallen was out the door. "You really need to be nicer to him. He admires you."

Othello ignored him and moved to the kitchen. "What did you cook?" He was starving and hoped the doctor had cooked something, better yet, something edible.

"No, you don't," Des said, pulling on his arm and turning him around. "Go get cleaned up, and I'll set the table."

"But I'm hungry," Othello grumbled.

"Is that why you're in a bad mood?" Des said, cupping his face. "Aw, poor baby."

No, I'm fucking pent up, and the way you look right now, I'm fighting every bone in my body not to fuck you despite what I told you about being friends, Othello thought, but instead, he said, "I'm really starving since I forgot to eat lunch, and everything smells so good." Othello's eyes lingered on the beads of sweat clinging to Des's creamy skin despite the airconditioning. His gaze appreciated the white T-shirt stretched across Des's lithe chest and the black jeans riding low on his hips.

"Yeah, well, me too. But I want this to be a special dinner."

"Why?" Othello asked.

He watched the little doc chew on his bottom lip, a sure sign that he was nervous about something. He looked anywhere on Othello but on his face. Reaching up, Othello pressed his thumb to Des's lip, stopping him from ruining his kissable mouth.

"Tell me," Othello whispered, removing his thumb and lazily grazing it against Des's cheek.

"This is my way of repaying you for that one dinner."

"How many times have we been out since then?"

"Quite a few times, but you always pay."

Othello stared at Des—not for the first time in the past few weeks. He wanted to pull the man into his arms and kiss him until he was breathless, especially when he was this submissive. Othello had been holding back on his attraction to Des. There were a couple versions of him: the one that was shy and naive, and then there was the side that showed his confidence and demanding nature.

"Fine," Othello sighed, lightly pinching his cheek, smiling when the man still didn't look up at him.

Fuck, he really makes me want to eat him up. It's too bad that I said he was off-limits.

Shaking his head, Othello went into his bedroom, unbuttoned his shirt, and shrugged it off before throwing it in the hamper. Unbuckling his belt, he grabbed the buckle, turning just as he was about to pull it from the loop. He paused when he saw Des still in the same spot, watching him. The little doctor's ears were bright red, the flush moving down his neck.

I know I've thought it, but could he really be submissive?

Othello needed to test the waters. Not taking his eyes off Des, he dragged the leather out of the loop, watching and listening to the little doc's breathing change and his cheeks blush. The little doctor gasped and clutched his chest when Othello slashed the belt through the air, making it snap like a whip.

Des raised his gaze, and their eyes locked on each other, and Othello couldn't deny the tension that rose between them. The lustful look on Des's face, his kissable lips parted as if wanting or needing to be filled with something dark, long, and thick. Othello's cock twitched just at the image. He traced his fingers along the smooth black leather, imagining the sweet pleasure of reddening the doc's creamy ass and back, pulling sweet sounds from him before he fucked him raw, leaving his cum inside, marking him.

Fuck, I need to get laid.

Reaching for the curtain rope, Othello pulled it, letting the curtain fall close and blocking them from each other. He stood there for a few seconds, not ashamed of what he'd done, but now he questioned whether he did the right thing by drawing a line between them so early. He had been looking for someone to play with, and the doctor checked off all his boxes. He was cute, funny, super intelligent, and a natural-born submissive he could mold to be his.

Othello wasn't looking for a relationship, especially not after the last one practically broke him, and it had taken him years to get over. Phillip was a trained submissive, and Othello was ready to give the world to him. He thought that Phillip understood him, the world he was from, and that their future was set. Plus, he was just as kinky as Othello. Hell, he'd been about to propose marriage to him but tore him apart instead when he caught Phillip cheating on him with another man. Trust was very important to Othello and what Phillip did meant he could never trust him again.

He hadn't closed his heart to the prospect of falling for anyone, simply placed love in the category of out of sight, out of mind. He tried playing with others after Phillip, but it didn't feel the same. There wasn't a connection. So, Othello simply focused on his work. He had never hidden his proclivities from his family. It was why they were encouraging him to date. They knew how badly Phillip had hurt him. They became worried when all he did was work. It had been a while since he'd felt anything toward anyone.

Finally, moving from where he stood, he undressed and headed to the bathroom. The image of Des standing there looking at him with want and desire in his eyes woke a forgotten desire in Othello, and now he had to choose whether to go with the feeling or ignore it and keep the line drawn between them. Maybe he'd see how the night went before he made another decision.

* * *

DES PANTED, leaning on the counter and holding his chest. *What the fuck just happened?*

A reel of Othello snapping the leather belt in the air played continuously in his mind. Othello's powerful appearance, shirtless and showcasing his well-defined chest and abs, was something he couldn't get out of his thoughts. He licked his lips, thinking about licking the sexy man's mermaid line. Des wasn't sure what was happening. He had always thought Othello had a dominating aura, even the night the man was laid out on his operating table.

It was what drew his attention. It made Des want to kneel at Othello's feet and be his everything. But from the moment Othello walked into the apartment, there was an air around him that he couldn't explain or put a word to. He looked back toward the bedroom and wondered if Othello was trying to tell him something. Des wasn't opposed to something happening between them. In fact, he'd been hoping for it.

But isn't he the one who keeps building a wall between us? Is he now erasing it?

Des was so confused about what to do. The more he

got to know Othello, the more he wanted to be with him. They talked about their lives over time, and there were times Des wanted to ask him about the night he got shot, but in the back of his mind, he knew he was digging into territory he shouldn't. But even with that nagging thought, Des didn't care.

It might be dangerous or foolish of him because he was so inexperienced regarding matters of the heart, but for the first time in his life, he knew who and what he wanted. He just didn't know how to go about getting it. Othello seemed like the kind of man who would stay strong in his word. However, after what had just happened, he was feeling hopeful. He took a deep breath and collected himself, and the scent of dinner reminded him that he needed to get it on the table.

With Tallen's help, he had made a simple dinner. It felt good to cook since he hadn't done it in a while. Thanks to the nanny his parents had hired to care for him, she'd taught him how to cook Italian, Spanish, Greek, Jamaican, Portuguese, Italian, and even Arabic and African meals. But tonight, he mixed it up a bit with an easy Caprese salad, lemon herb chicken with roasted vegetables, and chocolate strawberries for dessert.

Just as he placed the wine on the table, Othello entered the dining room dressed in a red silk shirt with a few buttons open, giving him a clear view of his chest. Des's gaze moved past his black slacks and ended on the taller man's bare feet. He had never thought he'd have a foot fetish with how cute they looked, not to mention the thoughts that ran through his head of licking and sucking on his toes. Or maybe he just had an Othello fetish.

"So, what did you make for dinner?" Othello's deep voice reached his ear, and Des gasped when he realized the man had gotten close without him noticing. That dominating aura surrounded him. Des took in a deep breath, hoping to center himself, but it was a big mistake because whatever cologne Othello was wearing made his cock twitch.

Fuck, he smells so damn good.

"Better yet, what's for dessert."

Me, Des wanted to say, but said, "Chocolate-dipped strawberries."

Othello tilted his head to the side. "Are you trying to seduce me, Doc?"

"Is it working?" Des smiled.

"We'll see how the night goes."

"Uh-oh, the last time you said that to me, things didn't turn out how I hoped."

"Well, things might turn out different this time."

Des shook his head, wondering if he could believe what Othello said. He knew how much the other man liked to joke around, and even though they were friends, they flirted constantly. But he couldn't help but wish and pray that things would change between them.

"Okay, enough joking around. Sit so we can eat."

They sat down and started eating. Since they were both hungry, there wasn't much conversation. He had just taken the last bite of his chicken when Othello broke the silence between them.

"I admit, it shocked me that you can cook, but I have to say, this was good." He leaned his elbow on the table. "What else do you know how to cook, Doc?"

"You'll have to date me to find out."

Othello responded with a smirk that Des couldn't figure out. They stared at each other, and he could feel the air crackling between them. Des wanted to straddle Othello's legs and kiss him hard while rutting against his cock.

Fuck, I need to do something before I embarrass myself.

Des stood and grabbed the dishes, but Othello placed a gentle hand on his. His breath caught in his chest, and he raised his gaze to meet honey-colored eyes. "Let me do it," he said. "You cooked. Go sit on the couch. I'll be there after I put these in the dishwasher."

Des nodded and did what he was told. He tried to get comfortable but couldn't. He kept looking back at Othello, who seemed completely unfazed, as if he hadn't noticed anything happening between them. Hoping to get his mind off his wandering thoughts, Des grabbed the remote sitting on the coffee table and switched on the television. The news was on, and the second the reporter mentioned his father, Des turned it off, throwing the remote to the couch.

Even after switching his profession, he hadn't heard from his parents. He guessed they were too busy trying to take over the world to notice. At the moment, his father was down in the polls and, by all appearance, wouldn't win. But who knew what his parents had up their sleeves?

Des also noticed that since quitting his job, he hadn't been wallowing in self-pity about Mr. Alverez. He wondered if that made him a terrible person, but he had been too caught up in living his new life, trying to put the past behind him. Funny enough, since leaving his job, he had been getting calls from private medical firms and corporations offering him a job. Even his grandpa, Douglas, offered him a position in his company as the head of the research department. Des wouldn't deny that it was weird that his grandfather would call him when they didn't have a relationship whatsoever. Des couldn't help but think it was his parents' doing. He couldn't chance working for his family again, so he turned all the jobs down.

Although he had money thanks to his grandfather, and with all his plans for the future, Des didn't want to run out of money. Although he wasn't looking for stardom, it didn't mean he didn't want to sell his paintings, but he was nowhere ready for all of that. In all honesty, he shouldn't even be thinking about wanting a relationship with anyone, much less Othello, with how flaky he'd been lately, but he would be a fool if he didn't try and get the man to notice how good they could be together.

He was so lost in thought that he gasped in surprise when he felt something cold graze his bottom lip. Slowly, he turned his head and connected again, this time with eyes that reminded him of the sweetest honey.

"Bite," Othello softly ordered.

Not taking his eyes off him, Des parted his lips and gently bit into the tip of the strawberry, sucking the juices into his mouth. He moaned as the sweet and slightly tart liquid filled his mouth.

"Does it taste good?"

Des was certain he nodded, but when Othello chuckled and then spoke, he realized he hadn't said anything.

"So?" he said. "How does it taste?"

"Sweet," Des whispered, finally finding his voice.

"Really?" He quirked a brow. "Maybe I should taste it for myself."

Before he could ask what he meant, Othello licked the corner of his lips and groaned deeply, as if liking what he tasted. Des's breath hitched, and his eyes widened, but the fruit was removed before he could comprehend what was happening. Othello's tongue swept into his open mouth, sucking and savoring the strawberry flavor off Des's tongue, pulling a deep moan from him. Des panted, feeling breathless as Othello went from sucking on his tongue to nibbling on his bottom lip before pecking at him gently on the mouth, making him tingle, then pressing their mouths together.

Their eyes remained open. He could feel the air crack-ling around them. Othello's gaze was so intense it felt like he was peering deep into his soul, burning with desire for him. Des wanted to close his eyes, but he couldn't. He felt trapped in a web of need and lust. Just one touch from Othello and Des was hooked on the man. Just when Des thought Othello was about to take their kiss further, he pulled back, releasing his mouth, to his disappointment. Before he could complain, Othello cupped his cheek, grazing his face with his thumb.

"It was you, wasn't it?"

"What?" Des asked, thoroughly confused.

"When I was in the hospital, I thought I had died and gone

to heaven, only to be greeted by an angel with bright green eyes, but now I know it was you."

"Yes," Des answered, not playing coy. "It happens to patients sometimes…" Othello placed a finger to cut off his rambling.

"I don't care about that," he said, removing his finger.

"Oh," Des said, turning his head away. "When did you figure it out?"

Othello turned his face back with a finger. "Does it matter?"

Des chewed on his bottom lip, staring into Othello's eyes. "I guess not."

"Des—"

"Othello—"

They chuckled, realizing they'd spoken simultaneously.

"Go ahead," Othello said.

"Why did you kiss me?"

"You know the answer to that," Othello told him.

"But—" he started, and once more, he was stopped with a kiss that made him see stars as Othello devoured his mouth, pulling chords of moans and groans from him that sounded like pleasurable music to his ears. Othello's tongue mapped out every corner of his mouth. Just as Des draped a leg over Othello, the man pulled back from their kiss, surprising Des, who gasped for breath, looking into his amber eyes.

"I want you, Des, not just for one night, but I'll warn you now, I'm not a good person. I'm jealous, possessive, and over-bearing, but I know when to back off. I don't do one-night stands. Or trying to fuck each other out of our systems. Once I claim you as mine, you'll never want to be anyone else's. If you stay, be prepared to stay no matter what you learn about me. If you cheat or lie to me, we're done."

He kept staring into Des's eyes.

"This is your time to walk away, Doc. Because if you stay, we can't return to the way things were. Think carefully before we go any further."

Des's mind raced. *I don't want to go back.* He licked his tingling lips, tasting the remnants of their kiss. His earlier reasoning returned to him. And although he wasn't expecting it, he'd been hoping for it, so why would he walk away now?

Othello went to pull away, but Des grabbed his hand.

"Just promise not to hurt or use me," Des whispered. He had been used by his parents far too much. He'd lived by their hand, and on moments when they wanted to impress their friends, he would be placed on a pedestal; it was the only time they would show him any kind of affection, only to ignore him and forget he was there the next.

"I told you before, I've never been in a relationship, but I know there are certain things I want from my lover. Someone who is dominant in the bedroom but who sees me as his equal." He could feel his face growing warmer, hoping Othello wouldn't tease him like normal. Then, a thought came to him since they were laying things on the table. *I should tell him I'm a carrier.* He went to speak, but Othello beat him to it.

"I can't promise that I won't break your heart, but I can try not to. And I would never use you," Othello told him softly. "Hurting you is another matter, but it would only be in plea-sure." He smirked. "All naughty boys deserve a spanking, even if it's to be reminded who's in charge."

Des knew his face turned as red as a tomato, but his embar-rassment was overshadowed by the image of him draped over Othello's lap and being punished with a brush, his hand, or even a belt.

"All in good time, baby, then I'll have that pretty ass nice and red," Othello whispered in his deep voice, and his warm breath ghosted along the shell of his ear.

"I don't know what you're talking about," Des mumbled.

"Sure you don't." Othello leaned back, peering into his face. "We'll go slow."

Des nodded. "So, does this mean my cooking impressed you?

Othello smiled. "It was more than your cooking."

"Really?"

"What did you think was going to happen after weeks of us flirting with each other?" Othello said, leaning close to him. Their faces were so close he could feel the warmth of his breath on his lips. "You look hot riding your motorcycle, by the way."

"I'm glad you think so," Des said. "But enough talking, kiss me more."

Othello chuckled. "I thought I was in charge in the bedroom."

Des went to speak, but Othello captured his lips, pulling a throaty moan from him as his hot wet tongue entered his mouth, stealing his breath away. Their kiss deepened, and sparks ignited inside him, winding their way around his body. His cock twitched in his pants, causing him to pivot his hips, seeking friction. As if knowing his thoughts, a large hand palmed his crotch, giving rise to his desire.

Des loved the taste and feel of Othello pressing against him. The firm softness of his lips as they moved expertly on his, taking full control of his mind and body. Their mouths gently ground against each other in a slow and seductive dance as he felt his body touch the soft cushions of the couch and Othello's muscled body lying on top of him. Des opened his legs but didn't know what to do with his hands, and it seemed the other man knew his thoughts. He grabbed his wrists and brought them above his head, keeping them locked with one hand while the other pushed up Des's T-shirt, revealing his chest. Othello trailed kisses down Des's chin, his neck, sucking and biting on every inch of visible flesh before pulling one of his nipples into his mouth. He couldn't hold back his reaction, arching his back and pushing his chest into Othello's mouth, wanting more.

He jerked his hips, rubbing his clothed erection against Othello's crotch, wishing they had no barriers between them. However, he couldn't deny that the fabric grazing against his sensitive cock made him even more aroused, and he couldn't slow his hips down; he wanted to cum. Othello went from one nipple to the other, biting and sucking on them until they hurt, but it felt so good.

"Oh, fuck, don't stop," he whimpered.

Othello moved down his body, pressing his face on Des's erection, groaning and lightly grazing his teeth along his shaft, making him shiver. His wrists were still held down, and he wished he could hold Othello, but he also liked being pinned down and letting the man do as he wished with his body. Des didn't regret that he had waited so long to have sex, but he didn't want to just kiss all night.

He wanted more.

"Othello," he whimpered. "Fuck me."

Othello raised his head, and their eyes met heatedly. "Are you sure?"

"Yes," he said, sitting up and cupping Othello's cheeks.

"I've waited twenty-six years and won't wait a day longer."

Des thought he would be rejected when Othello stood, but was pleased when he held out a hand for him. "Come. The couch is big enough for us to do anything on, but your first time should be in bed."

Des took his hand and was pulled from the sofa, then lifted off his feet. Instantly, his arms circled Othello's neck and his legs around Othello's waist, and then he captured his mouth, needing to taste him. For the first time, he didn't mind being shorter than Othello, with the way the taller man was holding him as they slowly made their way to the bedroom.

Des sighed against Othello's mouth when his back touched the smooth, cool, silk sheets. His legs tightened around Othello's waist, pulling the other man down on top of him. He groaned in delight when their clothed erections came in contact. He tightened his arms around Othello's neck, loving the weight on him. He could feel Othello's big, thick, hard cock pressing against him, and he couldn't wait to have it pounding inside of him. He was certain the man would ruin him, and he wouldn't regret it.

ACT III

*"It gives me wonder great as my content / To see you here before me!
O my soul's joy! / If after every tempest come such calms, / May the
winds blow till they have wakened death!"*
Othello (Act 2, Scene 1)

*H*e's so arousing and sensitive, Othello thought. *Why did I fight myself all these weeks?*

Othello leaned back and quickly helped Des out of his shirt, throwing it to the side. He trailed a finger on Des's chest, circling each of his nipples, pleased with how flushed his skin was, his breathy moans, and his dilated, needy eyes looking back at him. Leaning down, Othello captured his lips, groaning at Des's delicious taste. He reached between them and then unbuttoned and unzipped Des's jeans, pushing them and his underwear down below his ass. He palmed the doctor's hard, weeping cock, deepening their kiss and capturing his whimpers as he rubbed against his shaft and balls.

Each time, he would dip a finger lower, lightly grazing his perineum, aiming for his hole. Although he'd asked, Othello didn't plan on fucking Des tonight. As much as he wanted to be buried cock and balls deep inside of Des, he didn't want to rush things. Taking a man's virginity took finesse, and not to brag, but he had a big dick. Not to mention he liked fucking his partners three or four times, making them cum as many times or more until they were both satisfied. His ex needed at least two days' rest before he could get out of bed.

"Oh, Othello," Des breathed against his mouth. He widened his legs as far as they would go, allowing access to his hole. "Need to c..."

Othello hummed, knowing what Des wanted, but not yet. Othello enjoyed bringing his partners to the edge. Hearing their frustrated moans, begging and pleading to let them cum, brought a lot of pleasure to him.

"So eager," Othello said, kissing his way down Des's body.

"I've waited too long for this," Des told him.

"I'll make you feel good, baby," he said, moving down Des's body. He pulled himself off, then glided his hands up and down the man's toned legs.

Othello gazed into Des's lust-filled eyes that resembled sparkling emeralds, surrounded by long, thick, wet lashes. But he wanted to see them dripping with tears.

"Pull your legs to your chest and hold them there," Othello ordered as he stood from the bed and took off his shirt, smiling when he saw Des grew even hungrier. "Are you hungry, baby?"

"You know I am, so don't tease me," Des answered, widening his legs. "So come and feed me."

"When did you get so mouthy?" Othello chuckled, unbuttoning his pants and freeing his erection. Grasping it, he jerked his cock, pushing his pants down to his ankles and watching the doctor's eyes brighten at the sight of his erect member. He stood straight, palming from root to tip, using his precum as lubrication.

"I want," Des said, licking his lips.

"What do you want?" Othello's voice was thick with arousal.

"To taste, to feel, to suck."

"Turn around," he ordered. Des didn't ask questions. Releasing his legs, he flipped around, his head hanging a little off the edge of the bed and in the position Othello wanted, between his legs with his cock sitting on his lips. "Do you know how to suck dick?"

"No, but I know you can teach me."

Othello dragged the head of his cock over Des's lips. "Open your mouth." Des opened his mouth, and Othello fed the head of his cock into his mouth; he couldn't help the guttural moan that escaped. It felt so damn good. So wet and warm. Des swirled his tongue around the tip of Othello's cock, then wrapped his lips around it, taking in a little more. Othello wouldn't push Des to take him all tonight, but he couldn't stop cupping his face as Des moved his head up and down, leaving trails of saliva on his shaft. If this were his first time, he'd not be so bad, but Othello would help him improve.

"Open wider and stick out your tongue." Othello liked that Des was so obedient.

Othello pushed half of his cock in and out of those sweet hot lips and wet mouth, pushing more in with each stroke. "Fuck, baby, your mouth feels so damn good," he moaned, using Des's mouth any way he wanted but remembering he had to take things slowly. Des groaned around his cock, and Othello's knees almost buckled, causing him to pull out and step back, gasping.

Des sat up and looked at him with swollen lips and flushed cheeks. "Was I terrible? You didn't cum."

Othello cupped one of his cheeks. "No." He pecked him on

his lips. "You did fine, but I want to make you feel good right now." Othello kissed him again, pushing him onto his back.

Pulling back from their kiss, Othello stood and kicked

off his pants. Kneeling on the bed, he grasped Des's ankles and pushed his legs toward his chest. Lying down on his stomach, he grabbed Des's waist and pulled him forward, putting him at eye level with the man's ass. He hadn't noticed it before, but Othello spotted the iris-shaped mark next to Des's testicles, confirming that he was a carrier. Putting it to the side for later, he focused on the matter at hand, making Des cum hard, until he saw stars.

Othello separated Des's butt cheeks, groaning at the sight of his quivering hole. Leaning forward, he dragged his tongue along Des's hole up to his balls then back down again.

"Oh, fuck," Des screamed. His body was shaking. "Do it again."

Othello complied, this time swirling the head of his tongue around the head of Des's cock before sucking the shaft down to the hilt, touching the back of his throat. Des tried to move his hips, but it was impossible with Othello's tight hold.

"Othello," Des yelled. "Oh damn, so good."

Othello moved back up, spearing his tongue and dipping the tip of his tongue into the piss hole before he sucked him back down. Othello fondled and lightly pulled on Des's balls, bobbing his head up and down on the delicious cock in his mouth, fevered, moans coming from Des's lips as his body trembled, letting Othello know he was close to cumming.

Oh, sweet baby, this is only the beginning.

"Othello, oh fuck," Des chanted continuously, trying hard to thrust into Othello's mouth.

Des released his legs, and they fell on either side of Othello's head. He grabbed the back of Othello's neck, digging his nails into his skin, calling out his name, which sounded like music to his ear, but he wanted more. He was a greedy bastard, even with sex. Othello loosened his grip on Des, who thrust up, meeting his every move. Pulling off Des's cock, he glided his tongue back down his shaft, sucking on his balls, making them nice and wet before grazing his teeth on the iris.

He knew what the mark did to carriers. It gave them a euphoric high during sex. Othello was thankful he'd kept the soundproofing from the original building, with the way Des was calling out his name as ropes of cum shot out on his stomach and chest. Othello didn't let up. He sucked on the iris mark, leaving his own mark before moving back to his testicles, running his tongue along his perineum and then back up, licking the cum off his cock, stomach, and chest, swirling his tongue around the nearest nipple. Des's taste and scent surrounded him, and it turned him on more than he thought possible.

"Othello, please," Des whimpered. "Fuck me."

Othello raised his head and gazed at Des, whose eyes were lust-blown. Othello didn't respond; he simply moved up and claimed Des's mouth. He devoured his mouth, grounding his cock on the silk sheets, seeking friction. It had been a while since he fucked anyone, and even though he could wait a little longer, he couldn't deny how good Des felt writhing beneath him.

He sat back and reached for the bottle of lube and condoms on the nightstand. He threw the box of condoms to the side, broke the seal on the lubrication, and squirted some on his fingers.

"Put your legs on my shoulders."

Des did as he asked, and Othello hummed, placing soft kisses on his shins and moving his lips down to his thighs. He continued all the way down until he pulled Des into a sweet kiss as he pushed a finger into Des's hole, eliciting a throaty groan vibrating on his lips. Slowly, he moved his finger in and out of Des's hole, lightly brushing over Des's prostate, making him whimper, writhing and grinding his waist.

Othello pulled away from their kiss, and Des cried out his name, with tears streaming down the sides of his face, and Othello's cock twitched at the beautiful sight before him. When Des's muscles relaxed, he added another finger, stretching Des's hole. He leaned down and sucked Des's renewed erection into his mouth, grasping his own and jerking it in the same rhythm as his mouth and fingers.

"Oh fuck, oh fuck," Des chanted. "So good, so hot."

Othello added two more fingers and sucked harder, relaxing his jaw and taking Des's cock down to the base, the head touching the back of his throat and his pelvic hair brushing his nose. The scent of sex smelled so good on Des that Othello couldn't help stroking his cock faster. Des gripped the nape of his neck, thrusting into his mouth, fucking him with abandon.

He stroked his cock faster along with the fingers in Des's hole. The rigid veins on his tongue pulsated, and he could tell Des was on the cusp of cumming, and he wouldn't be far behind. He needed to cum to take the edge off, so they could do other things for the rest of the night. He rubbed on Des's prostate, pushing his fingers deeper, and was rewarded with thick white ropes of hot cum filling his mouth, sliding down his throat, and Des chanting his name like a prayer to his god. Othello growled around the cock still in his mouth, cumming in his hand.

Drinking Des's cum down, he moaned in sweet delight. Slowly Othello let Des's cock slip from his mouth and pressed his forehead on his thigh. He gently removed his fingers from Des's ass. Moving up his body, he captured his lips in a toe-curling kiss. Othello wanted more, but he could tell the doctor was tired. Des didn't need to say it.

Othello simply knew.

You need to work on your stamina, Doc.

"Be right back," he told Des, rolling off him and heading to the bathroom. He licked his lips, tasting the remnants of Des's cum. *Fuck, he is so delicious, and I want more.*

Othello washed his hands, grabbed a wet washcloth from the warmer, and returned to the bedroom. He smiled, seeing Des sprawled out on the bed, completely knocked out. Shaking his head, he cleaned up the sleeping form, stopping to inspect the carrier mark. He wasn't going to dwell on the mark but enjoy the moment. They had a ten-year age difference between them, and as much as he hated having flings and his words earlier tonight, he wouldn't force Des to stay by his side forever.

So the best thing was not to bring up the children talk. Besides, Des might change his mind in the morning. Throwing the washcloth to the floor, he crawled into bed, pulling Des close to him.

He really fits perfectly in my arms. And he's seriously my type.

"Don't disappoint me, Doc. Let's ride this relationship shit until the wheels fall off. I don't care if you're rich or poor; just don't cheat on me." He kissed Des's forehead, then settled down and went to sleep with the gorgeous man nestled against him—something he hadn't done in a long time.

* * *

DES GROANED, annoyed by the ringing and hoping that it would shut the fuck up.

"Yeah," came a deep, sleep-filled voice, causing Des to open his eyes and connect with unfamiliar surroundings.

Turning his head, he smiled, seeing Othello, and moved close, laying his head on his chest and listening as he spoke on the phone. The night's events came back to him. They didn't have sex, but oh gods, he couldn't believe how he acted. He buried his reddened face in Othello's chest, feeling his arms tighten around him.

"I'm taking a couple of days off, so set the meeting up for when I get back," Othello instructed.

The conversation ended, and Des looked up to see Othello gazing at him. Des leaned up and connected their lips for a quick kiss, then hopped out of bed and ran to the bathroom to clean up. Unlike the last time when he'd covered up his body, he didn't care this time. What was the purpose after all they did last night? When he returned to the bedroom, Othello was tying the sash on his robe.

"So am I to assume you taking time off has something to do with me?"

"You have a problem with that?" Othello walked over and handed him a shirt that looked familiar. It was the one he'd slipped on the last time he was here. "I figure you'd want to wear this."

Des smiled. "Are you trying to recreate our first morning together?" he asked, putting on the garment.

"You're thinking too much." Othello chuckled. "Think about what you want for breakfast while I get cleaned up."

"Okay."

Othello kissed him on the forehead and then went to the bathroom. Des hoped he wasn't imagining it, but it felt like there was a little distance between them. It wasn't what he had expected waking up in the arms of the man he wanted to be with, only to feel rebuffed the next day.

Did I disappoint him last night? Des sat on the bed and hissed, feeling the tenderness on his inner leg. *Fuck.* He got up, went to the vanity mirror, and looked at his mark, which had a bright red hickey. He remembered Othello sucking on it, making him cum so hard he almost passed out. *Could that be why he's so distant? He found out I'm a carrier?*

"Have you figured it out?"

He turned when Othello spoke. "Um...something simple."

"Alright."

They walked into the kitchen, and Des sat at the breakfast nook and observed the man making his coffee, wondering if he should bring up the whole carrier thing. He wasn't sure what to say. Besides, if Othello was bothered by it, then he should be the one to say something.

"Why are you staring at me like that?"

"Can't I look at you? You're a handsome man."

Othello smirked, then leaned over, pecking him on his lips. Des hummed, wanting to take the kiss longer, but Othello pulled away. "Since I took a couple of days off, what do you want to do? And please don't say the amusement park."

Des smiled wide. "I knew you took time off for me."

"Fine, since you figured me out, what's the plan?" Othello grumbled.

Des walked over to Othello and wrapped his arms around him from the back. "What if I want to stay indoors and have you make love to me."

Othello turned in his hold and encircled his waist. "As long as that's what you want."

"It is," Des whispered, staring into his handsome picture-perfect face. "Maybe during our breaks, I can draw you."

"That part, Doc, might cost you." Othello smiled.

Cupping the back of his neck, Des brought his face close to Othello's. "I can pay the price you offer."

Othello smirked, tightening his hold on him. "Is that so?" He pressed their mouths together.

Des hummed in their kiss, opening himself up to Othello. He pressed his body flush against the larger one, wanting and needing the man's touch. Just as their kiss deepened, Des's stomach rumbled loudly, breaking the mood.

"Maybe I should feed you before I fuck you," Othello said, breaking their kiss.

"I curse my need for nourishment," he pouted.

"Trust me, for what I have planned, you must eat to keep up your stamina."

After another kiss, Othello returned to making breakfast, and Des grabbed his phone. He noticed he had a call from his friends and his mother. Since the calls weren't back-to-back, he figured he'd return their calls later. Bringing up the news, Des scanned through some of the reports about a robbery here and there, then stopped when he saw an article about a suspicious incident that happened in a warehouse on the west side of the city that happened six months ago. The reporter had been investigating the incident for the past few months and found no clues about what took place. The article stated the police hadn't gotten any leads and that if anyone had witnessed or heard anything, they should report it to the authorities as soon as possible.

According to the report, gunfire was heard by the cops. When they arrived, the place was empty, and so damaged that it took the cops weeks to figure things out. Other than bullet holes littering the place, they couldn't say what really happened. Des's brow furrowed as he read on.

But if this reporter is free to say, I believe it was about the mob. In recent years, the mafia elements in Verona Heights have been making themselves known. People believe the three heads of the major families died out in the early 1980s, but I believe a new set has taken over and has been working in the shadows for years, and they are more dangerous than the old guards.

"What are you reading so intently?"

Des looked away from his phone, hearing Othello's question. "The news. It was about some shooting in a warehouse that happened some months ago." "Oh?" Othello quirked a brow.

"Yeah, the media thinks it's mafia-related."

"What do you think?"

"Not sure. If the mafia is still around, wouldn't the police have already arrested them? That reminds me, that night you showed up at the hospital was the night things went down at the warehouse. It would be crazy if that were the reason you were shot."

"And if it was?"

Des was about to ask Othello if he was kidding, but his look told him otherwise. However, Des was learning that it was better to ask the tough questions than to hide. This was the reason he had ended up not knowing about what was in his grandfather's will. He grabbed Othello's hand and looked him in the eyes.

"The night you were shot, was it because you were at the warehouse?"

"Yes," Othello responded, and Des was surprised he was so straightforward. "But it was an ambush."

"Wait...wait a second. Are you saying you're really in the mob?"

"I planned on telling you. We don't keep it a secret or blast it everywhere. We like to be discreet in our movements. But yeah."

Des was surprised and didn't know what to say. He'd always thought all the mafia stuff was just on movies or television shows, but to know that serious criminal organizations were operating freely and without repercussions, he could say he grew up way too sheltered. But now it explained things—the men who followed him around or the reverence Tallen had shown him.

"I won't go into details about my family dynamics or what happened that night, but I'll understand if you don't want to see me anymore." He kissed Des on the forehead and then went to walk away, but Des stopped him.

"If this is your way of breaking up with me before we truly get started, it's not working. I don't want to know the intricate things of how your family works, but I want to know you and how you got shot that night. That's it." Othello stared at him for so long that Des wasn't sure if he should say more.

"You shouldn't ruin your kissable lips by chewing on them like that," Othello said, his voice thick with arousal.

"I might not understand the whole mafia thing, or maybe I'm romanticizing things with the mob boss and the naive love interest trope, but I don't care. Like I told you for so long, I never got to choose what I want to do with my life. I know we're not in love, but I want to give us a chance to see where or how far we can go instead of walking away."

"You're not as naïve as you think, Desmond Ellington."

"That's nice of you to say, but I know what you and many others think of me. I'm book-smart but far from street-smart. And although this isn't what I expected to find out so soon after the night we had, I want to be with you,

Othello. I've wanted it since the night we met." "What?" Othello asked.

Des smiled and stood, wrapping his arms around Othello's neck. "It might sound weird, but the first time I saw you lying on the operating table, I fell in lust with you." Othello smiled, pulling him close. "So you thought I was sexy even with a hole in my chest?"

"Don't be so full of yourself, but essentially yes."

Othello pressed their foreheads together. "I like you too, Doc."

Des leaned in to kiss Othello, but his stomach made itself known once again, intervening in their intimate moment. Othello smiled, stepping back, and taking Des's hand. "Come on, let's eat." They walked over to the nook, sat down, and started eating.

The first half of the meal was quiet since they were both starving, and it was Des who spoke first.

"Have you ever killed someone?" He quickly clamped his

hands over his mouth and widened his eyes just as the bite Othello was about to take paused at his lips.

Fuck, did I just ask that? That's not what I was going to ask. Is he going to kill me for asking that?

Othello slowly put his fork back down and turned to look at Des.

"I didn't mean..." he said, removing his hands from his mouth and stuttering nervously. "I mean, I wasn't going to ask? Shit, I-I..." He stopped and glared at Othello. "Will you say something and stop making me think you'll cut my tongue out for asking that?"

Othello smirked and grabbed Des's chair, pulling him and it closer. Leaning forward, he somehow caged him between the nook and his larger body. "Stick out your tongue," he ordered. Des swallowed and nervously stuck out his tongue. Othello licked Des's tongue, then sucked it into his mouth, moaning as he was pulled into a kiss, but before Des could enjoy it, Othello pulled back.

"I doubt I'd want to cut out something that delicious," Othello said, then gently pecked him on the lips. "Besides, there's something else I'd rather do with your tongue." "Huh?"

"Good boy," Othello said softly, and Des wasn't sure if he had been drugged by the man's lips. However, he couldn't hold on to that thought because Othello pressed their mouths together. Othello expertly pulled, played, and teased his lips and tongue. Des's arms circled Othello's neck, deepening their kiss. Othello lifted Des off his seat and sat him on the counter. He groaned, feeling the man's large hands slip under his shirt, caressing his skin, moving toward his chest, and tweaking his nipples. He reached back down and grasped his waist. Othello pulled his shirt to the side as he trailed kisses down to his shoulder, then to his nipple. Des hissed, grasping the back of Othello's head, keeping his lips on the sensitive nubs.

"Othello, I want."

Othello raised his head, and Des opened his eyes, connecting with sweet amber. He was feeling dazed.

"What do you want?" he asked in a husky tone.

"Do I need to say it?"

"I need to hear it, Doc."

"I want you to fuck me and make me—" He licked his lips because it stopped him from saying yours. Because that was how he felt when he was with Othello, even when they tried to be friends. "—Feel good."

Othello smiled, and Des found it very charming, then lifted him off the counter. Des wrapped his legs around his waist. "Let's take this elsewhere. There's something I want to teach you."

"Oh, really?"

Othello kissed him again. "Yeah."

Just as they were about to walk into the bedroom, there was a knock on the door. They both remained still. Des was hoping whoever it was would go away, but he was sorely mistaken when there was another knock, this time more forcefully, that seemed like they were banging on it. Othello set him on his feet and stepped back.

"Go to the bedroom and wait there. Don't come out. I'm pretty sure it's someone from my family, and I'm not ready for you to meet them."

"Are you hiding me? Or ashamed of..."

"Get that thought out of your head right now," Othello cut him off. "I'm just not ready to share what this is yet. I want us to have time together before they start filling your head with craziness. Especially my folks, who've been begging me to start dating."

Des stared into Othello's eyes, seeking the truth. He was certain the man was telling the truth, so he leaned in and kissed him. "Get rid of them quickly."

"I will. Now go."

Des nodded and walked into the bedroom, pulling the sash on the curtain, letting it fall, and blocking the bedroom's view. He sat on the chair close to the window, looking out as a thought came to him. He had been infatuated with Othello since they met but had never done any research on him. Des reached for his phone, realizing he had left it in the living room when he heard Othello's voice.

"You came here to talk to me about that fucker Roderigo? This conversation could have been a damn phone call."

"*I* tried calling you, but you didn't answer."

Othello pinched the bridge of his nose. He couldn't believe Iago had shown up at his home to ruin what was going to be the best after-breakfast fuck to talk to him about the asshat, Roderigo.

"Did you really have to do that to him?" Iago said.

Othello glared at his brother. "I simply gave him the same lesson he was trying to give to Lucy. Maybe next time he enters my establishment, he'll remember the damn rules."

"Why are you bothered if he smacks up some whore?" Iago snapped.

"Don't call her that," Othello growled. "Lucy makes me more

money in one hour just smiling at the clients than anyone else in that club."

"Your defense of her makes it sound like you have feelings for her," Iago said in a calmer voice.

"And you're overthinking things, as always. Lucy and I are strictly professional." It was so professional that Othello considered giving her a managerial position. Lucy was much more than an escort. She kept all the others in line when he wasn't around. It was time he gave her a glow-up. It would help her and her five-year-old son.

"Speaking of which, when are you going to give him back his club? Haven't you done more than enough?"

Othello tsked and shook his head. "You know, Iago, some-times I wonder whose brother you are, mine or his?"

"Yours, of course."

"Then why the fuck are you here being an attorney for him? He lost it fair and square. Hell, the club wasn't even in his name but his dear old dad, who was happy to sign the deed away to me. He better be grateful I haven't
banned him from the place."

"Come on, O, don't do this," Iago said. "The Mirage means a lot to him."

"Yeah, well, it means the whole world to me, Iago. Now, if that's all you came here to talk to me about, leave. I took a couple of days off for a reason."

"I heard, and I'm surprised, so I wanted to check and make sure you were okay."

"I'm fine," Othello said, feeling quite annoyed by his brother.

"You're awful grumpy. Maybe you should really find someone to take the edge off."

What the fuck did you think I was about to do when you knocked on my fucking door? Hopefully, Des isn't paying attention to this conversation.

"Maybe you should have one of the escorts from the club come over and—"

"Enough," Othell said, cutting him off. "I don't need an escort. When I'm ready to date again, I will, so back off."

Iago was silent again, and Des thought he would drop the subject and leave. "I'm worried about you, O. Hell, we all are. Don't let the clan be your life. We all need companionship. I know what happened with Phillip years ago is still with you, but he was a bastard. I would kick his ass if I could."

"Yeah, well, he went missing, and no one can find him to stomp him into the ground," Othello said, feeling his irritation slip away. "Look, I know you all mean well, but I'm fine."

Iago nodded, then grabbed him by the back of the neck, bringing him close and pressing their foreheads together; their eyes locked on each other, and Othello could see worry looking back at him. "I love you, little bro."

"Love you, too." Othello held Iago's head. "Now go. I'm tired, and I want to rest. You tire me the hell out."

They both chuckled, breaking their contact. "Alright. I would stay and have lunch with you, but Emilia has a doctor's appointment. Then I'm taking her ring shopping."

"I want to say make sure the diamond is big enough to see from Mars, but I know my soon-to-be sister-in-law isn't the flashy type, so just make her happy.."

"I will."

Othello walked Iago to the door and saw him off before going to the bedroom and spotting the doctor fast asleep on the chair by the window. Othello knelt next to the chair and stared at Des as the man's question returned to him.

"Have you ever killed anyone?"

Othello hadn't been expecting the question, but for some reason, he didn't think he could lie to Des, which was why he'd told him the truth about being a part of a mafia organization.

Othello had done much since being a minor and major player in the family, and it was hard to let an enemy walk away. But he was not above torturing them for fun. The things he'd done, they'd wished they were dead, fulfilling his blood vow to the family. Othello preferred torture and letting the person live in regret for their misdeeds against him and hisfamily.

Looking at Des, he smiled. The man really surprised him with how easily he accepted everything. He had a good heart, and maybe Othello shouldn't have taken things further, but he didn't want to end things. He felt the doctor was good for not only healing his body but also his heart. Or Des could be right, and he was romanticizing things. Iago had been right. He'd held on to Phillip for so long he didn't want to let anyone else in.

Yet, here he was, opening the door to his heart for someone to either love him or hate him. Othello might have a tough exterior, but deep down, he was like any man looking for companionship and affection. It didn't have to be love. Just someone to hold in his arms while he fell asleep. Othello knew he shouldn't be starting a relationship because things were so tense in his and other clans, and he could be putting Des in danger. Othello began formulating a plan to protect Des without impeding his personal life. Standing, he picked up Des, walked with him, and laid him on the bed. Covering him up, he kissed him on the forehead.

I guess fucking you hard will have to wait until later.

Chuckling, he walked out of the bedroom and cleaned up the breakfast dishes that he had chucked in the sink before opening the door. After cleaning up, he headed up the stairs to the part of his apartment that doubled as his office and gym. Although he hadn't planned on getting any work done today, he figured since he had time, he might as well look through the paperwork he had been putting to the side for a while.

* * *

DES GROANED, rolling, then opened his eyes, and felt a sense of déjà vu staring up at the ceiling of Othello's apartment. He recalled what had happened earlier and realized he must have fallen asleep while waiting for Othello. He had heard some of their conversation but had no clue what Othello and his guest were talking about. Since he woke up in bed, the other man must have put him there.

Sitting up, he looked to the other side of the bed and found it empty. Getting out of bed, he searched for his man. He smiled at his thoughts when he walked into the living room but was disappointed when no one was there. Seconds later, he heard a thumping sound in rapid succession coming from upstairs.

Des headed up the stairs, and the noise grew louder. Then, he saw Othello's form standing before a standing body bag, hitting it hard. He was shirtless, drenched in sweat, with muscles in his arms, shoulders, and back popping with every powerful hit on the bag that trembled as if it was going to fall apart. Des bit his bottom lip, unable to take his eyes off the sexy-as-fuck man who had no idea he had an audience.

After a few minutes, Othello stopped and took off his gloves. Seeing the towel hanging on the rail, Des grabbed it and walked over to Othello, who had just turned around. His panting breath tickled Des's cheek. Neither spoke as Des reached up and patted the towel on Othello's face, their eyes still locked on each other. *Why does he smell so good?* Othello leaned down and brushed their lips together but took their connection no further. Othello took the towel and started wiping himself off.

"Did you enjoy your nap?"

"Hmm..." Des nodded. "Why didn't you wake me?"

"You looked tired, so I let you sleep." He smiled.

"It's not fair. You took the day off to spend with me, and I fell asleep."

"The day's not over yet."

Des moved closer, wrapping his arms around Othello, not caring that he was still a bit sweaty. "What do you have in mind?"

"How about after I shower, we go out for a bit? I think that now that we're together, I should truly wine and dine you."

"You weren't doing that before?"

Othello grasped Des's waist lightly. "Yeah, but this time it's different."

Des smiled, getting Othello's meaning. "Okay," he agreed, then a thought occurred to him. He didn't want to wear what he had worn yesterday.

"What's with that look?" Othello asked, getting his attention.

"If we're going out, I will need something to wear. I doubt jeans and a T-shirt are what you had in mind."

Othello leaned down for a kiss. "I took care of that while you were sleeping. I had my personal shopper grab a few things for you."

Des quirked a brow. "Personal shopper. Huh, it just occurred to me I have a rich boyfriend."

"You better believe it."

Des shook his head. "And not modest at all. But I like your cocky swagger, so I think you deserve a reward." "Is that so?" he said.

"Yes. I'm feeling very sweaty." He stepped out of Othello's arms and removed the shirt, dropping it to the floor, turning, and walking to the steps. "Want to join me in the shower?"

Othello smirked, and the look in his eyes scared and excited Des. It was the expression of a predator who had trapped its prey. "I thought you would never ask," he said.

Othello stepped forward, and Des had the bright idea to run from the big, hungry wolf who wanted to eat him. He shivered in sweet anticipation, knowing that by the end of the night, Othello would have him any way he wanted.

* * *

DES GASPED when his back hit the shower wall. He tilted his head back, and Othello licked, sucked, and kissed from his neck down to his nipples as his fingers pinched and tweaked the other one. Gasping, he grasped some of Othello's wet hair, pulled his head back, captured his mouth, and kissed him hard and needily.

Othello circled his arms around Des's waist, flipping them around. He moaned against his mouth, loving the hot kiss as well as the water beating down on his back. He pulled back and stared into Othello's eyes.

"You know, last night, I think I gave you a terrible impression of me," Des said, reaching down to press and rub on Othello's erection.

"Yeah, about what?" Othello cupped the back of his head, brushing his lips against Des's, moaning when he lightly pinched the head of his cock.

"I know I can pleasure you with my hands, but—" Slowly, Des went to his knees, putting his face to Othello's hard dick. "—I want to be able to do the same with my mouth." He looked up at Othello, rubbing his lips and then swirling his tongue around the head of his shaft. "Better yet, teach me how to make you cum. I want you to use my mouth however you please."

Othello stared at him, rubbing his thumb on his cheek.

"Are you sure?"

"Yes."

Othello said nothing for what seemed like minutes, turning into hours.

"No matter what happens, you're not allowed to touch your cock. Can you do that?"

"Yes, I can."

"If it gets to be too much, pinch my ass and I'll stop."

Des smiled and nodded, knowing that no matter what Othello did, he wouldn't stop him.

"Open your mouth and suck me inside."

Des grasped Othello's shaft, jerking him gently, and moved forward, opening his mouth and circling his lips around the head.

Othello gasped. "Take me in a little bit at a time, pulling back each time," he instructed, his voice hoarse but gentle. His hand was on the back of Des's head, guiding his movements.

His hand and mouth met as he sucked and jerked Othello's shaft, feeling the man move his hips, and his fingers tightened on his head.

"Fuck, your mouth feels so damn good," he moaned. "Give me a little teeth, baby."

Des moaned, releasing Othello's cock, pressing his hands to the man's thighs, and sucking him down as far as he could go. He loved the feel of Othello's erection in his mouth and made a plan to suck his man at least once a day.

He pulled back lightly, dragging his teeth along the veined, thick, and heavy shaft, swirling his tongue at the tip, lapping up the precum. Des could not help the groan that escaped his lips, but Othello's reaction made him want to do more. Suck him until he was weak and begging to cum. Des's hard cock twitched at the thought.

"Fuck, yeah," Othello growled. "Shit, baby, gonna cum."

Des reached up and cupped Othello's balls, tugging them gently as he sucked a little harder, adding some teeth but not enough to hurt. Othello moaned and grabbed his head, moving in and out of Des' mouth.

He circled Othello's legs, sucking his dick down, and it hit the back of his throat, surprising him, and for a second, he wanted to throw up but heard Othello growl as he shoved his hard pulsing cock down his throat, gagging him. Tears mixed with water streaming down his cheeks. His chest burned, and that was when he remembered to breathe, just as Othello pulled back and pushed in again.

Othello fucked his mouth hard and rough, and it made Des's cock grow painfully hard, and he wanted, no, he *needed* to touch himself. Still, he remembered Othello's words and focused on pleasuring the man who was ramming his cock in and out of his mouth, growling his name, cumming down his throat.

Des greedily drank Othello's cum, loving the taste of his masculinity, his strength, and his dominance that was claiming him inside and out. Othello pulled his cock out of Des's mouth, and before he could catch his breath, his mouth was captured.

Othello's tongue swept into his mouth, taking and tasting everything Des had drunk from him. He moaned, bucking his hips when Othello grasped his cock. It only took a few strokes, and Des came into Othello's hand with his lover's name on his lips. Panting heavily, he sagged against the larger man's body, smiling in satisfaction with Othello's deep voice rumbling in his ear.

"Well done, Tesoro."

* * *

"TASTE THIS," Des said, bringing his fork to his mouth.

He smiled when Othello hummed in appreciation. Des loved that Othello was a foodie like him. It ruined the mood to eat with a picky eater. Othello had taken him to Ouro e Vinho, which meant "gold and wine," a Portuguese restaurant with a mile-long waiting list. It had a magnificent city view on the forty-fifth floor of the Celeste Grand Plaza. Des was curious to know how Othello had gotten a reservation when not even his father, the good doctor David Ellington, could get a reservation on the fly.

Ouro e Vinho was quite elegant, and a suit and tie were necessary. Not only that, the owners prided themselves on keeping their guests' privacy since many politicians, celebrities, and bigwigs frequented the establishment. The ambiance was romantic and exuded sophistication, with marble floors and gold accents. Soft, warm lighting cast a gentle glow throughout the restaurant, aiding the romantic atmosphere of the lit candles on the table flickering off the clear wine glasses.

He and Othello were seated next to each other. Des did not want to sit across from him. He wouldn't deny feeling clingy toward Othello and hoped it didn't scare him off. He felt like this was a dream, and if he blinked too quickly, he would wake up stuck in a job he hated and alone. But it wasn't his imagination, and Othello Moor was the one to set this all up, which made him a little giddy.

"You impress me, Mister Moor," Des said.

"Really?" Othello put his utensils down. "What exactly did I do to earn your favor?"

"Everything." Des leaned closer, brushing their lips together. When he pulled back, he noticed Othello staring at something other than him, with his brows furrowed.

Although he felt slightly jealous, he couldn't hide his curiosity. "What's the matter?"

"Nothing. I thought I saw someone I knew."

"Must be someone important if they pulled your attention away from me."

"If I didn't know any better, I'd say you're jealous." Othello smiled.

Des scoffed, turning away from Othello's penetrating but playful gaze. "You're reading into things."

"Is that so?" he said, gently pinching Des's chin. Turning his face to his, Othello kissed his mouth before he could say anything. Des wrapped his arms around Othello's neck, deepening their kiss. Their lips slowly separated, and Des opened his eyes. "No one is more important than you right now." Othello pecked him on his lips. "Finish your meal."

"Underboss Moor, it's good to see you."

Des felt Othello stiffen and watched him place a smile on his lips that he knew wasn't real. Othello looked away from Des and faced not one but two men standing in front of their table. Othello stood and greeted them.

"Boss Antonio Greco, Underboss Cassio Ricci, it has been a while."

Des silently watched Othello ball his hands into fists as he put them in his pockets. A tense aura enveloped the three men, and Des wasn't sure if he should speak up. He should have felt offended for not being introduced, but he didn't mind with how the men glared at each other.

* * *

"I HEARD that you were injured some time ago, but I see that you're doing fine," Cassio said to Othello, but his eyes strayed to Des.

"Well, you should know I'm a hard man to kill," Othello said, shifting slightly to the side, blocking their view of Des.

When he made the reservation, he knew there was a chance he'd bump into someone from his world, but he wasn't expecting it to be a big boss. Most men trembled and stuttered in the presence of Boss Greco, but Othello wished he could shoot the man square in his face. *Fuck, I sound homicidal.* But he couldn't help it. Since his shooting, he'd thought over the events and concluded that the only forces that could have gotten away with what happened that night had to do with Greco and Ricci. Othello knew the two clans worked together as one, seeing that Cassio was their most trusted advisor. He just needed to find out who was working with them.

"We received an invitation to your boss's anniversary party. My wife and I look forward to being there," Greco said. "Unfortunately, Don Ricci will not be able to make it."

"My parents," he stressed. "We'll be sad Don Ricci won't be there, but with you there, I'm certain it will still be a happy event, Boss Greco. I'm sure my father cannot wait

to sit and talk about the old days with you."

"Ah, the old days when people knew their place. It's a shame some animals feel they are superior when they should be grov-eling at the feet of those of higher standing. Don't you think, *Moor?*" Greco chuckled as if he'd said something funny, but Othello knew damn well what his words meant. Maybe the man was hoping for him to react, but he wouldn't give the old fucker the benefit. The day would come when he'd wipe the smug smile off his face.

"Yes, I agree," Othello said, staring Greco dead in his eyes. "The old should stay in their place and let more intelligent people run the show. Don't you think, Boss Greco?" Othello smirked when the smile fell off the fucker's face.

"Why you—" Greco started no doubt to spout something insulting, hoping to bring Othello down a peg, but his under-boss interrupted him.

"Don Greco, our table is ready."

Greco scowled, then walked away rudely. Othello's eyes stayed on the man, plotting his sweet death.

"You're playing with fire, Moor," Cassio growled.

"I didn't light the match, Cassio," he told the man whose gaze kept straying to Des. The last man Othello had given his heart had also been sleeping with Cassio; he wouldn't let that happen again. "Keep staring, and I will pluck them out."

Cassio snapped his eyes away from Des and looked at Othello, seeing he wasn't joking. "Don't act like a barbarian,

Moor. You're in a civilized society. At least pretend like you have manners." Tsking, Cassio walked away, just as rude as his boss. Othello watched to make sure both men disappeared to wherever their table was before he sat back down next to Des. He despised them just as they did him. Othello was counting the days until he could make those two men and others who thought like them beg for mercy.

"Are you okay?" Des asked, touching his shoulder.

"I'm fine." Othello turned to him, offering a real smile.

"I don't know what that was all about, but it was pretty intense."

"Don't let them bother you," he said, not letting his conversation with the two older men ruin the mood. But then, a thought came to Othello. He didn't like the way Cassio was looking at Des. "If any of them approach you, don't entertain them."

"Why would they want to talk to me? I'm a nobody in all of this."

"Being connected to me makes you somebody, Des. They are dangerous men and will use you to get to me."

Des stared at him, then nodded. "I will listen to what you say."

"Good." He smiled. "Now, let's finish our meal; there's somewhere I want to take you."

Des hummed and leaned closer to him. "Really? Where are you taking me?"

"It's a surprise." Othello chuckled.

"You're no fun." He pouted.

"You weren't saying that earlier." He moved his lips closer to Des's ear. "I think your exact words were, 'Othello, please, make me cum. Don't stop…'" "Alright, enough," Des snapped.

He leaned back, laughing at Des's red ears and face. Othello leaned in and kissed him on his neck. "I'm sorry, baby. I won't tease you anymore."

Des turned his face to his. "Yes, you will. You love messing with me."

"I do because you make it easy. But it's one of the things I find enduring about you."

"You're telling the truth, aren't you?"

"I am."

Des smiled. "Okay, I forgive you." He leaned in and kissed Othello before returning to his meal.

* * *

DES COULDN'T REMOVE the smile from his face as he walked around. This was indeed a pleasant surprise. Othello continued to impress him that night and arranged for him to view and purchase rare art, books, and other things that might catch his eye. He knew there would be an auction at the end of the year, but it was only by invitation.

Des wasn't notable enough to get an invitation. So he was surprised to get this close, but who knew his new boyfriend was in charge of organizing the auction and got to see all the products before anyone else?

"If you see something you like, let Devin know, and he'll take care of it," Othello told him.

"Are you sure?" Des asked.

"Yes," Othello responded.

"What if I want the most expensive thing on the bidding block?"

"It's yours." Othello shrugged.

"You're being far too kind to me." Des smiled.

"I told you things are different now that we're together."

"I like this new phase between us." He leaned in and kissed him. "Thank you."

Othello grabbed his waist and pulled him close. Des moaned when Othello swept his tongue into his mouth, deep-

ening their kiss and making him shiver all over. Des grasped
Othello's jacket, wanting more. Slowly, their mouths separated,
and Des opened his eyes as he tried calming his breathing and
rapidly beating heart.

"I feel a bit ungrateful," Des said.

"Why?"

"Because you planned all of this for me, and the artist in me
wants to take advantage of this wonderful moment, but right
now, all I want is to go back to your place and

have you make love to me."

Othello smirked devilishly. "Devin."

"Yes, sir."

Des's eyes widened when the auction curator appeared out
of nowhere as if by magic or something. "Is everything
prepared?"

"Yes."

"Good. Send everyone home. I'll take care of Mr. Ellington's
needs."

Devin bowed like a butler he'd seen on television. "As you
wish." He turned on his heel and walked off, leaving them
alone.

Othello stepped back and took his hand. "Come on, let's
look around."

"But," Des started but stopped when they walked toward a
beautiful picture that should have captivated him, but he didn't
care. He was confused about why Othello wasn't dragging him
out of the place and taking him. They went from one picture to
another, yet none caught his attention.

"What do you think of this one?" Othello asked, breaking
into his thoughts.

"It's okay," he said softly with his head down. He knew he
was pouting, but he didn't care. He wanted to go home and
have Othello take his mind and body to a new place, but he
seemed more interested in the artwork on the walls. Why send

home the staff if they weren't leaving as well? As an artist, he should've been over the moon at all he got to see, but how can he?

He heard Othello chuckle, and Des wanted to smack the taller man. "I don't think you're paying attention," Othello whispered in his ear.

"Of course I'm paying atten..." Des raised his head and gasped mid-sentence when he saw the antique four-poster bed intricately designed, with a mahogany wood frame adorned with gold leaves from the canopy to the bottom. "Wow, this is gorgeous. It looks like something out of the 1600s, flashy but not as tasteless as one would imagine." Stepping away from Othello, he moved to the bed, lightly threaded his fingers through the thick red-and-gold drapes, then to the headboard with a more detailed design with what resembled a coat of arms. He brushed his fingers against the neatly made white silk sheets. He was surprised when he pressed into bed. It wasn't hard, but it was a soft plush mattress that seemed to be made for a king or queen.

"Gods, this is beautiful," he whispered, stepping back from the bed and taking in the rest of the room, which he'd just noticed was surrounded by red roses and candles of all sizes lighting the room, aided by the full moon seeping in from the window. On a gold ornate end table were two glasses and a bottle of wine chilling in a bucket of ice. It was so romantic, perfect for a night of lovemaking. Then, a thought came to Des.

Could all this be for me? For us? He had it all planned. He messed with me again by dragging me around the auction house, leaving this room for last.

Des had to admit it was romantic and couldn't get mad at the other man. A smile crossed his lips, but he hid it as he turned to face Othello. "Will this be auctioned off?"

Othello smirked as if seeing through Des but not calling him out. "You're right, it is gorgeous. The frame hails from Italy and was once owned by some royal noble. When we got it, it was pretty banged up. My people refurbished it, maintaining all the original aspects. But

auctioning it depends on you."

"Me? What do I have to do with your decision?"

Othello moved closer to Des and pulled him into his arms. Des moaned, unable to mask his response, melting against the man's larger frame. "Because once I make love to you in this bed, it will become ours." He leaned in and captured Des's lips with a kiss that made his knees weak. His tongue did things to his mouth as if he had a G-spot that led right to his cock that was already hard. Before their kiss got deeper, Othello pulled back, and only their panting could be heard in the silence of the room.

"Fuck," Othello said, his voice husky and deep. His fingers dug into Des's waist as if he was holding himself back.

"Is that what you plan on doing?" Des opened his eyes, wrapping his arms around Othello's neck.

"You are driving me crazy, Tesoro."

Des smiled at the endearment, leaned up, and brushed his lips against Othello's."Then let's go insane together." Their mouths met, and Othello picked him up and carried him to the bed. Without taking a breath or separating from their kiss, Des reached between them and tried to unbutton Othello's shirt, or at least he tried to.

Growling in frustration, he ripped the garment open. Hearing the tearing of fabric and the popping of buttons brought more joy to him than it should have. Othello pressed his weight on top of Des, holding him tightly in his arms, pulling a deep moan from him, feeling the man's heated skin even through his own clothes, making him feverish and needy. Othello flipped them over, and Des sat up, straddling his hips.

For the second time that day, he enjoyed seeing the look of lust in Othello's light amber eyes, which became darker the more aroused he got. Being on top of Othello made Des feel in control of the man's pleasure. To prove it, he wound his hips, grounding his ass on the hard cock, making the man underneath him groan and grab the front of his shirt, pulling him down for a searing kiss that had his lips burning as if he were scorched by fire, but it left Des wanting more.

SCENE III

OTHELLO

Othello bit his bottom lip, grabbing Des's hips and stopping his movement. He didn't know how long he was going to last. The entire night, Des had been teasing. Othello had to admit he'd made the mistake of picking out the perfect outfit that showed off Des's figure. Flipping them over, he sat on top of Des, grasping his wrists and placing them over his head.

"Don't move them," he ordered, liking the glint he saw in Des's eyes. Othello unbuckled his belt and slowly pulled it from his loops, watching Des's chest rise and fall, and his pretty green eyes darken to a color Othello hadn't seen before. Once the leather was pulled through the last loop, he lightly dragged it against Des's soft skin. Des gasped and closed his eyes.

"Look at me, Tesoro," Othello ordered. Des opened his eyes and looked directly at him. "Do you want me to spank you with this, baby?" Des nodded, and Othello chuckled. "Do you trust me so much?"

"I do," Des answered, not stuttering or turning his gaze away.

Othello didn't know what to say. Not since his last relationship had he played in the BDSM area. Despite what he'd claimed the day he woke up in the hospital, he knew Des was his type. Getting off Des, he unbuttoned his pants and slid them off, throwing them to the floor. Othello returned to the bed and did the same to Des, removing his pants and underwear.

"Roll over," he told Des.

He smiled when his Tesoro eagerly did what he told, no questions asked. Des's trust in him was so powerful it left him breathless. Othello folded the belt and trailed it down the center of Des's back, pulling a sweet gasp from him. He stopped at Des's lower back and lightly tapped the belt on his left cheek, watching his reaction.

Des wiggled his ass, and Othello did it again, this time adding a little more force, enough to sting but not leave a mark, pulling a hiss from his lover. Othello wouldn't go too far tonight; he simply wanted to test the waters. It was Des's first time, and he promised he would take it slow.

Othello leaned down and kissed the spot where he hit, then moved up his body, nipping at his shoulder. He kissed the back of his ear before sucking gently on his lobe.

"One day, I'm going to tie you to this bed and spank you with this very belt," Othello whispered in his ear.

"Why not tonight?" Des asked in a raspy voice.

"You're so eager to feel pain." Othello chuckled, trailing his lips to Des's cheek and placing a soft kiss.

"Only when you're the one making me hurt," Des responded, turning his head and connecting their mouths.

Othello moaned, taking every bit of what Des was willing to give. He lay on top of Des, and he sandwiched his cock between Des's legs rubbing his weeping erection on Tesoro's balls. Des groaned in his mouth and tightened his legs, slowly circling his waist.

Their bodies moved together, and their kiss became sloppy. Othello grabbed Des's hand and brought them up, silently instructing Des to hold on to the headboard. He sighed in satisfaction when wrapping his hand around the lube and condom packets. Their cocks ground together, rubbing against the soft sheet, sending waves of sensation throughout his body, and their breathing became ragged. Othello knew the signs and could tell Des was not far from coming, which caused him to stop and sit back on his knees.

Des growled in frustration, and Othello would have laughed if he wasn't in the same situation. Othello rubbed soothing circles on his back.

"Calm down, Tesoro," he said in a soft voice.

"Please don't tease me anymore," Des moaned. "I can't take it."

Othello reached for a pillow and tapped Des's hips. "Lift up." Des did as asked, and Othello fit the pillow underneath him and widened Des's legs, giving Othello a nice view of his puckered hole and the pretty iris mark on his leg. Leaning down, Othello spread Des's legs and buried his face in his butt cheeks, dragging his tongue along his hole. They both moaned at the touch and taste.

"Othello, fuck," Des groaned his name.

Othello swirled the tip of his tongue around Des's hole but didn't go any further. He loved eating ass, and as much as he wanted to fuck his lover with his tongue until he came, Othello was dying to bury himself into Des, feeling him tighten around him.

Leaning back, Othello tore the lube packet open with his teeth and let the liquid dribble over Des's butt crack, and watched it move down, soaking his hole. Othello placed a soft hand on Des's lower back as he circled a finger around his moist hole before pushing it in.

* * *

"OH," Des moaned, pressing his face into the pillow, feeling the sting from the finger moving in and out of his hole.

He had been prepared for this and knew that it would hurt. He was grateful that Othello was gentle with him, but Des wanted more.

"Othello, don't stop," he rasped. Othello grunted, and another finger joined the first one. He didn't stop this time, but he pumped them in and out of him. Des closed his eyes, enjoying the sensation of grinding on Othello's fingers and his cock on the pillow.

Distantly, he could hear Othello ripping something open and could only guess that it was the condom and was thankful that one of them had more sense to protect themselves. Des was too caught up in the pleasure to think clearly. The heat they'd created earlier hadn't disappeared. It was so heightened, that Des was close to coming.

Othello leaned over him and captured his mouth. His body relaxed completely at Othello's touch and kiss, and he felt like he was being taken to a new world. His body moved with Othello's fingers, as if the man were playing him like an instrument.

Des wasn't sure how many fingers were added since Othello kept him distracted, but he whimpered against Othello's lips when he felt the soft, blunt head pushing into his tight hole, stretching him, causing his erection to soften and his body to stiffen.

"Hurts," he softly cried.

"I know, Tesoro," Othello said. "Breathe," he soothed, giving him a peck on his lips and the tears that pooled in

the corners of his eyes. "I can stop."

"No, don't," Des said quickly. "Just give me a minute." Othello didn't stop touching him, and Des could feel his body relax. After a few minutes, he was ready and told his lover so. "Okay."

Othello didn't move immediately but looked into Des's face as if seeking assurance. Once he got what he wanted, he slowly pushed his cock in and out, sending tingles all through Des's body, pulling soft moans from him as his cock started coming to life.

"Othello, oh fuck, so good," he moaned, squeezing the head-board, but he wanted to hold onto his lover.

As if knowing what he wanted, Othello pulled out of Des, gently flipped him over on the pillow and grasped his condom-covered cock, and slowly pushed back into Des, not giving him a moment to breathe.

"Fuck, Tesoro, so tight, you feel so good squeezing my cock," Othello groaned before taking his mouth in a heated kiss.

Des wrapped his arms and legs around his lover as their bodies rocked together, shaking the sturdy bed and filling the room with their lovemaking and scent. Des had never felt this treasured before.

The way Othello held him while they made love brought tears to his eyes. He knew he would fall in love with Othello and be shattered if they ever broke up. His body wasn't the only thing that ached for Othello. It was his heart as well.

"Othello...Othello..." he chanted like a prayer as shivers

wracked his body, meeting his lover's every thrust. "Slow," he moaned. "Slow down, please."

"I can't," Othello grunted. "You feel too good." He held Des so tight he was sure he would lose his breath, but the pleasure was more important.

Des dug his nails into Othello's back, feeling his precum pooling between them, becoming lubrication as his cock jerked and rubbed against Othello's muscled stomach, sending delightful sensations all over him. With the added stimulation of Othello's large cock pounding into him, brushing against his prostate, he couldn't hold back, cumming and soaking their stomachs.

Othello grunted Des's name and buried his face in Des's neck, cumming and filling the condom, and Des wished he could feel his lover's hot cum filling him. Othello didn't stop moving his lips; he continued to fuck him through both their orgasm. Othello raised his head and looked into Des's face.

"Can you go again, Tesoro?" he asked, breathlessly. "I haven't had my fill of you yet."

"Good, because I need more of you," Des said, claiming his lips. They kissed for a little longer before Othello pulled out and changed the condom before pushing back inside of him.

Des wasn't sure how long, which positions, or how many times they went at it before he fell asleep, but one thing he knew was that he was becoming very addicted to Othello and his cock.

* * *

A FEWHOURSLATER, Dessnuggledhisbackinto Othello's chest, who had an arm wrapped around him. He had fallen asleep and woken up with Othello holding him like a precious gem. After a few hot kisses, they were basking in the afterglow of their lovemaking, and Des was glad that he had waited to be with someone who would take him to heights that had his body still tingling.

He hummed, feeling very content, even with the pain in his hips and ass as evidence that Othello didn't have a pencil dick. He mentally shook his head, recalling that morning after his drunken stupor. Sighing, he looked around the room and noticed that the candles had burned to almost nubs during their intimate moment, but the moon seemed much brighter. Des hadn't expected their night to turn out so beautifully.

"You look happy," Othello whispered in Des's ear, his voice tender and bringing a smile to Des's face.

"I am." He looked up at Othello, his eyes reflecting how happy he felt. "I guess this bed is ours now, right?"

"I'm a man of my word, Tesoro," Othello told him.

"And whose apartment will it be going to?" Des inquired, his curiosity piqued and anticipation evident in his voice, but he hoped Othello didn't get the wrong idea. He liked the man and wanted their relationship to blossom, but he wasn't ready to move in with him.

"I can have it sent to yours," Othello stated.

"Really?" Des asked, excited. He really liked the bed, and the artist in him couldn't let it go to someone else. But the significance of keeping the bed he and Othello made love in made him feel warm and tingly inside and out.

"Yes." Othello chuckled.

"You continue to impress me, Mister Moor."

"I aim to please."

"But when did you plan all of this?"

"While you were napping." Othello dragged his tongue along Des's neck, sucking up a mark before settling back into his pillows, holding Des tighter.

"Was I sleeping that long?"

"Mm." Othello chuckled. "Are you in any pain?"

"A little, but you were gentle."

"We should head home so I can get you in the tub. Then put some more ointment on it." Othello made to get up, but Des stopped him.

"No, not yet." Othello looked at him. "I'm not ready to leave yet."

"Are you sure?" he asked.

Des nodded. "I want to stay in your arms a little more."

Othello palmed one of his cheeks, then leaned down and kissed him. "Okay, we'll stay a little longer."

He settled back into bed with Des in his arms like before. Sighing happily, Des clasped their fingers, admiring the tattoos on Othello's fingers that were in Portuguese, but meant death, and a passage in Arabic on the backs of his hands.

"What does it say?" he asked Othello, rubbing the tattoo.

"Never forget, never regret, never forgive," Othello answered.

"Does it say the same thing on both hands?"

"No." Othello kissed him on his shoulder. "The other says no regrets, no hesitation."

Des turned his head and observed Othello's handsome face, wondering what could have made him make those personal vows.

"What?" Othello quirked a brow, looking at Des.

"I want to know everything about you," he said. "I know we talked a lot before we got together, but we've kept some personal stuff from each other. If this is going to work between us..." He chewed on his bottom lip, staring at Othello, not sure if he should continue or if he was asking too much.

"What do you want to know?" Othello asked.

"Where were you born?"

"Here in Verona Heights. My real parents died when I was young."

"Wait, I thought..." He stopped speaking, brow furrowed, showing his confusion.

"Alessandro and Maria adopted me and Iago."

"Oh. That makes sense. I'm sorry about your real parents," Des whispered.

"Don't be. I don't remember much about them." A look crossed his face, and Des could tell he was trying to recall a memory or two, but nothing of significance came to him. "Anyway, when they died, I was sent to a group home, which is where I met Iago." His face brightened at the mention of Iago's name.

"You two are really close, huh?"

"He's my best friend, brother, and the only man I trust to watch my back," Othello explained. "We fight, we love, and encourage each other. Growing up, we were fucking hellions. It hasn't changed much. We just found a different way to terrorize people." He chuckled. "Iago's about to be a father, and I'm happy for him."

"So you're going to be an uncle? Congratulations."

"Yup, and I plan on spoiling the kid rotten, no matter what Iago says."

It would have been the perfect time to ask if Othello wanted kids of his own. Instead, Des smiled at hearing Othello talk about his brother. "I'm kind of jealous of your relationship with him. Being an only child was hard enough, but being ignored and feeling unloved by my parents was worse."

"I don't think your parents hate you," Othello commented. "They were just trying to..."

"Stifle my creativity," he snapped, sitting up and ignoring the pain in his ass, but he was suddenly feeling fired up that Othello was taking his parents' side. "I told you just a little of what my parents did. But they lied to me for years, forcing me into a career I never wanted, and now I have to start from scratch to catch up to where I should have been. How can you take their side?"

"I'm not taking their side, Tesoro." Othello pulled him back into his arms. "Your parents were wrong with their approach, but answer me one question. Was being a doctor really that bad? And be truthful," he said, lightly tapping the tip of Des's nose.

Sighing, he shook his head. He'd always said that although he hated his job, he knew he was good at it. "It wasn't so bad."

"I think the reason you hated it was because your parents pushed you into it. If you had chosen it for yourself, things would be different."

Des couldn't argue with Othello's logic. "Why do you have to sound so sensible," Des told him. Othello chuckled, then kissed him on the forehead. "I'm not going back, Othello. I know I was good at my job, but I don't want to be responsible for another person's life that way again. And I won't forgive my parents. For years, I did what they

wanted. Now it's time for me to live for me."

"You don't have to do anything you don't want to, Tesoro. You've made your decision, and now the only thing is to move forward. As for your parents, I won't comment on that." Othello pulled him close. "One day, you might forgive them, but there's nothing wrong with letting your anger out occasionally. If Alessandro and Maria did the same to me, I doubt I'd speak to them again."

Des looked at Othello and saw the truth in his eyes. "Thanks for listening."

"Anytime, Tesoro."

"I like that," Des told him between yawns, pressing his face into Othello's chest, as his eyes suddenly grew heavy, as if he'd been drugged. "I like it when you call me your treasure."

As he closed his eyes, a soft kiss touched his forehead. "That's because you are," Othello whispered as he fell asleep.

* * *

CASSIO GLARED at the man in front of him. "When you agreed to work with us, it was with the understanding that you needed to give us everything on Moor."

"And when have I gone back on that deal?" his companion stated.

Cassio went to slap the man in the face, but Antonio Greco stopped him.

"So you didn't know he was dating?" Antonio asked.

"Dating who?" the man said, standing.

"You really didn't know?" Greco said.

"No, but how did you find out?" the man said.

"We saw them tonight at the Celeste Grand Plaza," he said. "They were pretty cozy. It's a side of Moor I've never seen before. We almost didn't want to interrupt them. It's a shame Moor is probably fucking that little sweet body right now. I must say, Moor knows how to find good-looking companions." He smiled. "I can't wait to take this one

away and ruin him like I did the last one."

"You better not let Stephania hear you say that." Greco chuckled.

"Man can't live on bread alone, my friend. Every now and then, he also likes a little meat." He chuckled and looked at their companion. "Find out who he is. I want to know all I can about him before I make my move." "Yes," the man said with no hesitation.

Cassio stared at their companion, wondering if he felt guilt for his actions. He didn't think he could go against his family. With his brother terminally ill, it was up to him to look after the clan. Now, Cassio was protecting his brother from all who would use his illness as the perfect time to strike their family. As much as he trusted Antonio, not even he knew that Dominico wasn't just working from Italy but bedridden for the rest of his life. Dominico taught him to protect everyone in the family, from the top to the lowest soldier, so they would never think to betray them.

It was evident the Romanos did not have the same ideals since the man in front of him portrayed no remorse. When he first came to them, he'd said he wanted to take down the Romano clan, or to be more specific, Moor. When they asked why, their companion asked that his reasons remain personal.

His answer only made Cassio and Greco suspicious since they knew how dedicated he was to the family. They had given him a test to bring back information on what the Romano clan was up to. When he came back with what they wanted, they decided to help him. That was a year ago, and so far, their cooperation had borne much fruit.

"Another thing," Greco said. "For your information on the Kurohue, we'll give you the resources you need for your next plan to take Moor out."

"Thank you, but I'll wait to take those resources."

"Why, are you giving up?"

"Hell no, but for now, I'll shift my focus from him to someone else," the man said.

"Dare we ask who?" he said.

Their companion smiled. "Pay attention to the news in the coming weeks, and you'll get your answer. Until then, good night."

They watched him leave before Cassio spoke. "When can we kill him?"

"Once he gives us what we want," Greco responded. "Back in the day, I had high hopes for Alessandro, but he lost my respect when he adopted that little thug and announced he'd be the next successor," Greco snarled. "How dare he ruin a tradition of only our kind sitting at the head of the family?"

"Is that why you agreed to give resources to the little rat?"

"Yes," Greco said, standing. "What about you?"

He stared at his boss for a few seconds. "Honestly, I don't care about all that shit; I simply hate Moor and want to see the cocky bastard on his knees, begging me to spare his life before I kill him."

Greco smiled. "Come to my bed tonight."

"I should update my brother on what's going on."

"Do it tomorrow tonight. I need to be inside of you," Greco said.

Cassio smirked. Greco was a good-looking and fit man, even in his fifties. They had been on-and-off-again lovers since he started working for the Greco clan. Cassio didn't deny that he enjoyed going to bed with Greco but wanted to sink deep into someone younger tonight. Or maybe he could imagine it. "What of your wife?"

Greco leaned down and kissed him. "Remember the rule. Never mention Phillipa when it's just us."

Greco captured his mouth before he could say anything else.

* * *

"Is this all the information you could dig up on
Doctor Ellington?" Jackson Durrant asked.

"I wouldn't be here if it weren't," Othello snapped, annoyed that he left the comfort of his bed with Des wrapped around him not only to go to work but to meet with the asshat sitting across from him. For the past couple of days, he had put every-thing on hold to spend time with his new lover. He'd forgotten what it was like to wake up with someone in his arms, and for the past two days, it was a dream. He couldn't wait to end his day to see his lover.

"I see a lot of things here about Ellington, but nothing about his wife and son."

"Because there's nothing to see," Othello sighed.

"There's got to be something," Durrant said. "Nobody is clean. He's got to have something in his closet."

"Yes, he does," Othello said, leaning close. "Me." He ignored the surprised expression that crossed Durrant's face. "If I hear you're looking into his background, or you let the dogs sniff in his direction, I will come for you. " "I—I—I mean, I didn't. I wouldn't—" he stuttered.

Othello stood along with his men, who came with him. He fixed his jacket with his eyes on Durrant. "Don't be too quick to use what I gave you. Let the information out slowly, then let everything explode at the right time." "I know how to do my job," Durrant snapped.

"I hope you do, because if you don't heed my warning…"

Durrant nodded, and Othello walked out of the coffee shop with Tallen next to him.

"Boss, are you sure the doc won't be mad about the information we gave to Durrant?"

"He gave up his chance to be mad at me. He told me he didn't want to know what his father was up to, and I stuck to my word."

Othello didn't know when the information on Ellington Sr. would be revealed to the public. Still, it would damage not only his career as a doctor and politician but also his family.

"Tallen, from now on, I want you to look out for Des when I'm not around," he said, getting in his car.

"Okay, boss." Tallen got in the driver's seat and drove them to the office, where Iago was already working hard.

"What are you doing here?" Iago asked.

"I feel like you ask me that every time you see me," Othello told him.

Iago chuckled. "Don't take it to heart. It's that lately you're either working or taking time off."

"Hey, I only took two days off, not a whole year." Iago nodded.

"Alright, what's on today's agenda?"

They walked and talked about what they had to do for the day. A few construction projects were currently in the works, and a few were finishing up.

"The Kurohue-gumi clan canceled the meeting," Iago said.

Othello stopped walking and looked at his brother. "Why?"

Iago shrugged his shoulders.

Othello furrowed his brows. He had been looking forward to making a deal with Takashi Kurohue, the leader of the Kurohue clan. Othello wanted to expand their operation to Japan. He'd rather not work with Kurohue, but Alessandro's close friend had convinced him that Kurohue would be good to work with. Othello couldn't put his finger on it, but something about Kurohue rubbed him the wrong way.

"I hope they aren't going to be working with someone else?"

"I don't know," Iago said.

Now that Othello thought about this, it was the third time he was supposed to meet with another boss to discuss business cooperation, only to later find out they went and made a deal with Greco and Ricci. Someone was fucking with his bag, and Othello didn't like it one bit.

Fuck, how did it take me this long to realize the traitor was working with them? When I find the rat, I'm going to kill them with my bare hands.

"What are you thinking?" Iago asked him.

Othello looked at his brother. "Find out why they canceled."

"I'm already on it, but what will you do in the meantime?"

"Nothing," he said, not sure why he was lying to a man he trusted with his life. Right now, he wasn't sure if he could trust anyone until he found out who the Judas was in the clan. "I'm going to let you handle this."

"Are you sure?"

"Of course." Othello smiled. "Alright, I'm going to get some work done."

Before he could enter his office, Iago stopped him and stared at his face. "There's something different about you. Two days ago, you were all grumbly and ready to cut my head off, and today, you seem easygoing. What did you do those two days off?"

"I relaxed," Othello said. "Something you should think about doing?"

Iago went to say something but was stopped by his ringing cell phone. "I have to take this," he said, looking at the screen.

"Do you, man. I'm going to get some work done."

Othello stepped into his office and did just that.

Later that night, Othello entered Des's apartment, shaking his head at Des for not locking the door as he set the grocery bags on the counter. The neighborhood was safe, but you never knew what could happen. He then went and searched for his lover. He had texted Des and told him he'd be stopping by after work, so maybe that's why he left the door unlocked.

Othello looked around the apartment and noticed that Des had unpacked more boxes since the last time he had been there. It didn't look like he had a lot to fill his large apartment. Taking the stairs two at a time, his brows creased together when he got to the top of the stairs, hearing voices that not only belonged to Des. He walked down the hall. They were in the part of the apartment that Des had designed as his studio. He was about to interrupt but stopped when he heard his name mentioned.

"Do you think Othello will like it?"

"I do. This is brilliant work, Des. When you quit working at the hospital, I doubted that you could do this, but after seeing this, I believe you can make it as an artist."

"Thanks, Gray. I needed to hear that. To be honest, I doubt myself. I still do. I keep wondering if my parents

were right and I'm no good at this."

"Hey, man, don't do that to yourself. This is your dream. This is something that you've wanted to do your entire life.

Remember, your grandfather believed you could do this, or he wouldn't have defied your parents."

"I know. And I just don't wanna let him down. I want him to look down from wherever he is and be proud of me. Be proud that I put my everything into this."

"He is, and he will be. Just keep doing what you're doing. And when you become super famous and mega

rich, I'll be able to say that's my best friend."

"Quit that. I'm not doing this for fame, but I don't mind the mega-rich part."

Hearing the silence between them, Othello pushed the door open. "He's right, you know."

Both men gasped and turned to look at him. "Othello, what are you doing here?" asked Des.

"I texted you and told you I was coming. Your door was unlocked, so I let myself in." Although he was speaking to Des, his eyes zeroed in on the man who called himself his lover's best friend. Who would've guessed it was someone he'd had run-ins with.

"Oh, damn," Des said. "I was so focused on finishing up the painting that I didn't hear my phone."

"Detective Gratiano, I didn't expect to see you here," Othello said, moving farther into the room.

"You know each other? Gray, you never mentioned that."

"Only in passing," Gray answered, glaring at Othello, who smirked at his feeble attempt. "Mr. Moor and I have spoken a time or two."

Hearing that, Othello quirked an eyebrow in the man's direction. *Is that what he wants to call it? Fine, then we'll go with that.*

"Alright, I can tell you to have plans, so I'm going to head out," said Gray.

"Are you sure? Don't you want to stay for dinner?" Des said. "I would love for my best friend and my lover to get along."

"I bought enough groceries for only the two of us," Othello added before the detective could respond.

"Oh." Des sighed, then turned to look at Gray. "How about we change plans and meet for lunch or dinner some other time?"

"That sounds great." Gray smiled, then leaned in and kissed Des on one cheek. "Don't give up on yourself, Des."

He looked at Othello, this time less threatening, and nodded as he walked by him.

"Let me walk him out," Des said, coming over to kiss Othello.

While he was gone, Othello took the time to observe the painting Des had done for him. Weeks back, he'd commissioned a painting of Alessandro and Maria on their wedding day. To be given to them at the anniversary party. Othello had taken a gamble since he had never seen Des's work, but looking at the artwork, he could only say he'd made the right decision.

Des had captured the essence of the couple's love. He had gone a bit further by incorporating a pose of them now, with Alessandro holding Maria possessively, staring deep into her eyes with admiration that would make anyone jealous, desiring the same kind of affection just standing in front of the artwork. Othello had only given Des the wedding picture, so the other pose had to be taken from his heart.

"I hope you like it," Des said, standing beside him. Othello heard the slight tremor in his voice, and he could tell the man was nervous.

"I feel that it is wrong you won't let me pay you for this," Othello said, gazing at Des. "The detective is right, and as someone who appreciates fine art, your confidence comes out in your work. Don't sell yourself short, Doc."

That brought a genuine smile to Des's face, and his cute dimples became more pronounced.

"Thanks for saying that. And I knew there was a reason I was so attracted to you from the beginning."

"So you'll let me pay you?"

"Hm...only with kisses." He smiled. "And lots of them."

"Gods, you're so cheap." He chuckled. "But someone I can definitely afford." Othello wrapped Des in his arms, pulling him close and claiming his sweet lips.

* * *

A COUPLE OF DAYS LATER, Othello sat in the far back corner of a dive bar on the other side of town, looking at the person who had just sat before him.

"I'm sorry I'm late. I had to ditch my partner to meet with you."

"It's fine. I called you out on short notice," Othello said, leaning back in his seat. "When were you going to tell me you and Des were friends?"

Gratiano sighed. "I mean no disrespect when I say this, boss, but I didn't expect you two to get together. Des told Bianca and me about his attraction to you, and I guess I wasn't expecting him to follow through and pursue you. I love him as a friend," he added quickly. "But when it comes to putting himself out there, he doesn't for fear of rejection. It's why he never fought his parents when they pushed him to become a doctor. He's changed since he met you."

Othello nodded. "I don't think I can take credit for that. It's always been inside of him. I assume you don't want him to know about our connection?"

"Not yet." Gratiano sighed. "He's not ready to hear that his best friend has been a part of the mob since he was sixteen and only became a cop so that he could watch his boss's back. Maybe one day I'll tell him, but not yet." "He knows about me, Gratiano," Othello said.

"You told him?" Gratiano asked, seeming surprised. "When have I ever lied about me or my family?"

"Forgive me, but that's not what I meant. It's just that, I figured Des would have walked away once he found out you're a mob boss." He sighed and sat back in his chair,

hard. "I guess he's really changed."

"He took the news pretty well," Othello said with a smile. "But he did ask if I killed anyone."

"What did you tell him?"

"I found ways to distract him." He waggled his eyebrows at his friend.

Gratiano chuckled. "You might think he forgot, but he'll bring it up again."

"Then I'll keep distracting him until he stops asking. Alright, enough of that. There's another matter why I called you out here."

"Okay, I'm listening."

"I need you to go undercover and investigate who is working against us. There's a rat amongst our midst, and I want you to sus them out."

"Okay, how?" Gratiano asked.

Othello reached into his jacket pocket, pulled out an envelope, and handed it to Gratiano. "This is some information on the shooting from the warehouse six months ago. We're still trying to figure out who ambushed us. My money is on the Ricci and Greco families. Find the link between them and our rat. Report anything you find to me and no one else. Right now, I don't know who to trust."

"Yes, boss."

Othello stood, but before he could walk away, Gratiano spoke.

"I'm loyal to you and have been since you first took me in as a friend. I owe you a lot, Othello. And although I might not be able to kick your ass, if you hurt him, nothing will stop me from trying to kill you."

Othello smiled. "Then you're no longer loyal to me, Gratiano, or should I call you Gray from now on?"

"Anything that makes you happy, boss," Gratiano said, looking at him.

"Contact me when you have something significant."

This time, Othello walked away, feeling the need to see his little treasure.

SCENE IV

DES

*D*es sighed, stretching out the kinks in his back. It was a couple of weeks later, and he had been sitting in the same spot, working on a painting for class. After finishing the last part, he cleaned up, left it to dry, and went to eat.

Once he got to the kitchen, he made a sandwich and picked up his phone. He then scanned his social media accounts, where he had posted a few of his paintings under a pseudonym. He had garnered a small following that he wouldn't call a fan club, but they loved his work.

He thought about selling the little stock he had but wasn't sure anyone would buy his work. He knew he needed to improve his technique but wasn't in a rush. Des almost choked on his sandwich when breaking news flashed across the screen.

Senate candidate David Ellington's home was just raided and searched today by the FBI under the suspicion of running a Ponzi scheme, defrauding his investors out of millions.

"Holy shit, Dad, what the fuck did you do?" Des whispered as he furiously scanned the article.

He got up from the table and hurried into the living room, switching on the television. Since it was breaking news, he didn't need to search for any other channel. Des sat transfixed, listening to the report, and couldn't believe what they were saying about his father.

He was startled when there was a knock at his door. Frowning, he put the remote down and went to answer it, becoming equally confused when he didn't recognize the person.

"Yes, can I help you?"

"Desmond Ellington," the man said.

"Yeah, that's me."

The man reached into his coat pocket and took out a wallet with a police badge. "I'm Detective Leonard Oz. Is it alright if I come in and ask you some questions regarding your father?"

Des looked into the tall detective's brown eyes. "You don't need to come in. I can answer them right now," Des said.

"What's going on here?" said another voice that Des recognized.

Detective Oz stepped to the side, revealing Othello standing there.

"Othello Moor," Oz said in a tone that Des could only describe as unfriendly. "What the hell are you doing here?"

Othello quirked a brow, smirking. "Is there a problem with me coming to see my lover, Detective?"

"Lover," Oz gasped, then looked at Des. "Is what he said true?"

What the hell is wrong with this man? "Yes."

"Do you know who he really is, Mister Ellington?" Oz asked. "How he makes his money?"

"What does me knowing what Othello does for a living have to do with why you're here? You came to ask me questions about my father, which I know nothing about."

While Des spoke, Othello approached him, kissed him on the side of his head, and entered his apartment. The detective didn't take his eyes off Othello the entire time.

"Are we done here?" Des asked, getting the detective to focus on him.

"No," Oz answered. "When was the last time you spoke to your father?"

"Six months ago when I told him to stay the fuck out of my life."

"Why's that, if you don't mind me asking?"

"That's personal," Des responded. "But if you have any more questions, you can contact my lawyer, Erin Graham." Before the detective could say more, Des closed the door in his face. Turning, he faced Othello, who had removed his coat and jacket, loosened his tie and the top three buttons on his shirt, and was lounging on the couch with his eyes closed, but Des knew he wasn't sleeping.

"I have one question for you," Des said.

"Only one? I figured you'd have more," he said, opening his eyes and looking at Des.

"I do, but I don't want to know why that detective has a problem with you."

"Okay, so what do you want to know?"

"Was the raid on my parents' home caused by you?"

"I simply passed on some of the information; what the other party wanted to do with it is their business."

"So there's more that could bury my father?"

"Not just him, Tesoro," Othello said. "Your mother as well."

He stared at Des for a few seconds before speaking. "I can tell you what else I have on them, and you can do whatever you want with the information."

Des shook his head. "No, I made a deal with you that whatever you found out, I didn't want to know. It might sound crass, but my parents made their beds, and now they must lie in them."

"Are you sure?"

"I am. As long as they leave me out of it the way they have my entire life, I don't care what happens." He bit his lips, wanting to feel a little pain. "Does that make me

sound like a terrible person or son?"

"That's not for me to answer, Tesoro." He stretched out a hand, and Des, like a magnet, went straight to him, straddling Othello's legs. "You know that you can ask me for help, and I can make it all go away. Your father can win the race, and everything will be as it was. Or you can use me to exact your revenge for the hurt they caused you." He cupped one of Des's cheeks. "I am your sword, Tesoro. Use me to strike your enemies no matter who they are, and I will make them bleed."

Des had never had anyone speak in such a manner to him or want to fight his battles for him. Common sense said he should be afraid, but he was so aroused he wanted to give and bear all to Othello.

"And what should I give you in return?"

Othello smiled. "The one thing no one else can have." He placed a hand on Des's chest. "Your heart."

Des leaned forward and pressed their foreheads together, wanting to tell Othello that he'd had it from the moment they met, but all he could muster was a nod as he tightened his arms around Othello's neck.

"Hold on to the information for now. Let me see how he digs himself out of this hole."

Othello pecked the tip of Des's nose. "As you wish."

* * *

DES SIPPED HIS COFFEE LEISURELY, looking at the two people across from him who appeared as if their world wasn't slowly crashing down around them. It had been a few days since the news came out, and although things had died down, it was still a topic of discussion.

The detective didn't return to talk with Des, nor did the press. He was thankful that his parents kept him somewhat away from the public eye, and no one bothered him. So, of course, he was curious when his mother called earlier that morning and asked that he meet with them.

Feeling spiteful, Des asked Othello to tag along, who'd only chuckled when he made the request. By the way his father was glaring at Othello, and it seemed his effort wasn't in vain. They had been sitting at the table for over five minutes with neither party saying a word. "Desmond," Ava said, clearing her throat.

"Yes, Mother."

"Aren't you going to introduce us to your companion?"

Des looked at Othello, noticing the sly, playful smirk on his lips. He grabbed Othello's hand, steepling their fingers together and putting it on the table for his parents to see.

"He's my lover, Othello Moor," Des said.

"I forbid it," David growled just as Ava spoke. "Lover?"

"What the hell do you forbid?" Des said, facing his father. "You no longer have a say in my life."

"You have been nothing but a damn disappointment from the day you were born," David hissed. "No carrier has been born into our bloodline, and to make matters worse, you're with a man, utterly disgusting."

Months ago, those very words would have crushed him to the bone, but now he could face the words head-on.

"Why did you call me here? Because if it's to insult me, you could have done that over the phone," Des snapped.

"Moor," his father said, ignoring his question. "Are you, by chance, Othello Moor, son of Alessandro

Romano?"

"I am."

David huffed, eyeing Othello. "Word on the street is your company deals in unsavory business."

Othello chuckled. "Well, we can't all be as ethical as you, Doctor Ellington. Who else knows what other skeletons are hiding in your closet?"

"I've committed no crime, not like some people," David countered, then turned to Des. "You idiot boy have no idea who you're sleeping with."

"Unlike you, I have no evidence against me," Othello said smoothly. "And Des knows exactly who I am. I am the CEO of Romano Construction. No job too big or small is our motto."

Des would have laughed, seeing the sneer on his father's face. "You bas—"

"David, that is enough!" Ava growled, which shut his father up completely. "First, let me apologize to you, Mister Moor. My husband is under a lot of strain, and well, his mouth gets the better of him."

"I don't need you to apologize for me," his father growled.

"Second," she continued as if her husband had not spoken. "Desmond, we wanted to see you because your father needs your help. We need the money your grandfather left you. We..."

"No," Des said before she could go any further.

"Don't you want to hear why we need it?"

"Nope. Whatever you two are involved in has nothing to do with me."

"But we're your parents," she shouted.

"And I was your son who you've ignored, seen as a disgusting disappointment, only to be called upon when you need something. I'm no longer the kid who yearns for your affection and approval."

"But your father might go to prison. Don't you have any feelings about that?" Ava asked.

Des stood, and so did Othello, following his lead. "If he broke the law" —he looked directly at his father— "he should rot in jail for his crimes. Don't ever call me again. As far as we're concerned, you are strangers to me." His mother gasped, clutching her expensive pearls. "You don't mean that," she said, a slight tremor in her voice.

"If you've never taken me seriously before today, I suggest you do it now."

Des was about to make a grand exit, but Othello pulled him back, hugging his waist. "Maybe the person you should have apologized to wasn't me," he said, "but to your son. If you had shown him some courtesy, you might have gotten what you wanted."

After he said his piece, they walked out of the diner, holding hands and remaining silent until they were in the car driving down the highway.

"Are you okay?" Othello asked.

"Yeah," he sighed. "They never cared about me."

"Your father is a piece of work, but your mom is different. I don't think things are as harmonious as they appear."

"What do you mean?"

"I feel like she's going along with your father to keep the peace between them. Your mother loves you, Tesoro. If I were to guess, I'd say she regrets how the relationship between you both turned out."

"I don't know about that. My mom has always taken my father's side."

Des had no one to defend him growing up except for Nanny Cee. When his parents found out, Nanny Cee was fired, and they left him alone while his parents did whatever they wanted.

"Promise me you won't let them come between us," he said, looking at Othello.

Othello smiled. "The only one who can ruin what we have is us, Tesoro." He reached over and grabbed Des's closest hand, bringing it to his lips and kissing the back of it without taking his eyes off the road. "Remember, I am yours to use. And I'll stay by your side for however long you need me."

"Thank you," Des said, squeezing Othello's hand.

* * *

DES TILTED HIS HEAD BACK, giving Othello access to his neck, moaning loudly. He was straddling Othello's lap with his lover's hard cock pounding inside of him.

He'd been surprised when he opened the door, and Othello stood on the other side. He hadn't expected to see his lover that night. Since they met up with his parents, they had been going hot and heavy over the past few weeks, with Othello taking him on romantic dates and even taking a quick weekend trip.

But tonight, Othello told him he would be working late and that they might not see each other. When he opened the door, he hadn't gotten one word out before Othello pulled him in his arms and claimed his lips; before he knew it, he was straddled over the man's lap with his cock buried inside of him.

"Othello," Des whimpered as Othello's cock hit his prostate each time it went in and out of him. Othello growled against his skin, grasping his waist and digging his nails into Des's flesh.

"Oh fuck, right there," Des groaned, swerving his waist, holding on to the back of the couch, meeting Othello thrust for thrust. He reached back with a hand and grasped one of his balls, massaging and gently pulling on it as he rode Othello's cock, feeling his orgasm building. Their bodies move in sync, his heart beating loudly, his skin flushed with heat and drenched in sweat. Othello's tongue trailed down and captured a nipple in his mouth, biting on the nub. His cock was sandwiched between them, rubbing on the firmness of their abdominal muscles, bringing him even closer.

"Mmm..." Des moaned as Othello's cock went so deep inside of him it felt as if he were rearranging his guts. "O, I'm—fuck," he whimpered, unable to finish his words, cumming between them. His body shook just as Othello's teeth bit on his nipple, just as his nails dug deeper into his flesh. Othello's thrusts didn't stop. He hummed against Des's skin when he gently pulled on Othello's balls, circling his hips, fucking his cock.

Des wanted to pull all pleasurable sounds from Othello, and he wanted to drive the man so fucking crazy that he would become an addict for him and no one else. They had made love so many times over the past few weeks that he had become accustomed to Othello's large cock pounding inside of him and didn't think anyone could be compared to him. He knew he was falling in love with Othello. Des knew it was early in their relationship, but he couldn't help it. He wanted to be with Othello no matter what the future held for them.

"Tesoro," Othello growled against his chest. His balls drew tight in Des's hand, and his body stiffened beneath him as hot cum seared his walls, bringing a pleasurable hum from Des's lips, not caring that neither thought about a condom.

Des fell on top of Othello, panting heavily. Othello wrapped his arms around him, kissing his sweaty hair.

"I told you this was a good fucking couch," Othello rasped, and it made Des chuckle and closed his eyes, snuggling against his lover whose cock was still buried inside of him.

* * *

SOMETIME LATER, after they had cleaned up, they were back on the couch with Des sitting between Othello's spread legs and his back against his bare chest. They'd ordered Portuguese takeout, polished off a bottle of red wine, and were working on their second. He was feeling a nice buzz along with Othello's hard cock pressing and pulsating against his ass.

The man is insatiable. He couldn't deny it, but so was he. Each time Othello was near, his body hummed with excitement. "You still haven't told me why you're here," Des said, breaking the silence between them.

"Do I need a reason to see you?"

Leaning his head on Othello's shoulder, Des looked at the handsome man. "Of course not, but you told me you would be busy tonight."

"I finished my meeting early, but I had to see you before I left the country."

"Are you running away without me?" Des sat up and straddled Othello's legs, draping his arms over his shoulders. "Where are you going?"

"Japan. I need to handle some business." Othello chuckled, grabbing his hips, bringing Des's ass over his cock. "I'll be leaving early in the morning. But I'll only be gone for a couple of days, back in time for my parents' anniversary party."

"Oh," Des said, suddenly feeling upset, not because Othello was leaving town. But he didn't know if he should feel annoyed that Othello hadn't asked him to be his date. Des didn't want to assume they were at the parents-meeting-each-other phase yet since they hadn't been together that long. Also, it wasn't as if he hadn't met Othello's parents before, but if he went to the party, it would be as his lover and not his former doctor. "I hope you and your date have fun."

"I'm sure we will," Othello said.

Angry, Des got off Othello and the couch and then started cleaning up. *How dare he not ask me and take someone else?* He mentally grumbled, throwing the empty dinner containers in the trash. He began washing the dishes when strong arms slinked around his waist, and Othello's chin rested on his shoulder.

"It's a black-tie affair, so make sure to look extremely handsome when you officially meet my folks," he said softly, causing Des to stop what he was doing and turn his head to glare at the man smirking cheekily at him.

"Why are you such an asshole? Couldn't you say I was your date rather than make me think you're taking someone else?" Des argued.

"Who else would I take?" Othello chuckled.

"I don't know, what if I'm..." He never got a chance to finish his statement since Othello turned him in his embrace.

"I might not be a nice person, Des, but when I'm with someone, I would never cheat on them," he growled. "So get that fucking thought out of your head right now."

Des was about to apologize but held back from saying anything. What was he apologizing for? Their relationship was new, and he was inexperienced. Who's to say a more experienced man wouldn't catch his eye? At that thought, Des realized that he might not fully trust Othello and didn't know why. Looking into his lover's face, he hoped Othello would see his unease and say something assuring that he had nothing to worry about, but he released Des and walked to the bedroom, coming back with his shirt on and buttoning it up.

"Why are you getting dressed?" Des asked.

"I have to go home and pack for my trip. My flight leaves in a few hours, and I have things to take care of before I go," he explained, moving closer to Des and gathering him in his arms. "Be good while I'm gone. I'll have

Tallen come and hang out with you."

"You don't have to do that," Des said, still feeling out of sorts. "I have friends, you know?"

"I'll feel better knowing one of my guys is with you." He kissed Des on his lips softly. "Don't drink too much while I'm gone. You know how you get when you're drunk. I don't want to return to hear you've been in a fight with the Beast again."

"That was not my fault, and you know it," Des pouted.

"Maybe not." He released Des and then grabbed his jacket off the sofa. "I'm heading out. See you in a couple of days." Othello was out the door with one last kiss, leaving Des with conflicting thoughts, like whether he was good enough to hold on to a man like Othello. Or better yet, could he trust him not to break his heart? Maybe it was finally hitting him that he'd jumped into things too quickly with Othello and should have taken things slower than they did; maybe he wouldn't feel so out of sorts.

IT WAS late into the next evening when Othello got to Tokyo, Japan. He had thought about calling Des, but it was too late in the States, and he didn't want to delay things. The sooner he was done with his business, the quicker he could return to his sweet lover. Not only was he meeting with the Kurohue clan leader, but he'd made an appointment with the Kurohue's rivals.

He hadn't told Alessandro or Iago what he was doing and only brought two of his soldiers with him. He was supposed to be in England, but he was far away from where he was supposed to be. He had a reason for his subterfuge. Although he had told Iago to look into why Kurohue had backed out of their meeting, Othello couldn't wait for the results and needed to speak with the man face to face. Othello might not have lived in Japan, but he knew of Kurohue's habits. He liked to frequent Kuroyuki, a host club that offered more than just a friendly ear. Before he could take a step into the club, he was stopped by the bodyguards. His men went to reach for their weapons, but he stopped them and spoke to the guards.

"Tell your boss The Shadow is here to see him," Othello said in fluent Japanese. After the Romanos adopted him, Othello took advantage of the privileged education and learned everything he could. From art to different languages, he even traveled in college to learn about different cultures before returning home and immersing himself in the family business.

One of the guards went inside and came out a few minutes later. "Come this way," he said, stepping aside for them to enter. Then, both guards escorted them to their boss. He recognized the elegance in the decorations but knew there was more to it, such as a bathhouse and special rooms that offered the guests a happy ending before they walked out the door. Not to mention, the club was a front, similar to his own establishments. So, there wouldn't be any security cameras anywhere in and out of the building. Othello and his men were led to a private room, with Kurohue sitting on the couch, surrounded by gorgeous men and women.

"I didn't expect Othello the Shadow Moor to appear on my doorstep?"

"Get rid of them," Othello told him.

"You dare to walk into my club giving me fucking orders," Kurohue said, but Othello leisurely sat down and waited for the man to do as he said. Kurohue waved his hand, and the people fawning over him got up and left, except for the bodyguards, who stayed while they talked. "You didn't have to come all this way for a canceled meeting."

"Why?" Othello asked. "We had an agreement, and you backed out at the last minute. I get annoyed when shit like that happens."

"I was offered a new deal I couldn't refuse," Kurohue smirked. "I was willing to meet with you until I found out some things about your family."

"Oh yeah?" Othello asked. "And what's that?"

"Your family is too clean for my kind of business," Kurohue

told him, then snorted a line of coke. "Arms and weapons are all good and shit, but do you know what makes money flow into your hands like water?" He paused as if waiting for Othello to respond, but continued, knowing that he wouldn't. "People, it's what makes the world go round." He cackled.

"It seems my trip here was truly a waste of time," Othello said, flicking lint off his pants.

"I wouldn't say that. Give me a better offer, and I will go with you. Just like that." He snapped his fingers.

"I can't trust you to keep your word anymore, Kurohue." Othello watched as the man snorted another line and as the drugs took effect.

"I like you, Moor, so I'm going to help you out. You have a rat in your nest, Moor," Kurohue said, slumping in his seat, leaning his head on the back of the couch.

"How do you know that?" Othello asked, feeling pissed that family business got out, and he didn't even know who the fucker was.

"They were the ones that put me in touch with my new business partners."

"Who are they?"

"That I wish I could tell you," Kurohue said. "I simply got a text saying to cancel my appointment with you, and that someone else would contact me later."

"And you followed through, just like that?" Othello asked, snapping his fingers.

"No, I waited to hear the deal and went with them because it sounded too good to pass up. Like I said, people make the world go around, and put money in my pockets."

Othello really hated men like Kurohue. They had no loyalty. "Give me the number."

Kurohue stared at him for a few minutes, then reached into his pocket, pulled out his phone, and rattled off the number.

Othello dialed the number, with Kurohue watching him, and remained stoic when he dialed an outof-service number.

How clever of him.

Putting his phone away, Othello stood. "You said my family is too clean for your business, but do you know what I detest? It's people like you who don't keep their word. When you make an appointment, it might sound silly to you, but I live by a code of ethics. Never break your word."

Just as Othello finished speaking, two of Kurohue's body-guards were dropped, followed by two more before the drug-addled man knew what was happening.

"What the fuck a..." A silent bullet entered the center of his forehead, stopping anything else he had to say.

"Search his pockets and bring me his phone," he told the man closer to him. Othello smirked. His people really knew him well. No one would call him sensible, traveling so far to get answers, and then having the man killed. But Othello had every intention of finding out why he canceled the meeting and nothing else. But who told him to try to pull a fast one on Othello?

"Here you go, boss," his subordinate said, getting his attention. "I already unlocked it."

Taking the phone, Othello scanned through his contacts, feeling annoyed when he didn't see a name or number he recognized. That meant a couple of possibilities: Kurohue had another phone that wasn't on his person. He wouldn't spend more time searching for it when he had other places to be and new deals to make.

"Let's go," Othello ordered, shaking his head. *What a waste of fucking time.*

SCENE V

DES

es woke up to his phone alarm. Turning it off, he
snuggled under the covers, wishing Othello was
there. How weird was it that the other man hadn't been gone a
full day? It felt like forever to Des. Groaning at the sound of his
phone ringing, he was tempted to ignore it but thought better,
thinking that it was Othello calling him. Sitting up, he reached
for his cellphone and blinked in surprise at the name on the
screen.

Ava.

He didn't want to speak to his parents since not after their
last meeting. He also hadn't kept up with his father's campaign
because he wanted nothing to do with it. Why should he

support a man who never cared about his dreams? Des didn't hate his mother, but he couldn't trust her. Ava had aided in suppressing Des, but he couldn't forgive that. He didn't know how long he stared at the screen, but it stopped ringing just as he was about to answer. He debated on whether he should return the call.

However, it rang once again. This time, it was Othello.

"Hello?" Des answered.

"Don't tell me you're still in bed."

Des smiled and felt his cheeks flush, hearing Othello's deep, soothing voice in his ear. "If I am, are you jealous you're not here to snuggle with me?"

Othello chuckled. "Who knew the good doctor was such a teddy bear in bed?"

"That's only because you turned me into one." Des loved cuddling next to Othello, feeling his warm body pressed against his. "Are you done with your trip?"

"Almost. Why, do you miss me?"

"Would you consider me weak if I say yes?" Des bit on his bottom lip.

"No," Othello whispered. "Because I miss you too. In the short time we've been together, I've grown accustomed to having you in my arms."

Des grinned. Despite his minor freakout the night before, hearing Othello say that put some of his doubts to rest. "Are you saying you like me, Mister Moor? Or maybe

you're falling in love with me?"

"Are you fishing for compliments, Doctor Ellington?" Des could hear the smile in his voice.

"What if I am? "

"You should already know the answer to that, Des."

"Should I?" He ran his hand over the cold sheets where Othello usually slept when he stayed at Des's place.

"7458," Othello responded, confusing Des.

"What are those numbers supposed to mean?"

"It's the pin number to my credit card," he said. "I'll see you soon." He hung up before Des could respond.

What the fuck? Why would he give me his PIN? I don't even have his credit card. Just as the thought crossed his mind, he received a text.

Tallen will give you my card. Use it to buy your suit for the anniversary party and whatever else you need.

Des furrowed his brows, not comfortable taking money from his lover. He wasn't sure how to define the status of their relationship. He liked Othello, and even though they hadn't been together long, he could feel himself falling deeply in love with the man. But what about the things they needed to work on, like whether there was a future for them? It hadn't escaped his notice that neither had mentioned that he could get pregnant, and the night before, when they fucked, Othello hadn't used a condom.

The only plus to the situation was that Des kept up with his suppressants, but it was not foolproof, and he could still get pregnant. Although Othello hid his family dealings from him, he couldn't ignore the fact that his lover might be a killer. He was a doctor, a person who saved lives, and he was falling in love with someone who took them. Othello had yet to answer the question he'd posed at the beginning of their relationship. Des wasn't sure what he would do if the answer was yes. Could he walk away? He wasn't confident that Othello would leave the life he'd built for himself just because they were in love, and Des didn't think he could ask Othello to do it. Not when his own parents had forced him into a career he never wanted.

"I'm not going to solve that right now, but I might as well get out of bed."

After going through his morning ritual and a hot shower, Des walked into his bedroom with a towel wrapped around his waist and another drying his now shoulderlength hair, when he heard voices coming from the other room. Listening closely, he could pick out Bianca's voice and wondered who she was talking to and who she'd let into his apartment. Grabbing a pair of sweats from his dresser drawer, he pulled them on and went to see what was going on. He headed to the kitchen, where he heard the voices and saw Bianca talking with Tallen, who wasn't wearing a suit like normal but jeans and a button-down shirt with the sleeves rolled up to his elbows. Tallen was looking far more relaxed than Des had seen him before.

"What are you two doing here?" he asked.

"Des," Bianca said, rushing over and hugging him tightly. "You're awake. When did you get an assistant?"

Assistant? He quirked a brow, looking at Tallen over Bianca's shoulder. Tallen shrugged his shoulders, looking sheepish. *I suppose he couldn't say he works for a mob boss.* "I guess it slipped my mind," Des said, stepping out of her embrace.

"And I'm here to drop this off and take you shopping." Tallen reached into his pocket and handed Des the credit card. Not even looking at it, he put it in his pocket.

"When the hell did you get a black card?" Bianca asked.

"A what?" Des wasn't sure what the heck she was talking about.

"The credit card he just gave you is a black card, so either you started dealing drugs, became a high-paid escort, or you have a sugar daddy you forgot to tell me about; there's no way you'd have a card that has its own zip code."

"How is it the first two things you could think of is me selling drugs or my body?" Des asked, shaking his head. "Did you forget my grandfather left me money to take care of myself for life?" He didn't say anything about the sugar daddy part. Or he didn't consider Othello to be one.

"Cut the shit. Number one, you hate credit cards and prefer using the app because you said fewer things in your pockets so they won't hold you down. And two, you're hiding something from me, Desmond Ellington. Now, spill."

"I'm not hiding anything," Des said. Well, he kind of was. Besides Gray, he hadn't told anyone that he and Othello were dating, though she knew he'd wanted to ask the other man out. He loved Bianca. She was a good friend, but she tended to mother-hen him or ask questions he couldn't answer or wasn't ready to.

"Fine." She smiled, and Des knew it didn't bode well for him. "Tallen dear, where are you going shopping today?"

"Wherever the doc wants to go, I'm just there to carry his bag," Tallen responded.

She circled one of Tallen's arms, resting her head on his shoulder and looking adoringly at him. "Do you mind if I join you both?"

"Um...sure—I don't mind," he stuttered, unable to defend against her cuteness. Des had to admit Bianca had a way with people he often envied.

"Don't you think you should ask me if I want to go shopping?" Des snapped.

"You have no choice, Doc," Tallen said, looking at him with pleading eyes, practically saying Othello had given him an order he could not go against.

"Fine," he sighed. "Let me get something to eat, and we'll go."

"I brought you breakfast," Tallen said, pointing to the bag on the counter.

The logo on the bag told him Othello had instructed Tallen where to go. It was probably filled with his favorite sweets since it was from a bakery Des loved. He couldn't help but smile. They had a lot to work out about their relationship, but it seemed Othello knew him well and took far better care of him than he did himself.

"What's with that smile?" Bianca asked, standing beside him.

"My boyfriend knows me well," he mumbled.

"Boyfriend?" she asked, looking from him to Tallen, whose face grew pale, quickly picking up on what was happening.

"It's not him, but someone else."

"Wait, are you telling me you finally had sex?" she shrieked excitedly.

"Oh, for fuck's sake," Des said, just as Tallen mumbled something and ran out of the kitchen. "Look what you did. You scared off the poor guy."

"He's not the one you're fucking, so it doesn't matter." She grabbed his hand. "Now tell me, who is it? And be honest with me, that's his credit card, and Tallen isn't your assistant?"

"It's Othello Moor, the guy I told you I liked a few weeks back. Yes, it's his card, and no, Tallen isn't my

assistant; he's more of a friend."

"You've been a busy boy while I was away." She smiled, grabbing his hand and pulling him to the kitchen table. Bianca was a flight attendant who worked for a private company. When she wasn't wrapped up in a new boy toy, she was busy at work, where she'd been for the past few weeks. "Spill, I want to know all the tea."

He was about to speak, but his stomach rumbled. "Can I eat while we talk?"

"Of course, we don't want to waste your *boyfriend's* efforts, do we?"

"Does it sound weird that I call him that? It's like I'm in high school," he said shyly.

Bianca shrugged her shoulders. "Who the fuck cares? Call him what feels right to you, as long as he doesn't care." She got him a few pastries, and he made tea for both of them while he told her everything he could about Othello, leaving out the whole crime family thing. As he talked about his relationship with Othello, the more he realized his doubt was seeping away. Sure, they would have problems, and Othello's occupation might rear its ugly head one day, but he couldn't run at the first sign of trouble.

Othello had allowed him to walk away before they started out, and he was the one to pursue a relationship. With his mind made up, Des enjoyed his Baklava and pastel de Nata and hung out with his friend. Before they left for their shopping trip, he took Othello's credit card out of his pocket and set it on the counter. It was a nice gesture on his lover's part, but Othello didn't need to take care of him financially; he could do that on his own. Maybe if their relationship was deeper or they were married, he wouldn't mind.

Marriage. The word echoed in the back of his mind for the first time in his life, and he grinned when it didn't scare him in the least.

* * *

OTHELLO SIGHED TIREDLY, slumping down in his seat as the car drove out of the airport parking lot. He was running on so little sleep and couldn't wait to sink balls deep inside Des the way he was strung so tightly. But it would have to wait until later since they had his folks' anniversary party to attend. His meeting with the Zoraki Law clan went far better than he expected. It could also be that Othello and their leader once knew each other in college but had lost touch since Zoraki changed his name and clan. As a boon for taking out his competitor clan, Zoraki ensured that the authorities wouldn't be looking in his direction or even know that he was in the country. All records of his presence would disappear. Othello pulled out his cellphone and called his father, who had called while he was on the plane.

"Was your business trip fruitful?" Alessandro asked. "Of course, I'll tell you the details later."

"Good. On a different subject, tell me, Son, will I meet your young man tonight?" Alessandro chuckled.

"I still want to know who told you about the party," Othello said.

"I have my ways of getting information," Alessandro said. "And don't try to evade my question."

"You already know him." Othello shook his head. Alessandro had been curious about who he'd been seeing, but Othello had been mum about it, even going so far as to tell Tallen and Marco not to say anything. "It's Doctor

Desmond Ellington, or should I say former doctor." "Tell me it's the son and not the father." He laughed.

"You have jokes, old man." Othello smiled.

"Why shouldn't I joke around? I'm celebrating love, and both of my sons are also in love or starting to figure out what it is. Someday, I'll be a grandfather of one, hopefully, two."

"Don't you think you should wait a little for Emilia to have this baby before hoping she'll get pregnant so quickly?"

"Now look who's got jokes," Alessandro grumbled, making Othello laugh. "You know damn well I was talking about you."

"Papa, Des and I aren't ready for children. Plus, we have more pressing issues to take care of. Not to mention, I'm not sure if Des wants kids. He has his new life all planned out, and I don't want to delay it any further. If we ever get to that point, then we'll get there. If not, there's no rush."

"You were always a sensible child and even more so as

an adult. Anyway, your mother is calling for me. I'll see you tonight."

Throwing his phone on the seat next to him, Othello closed his eyes, hoping to get a quick nap before he got to his place. The conversation with Alessandro came back to him. Since he'd broken things off with Phillip, Othello hadn't thought about children. Did he want a couple of rugrats? Sure, but he wasn't kidding when he said he wasn't in a rush. Neither he nor

Des seemed to be in a hurry to have them, and they hadn't even talked about it. He was enjoying the pace of their relationship. There was no need to change what was working.

* * *

LATER THAT EVENING, Des and Tallen pulled up to The Gilded Orchid Hotel and got out of the car. Des stared at the large, imposing building as he tried to avoid the flashing cameras. Over the past few weeks, he'd come to know that Othello and his family were well known, but he hadn't expected the press to be here. Even with all his money, Des never considered Othello's family to be local celebrities. Seeing the press made him more nervous and excited at the same time.

He knew Othello was back since Tallen had told him, but he was on pins and needles since he would officially meet Maria and Alessandro. He brushed the creases out of his pants. He was grateful for Bianca, who'd helped him pick out his suit. Since Des wasn't up on fashion, according to Bianca, he must go with a famous Italian designer named Aurelio Di Firenze for a midnight-blue singlebreasted three-piece suit. He'd combed his hair back, pulling it in a low bun, showing off his features and diamond studs.

"Are you ready?" Tallen asked as they made their way up the stairs.

"Yeah," he said, carrying the gifts he'd bought, praying that Othello's parents would like them. "Do you think we can avoid the press?"

"Sure, come on, I know another way in."

Tallen led him to the back, bypassing the press, and entered through the kitchen, and no one batted an eye at them or asked them questions, so it was easy to guess that Tallen had done this before. In the past couple of days, he and Tallen had grown close. He didn't talk about Othello as much, but Des could see he truly respected the man. Des had found out that Tallen had a crush on a manager from Othello's club named Lucy, and they are slowly moving from being friends to something more.

When they walked into the hotel, Des couldn't stop staring at the grandeur of the design, a mixture of old world and new. The marbled floors, silver- and purpleaccented walls, and soaring ceiling, and the impressive crystal chandelier hanging in the center gave off a warm golden glow in the reception area. Tallen led him to the ballroom, which was equally elegant as the rest of the hotel, but what really caught Des's eyes was the handsome man who stood out among everyone in the entire place.

He was dressed in an all-black pinstripe suit except for the blood-red tie, which added a splash of color. He looked so good from head to toe that Des couldn't take his eyes off him. Othello was standing next to his parents and brother, with a beautiful pregnant woman sitting beside them. They were greeting the guests as they came in.

As if knowing he was being stared at, Othello looked away from the person who had walked over to his group, and their eyes connected. Des wanted to rush over and kiss the ever-loving daylights out of him, but he held back. "Hey, Doc, you should go over and say hello to Miss Maria and the don. I can take the gifts you bought," Tallen said, causing him to look away from Othello.

"Uh...that would be great, thanks." He handed the neatly wrapped boxes over to Tallen."Do I look good enough to meet the parents?"

Tallen smiled. "You look better than good. Plus, with the way the boss is staring at you, I'm sure he's going to drag you to some dark corner and devour you whole."

Des smiled shyly hearing that and looked down, hoping his cheeks weren't flushed at how happy the thought made him.

"Go on over. I'm sure he's wondering what's taking you so

long." Tallen patted him on his shoulder, chuckling as he walked away, leaving Des alone. Just as he was about to walk over, someone else interrupted him.

"We meet again, or should I say formally, meet for the first time."

Des turned to the person who had stepped up beside him and couldn't for the life of him figure out who the person was or why he was talking to him.

"I'm sorry, but I think you've confused me with someone else," Des said.

"I feel hurt, Doctor Ellington. Ah, that's right. You aren't a doctor anymore." The man grinned, showing his pretty white teeth.

"Okay, now that you know my name, who the hell are you?" Des didn't raise his voice because of where they were.

"I'm Cassio Ricci," the man said, and Des shrugged when nothing came to him. "We met at the Celeste Grand Plaza a few weeks ago."

"I hate to be rude, but I still don't know who you are," Des told him.

"That's fair," Cassio said, moving in front of him and blocking Des's view of Othello. "How about we take the time to get to know each other?"

Des smiled, really trying not to scream and get the fuck out of his face because he needed to make a good impression on Othello's parents. Although he didn't get along with his own parents, he was taught manners, and it was rude to enter a person's home and not speak to them. Even though it was not the Romanos' home, it was their event.

"Can we do that some other time? I need to greet the Romanos."

"What a coincidence, so do I. Should we go together?" He smirked. Des really hated his smug expression for some odd reason.

"Do as you wish." Des stepped around him.

As he walked away, he felt a hand touch the small part of his back, making him flinch, but Des didn't move away immediately because he didn't want to draw attention to them.

However, when he locked eyes on Othello, there was no missing the storm brewing in his honey eyes or the ticking in his chiseled jaw. Clearing his throat, Des moved a little faster, wishing the Romano family had stood at the door to greet their guests and not at the far end of the large hall.

Fuck, I'm going to have to find a way to soothe the angry beast.

* * *

A FEW MINUTES earlier

"Oh, that's interesting," Iago said, catching Othello's attention. "When did Tallen and the doctor who operated on you start dating? I thought he was into Lucy."

Othello scanned the room, and his eyes landed on Tallen. They instantly shifted to the gorgeous beauty dressed in dark blue that made his eyes sparkle in the golden glow of the ballroom.

"Are you sure he's dating Tallen?" Othello asked Iago, not taking his eyes off Des.

"How else would he get an invitation? I didn't see his name on the guest list."

"What if he's here with someone else?"

"You think?" Iago said thoughtfully. "Oh, I think you're right. I mean, look at the way Underboss Ricci is eyeing him. Or maybe he's doing them both. I didn't think the doctor had it in him to be a tease."

Othello ignored Iago's words and continued watching Des. He could tell his lover was nervous and wanted to go over and ease his worries, but he'd promise Maria he'd stay and greet the guests. However, Othello became irritated when Cassio stepped beside Des and moved to block his view so he couldn't tell what they were discussing.

Fucking asshole.

A minute or two later, they began to move through the crowd. Othello had put his hand in his pocket, hiding his fist, when Cassio placed a hand on Des's back. Then he looked at Othello, smirking as if daring him to do something. But he had to keep his cool for now.

The second they made their way over, Othello reached out and pulled Des into his arms, kissing him before his lover could speak. He heard gasps around him as Des's arms circled his neck, and he cupped the back of Des's head, deepening their kiss.

Tasting and feeling his lover's lips moving against his felt like coming home after a very long trip, not a couple of days. He wanted to continue kissing Des but knew they had to stop because of where they were, but with one last lick of Des's mouth, he promised that he was going to fuck him raw until he couldn't walk later tonight.

"What took you so long to get to me?" Othello asked, watching his lips and waiting for Des to open his eyes and catch his breath.

"Sorry for the delay," he responded breathily.

He smiled, leaning back, and gently pinched his chin. "It's okay; it just means I'll punish you later." He chuckled when Des's face turned as red as his tie.

"Do you plan on holding the man hostage all night long?" Maria said, and he could hear a slight chuckle in her voice.

"You know," Iago said next to him, "you could have just told me he was with you and not let me speculate."

Othello looked at his brother, grinning. "What would be the fun in that?"

Iago rolled his eyes, chuckling. "Asshole." "Iago," Maria admonished softly. "Sorry, Mama."

Othello was about to speak when he heard a throat clearing. He looked up, noticing that Cassio was still standing there.

"Underboss Ricci, pardon my son," Maria said. "As you can see, he forgets himself when he is with his lover."

"You have nothing to apologize for, Lady Maria." Ricci smiled, making Maria giggle like a young schoolgirl. However, despite his complimentary words, Othello could see the tension coming off Maria's body in waves.

"Yes," Othello said, looking at Cassio. "Pardon my rudeness."

"I don't blame you." His eyes drifted to Des, who was in his arms. "If I were you, I wouldn't let him out of my sight even for a minute." He looked at Othello daringly. "Who knows, someone might try to steal him away. We wouldn't want that to happen again."

Othello smiled, even though he wanted to punch the man's face or put a bullet between his eyes. His arm tightened around Des, and he felt his possessive nature take over. "I doubt that would happen. Unlike most, Des is not easily swayed."

"I have no idea what you two are talking about, but I'd rather you not involve me. And I'd rather you both not talk about me as if I'm an object," Des added just as Cassio spoke.

"We shall see," Cassio said, then turned his attention to Maria and Alessandro. "Boss Greco and Ricci send their regards, congratulations, and gifts for being unable to attend the festivities. They had to attend a business meeting."

"It's quite alright, and thank your bosses for me," Alessandro said.

He nodded and then looked at Othello and Des before walking away.

"You're going to have to watch your back and protect your guy," Iago whispered in Othello's ear. "You don't want him seducing the doc like he did Phillip."

That shit won't happen again, Othello mentally vowed. He

wasn't sure what the future held for him and Des, but he'd kill Cassio first before the man had a chance with Des.

"Are you going to hold the doctor all night or introduce him to the family," Alessandro said.

"Don't you already know him?" Othello grumbled.

"As your doctor, not as your lover," Maria said. "Now, use some of the manners I taught you."

"Yes, Mama." He smiled, taking Des's hand and leading him over to his parents, then Iago, and lastly, Emilia, who Des seemed interested in. He would have been jealous if he didn't know how much his lover liked riding his cock and screaming his name.

He watched and listened to Des talk to Emilia about her pregnancy. He didn't know if his lover realized it, but he was using the concerned doctor's voice. Sometime during the festivities, during the speeches and dancing, Des disappeared and quickly returned with a large glass of ice, which he handed to Emilia before coming to Othello.

"I don't want to alarm anyone, but Emilia is going into labor. She's been having contractions fifteen minutes apart. She thought it was Braxton-Hicks, but her contractions are now ten minutes apart. I've already called the hospital and told them we're on our way."

Othello listened and didn't overreact because Des explained everything calmly. In a split second, he knew what had made him a good doctor.

"Othello, did you hear me?" he asked sternly.

"Um...yes."

"Go, let the family know, and send the baby's father my way. He needs to be by her side."

Othello's brows furrowed when he noticed something was off with Des, he was worrying his bottom lip like he always did when he was nervous or thinking deeply about something.

"What's wrong?"

Des sighed and looked at Emilia. "She's been having contractions all day but didn't tell anyone because she

didn't want to ruin the party." "But?" Othello prodded.

"I don't know if I'm overthinking, and I'm not an obstetrician, but I don't like how pale she looks. We need to get her to the hospital quickly so the doctors can get a better look at her."

Othello glanced at Emilia and noticed her normally pink face was a bit ashen, even with makeup on. "Okay, I'll get the family."

He kissed Des on the forehead and left to find his family. It didn't take long to find Alessandro and Maria, giving them the news, but no one knew where Iago was, nor was he picking up his phone. Othello's only choice was to text him and get Emilia to the hospital; hopefully, he'd be there before the baby was born.

He better be dying, or I am going to kick his ass.

ACT IV

"Reputation is an idle and most false imposition; oft got without merit, and lost without deserving."
Iago (Act 2, Scene 3)

Des kept talking and encouraging Emilia on the way to the hospital, which should have been the father's job. When he was introduced to Emilia, Des immediately noticed that something was wrong and struck up a conversation with her. When Emilia mentioned she hadn't felt the baby move since her last checkup a couple of days ago, Des found that concerning, along with her pale features.

"Des, it hurts," Emilia panted. She gripped his fingers tightly, and he prayed to every god in the universe that she wouldn't break them.

"I know, we're almost to the hospital," he told her. "Breathe for me, okay."

She nodded and let out a slow breath. Des looked at Maria, who had been dabbing the sweat off Emilia's face. Othello was driving with Alessandro, who was a Mondaymorning quarterback. Des wanted to ask where Iago was, but his curiosity had to be put on hold for now.

Des focused on Emilia, who needed his help. Rubbing her stomach, he was grateful when they finally pulled up to the hospital. Des didn't wait for it to come to a complete stop. He hopped out, grabbed a wheelchair, and pushed it over as they helped Emilia out of the car. They hurried into the hospital, and Des sighed in relief when a familiar face came over to him.

"Doctor Ellington, are you back?" Chloe asked.

"Not quite. I called and informed the staff I was bringing a patient who was eight and a half months pregnant. Contractions went from thirty to five minutes apart. I was able to slow them down, but I don't know for how long. Her water hasn't broken..." Chloe followed beside him, getting Emilia to a bed. Des continued rattling off what he'd observed all night.

Des issued some commands when he noticed two other people in the room. Chloe worked quickly, setting up the fetal monitor, and Des went into action. He did his check and was surprised when he saw that they were monochorionic twins sharing the same placenta.

Fuck.

"Emilia, you're having twins?" he said, looking at her in shock.

"Yes," she whispered, seeming ashamed, which Des couldn't understand.

"They'll be happy when they find out," he comforted her.

"Okay, Ellington, step back," someone said to him. "You're no longer a doctor here."

Des ignored whoever it was and continued to perform the ultrasound because his gut was telling him something more serious was going on. It didn't take Des long to see the problem. A partial placental abruption. Des wasn't an OB and would rather have a second opinion just to be sure.

"Nurse Chloe, who's the OBGYN on call tonight?"

"That would be Doctor Stephen," she responded.

"Get him down here, now," he growled.

"Des, is everything okay?"

He looked at Emilia and tried to smile. He didn't want to lie to her or scare her. "We need to contact your doctor; by the look of it, you might be spending the night."

"Is it serious?" she asked. "Are the babies alright?"

"The twins are fine, but they are just putting a lot of strain on your body. I'll make sure things don't get worse," he reassured her.

"Someone called for an OB?" a handsome doctor Des had never seen before entered the room.

"Yeah, that would be me," Des responded, explaining who he was and Emilia's symptoms.

"Let me take a look," Doctor Stephen said, and Des stepped aside.

Des held Emilia's hand and watched Stephen work. It also didn't take him long for him to confirm Des's diagnosis.

"You're right." He looked at Emilia and explained everything that her placenta was pulling away from her uterine wall, that was putting a strain on not only her but the babies as well. "The good thing is it's minor. Both you and the babies are stable. With Doctor Ellington's quick thinking, he slowed your contractions down. However, I wouldn't advise sending you home. We will need to monitor you for the rest of your pregnancy. The other option is we induce you, and you give birth tonight."

"I'd rather you take the babies out now," Emilia said, not taking the time to think about it. "I'm ready to meet my babies."

Stephen gave her a calm smile that could melt ice. "Very well. Although the abruption is minor, and most doctors would rather go with a vaginal birth, I'd rather err on the side of caution and recommend a Cesarean."

"Okay," Emilia sighed, relaxing for the first time since Des brought her in.

"It will be a couple of hours before we get you into surgery." He glanced at Des. "As the father..."

"I'm not the father," Des said as Emilia spoke. "He's not the father."

"Oh." Stephen chuckled.

"I'm a family friend. The baby's father should be here soon," he said, remembering everyone was outside waiting, probably about to jump out of their skin. "I'll inform the family of what's happening. I'm sure they are anxious."

Just as he was about to leave, Emilia grabbed his hand. "Can you be in the operating room with me?"

"What about Iago?"

"Right now, he's not my main concern," she snapped.

"I—" He was about to tell her no, but her anxious expression returned, stopping him. "Okay."

"One more thing. Don't tell the family about the twins," she smiled. "Iago and I wanted to surprise them, so each time we gave them a photo of the ultrasound, it was of one baby at a time so they wouldn't know."

"You got it." He leaned down and kissed her forehead. "I'll be right back."

"How are Emilia and the baby?" Maria asked the instant he walked into the waiting room, her anxiety seeping off her in waves.

"They are doing fine. But the doctor is going to induce her, and she'll be giving birth sometime tonight." He explained the complications, which was why the doctor wanted to perform a Cesarean. As he spoke, his eyes searched for Othello and Alessandro, wondering where the two men had gone off to. "Where's Othello and your husband?"

Maria's face changed from worry to anger. "They're talking with Iago."

Once more, Des wanted to know what the fuck was going on but knew he had to put things aside. "The doctor will be out to speak with you all in a few minutes."

"Tell me something, Mister Ellington," Maria said.

"Des or Desmond, please," he said gently. "People will think you're talking to my father."

"Des," she smiled. "Will Maria and the baby be okay?"

"I won't give you false hope and say everything is certain. Although it was caught in time, factors can still occur."

"Then, can I ask a favor?"

"Sure," he responded before his brain and mouth could communicate with each other.

"Can you be the one to deliver the baby?"

"Uh..."

"I know the doctors here are good, but you saved my son, and now I'm asking you to do the same for my grandchild and his mother. It's selfish of me, I know. Othello said you no longer want to be a surgeon, and here I am asking you to do the one thing you probably didn't want to do. But I trust you, Des, especially with the people that are most dear to me."

"I...uh...I..." Des stuttered.

"Doctor Ellington?" A voice calling his name saved him from answering Maria.

"Yes," he said, excusing himself from Maria's side to join Stephen's side.

"I was wondering if you could assist me with the delivery?"

Des stared at the handsome doctor, and a certain expression in his eyes told Des that the good doctor had been listening to his conversation with Maria.

"I'm not sure that's a good idea," he said. "I haven't held a scalpel in months."

"If it's less than six months, I'm sure you'll do fine. Besides, I think it would put my patient at ease to have someone she knows deliver her baby. Let's leave the handholding to the father or another close family member." He winked.

"I guess you're right," Des said, chuckling. Heading back to Maria, he told her he'd do as she asked, which made her happy. He led Maria to Emilia and returned to the waiting room, surprised to find Stephen still there.

"I'll get you some scrubs," Stephen said.

"That would be great, thanks," Des absently responded, looking down the hall, hoping Othello would return. Sighing, he looked away and caught Stephen's eye, noticing that he was staring at him. "Is there something else, Doctor Stephen?"

"You're not at all what I imagined," Stephen told him.

"I'm not sure what you mean." Des furrowed his brows.

"I was told you're cold, rude, but the devilishly handsome part they got right." He smiled. "But you're a damn good doctor. Maybe you should consider coming back. If you haven't noticed, the nurses miss you and some of the doctors as well."

Is this guy flirting with me right now? "I..." He was cut off just as he was about to tell Stephen he was dating someone.

"Don't get me wrong, I'm not coming on to you," he said quickly.

"Okay, so what do you want?" Des folded his arms over his chest, staring the man down.

"I'm just saying that people have you all wrong, and I can't wait to do this delivery with you, Doctor Ellington." He left before Des could say anything.

"What a weird guy," Des mumbled. He was about to go be with Maria and Emilia when Chloe came over and handed him a set of scrubs.

"It's good to have you back with us, Doctor Ellington," she said.

"I'm not really back, but thanks." He smiled. "It's good to see you, too," he said and went to get changed, hoping that by the time he was done, Othello and the rest would be back.

* * *

"ARE YOU FUCKING KIDDING ME, IAGO," Othello growled, trying his best not to slap the snot out of his brother.

"I didn't expect her to go into labor," Iago slurred.

Othello pinched the bridge of his nose, so frustrated with his brother. He was trying to figure out why he thought it was a good idea to show up to the hospital drunk, high as a fucking kite, and smelling like cheap perfume from the bitch he was fucking in one of the hotel rooms.

"You didn't expect her to go into labor! She's almost nine months pregnant. Since the day we found out she was pregnant, I told you to stay by her side. I begged you to stop fucking around on Emilia, and on our parents' anniversary, you bring your mistress to the party, and for what? A quick fuck while the woman you claim to love is in pain!"

"Alright, stop lecturing me! We can't all be fucking perfect like you, Othello," he shouted. "I made a mistake, okay, and I promise I'll make it right."

"That's what you said months ago," Othello snapped.

"Hey, lay off him," Roderigo shouted.

"Why the fuck are you here?" Othello yelled, wanting to punch a hole in the man's face.

"Does it make you jealous that he wants me here, Moor?" Roderigo countered.

"What the fu..."

"Othello, that's enough," Alessandro said, stopping him from saying more. "We need to get some coffee into him and clean him up. I'm sure Emilia is worried about him and doesn't need the added stress right now. I'll go and get him some coffee."

Othello nodded, watching the old man leave, grabbing Roderigo with him before the man could protest.

"She's not, you know," Iago whispered, his head down.

"Emilia turned down my proposal." "When?" Othello asked.

"The day I took her to buy a ring, she said she didn't want to marry me," Iago cried. "She's leaving me."

"Do you blame her?" Othello scolded, recalling Iago's excitement that he would finally propose to Emilia. But that was a long time ago. Had he been holding on to the hurt for so long? "And you had to make it better by inviting your lover."

"I didn't invite her. She just showed up," he explained, looking up at him. "O, I love Emilia, I really do. It's just I can't seem to do right by her. But she's also changed."

"What do you mean?"

Iago shrugged. "I don't know how to explain it. She won't talk to me or let me touch her."

"Then maybe you need to let Emilia go or figure your shit out."

"You're right," Iago said after a few moments. "But I can't. She's my heart and the reason for everything I do." Othello said nothing. Love was a crazy thing, but one thing he was sure of was that if a person really cared about someone, fucking another person wasn't the way to show it.

"He's going to cheat on you," Iago said out of nowhere.

"What the fuck are you talking about?"

"That doctor. He's good-looking, fuck, bordering on pretty. If I were into guys, I would have..." He paused and cleared his throat when Othello growled, warning him to tread carefully. "Anyway, you need to watch him carefully. I saw the way he and Cassio were eye-fucking each other. It's going to be the Phillip situation all over again."

"Des isn't anything like Phillip. Don't talk about shit you know nothing about," Othello snarled.

"Hey, don't get mad at me. I'm just telling you what I saw tonight."

"Was that before or after you were drunk off your ass?" he snorted.

Iago stood and moved closer to the window. "Fine, don't believe me. I'm just trying to be a good brother and protect your heart. But mark my words, he will fuck around on you. Take it from someone who can spot one of their own."

Othello didn't want to listen to more of Iago's ramblings and was thankful when Alessandro returned with a large coffee for Iago. Not saying a word to his father, he left them alone and went to find Des to get some information.

When he found his lover, he was standing by the nurses' station dressed in scrubs, chatting and smiling with another doctor. Othello stood to the side and watched his lover, who seemed very at ease, as he tried to not let Iago's words affect him. Othello wanted to say he was sure Des would never step out on him, but even he couldn't be certain.

Fuck, what the hell am I thinking? Des wouldn't do that to me. He's nothing like Phillip. Unlike that bastard, Des trusts and cares for me.

Pushing that out of his mind, he walked over to Des.

"How is Emilia?" he asked, getting his lover's attention as he gently slipped an arm around his waist.

"Oh, you're here, finally," Des said, turning in his embrace and ignoring the doctor and nurses he was talking to. "She'll be fine soon. We're about to operate in another hour or so. Doctor Stephen is simply waiting for her to relax."

Othello frowned, not hiding his concern for Des. "You're going into the operating room?"

"Just this once. The women in your family made a request, and I found it hard to reject." Othello smiled. "You're such a softy." "Guilty." Des chuckled.

He pinched Des's chin softly, lifting his face to his. "Are you sure about this?"

"Yes, I am. It's just once."

"Okay." He leaned down and kissed Des on the forehead, hugging him flush against him.

This was the difference between Des and Phillip. Des would do things for people out of the kindness of his heart, while Phillip was selfish and required payment at the end. *No wonder I'm falling in love with him.*

* * *

DES ENTERED the operating room and waited for the nurse to finish gowning and gloving him up. While listening to the nurse's update, his mind drifted just a little. The last time he had been in the operating room, his patient died, and although he was partially settled with the thought that he had done everything he could, he was still nervous. But he couldn't deny the excited emotion coursing through him like he'd always felt whenever he was in the operating room, which shocked him.

Fuck, are my parents right?

Des didn't get a chance to dwell on that thought since the nurse had finished speaking, and the room grew silent. He noticed everyone, even Emilia, lying on the operating table numb from the waist down, was looking at him.

He locked eyes with Maria, who had taken Iago's place since Emilia was adamant Iago was not allowed anywhere near her or the babies. No one argued or tried to convince her to change her mind and did whatever she requested. But Des knew that Iago was still in the hospital waiting for news about his children.

"Are you alright, Doctor Ellington?" Doctor Stephen asked.

"Yes," he said, clearing his throat. "Let's get started."

Moving over to the table, he extended a hand. "Scalpel."

He swallowed, running a finger along the dull edge of the scalpel when handed to him. It felt just as normal as it did when he held a paintbrush. And just as when he made the first brushstroke, Des made his cut and focused on bringing the two healthy babies into the world.

* * *

OTHELLO LEANED AGAINST THE DOOR, his hands in his pockets, staring at Des gently rocking one of the twins. It was hours later, and to his surprise, he was an uncle of two boys, Antonio and Tybalt.

"The way you're watching him makes me wonder if you're changing your mind about the whole not-having-akid thing," Alessandro said, standing beside him.

"Maybe," Othello said, not refuting his father's words. After Phillip, he had closed off his heart and mind to love and wanting children, but with Des in his life, he was walking back on that feeling.

Des looked good holding the baby, and he could see Des pregnant with his child, who would be born with either of their features. As if hearing his thoughts, Des raised his gaze and smiled as their eyes met.

"He fits in well with our family," Alessandro told Othello. "I liked him from the night I met him." Alessandro squeezed his shoulders. "He's good for you, Othello. Don't let him go."

Alessandro walked over to Des, who handed the baby over to the giddy grandfather and then came over to stand in front of Othello.

"How does it feel to be an uncle?" Des asked.

Othello grabbed the front of Des's scrubs, pulling him flush against his body. "You did good tonight. Are you tired?"

Des turned in his embrace, pressing his head back into Othello's chest. "I'm exhausted, but seeing that makes me happy. Tonight also made me remember why I'm not cut out to be a doctor. It's a good profession, but not for me."

"I want you to be happy, Tesoro, so I will give you anything you want," Othello told him.

"Thank you."

Othello leaned down and kissed behind his ear.

"We've never talked about it, but do you want kids?" Des asked.

Othello looked at Tybalt and Antonio, who were being gushed over by their grandparents. "Maybe one day, but not now."

He might have opened his heart to wanting kids again, but not until he found out who was working against him. "Okay, let's wait until we're both ready," Des said, then looked up at him. "As wonderful as all of this is, I need you now. Take me home."

Leaning down, he gently kissed him on his lips. "Okay."

Saying nothing to the family, he got Des home in record time, naked and screaming his name before the sun hit the sky.

* * *

A FEW WEEKS LATER, Des and Alessandro met with

Devin as they toured the auction house, checking the crates and ensuring the weapons would be well hidden and secure when they shipped.

The art auction was a front for the shipping and selling of weapons. The art would be sent to the proper recipient, but someone from the organization would be there to deliver the guns to whoever bought them. At least three crates were going to Japan.

The priceless art and artifacts were obtained legally and would bring in enough funds, but the weapons were already bought and paid for, expanding the family's wealth.

"Are you sure you don't want me to stay?" Alessandro asked. "We can come up with a new plan."

"No," Othello said. "We've had this shooting hanging over our heads for long enough. I'm frustrated we still haven't found anything. We need them to make a move."

"Alright," Alessandro sighed. "It's going to be hard pulling Maria away from the twins."

Othello smirked. "She is enamored with them."

"I just wish Iago would get his shit together," Alessandro said heavily.

In the weeks since the babies' birth, Emilia had told the family that she and Iago were over, but she would not stop him from being a part of the twins' lives. Othello couldn't say he blamed Emilia, since she'd put up with his shit for a long time. They were co-parenting, but Othello knew Iago was trying to get Emilia back.

"He will," Othello said, trying to assure his father.

"Take care of him while we're gone."

"Of course."

"Alright, let's get this done. We still need to head to the docks after this to send out the shipment."

They spent the next few hours going through their stock. When they left the auction house to head to the port to check on the freight, the sun had just gone down. Since the workers had already gone home for the day, no one was at the docks but them.

"I want a thorough check," Othello said to Marco and Tallen, along with Vito and Nico, two of his other men who had come with them.

"Yes, boss. " They separated, and Othello scanned the area as a strange feeling crawled up his back.

"What's wrong, Son? You have that look in your eyes."

"Something doesn't feel right." He scanned the dark expanse of the docks. "Get back to the car."

Just as he said the words to Alessandro, the metal clanking of a container echoed throughout the silent docks, followed by the screech of tires. Othello's instinct kicked in.

"Get down," he barked, grabbing Alessandro by the arm and hurrying them both behind a stack of pallets just as a hail of bullets sounded throughout the docks. The gunfire reverberated through the air. Othello could tell his people were returning fire.

"Another fucking ambush," Othello growled, crouching low. "I'm getting sick and tired of this shit." "You and me both," Alessandro said.

"Are you carrying?"

"Of course."

"Good. Stay hidden," he ordered, pulling out his handgun, his grip steady. Unfazed by the chaos, Othello thrust himself into the chaos, returning fire at anyone he didn't recognize. This time, the men who attacked them were bold and did not wear masks, but still, Othello couldn't tell who they were or which family they came from.

All he knew was they weren't cops. Ducking behind one of the freight cars, he could feel his adrenaline pumping as the bullets ricocheted off the metal, but he had to take the chance to peek around the corner, hoping to figure out what the fuck was going on.

Several figures moved in the darkness, some hiding behind a few shipping containers. There was a rapid exchange of bullets, and that was when he noticed the scorpion tattoo on the side of one of the men's faces.

The last time he saw that tattoo was a year ago, when he and his people had a run-in with the Russian mafia, but he was certain they'd squashed any beef they might have had, so he pushed that thought away. No, this had to be someone else making it look like the Russians.

"Boss, what the fuck is going on?" Nico, one of his men, asked, moving to stand beside him.

"Your guess is as good as mine," he said.

"Someone must have leaked and told them we would be here?" Nico growled, firing a couple of shots into the darkness, hoping he'd hit his target.

Othello smirked. "It doesn't matter. None of them are leaving here alive." He looked in the direction of where Alessandro was. He was guarding himself well, but Othello didn't feel good about that. They were cornered and out in the open. "Nico, go and cover the don. Don't let anything happen to him."

"You got it." Othello covered Nico as he trudged through the multitude of bullets and ran to Alessandro's side. Raising his gun, Othello moved from out of his hiding spot just as he saw Vito get hit, collapsing, clutching his side. As far as he could tell, that was their first and only casualty.

Watching the scene, that feeling that something wasn't right nagged at him. He counted ten men to his five, himself included, and the odds weren't in their favor, but they weren't aiming for them or specifically him. Othello was sure there were more hidden, waiting for some signal.

The crack of gunfire continued to ring out, and a shout came from where Alessandro was hidden. Othello looked over to his father's side, as if he could see clearly in the dark. His heart stopped in his chest when he saw a figure standing over him and another lying beside him. There was a gun pointed at Alessandro's head.

Without hesitation, Othello raised his gun, finger pressing the trigger, shooting the attacker, dropping him. But Othello didn't let his finger off the gun's pulse until he was beside Alessandro.

"Are you hurt?" he asked worriedly, checking his father over.

"No, Nico blocked me in time," Alessandro said.

"Dammit, Nico," he cursed and checked on the man who had protected his father with his life. He thanked all the gods he was still alive. He was shot in the back, but they needed to get him to the hospital, or he could die.

"These guys aren't professionals," Alessandro said.

"No." He looked at the guy he'd killed. "Maybe he was, but these fuckers don't know who they are messing with."

"Go finish this up," Alessandro said. "I'll stay here with Nico."

"Are you sure?" Othello asked, worried.

"Yeah, we fight for family, just as they will for us, Othello. Remember that." Then he grinned. "Plus, I called for backup."

"You sly, old man," he mumbled.

"Idiots will always underestimate us. I know you're out for blood, but keep at least one alive. That way, we can get some answers."

"I make no fucking promises." No further words needed to be said. Othello reloaded his gun, stood, and aimed it at anyone who moved left or right. He hoped to capture one alive, but when someone aimed a gun at anyone deemed precious, they had to fucking die.

He fired a couple more shots, taking out two men. "The backup needs to get here quickly," he mumbled to himself. As if hearing him, the roar of engines filled the air, and two black SUVs tore onto the pier. Othello smiled as their headlights cut through the night. Before the vehicles stopped, their men spilled out, weapons drawn, turning the tide in the fight.

"Cover me," Othello shouted to Alessandro, then moved from behind the pallets, with his father giving him cover. Othello sprinted across the dock, moving behind the freight cars. It might have been his imagination or the night's light playing tricks on him, but he saw something shiny peeking out from one of the containers near the chaos.

Othello reached the side of a container, breathing heavily. He peered around the corner and saw one of the remaining gunmen reloading behind a stack of barrels. Without hesitation, he lined up his shot and pulled the trigger, shooting the gun out of his hand, then ran forward, barreling into him, bringing him down. Othello growled, raining down punch after punch, not letting up.

Blood splattered on his clothes and face, but he paid it no mind. He was too angry to care about his appearance. While using a gun was fine, Othello preferred smashing his opponent's face in. It helped get rid of his anger.

"Othello, stop," Alessandro yelled as the other men pulled him off the guy. "You'll kill him, and we won't get any answers."

Othello didn't struggle, but pulled away from his men and moved over to the guy who was moaning and groaning on the ground, the only sound that echoed on the pier that had been ablaze with gunfire and noise only seconds before. But he didn't pay the man any attention and grabbed him by his shirt collar, pulling him up.

"Who sent you?" he growled in the fucker's face.

The guy gave him a bloody smile, which made Othello want to hit him more, but he held back. Upon closer inspection of the tattoo on his face, Othello could tell that it was fake.

Amateurs, he mentally sneered.

"Do you really think I won't kill you?" he said in a deadly calm voice and slapped the guy in the face. Othello dragged him to where the chaos was, letting him see all of his friends lying dead on the ground. Othello enjoyed seeing the fear in his eyes. "You will tell me who sent you, or I promise you, after the torture I will bring you, you will wish for death." He remained silent, and Othello's patience was ready to pop until Vito spoke up.

"Boss, I recognize this guy," he said, pointing to one of the dead men.

"Yeah, who is he?" Othello asked.

"He's part of Falcon's gang. He was with me and the others outside, watching the door the night you got shot," Vito explained.

Othello looked at Alessandro. "It seems I pegged him wrong. Well, I won't be making that mistake again." Pulling out his gun, he pointed it to the man's head. Just as he was about to pull the trigger, he heard a jingly ringtone. Othello tilted his head, and Tallen ran over, searching through the guy's jacket, then pulled out his cellphone. "Say the wrong thing, and I will kill you on the spot."

Tallen swiped the screen, answering the call. "Sorento, what took you so long to fucking answer?" Falcon's sarcastic tone said on the other side of the line.

"I—I had to make sure they were dead," Sorento responded.

"Is Moor dead? Did you make sure?" Falcon asked.

Sorento looked at Othello, who quirked a brow. "Yeah, I killed him myself."

Falcon laughed. "You did good, Sorento. It's a shame. I really liked Moor, but he's not one of us. Plus, he was too fucking cocky for his own good." Falcon sighed. "Make sure our guys clean up the mess. We don't want evidence coming back to us. Bring Moor's body to me. I'm at the main house." Falcon hung up, not leaving room for further discussion.

Othello looked at Sorento. "Your boss really is an idiot," he said, then pulled the trigger, taking the man out and letting his body drop to the ground.

He looked at Alessandro. "I'm dealing with this tonight. Do you have any objections?"

"None, but you realize he's not working alone," his father said. "You're the boss now."

Othello nodded. "Don't worry, I won't kill him yet. I get the feeling he won't talk so easily."

Scanning the pier, Othello noticed most of their cars were

gone and suspected they had taken the injured to get patched up. Their cleaning crew was already fast at work. While he was on the phone, they already had the bodies squared away, ready to be taken to Falcon.

They couldn't hide the bullet holes in the containers, but getting rid of the pallets was easy—just dumping them in the water. Some of his crew were hit, but not to the point of death; however, he needed to be sure.

"How many of our guys were hit?" he asked.

"Two," Vito answered. "Marco took Nico to get treated since he was the worst one. Too bad the doctor isn't at the hospital anymore; he could have patched him up."

At Des's mention, Othello figured he wouldn't see his lover tonight. He couldn't let the Falcon situation sit for too long. It also meant that he could get answers about what was happening. He'd underestimated Falcon, but Falcon also didn't know him well enough.

"Get our people to do a better job with cleanup. We don't want to leave any evidence we were here." "Yes, boss," Vito said.

"Tallen, call up the crew and tell them to prepare for a hunt." Othello grinned, licking his teeth, feeling like a feral beast. He might not end up having a romantic night with Des, but once he got his answers, he'd be so fucking horny he would be sure to fuck him so good that his little doctor wouldn't be able to get out of bed for a week.

SCENE II

DES

"*A*re you sure my parents can't get their hands on my money?" Des asked Erin.

The money his grandfather had given him was now close to one hundred million dollars, thanks to some keen financial advice from Othello.

"Yes, for the fifth time," she groaned. "Why are you worried about this? We covered all of our bases."

"I'm being annoying, I know, but my parents are not to be trifled with. Look how easily my father evaded the allegations; from the looks of it, he's even gone up in the polls."

"I thought you weren't paying attention to the election," Erin said.

"I wasn't until they asked to see me again. This time without my boyfriend," he sneered, remembering hearing the slight distaste in his father's tone when referring to Othello.

"Speaking of which," Erin said, smiling. "When will you let me meet the guy you can't stop talking about?" "Soon." Des stood and grabbed his helmet. "Othello's pretty busy lately with the auction coming up."

"By the way, I got my invitation for it." She picked up the black-and-silver envelope off her desk, holding it in her fingers. "Thanks for getting me in."

"No problem, you're my friend and lawyer. I'd do anything for you, just like how you helped me." Looking at his watch, he headed toward the door. "I need to head to the store and get something for dinner."

"Alright, I'll see you next week for the other stuff." She met him at the door. "You're doing the right thing, Des."

"I've wavered on getting started long enough. Being in the operating room made me realize that although I loved and hated being a surgeon, I prefer being an artist. It's time I opened my studio. It's just fucking scary as hell."

"You're not doing this alone. You have me, your lawyer, and broker, not to mention your friends and lover boy. I'm sure once you tell them, they'll be there to support you."

"I know." He hugged her quickly and then left. Soon, he wouldn't be able to ride his motorcycle. The weather was getting colder, but Des loved feeling the cold wind gliding over him.

He pulled up to the grocery store, took off his helmet, and was about to put it away when he felt his cellphone vibrate in his jacket pocket. He smiled, seeing Othello's name.

"Did you miss me, Mister Moor?"

Othello chuckled, then sighed. "You have no idea."

Des relaxed on his bike after hearing that tone in Othello's voice. "I'm not seeing you tonight, am I?"

"Sorry, Tesoro, some work stuff came up. I may not see you for a few days."

He was a bit disappointed, but Des could do nothing about it. Since the birth of the twins, Othello had been working more since he was doing his and Iago's jobs, even though Des had no idea what that was.

"I'll send someone to watch over you while I'm gone."

"You don't need to do that," Des told him. "I'm a big boy, and I can take care of myself. Besides, I will probably be too busy on my end. Erin got all the paperwork I need to get the studio started."

"Okay. Call me if you need me, Des."

I always need you, Des wanted to say but said, "Alright," instead.

They ended their call, and Des was about to put his helmet on, head home, and order takeout since he wouldn't see Othello, when a sleek black car drove up and stopped beside him. The car was expensive, like the ones you only see in movies, with black-tinted windows. The back window slowly rolled down, revealing a handsome man with wavy jet-black hair and gray eyes.

"We meet again," came a sultry voice that Des did not recognize.

"Do we know each other?" Des asked, staring at the other man who smirked, but he could see a slight irritation flash in his eyes.

"It would seem I didn't leave a memorable impression on you, Doctor Ellington."

"I think you have me mistaken with my father," Des responded.

The car door opened, and the man got out, showing his impressive height. He was still not as outstanding as Othello but good nonetheless.

"Cassio Ricci," he said, introducing himself, and a recollection returned to him.

"I remember now. We met at the Romanos' anniversary party."

"You could say that." He smiled.

"Well, it was nice seeing you again." Des went to put his helmet on but was stopped by Ricci.

"Wait, I don't see Moor. Did you two end your relationship, perhaps?"

A sarcastic smile graced Des's face. "He's busy tonight."

"Not with another lover, I hope."

Des didn't respond to that. He didn't doubt Othello's affection for him, and although he might be a fool in love, he was certain Othello wouldn't cheat on him.

"Okay then, I'll be on my way."

"I'm sorry," Ricci said before Des could make another move.

"What are you apologizing for?"

"For what I just said. It wasn't called for."

"No, it wasn't." Des sighed. "Look, I don't give a fuck what the beef is between you and Othello, but it has nothing to do with me."

"You're right. It doesn't." Ricci chuckled. "I like you. And I can see why Moor is drawn to you." He reached into his pocket and pulled out a business card, extending it toward Des. "I'd like it if we become friends. Word on the street is that you're looking for investors for your art studio. I'd like to lend a hand."

Since being with Othello, Des had learned a few things about business. It was better to ask other, more influential people to give him money for projects than to spend his own. So, he saw nothing wrong with taking the business card.

"I also heard you do commission work," Ricci said before Des could tuck the card away.

"You certainly heard a lot."

Ricci grinned. "I like to do my research. Do you have time to talk? I want to hire you to do a painting as a gift to my brother."

"I hope you aren't looking for anything too difficult. I'm still new at this," Des clarified.

"No," Ricci said, licking his lips. "I'm sure you'll be able to handle anything I require. So, are you free so we could grab a meal while we discuss business?"

Seeing that Othello would be busy for a few days and that it was work, Des didn't think it would be a problem to meet with a potential client and investor.

"Sure, where to?"

"Follow me; I know a quaint Italian restaurant that serves the perfect chicken parmesan that makes you want to kiss your own mama."

"Okay." Des watched Ricci return to his car. The driver waited for Des to put his helmet back on and rev his engine before he drove off with Des following behind him. On the ride to the restaurant, something felt off, but with the need to prove something to himself, he ignored the feeling.

* * *

OTHELLO SAT LAZILY in the chair with one leg crossed over the other, smiling as he scanned through his cellphone, looking for a gift for Des. He was utterly unfazed by the sound of a fist meeting flesh or Falcon's painful groans. Falcon was indeed the idiot Othello thought him to be.

Thinking Othello was dead, he'd left his compound unguarded outside, with only a few men inside with him. It made it easy for Othello and his men to enter his home, capture Falcon, and kill the soldiers with him.

They had taken him to The Pen, where he was stripped and strung up by chains, hanging from the ceilings by his arms and with his toes barely touching the ground. Othello didn't need to give the order; his men proceeded to beat him until he decided to talk.

"Aren't you going to say something, Moor!" Falcon shouted between punches.

Without lifting his eyes off the phone screen since a watch caught his eye, he asked, "Are you ready to talk?" Othello clicked on the purchase, not batting an eye at the price. He was formulating the perfect moment to give the gift to Des. It had been a while since he had wined and dined his lover.

Maybe I should take a quick trip?

"Moor, you fucking asshole, call off your fucking dogs and look at me," Falcon shouted.

Othello sighed and waved a hand as he raised his gaze, looking at a bloody Falcon. "You have my attention."

"I didn't want to do it," Falcon said. "I'm serious, but it was too good to pass up."

"Tell me who your contact was," Othello said.

"I don't know," Falcon responded instantly. "Everything was done via text. They kept things short but told me of your every movement."

"When did it start?"

"Before we struck our deal. It was all a setup to get you to that location and have you killed."

"How did you find out that we would be at the docks today?"

"The same way I get any information on you and your activities, through text." He gave Othello a bloody smile. "You have a rat running around in your midst, and they aren't working alone."

"Do you know who they are working with?"

Falcon huffed. "If I did, I wouldn't be working with your rat. I'd simply go to them."

"The night we met, you were stalling, which was why you

argued about the negotiation." It wasn't a question, so he wasn't expecting Falcon to say anything.

"Of course I was, but my guys were supposed to show up as soon as we sat down. There shouldn't have been any negotiation." He tsked. "You were supposed to die, Moor. I don't know what kind of star you were born under to survive every attempt on your life, but it's a lucky fucking one. You were supposed to die on the operating table. My cousin made sure the second bullet was left inside of you. Who knew that the surgeon would find it? Maybe I should have killed him."

Sharp gasps filled the room, but Othello ignored them. He was certain Falcon had no clue who Des was or what they meant to each other.

"You sound jealous," he said.

"I am," Falcon whispered. "You were adopted into an influential family, and your father respects you to the utmost, and you're not even his flesh and blood. Even my father gave everything we owned to you before he died. I had to forge my father's will to keep our family properties together. So when a message came to me to set up a meeting for us to set you up, I jumped at the chance. Getting my hands on Rizzo's property wasn't as important as taking you out. I respect you, Moor, but I don't like you. I suppose many others feel the same way I do."

Othello stared at Falcon for a few minutes before he spoke. "I told my father you would be dead by the end of the year, and although I was willing to give you a chance to build up your clan and then take you on, after this, I can honestly say you're not worth it. Fuck, Julian, I almost forgot you existed." Othello shook his head. "All you had to do was stay quiet and live your life. But when you threaten me and mine, you suffer the consequences." "What of yours did I threaten?" Falcon growled.

"First, my father, then my brother, and last, the doctor who saved me is now my beloved."

"I don't care!" Falcon shouted. "How the fuck could I live a good life when I knew sooner or later you would come after me and my family?"

"But no one told you to put yourself in front of me. You're weak, Julian. I'd expected it would take you days to crack, and I ended up breaking a date with my beloved; who knew you couldn't take a few fucking licks, and you'd start squealing like a little piggy." Othello huffed.

"I'm not weak!" Falcon shouted. "Let's change positions and tell me how it feels."

"I've had worse," Othello snapped, not going into details, but the surrounding men knew the truth. Alessandro loved him and Iago to death, but he was tough on them, especially regarding training. Growing a thick skin wasn't just for insults.

"You're pathetic." Othello stood, brushing off his clothes just as Tallen came over and handed him a stack of paper. "As for your father's will, we found it, which makes you insignificant."

"How did you get that?" he asked, looking at the folder, wide-eyed.

"I told you that you weren't smart. When you want to hide important documents, you put them in a safe far away where no one can get to them. Not in the bottom of your fucking desk drawer. Enough talking."

Falcon trembled and shook the chains holding him. "Please, Moor, don't do this," he begged. "I—I can be useful. You still need me. You know the commission won't stand for this. Sure, they turned a blind eye when we took out Rizzo, but they will come for you, Moor. Listen to me!

I—I can find out who the traitor is."

"Really?" Othello said, ignoring all the other parts of his ramblings. "How?"

"T-tonight, they are waiting for me to text them at ten with confirmation of your death. They'll know I failed if they don't hear from me."

Othello tapped his thumb on his leg, growing more

annoyed at this man's stupidity. "They already know I'm alive. It's now eleven thirty." The fear in Falcon's eyes excited Othello, reminding him of the first time a man knew he would die. He looked at Tallen. "You want to

move up in the ranks, right?"

"Yes, boss," Tallen said, moving forward and standing beside him.

Othello pulled his gun from its holster and handed it to Tallen, who took it. "Then you know what you must do." He stepped back and waited for Tallen to act. The man had been by his side for quite some time. He'd been hesitant to move Tallen up in the ranks, but maybe it was time.

"P—" was all Falcon got out before the gun went off.

Othello smiled and moved next to Tallen, clasping his shoulders. "Well done. Today, you are no longer a made man but our youngest capo. Don't disappoint me, Tallen. We'll have your official party in a few days. After getting rid of the body, you are all free to celebrate." "Thank you, boss," Tallen smiled.

There were smiles all around. Othello turned and whispered in Vito's ear. "Make sure Falcon's cousin never sees daylight again." He glanced over at Falcon's body. "Bury them in the same pit. They can suffer in hell together."

"Yes, boss."

With that last instruction, Othello left The Pen. He needed to report everything to Alessandro before taking him and Maria to the airport in the morning. It was even more important that Alessandro and Maria get out of town after the shooting at the docks.

Othello knew that his actions tonight would definitely reach the ears of the commission and would cause problems for the family, but he didn't fucking care. It was time for him to take the Ricci and Greco families down.

But before going to his parents' home, he stopped by the

hospital to check on Nico, even though visiting hours were over. He wasn't surprised to see Marco at his bedside.

The story they told the hospital and the cops was that he was shot in the back by some unknown person while they were taking a romantic walk on the pier. The bullet didn't hit any major organs, so his recovery would be quick and smooth.

* * *

WEEKS AFTER THE AMBUSH, Othello groaned, rolling over and reaching for Des, but he opened his eyes when he came up empty. Sighing, he sat up and looked around the moonlit bedroom, not seeing Des anywhere, but he had a feeling where he was. He'd been painting a lot more, even picking up a few commissioned works, which made Othello proud.

He had noticed that Des had been a little restless since the ambush. He was certain that Des didn't know about the shooting, so he was at a loss. *Maybe it has something to do with his parents.* Othello knew his mother had been calling Des quite a bit over the past few days.

Or the fact that we haven't been spending much time together. After the ambush at the docks, he'd made sure Alessandro and Maria got on a plane and drove himself into work, making less time for his lover. Iago was still busy trying to get back into Emilia's good graces, plus the twins. Othello hadn't updated him on what had been happening.

Sighing, Othello threw the covers back, got out of bed, and was about to find his lover when his cellphone vibrated. Grabbing it, he recognized the number and knew it had to be important if they were calling so late.

"What is it?"

"The department got an anonymous tip for the weapons sale for the auction. They are trying to get a judge to sign off on a search warrant. I can't stop or stall them, but you must move quickly."

Othello pinched the bridge of his nose. The anonymous person had to be their rat.

"Thanks, I'll take care of it. How are you doing with the other thing?" By Gratiano's silence, Othello knew he'd found something. "Tell me."

"Boss, I'm not sure about the information I gathered. I need more time to confirm a few things."

"How long do you need?"

"A few days or less, to be sure. I checked out all the leads you gave me from Falcon, but I don't have any more information to give you right now."

Othello nodded. "Okay. Do what you have to do." He was about to hang up, but Gratiano stopped him.

"Boss, keep only those you really trust near you. I'm not kidding when I tell you a huge target is on your back. The two ambushes and this tip are just the beginning."

"I thought getting shot would be it."

"No," Gratiano responded. "That was just a warning." He sighed, and Othello could tell he wanted to say more. "Say it."

"If the information I have is correct, then I think you need to let Des get as far away from this for a while to protect him."

"Is this your way of telling me to break up with him?" Othello snapped.

"No," Gratiano answered quickly. "Boss, I know how

you can be, and blood is going to be spilled; I just don't want it to be his."

"What exactly do you think you have? Just say it."

"Please, let me confirm the information before I tell you everything," Gratiano said pleadingly. "I'm asking you to trust me, Othello. Let me do the job you hired me to do, and that is to look out for your best interest."

Othello's brows furrowed. The only time Gratiano referred

to him by his first name was when he wanted Othello to pay attention.

"Okay," he conceded. "Hurry and do what you need to do. I'm sick of not knowing who is working against me." "Will do. And think about what I said about Des."

"Alright."

They hung up, and Othello made a few phone calls to get the ball rolling on getting the weapons out of the auction house. He needed to leave, but before that, he needed to talk with Des. Grabbing his robe, he shrugged it on, and putting his cellphone in his pocket, Othello went to see his lover. The closer he got to Des's studio, the more the scent of fresh paint hit him, along with smooth jazz playing in the background.

The door was open, and Othello saw Des naked, sitting on the stool, gently brushing the paintbrush on the canvas. Not far from him was a glass of whiskey on the small desk that fit neatly under the windowsill. It wasn't a big room, and most things were within easy reach. Othello mentally sighed.

Although he didn't drink much, he had nothing against people partaking in their vices, but he couldn't deny his worry about his lover. He'd noticed Des had been drinking excessively lately, which was a sign that something was bothering him.

When Othello questioned him, Des told him he was fine. Nothing was okay; something was eating Des up inside, and Othello knew he couldn't ignore it any longer. Quietly, he moved further into the room and stood next to Des, who was so engrossed in his work that he hadn't noticed he was there.

Othello looked at Des and was a bit taken aback by the serene expression on his face. His eyes glazed as if he had taken a drug, and a slight smile on his lips as if he was lost in a dream or a fantasy that he couldn't keep to himself. Othello moved his gaze from Des to the canvas that was starting to take the shape of a figure.

Des continued to paint, and instead of interrupting him,

Othello walked toward the door, figuring he'd send him a text or call him later. Just as he was about to leave, he stopped when he noticed a familiar card sitting on the only table in the room. Moving over, he picked up the card, scowling when he saw Cassio Ricci's name and personal number.

He looked back at Des, who still hadn't known he was in the room. Glancing back to the card, he wondered when Des had talked with Cassio Ricci long enough to get his business card.

"Hey," Des said, getting his attention.

Othello turned to Des, who had stopped working and was looking at him.

"Hey, yourself," he said, putting the card in his robe pocket and walking to Des.

"What are you doing up?"

Kneeling between Des's open legs, he kissed Des's chest. "I woke up and found my lover missing." Grabbing him by his waist, Des wrapped his arms around his neck. "What are you working on?"

"Let's not talk about it." Des sighed. "Instead, I want us to do something more pleasurable with our mouths." He leaned down, brushing his lips against Othello's, who moaned, tasting Des and the expensive whiskey on his tongue. He cupped the back of Des's head and kissed him deeply.

He trailed soft kisses down his body, pressing a tender kiss on the head of Des's cock before sucking the shaft down into his mouth, feeling it swell and pulsate on his tongue. Des groaned, dragging his nails along Othello's back.

Des grabbed a handful of his hair, pulling his head up and off his cock, then claimed his mouth in a rough kiss, taking what he wanted and needed from Othello. Des had grown more confident in his desires since their first time together. Othello tightened his arms around Des and pulled him down on top of him.

Their kiss grew more intense. A moan escaped his mouth

when their cocks rubbed together. Reaching down, he circled a finger around Des's hole that was still wet and loose from their earlier lovemaking. Othello grabbed Des's waist and flipped them over. Breaking their kiss, he leaned back, staring at his gorgeous lover.

"Turn over," he said.

Smiling, Des got on his hands and knees. Othello grabbed and then smacked one of Des's ass cheeks, rubbing it and soothing the sting before doing the same to the other. Des whimpered as he did it once more. Othello wished he'd brought his leather belt.

"Othello," Des moaned. "Please, don't tease me."

Othello chuckled and kissed the base of his back, then the crack of his ass, moving down, swirling the tip of his tongue around the hole.

"Oh fuck," Des whimpered when he stuck his tongue inside, moving, bobbing his head, moving it in and out.

Des moaned and groaned his name, moving his hips, fucking himself on Othello's tongue. He grabbed Des's hips, steadying him, adding more of his tongue and saliva, wetting his hole. He grabbed and separated Des's buttcheeks, going as deep as he could. Des's body shook, and Othello knew his lover was close to cumming. Slowly, he removed his tongue and gazed at Des's moist hole. His handprints marking Des's ass cheeks made him grow even harder.

"Let's go to the bedroom," Othello said in a raspy voice.

"No," Des said, looking over his shoulder at him. "Take me here and now."

"Are you sure?" he asked.

"Yes, I have lube in the drawer next to you." Des leaned up and kissed him.

Othello quirked a brow. "Were you hoping I'd fuck you in here?"

"Of course, one of my top fantasies." He smiled.

Othello chuckled and kissed him once more, pushing Des back down and rubbing his back as he reached into the desk, grabbing a lube packet and tearing it open, squeezing it on his cock and Des's hole. Othello jerked his erection a couple of times, positioning it to Des's entrance, and pushed the head inside his hot, tight heat, making them both moan. Pressing his hand on the small of Des's back, he pushed all the way in and waited for a spell for Des to adjust.

"Shit, Tesoro, you feel so good squeezing my cock," Othello whispered, grabbing Des's hips and slowly moving in and out of him. Othello's eyes grew hazy as he panted heavily. His hips moved a bit faster with each thrust."So tight. Shit."

"Oh, fuck…oh fuck," Des whimpered, grinding his waist and meeting Othello's movements.

The sound and sweet aroma of sex filled the room, their desire for each other building as well as their orgasms. Othello grabbed Des's shoulder while keeping the other on his hip, changing the angle of his thrusting, brushing his cock over Des's prostate. His heart was pounding so loudly in his ears it was a wonder he could hear Des's pleading and begging.

"Othello…I need…I need."

Usually, Othello wanted to tease Des a little longer, bring him to the edge, then pull back, torturing them both with pleasure, but not tonight. He could feel his own urgency to cum.

"Touch yourself, Tesoro," he groaned, quickening his thrusts, causing his hips to slap against Des's palm-printed ass. His movements were rough yet not enough to hurt his lover, who liked when Othello fucked him this way.

"Gonna cum," Des chanted, then cried out Othello's name. His walls tightened around his cock.

"Des," Othello growled, cumming, unable to hold back his orgasm, painting Des's channel with his hot seed and leaving his mark on every part of his lover's body.

Othello leaned forward, pressing his forehead into Des's

sweaty neck, licking and sucking up a mark. He peppered gentle kisses to his cheeks, meeting Des's lips for a slow kiss. They both groaned when his softened cock slipped out of Des. Their lips separated as they fell to the side, gasping but with bright smiles on their faces.

He leaned over and kissed Des softly, their tongues teasing each other's lips, neither in a rush to deepen the kiss. Des rolled on top of him, laying his head on his chest, and Othello wrapped him in his arms.

"Des, I..." He didn't get a chance to say what had been on his tongue for weeks because his cellphone rang, and he couldn't ignore it at a time like this. Without disrupting Des, he pulled it out of his robe pocket and saw Tallen's name on the screen. "Yeah."

"Boss, we're almost done loading everything on the trucks."

"Okay, head to Silver Port. I'll meet you there. Take the back roads and make sure no one is following you."

Silver Port was a two-hour drive from Verona Heights. Othello had a warehouse there where he could hide the weapons for now.

"You got it."

They hung up, and Othello set his phone to the side, hugging Des tightly.

"You're leaving again, aren't you?"

"I'm sorry, Tesoro," he whispered, kissing his forehead.

"I feel like lately we don't see each other, and when we do, it's for sex." He raised his head. "Maybe I should ask you when we can meet next, or should I make an appointment for a date."

"I'm sorry, Tesoro, things have been a little crazy right now."

"So crazy that you have to leave me at two in the morning." He got off Othello, standing, and walked over to the window, not caring about his state of undress. Othello licked his lips at seeing his cum sliding down Des's legs. "When will I see you again?" Des asked, pulling Othello from his naughty thoughts.

Othello sighed and got off the floor. "It should only be a couple of days."

"Why are you going to Silver Port?"

"I can't tell you that," Othello told him. "We've never discussed my family business, and I'd like to keep it that way."

"So I'm not supposed to worry that something major is going down for you to go to another state?"

"You don't need to worry about me or my family," Othello said.

"Why shouldn't I? I've heard things," he replied.

Othello furrowed his brows. "What things? Who are you talking to?"

"I don't know. I heard about some shooting at the docks a few nights ago, and it made me wonder if you were involved."

"How would you hear about a shooting that not even the news or the cops are aware of?" Othello asked, not liking the way he sounded suspicious.

"So you were there," Des said in surprise.

"Answer me, Des."

"I heard it from Tallen, okay," he said, gazing away.

Othello gritted his teeth and planned on punching the shit out of his new capo when he saw him.

"Tesoro, look at me." He waited for Des to look his way. "I'm fine, and nothing will happen to me."

"You don't know that."

"I do." He leaned down and kissed Des on the forehead. "After I settle everything, how about we go somewhere."

Des sighed. "I know this is your way of changing the subject, and I'll go along with it for now." He hugged Othello, wrapping his arms around him. "Just don't get hurt. I can't live without you, especially now that you've wrapped your way around my heart."

Othello pressed his face on the top of Des's head, closing his eyes. "You too, Tesoro."

They stayed like that for a few minutes before Des stepped back. "How soon do you have to leave?"

"I can spare a few more minutes. Why?"

"I need a shower. Want to join me?"

Othello smiled. "You never have to ask."

They made love again in the shower before Othello left for his drive to Silver Port. There, he met his team and had the weapons taken care of, but he had other things to take care of. He had to get them out of the country before the cops figured out what he was doing. So, in the following hours, he and his men worked tirelessly to get the weapons shipped out by land and sea before he could return to Verona Heights, just as the cops and feds pulled up at the auction house.

"What's going on here?" Othello asked, getting out of his car.

"Othello Moor," a familiar voice said as they approached him with a neatly folded paper in his hand that Othello didn't reach out to take. "We have a warrant to search your property."

"Why?" he asked calmly, staring at Detective Oz. "Has someone reported us for a forged painting or something? I can assure you that our collections are all genuine. So you

can take your men home."

"Are you hindering us from enacting a court-ordered warrant?" Oz growled.

"You haven't told me why you want to search my property," Othello said, putting his hands in his pockets. He leaned against his car as if he had no care in the world.

Detective Oz narrowed his eyes at Othello. "We got an anonymous tip that you are harboring illegal guns and

other weapons in this vicinity."

"I'm an upstanding businessman, Detective Oz. I wouldn't do anything to bring shame to my family's name," Othello told him.

"Businessman, my ass," Oz snarled. "I know what you and your family are into."

"I would never look at your ass, detective. I can honestly say you're not my type," Othello said, ignoring his men coughing to mask their laughter.

"I feel you're trying to stall for time, Moor. Whatever the case, my men and I will search every nook and cranny of this place."

"Far be it from me to stop you from doing your job, Detective. However, please be gentle with the priceless art. I promise not even two years of your salary would cover the cost." He waved a dismissive hand and watched as Oz huffed, then walked away.

The men searching his property were not as gentle as he had asked and broke at least one piece of the priceless collection worth over fifty thousand dollars and up. Othello remained silent, keeping his posture calm, especially when Oz moved the bookcase, revealing a safe where he had kept the weapons hidden.

If Othello had doubted that someone on the inside was working against him, he would have been more convinced now than ever. Only he, Alessandro, Iago, and a handful of his trusted men knew where they were. Three hours later, Othello was sporting a bright smile as he watched an unhappy Detective Oz leave the auction house.

His face became serious the second the cops drove off. "Fuck!" he cursed, kicking the broken piece of statue the cops broke during their search. "Get this place cleaned up." Looking around the showroom, Othello realized there was no way he could have the auction now. He had stock, but not as priceless as the ones the cops broke.

"Fucking cops," he growled, wanting to punch something or more like someone hard.

* * *

DES OPENED the door at the insistent knock, hoping that it was Othello returning quicker than he said he would, but he was stunned when he saw his mother standing at his doorstep.

"Mother," he said, not hiding the shock in his voice.

"Why do you look so shocked?" she asked.

"Um...because this is the first time you've ever visited me."

"Are you going to let me in, or should I stand out here for us to have our conversation?"

"Oh, come in," he said, stepping to the side and watching her walk in with a suitcase he'd just noticed.

"Are you planning on leaving for a trip? Does Father know?" he asked, noticing her gaze roaming around his apartment.

"How many bedrooms do you have?" she asked.

"Three, but I use the smallest one for my studio."

"Bathrooms?" Ava left her luggage and then went to the kitchen, opening and closing cupboards.

"Mother, what the hell? Why are you asking me questions about my place? It's not like you're moving in here."

Ava stopped what she was doing and looked at Des. "That is exactly what I'm doing here. You're an adult now, so I will tell you the truth. Desmond, I've filed for divorce." "Say that again," he said, thinking he heard wrong.

"I'm leaving your father."

"What the fuck?" Des cursed when he got over the oneminute shock.

"Stop cursing, dear. It's unbecoming," she admonished primly.

"Fuck that, Mother, you can't be serious."

"I most definitely am," she said, walking away. Des followed behind her, feeling as if he had entered a different universe.

Before she could get to the bedroom, Des stopped her. "Mom, talk to me."

Ava gasped and looked at him. Her eyes were a little wet, as if she was about to cry but held herself together.

"You haven't called me Mom since you were five."

"I didn't know it was important to you," he said. "But tell me what happened between you and Father."

"He cheated on me, Des." Her lips quivered as she spoke. "I sacrificed everything for him, especially my relationship with you, and for the last twenty-five years, he has been carrying on a relationship with some b—" she paused as he could see her anger building up, but she quickly collected herself, "—woman who gave him a son, who

right under my nose he took as his protégé." "What?" Des gasped.

"Des, dear, I'm feeling a bit tired; I'd like to get some rest."

He nodded without thinking and guided her to the guest bedroom. He realized that she had called him Des and not Desmond. Before he could close the bedroom door, she stopped him.

"I know I cannot apologize for all the years of turmoil I might have caused you, but I would like to try to make amends for my actions."

Des wasn't sure what to say, so he nodded and closed the door. His mind was swirling with what his mother had just told him, and as much as he hated to do it, he needed to talk with his father.

SCENE III

DES

Des got out of the car and walked into his parents' home without knocking. Since he didn't see his father anywhere, he went straight to his office.

"Father, what—" he said, bursting through David's office door but stopped mid-sentence when he saw Doctor Stephen and a strange woman sitting comfortably, dressed in an expensive pantsuit. At a quick glance, Stephen resembled the woman, so Des assumed they were related.

"Desmond, what are you doing here?" David asked, getting up from his desk and meeting him partway.

"I came to see Mother," he lied, not taking his eyes off Stephen and the woman. "She's been calling me to talk about—"

Des stopped speaking again and walked over to Stephen. "What are you doing here?"

Stephen glanced behind Des as if looking for permission to answer him.

"I came to see Doctor Ellington," Stephen responded.

"Really?" Des said, dragging out the word, then turned to David. "Father, you didn't answer my question. Where is Mother?"

"She's not here," he said, looking away sheepishly. "She walked out on me this morning."

"Oh, for fuck's sake, David, tell him the truth. He is an adult. He should be able to handle it," the lady said, standing up and standing next to Des's father, holding one of his arms.

"Mom," Stephen said just as David said, "Dawn, no."

"Your father and I are getting married after he divorces *her*," Dawn said gleefully.

"Her?" Des said, utterly disgusted with the way she referred to his mother. But Des ignored her and looked at his father. "After all my mother has done for you, this is how you treat your wife. The woman who has stood beside you and listened to every fucking thing you say. But in one split second, you turn your back on her and take up with some trollop."

"Watch your mouth, boy," David growled.

"The fuck I will," Des snapped. "You fucking disgust me."

"Des, don't talk to Dad like that," Stephen said.

"Dad—Dad—" he scoffed. "I remembered when I was five, I called you Dad. You shouted at me never to call you that, but this bastard gets the privilege of doing so."

He had already clocked that Stephen was David's son, but hearing the man call him Dad cut Des deeper than it should have. "All my life, I tried my best to get you to notice me. To see my worth, yet you already had the son you wanted."

He turned to Stephen. "Let me guess, you're following in the footsteps he laid out for you while I am a disappointment to him. The night at the hospital, you knew who I was. I kept thinking there was something off about you, but I never guessed we were related."

"It's not like that," Stephen said, looking at Des with pitiful eyes.

"The fuck it isn't," Des yelled.

"I want to get to know you," Stephen said. "I've heard so much about you from Dad and the people at the hospital—"

"Fuck you," Des growled at him. "I want nothing to fucking do with you."

"You do not get to talk to my son like that," Dawn shouted.

"I will talk to him however the fuck I want," Des argued back. He looked at his father. "Enjoy what little free time you have because I'm going to make sure you lose every fucking thing you worked hard to attain. You've hurt me all my life, and yeah, I cried over it, but I can tell my mother must have suffered just as much."

With that, he left, ignoring his father calling his name. Des didn't know why he had stood up for his mother like that when he knew she'd gone along with everything his father wanted. But thinking of Ava's face when she told him about their divorce made him feel that his mother was never strong enough to go against his father like he thought she was.

Des got in his car and pulled out his cellphone to call Othello, but paused his actions. He didn't need or want Othello to help him with this. Thanks to Erin, who had collected the information when she looked into his case, he had enough incriminating shit on his father to lock him up for a long time. But it made him wonder how they missed the fact that he'd had a fucking mistress for over twenty years.

"This better be good for you to call me on my day off," Erin said on the other end.

"How the fuck did you guys miss the mistress?" he asked Erin.

"What are you talking about? Who has a mistress?"

"My father. He's been seeing some woman for over twenty years and they even have a kid who works at the hospital."

"What? Wait, what's her name?"

Des sighed. "They called her Dawn."

"Dawn, Dawn," she chanted. "Let me look into it and get back to you."

"Erin, whatever you find, I want to take them down."

She was silent for a few minutes. "Don't do this out of anger," Erin warned.

"Erin, aren't you the one who told me you hate bullies? Well, my father is the biggest one of them all."

"What about your mother?"

"I don't feel sorry for her, but there's no reason for her to be caught up in my father's dealings. Who knew the man was so disgusting? I'm sure his other son has no idea what he's truly like."

"Are you sure you want to do this?"

"Yes, but I want it done strategically, not how those idiots on Benito Grant's campaign did it. I want his downfall to be slow and painful. Let my father think I forgot about him, and then *bam*, we bury him."

"Okay, we'll do what you want." Erin sighed. "But Des, what happened to you?"

He pressed his head into the headrest, closing his eyes. "I got tired, Erin. I don't want to be a pushover anymore."

"We'll meet at the cafe tomorrow at three."

"Okay."

* * *

OTHELLO SIGHED and shrugged off his jacket as he entered the Romanos' family home. Pulling off his coat and jacket, he dropped them over the railing as he made his way to the kitchen. He would have returned to his apartment, but he had work to do and knew it would take him into the night. He'd rescheduled the auction to a few months from now.

Walking into Alessandro's office, he stopped when he saw Iago sitting at his father's desk. They'd both been so busy they hadn't seen or even spoken to each other in days.

"I figured you'd show up here after the day you've had."

"So you heard?" Othello asked, moving over to the chair and sitting down.

"Nothing happens in this family that I don't know about." He looked at Othello seriously. "Are you ready for the consequences? We knew partnering with Falcon was also making a deal with Ricci and Greco since he was their ally."

"If a war is coming, then so be it," Othello said.

Iago smiled. "You're always steadfast in your words, and you have no regrets about your actions. Does your good doctor know how cruel you can be?"

"What I do for the family has nothing to do with Des."

"So the answer is no," Iago said. "How can you be yourself when he's never seen the real you?"

"Who says I'm not myself when I'm with him?" Othello shook his head, wondering why the conversation veered off into this topic. "I am me with the family and Des. I hide nothing."

"If you say so," Iago said. "Do you know who tipped off the cops?"

"If I knew that, I'm sure you'd have heard that they are already dead." He was happy that Iago changed the subject.

Othello got up and went to pour them both a drink. He shouldn't be drinking on an empty stomach, but after the day he had, he needed something to take the edge off his stress.

"I need to find out who is behind this, Iago." Othello sighed, sipping his whiskey.

"We will," Iago said, leaning back in the chair and swirling his drink. "I'll also set up a meeting with our allies; if we are to go to war with the commission, we must be prepared. I doubt they'll skip the warning or sanctions and go straight for taking you out."

What Iago said was true. The commission had rules for the families that could not be broken, and even though Romanos had been doing their own thing to acquire power, property, and resources, some were approved by the commission heads.

They did turn a blind eye to Rizzo, on that Falcon was right, but taking out an ally in the act of revenge was something that needed the commission's permission. Not to mention, he'd ordered the killing of a civilian, putting another red mark on the family. With those two actions, it might show strength, but his leadership could be called into question.

Putting the matter with the commission out of his mind, Othello studied Iago for a few minutes and could tell his brother had something on his mind.

"Everything alright with the twins?"

Iago beamed. "They are perfect little monsters who have taken over my heart."

"What about you and Emilia?"

"It's the same, if not worse," Iago said sadly. "She only talks to me when it has something to do with the twins. I know I fucked up, but she's forgiven me before."

Othello said nothing. He had no advice to give Iago to help him, so he simply poured them both another drink. "I will win her back, I'm certain of it. Emilia loves me." *But do you want to love her?* Othello mentally asked.

"Enough about me. Let's talk about you and your doctor," Iago said.

"My relationship with Des has nothing to do with you and Emilia."

"But can you trust him?" Iago asked.

Othello put his drink down, glaring at his brother.

"What are you getting at?"

"I don't trust him," Iago stated firmly.

"Are you saying this because of what's happening with you and Emilia?"

"No," he answered. "I've just been thinking a lot lately."

"That still doesn't prove why you don't trust Des." Othello took a deep breath, trying not to get angry. For whatever reason, Iago had a problem with Des. "What has he done to you?"

"I think he's bad news. Since you started seeing him, bad shit's been happening. I get that he saved your life, but knowing what I know now, I think he's working for theenemy."

"Take that shit back, right the fuck now," Othello growled.

"I knew you wouldn't believe me." He picked up his cell-phone, started scrolling through it, then stopped and handed it to Othello. On the screen was a video of Des and Cassio Ricci standing far too close to each other, conversing. He couldn't hear them or read their lips to figure out what they were saying, but by the comfort in body language, it was evident it wasn't the first time they had met.

"How did you get this?" Othello asked, glancing at Iago and then back at the screen.

"You should know by now that if something is bugging me, I don't let it go until I have proof."

At times, Iago could be like a dog with a bone when he was fixated on something.

"I think Falcon was working with Ricci," Iago kept talking as Othello tried his damndest to figure out what the people on the screen were saying to each other. "The night we were ambushed, Falcon's cousin worked on you, then Ellington operated on you. Six months later, he shows up at our club and works his way into your life. I strongly believe Ricci sent him to spy on you. How else would he know about you going to the docks? Or about the weapons at the auction house? Didn't you take him there?"

He stopped the video and looked at Iago. "You've put a lot of thought into this," he said.

"You don't sound convinced," sighed Iago.

"Honestly, no," Othello said. "Based on what you're saying, Des knew about all of my activities and made sure he would be on duty the night I got shot. It doesn't add up, Iago."

"How do you figure that?" Iago asked. Othello wasn't sure why he could feel tension from his brother when they were having a calm conversation.

"Des and I don't talk about family business." He shrugged his shoulders. "The leak is someone else."

"I don't believe it. How do you explain his relationship with Ricci?"

"What relationship?" Othello stood, shaking his head. "Just because you don't like Des, you're grasping at straws." He looked at Iago seriously. "I get you're trying to protect me because of Phillip. But for the last fucking time, they are not the same people. The more you talk about your lack of trust in Des when you don't even know him, the more I think you have ulterior motives. Don't make me think ill of you, Brother, so I'd advise you to drop it. Better yet, go home. You have your own relationship to worry about. Stay the fuck out of mine," Othello told him, no longer in the mood to listen to Iago's ramblings.

Iago stood and shook his head. "He's going to break your heart, O. And when he does, I'll be here."

Why the fuck isn't he listening! "Weren't you the one who told me to find someone to love? Why do you keep doubting him?" Othello snapped.

"Because he's not worthy of you. Okay, fine, you don't think he's working with Ricci. What about his father?"

"What about him?" Othello shouted, but Iago didn't back down.

"Are you an idiot?"

"Watch your words, Iago!" Othello growled.

"I won't," Iago argued back. "Someone has to knock some fucking sense into you. It's like when you get some ass, you forget you have responsibilities. You did the same thing with Phillip, and you're doing it with this guy. His father is running for senate, for god's sake. And by the looks of it, he'll win. What if your doctor tells him about us, and they bring everything we've built down? You can't tell me the raid on the auction house was a coincidence. After what just happened with Falcon, we're about to go head to head with the commission."

Iago pinched the bridge of his nose agitatedly. "You can't be distracted right now, O. Besides, are you sure he'll stay by your side when everything is said and done? You should dump him and find someone better before he does. Someone who wouldn't run to the cops the first time they see the real you. Let me set you up with someone, please, O. I'm just trying to protect my family."

"I heard everything you're saying, Iago, but there are a few things wrong with your logic." Othello sighed, reining in his anger. "One, there's no one better than Des. Two, there's no guarantee his father will win the Senate race. And three, I never have to ask Des if he'll choose me over his family because I know I will be his choice. What Des and I have cannot be compared to what I had with Phillip or anyone else. I'm not like you, Iago; I can't flit from one lover to the other when I know I have someone who loves me to hell and back."

"If you weren't my brother, I would punch the shit out of you for saying that," Iago spat.

"When has that stopped you," Othello shot back.

"Now, you have the power I don't have," Iago mumbled, but Othello heard him perfectly.

"What in the fuck are you talking about?" he asked, tightening his brows.

"You're in love with him," Iago said, not answering his question, but his face registered shock at the thought of Othello falling in love was a novelty.

"I am, and I am certain he loves me too," Othello said confidently.

"Have you told him?"

"No." He smiled. "I'm waiting for the perfect moment to tell him."

The tension that had enveloped them simmered, but he didn't want to deal with Iago anymore. He wanted to finish his work, head home, and sleep in his own bed, even though he still had a room at the Romanos' house.

"Go." Othello looked away from Iago.

Othello dropped in his chair, pinching the bridge of his nose. He didn't want to doubt Des, but he also didn't want to admit that some of what Iago said made sense; the shooting at the docks and the cops searching the auction house were the top two on his list. But as he told Iago, Des knew nothing about their family business.

Iago didn't know Des the way he did. Hell, his brother had never even spent a second with his lover, even after Des delivered the twins. If he didn't know how devoted Iago was to the family, Othello would think he was the one working against him. Shaking his head, Othello put a full stop to that thought. Iago might've been a bastard regarding his relationships, but family was very important to him, especially the one that rescued him. He appreciated Iago worrying about him, but Othello felt his brother should focus on his own relationship.

Late into the middle of the night, closer to the morning, Othello entered his apartment and instantly knew something was different. Although he didn't sense any danger, he didn't let his guard down.

He was about to reach for his gun but stopped when he noticed Des's coat thrown over the back of the sofa. A smile graced his tired lips. Des had planned to call him later, but this was a pleasant surprise. He removed his outer coat and jacket, threw it on Des's jacket, and headed to the bedroom.

Othello walked over to the bed and saw the lump on the bed. Slowly, he removed the cover and saw Des's sleeping face. When Othello trailed a finger down the bridge of his nose to the tip, Des scrunched it cutely. His long lashes trembled as his eyes tenderly opened, and he stared up at Othello with moist eyes.

"You're home?" he said in a sexy, sleepy voice.

"I am," he said, kissing him quickly. "I'm going to shower."

"No, come hold me," he said, pulling Othello to the bed. "I miss you."

Othello sighed, toeing off his shoes and allowing his lover to pull him easily to the bed, where Des snuggled into his arms. Although Othello was one of those people who had to shower before going to bed, he couldn't deny how comfortable he was at the moment. Or maybe he just enjoyed spoiling the former doctor.

"I can't say I'm unhappy to see you, but why are you here?"

"I needed a place to hide from my mother," Des responded groggily.

"What?" He sat up and looked at Des.

"Don't move," Des whined, pulling him back down and half-draping himself over Othello. "It's a long story I'll tell you in the morning. Now sleep."

Othello chuckled and held him tightly, listening to Des's soft snores as he drifted off to sleep.

* * *

DES GROANED SLEEPILY, wrinkling his brows as he slowly opened his eyes, expecting to wake up in his bedroom. Seeing the familiar dark red made him recall he'd shown up at Othello's place, needing somewhere safe to collect his thoughts and sanity after everything he had dealt with the day before. He was about to close his eyes and drift back to sleep when the scent of coffee reached his nose.

Othello, he thought, sitting up in bed. So it wasn't a dream. Des had sworn he was dreaming the night before when he felt Othello's presence. Giggling, he pushed the covers off and got out of bed, not even caring about his state of dress, and ran to the kitchen, stopping only for a second to watch Othello, who was standing at the stove with his back to him. Des hurried over, circling his arms around Othello's waist and burying his face in his rigid back.

"You're awake."

He hummed, feeling Othello's deep baritone voice vibrating on his face. They had only been separated for a day, but it felt like years. Lately, they hadn't been spending that much time together. Othello was always busy with family things, and Des was occupied with school, commissioned work, and now his mom. He just needed one day with his lover without any interruptions. Thinking of Ava, Des knew he had to meet with Erin later to discuss how to deal with his father.

"What's with all the sighing?" Othello asked.

"I was thinking about my mom," Des answered, pressing his cheek against Othello's warm skin. He didn't want to let go, but he knew he would have to eventually.

"That's a first. Holding me makes you think of a woman, and your mom at that." He chuckled.

"It's not like that," he told Othello, pouting. "I hoped to spend the day with you, but I have stupid errands." He went to say more, but his cellphone rang, and he knew he had to answer it because it could be his mother. Yesterday, after he returned to his apartment, she'd fussed over him. It was cute for about an hour until it became intolerable. He wasn't used to

Ava's affection, and so when she fell asleep on the couch, he escaped to Othello's apartment.

"Are you going to answer that?" Othello asked.

"I don't want to. It's my mom," he whined.

"I really need to hear the story as to what's going on, but you need to get that; it might be an emergency."

"Fine," he groaned, releasing Othello and hurrying back to the bedroom to get his phone. He was surprised to see that it wasn't his mother but Mr. Ricci, which caused Des to furrow his brows.

"Why is he calling me so early in the morning?" Des mumbled to himself. Des did not like Cassio Ricci. If it wasn't because he was trying to get his name out there as an artist, he would have told the man to fuck off.

Cassio Ricci always seemed to find Des wherever he was, as if he had a tracker on him. First, it was the time he bought him dinner, then at the grocery store, and the other day, it was the cafe Des liked to frequent. It was very annoying. Not to mention the sly touches or the flirting, which Des ignored or politely told him how much he loved his boyfriend. Des always smiled when he said Othello was his boyfriend.

"Everything alright with your mom?"

Des looked up when he heard Othello's question. "It wasn't her. It was a client. I missed his call. I'll return it later."

Othello nodded. "Breakfast is ready. Go clean up."

"Okay." He threw his phone to the bed and then ran to the bathroom, grabbing his towel as he went for a quick shower.

* * *

OTHELLO SMILED and was about to head back to the kitchen when Des's cellphone rang. He was going to ignore it, but that thought went out the window when he saw Cassio Ricci's name on the screen. Othello frowned and reached for the ringing device. His finger hovered over the decline button, but it instantly moved over and answered the phone.

"How the hell did you get this number?" Othello growled.

Ricci chuckled, and it irritated Othello more than it should have. "It seems the little dove is keeping secrets."

Between the business card, the videos, and now the phone call, Othello didn't have an explanation, and his curiosity was beyond piqued.

"Stay away from Des," Othello snapped. "I know what you're trying to do, and it won't work. Keep ignoring my words, and I'll make sure you pay dearly."

Ricci laughed loud and hard as if Othello were a comedian. "I'm not afraid of you, Moor. Besides, I can't stay away from your little doctor. He's quite intriguing. In the beginning, I was going to use him to get you, but now, I want him for myself."

"You really want me to put a bullet between your eyes." Othello wanted to growl or smash something but held it together. "Heed my warning, Ricci. Come near Des again, and I'll kill you."

Othello hung up before Ricci could utter another annoying word. He threw Des's phone back on the bed and went to the kitchen to grab his own cellphone, which rang as soon as he picked it up. Gratiano's name flashed across the screen.

"Do you have time to meet tomorrow?"

"I take it you have something for me?" Othello asked.

"Yeah, and it's not good, Othello."

"Alright, we'll meet tonight at the usual place."

"No, let's meet somewhere more private. I'm not coming alone," Gratiano said, causing Othello to furrow his brows.

"Who?"

"You'll see when we get there. Meet us at eight at the docks."

"Okay." Othello hung up just as Des entered and walked over to him, drying his hair that had gotten longer since they'd been together. He took Des's towel and finished up the job.

"Tesoro, there's something I need to ask you."

Des hummed, wrapping his arms around him. "Yeah, what is it?"

"What's your connection to Cassio Ricci?"

Des groaned. "He's my new and only client."

"Client?"

"Yeah." Des raised his head. "He's paying me a lot of money for a painting."

"How much is he paying you?"

"More than he should."

"I'll pay you double to drop him as a client," Othello said.

"What? Why?"

Othello draped the towel around Des's neck and looked Des in his eyes. "He doesn't care about the painting, Des. He's trying to seduce you to get to me."

Des furrowed his brows, stepping out of Othello's arms.

"What the hell do you have to do with this?"

"It's a game to him, Tesoro." Othello went over to the stove, grabbed the cooled pan with the vegetable frittata he had made for breakfast, and brought it to the table.

"Is that all you're going to say?" Des snapped.

"Sit down, and I'll explain things," he said to his lover, who seemed hesitant but did as Othello asked.

He plated the frittata, handed it to Des, and encouraged him to eat. "I say it's a game because he's done this before. The last person I thought I was in love with, Cassio seduced him. Most would say someone who didn't want to be seduced wouldn't have gone, and Phillip was very willing. I'm not sure how his wife put up with it, but Cassio paraded Phillip in front of me every chance he got." Othello smiled but felt no joy. "Now that we're together, he's playing the same games."

"Why would he do that?" Des asked.

"Because he hates me, Tesoro. He finds me unworthy of

taking my father's place. Or it could be that he's been holding a grudge since high school." "What did you do?" Des asked.

"I beat his ass so bad he couldn't show his face for a few months." Othello smiled, recalling the memory. "Look, I don't like him either. Just stay away from him. Besides, you don't want to be the third wheel in his marriage or deal with his other lovers."

If Ricci thought no one knew he and Greco were fucking, they were both stupid. It was talked about, just not within ear's distance of the two of them.

The silence dragged between them. "What happened to Phillip?"

"Honestly, I have no fucking clue. I broke off all contact with him after he fucked around on me. But not long after, he went missing. I think once Ricci realized that taking Phillip from me didn't affect me, he got rid of him." Othello looked at Des, who hadn't eaten a bite.

"When you say get rid of, you don't mean murder, right?"

"No other way to say it." Othello shrugged.

"I feel like I should be worried about how casually we're talking about someone killing another person. I don't want to be the kind of person who doesn't care about human life."

"This is why I don't discuss my family business with you, Des. I don't want to taint your view of the world or

me. In my world, it's kill or be killed." "I know," Des whispered.

"Stay away from him, Tesoro. I might not have cared that he stole Phillip, but with you, I will burn his world down if he touches one hair on your head in lust or anger."

Des remained silent, staring at him for a few long minutes before he spoke.

"Are you changing your mind about us?" Othello asked. He didn't want to admit how unsteady his heart was beating in his chest, waiting for Des to answer. If Des wanted to walk away from him, he would let him, but Othello knew it would break him.

Des shook his head. "No," he said. "I want to be with you, no matter what. You warned me you're not a good man. I know you hide that part of yourself from me, and I might not be ready to hear about your day, but I want to be your comfort, just as much as you bring me comfort."

Othello smiled. "You are. More than you know."

"You love me, don't you?" Des uttered softly, looking down at the table.

Othello stood and approached Des, reaching for his hand. He pulled him from his seat, circling his arms around his waist, and held him flush against his body. "If burning worlds down wasn't an indication, then let me be clear. I love you, Desmond Ellington."

Des's eyes glistened, becoming wet. "I might not have your powerful influence, but I feel the same way, Othello Romano-Moor. I love you too."

"I hope you don't regret saying that." Othello pressed his forehead to his.

"I won't." Des smiled, leaning up to kiss him.

They held each other for a few minutes, then sat down to eat. Just as they were finishing up, a knock came at the door. Des went to answer it while Othello cleared away the dishes. He returned a few seconds later, with Luca Rossetti following behind him. Othello knew why he was here. He was being summoned to appear before the commission.

And so it began. "When?" he asked Luca before he could take another step further and Des could say anything.

"You have one week," Luca responded as his eyes trailed to Des.

"How gracious of him to give me so much time,"
Othello said sarcastically.

He knew what that meant: the commission was planning on

killing him, but they were giving him time to get his shit in order as they would say, an eye for an eye, only on their timeline. Yet, they would realize it was a mistake to take so long to kill him, and he wasn't going down so easily or without a fight.

"Where?"

"The Black Anchor." *Just hearing the name of the place, they are certainly planning on killing me.* Everyone knew that the warehouse was where the commission did most of their killings.

"I take it you were the one to suggest that place?"

"Yeah. Look, Othello, if..."

"Don't get involved, Luca," Othello said, cutting him off. "Tell your masters I will be there."

Luca didn't have a comeback, knowing that his family could not oppose the Ricci and Greco families. They willingly adhered to the commission rules that kept their families in line, like giving half their profits to the two prominent families. Meanwhile, the Romano family went against them, wanting to change the system.

"If you become the head of the commission, Don Rossetti is willing to give you one-third of his property," Luca said.

"Why?" Othello asked.

"For protection. He wants to go legit."

"And you? What do you want?" Othello asked, staring at his once-friend.

"I will follow him to the end," Luca said, not looking away.

"Very well, I will take his request under consideration," Othello said after a few moments.

Having nothing else to say, Luca simply nodded and left.

"Want to tell me what that was all about?" Des asked when the door closed behind Luca.

"More game," he said as a simple explanation. "Just promise me you won't see Cassio Ricci anymore." "I can after I give him his money back."

"Let me do it for you." Othello smirked.

"You're going to cause trouble, aren't you?" Des said, squinting his eyes.

"Just a little." He chuckled.

"I don't believe you."

Othello pulled him into his arms. "Tesoro, I will never lie to you."

"Good."

Their lips met in a heated kiss, and Othello enjoyed the moment, forgetting about everything else as he dragged Des to the couch and made love to him, loving the sounds of his gasps and moans when he buried his cock deep inside of his Tesoro.

SCENE IV

DES

"*I* don't want to leave," Des said, wrapping himself up in Othello's arms.

"Then don't. Spend the day with me." Othello buried his face in Des's neck, making him giggle.

"I wish I could, but I need to meet with Erin about my mom." He sighed. "Stop that. I'm trying to be serious." Des playfully slapped Othello on his arm, then wiggled out of his hold.

"Me too."

Othello dived on top of him, holding Des down, and honestly, he didn't put up much of a fight. He enjoyed feeling his lover's strength pressing down on him. Othello snuggled into his chest, and Des circled his arms around him, giving comfort to his man.

"Tell me what's going on," Othello said.

"My dad cheated on my mom, and now they're getting a divorce." Othello didn't comment or move, which got Des's attention. "You don't seem surprised."

"I'm not. I knew about the mistress, and the son they had together."

Des felt his anger surge and tried to push Othello off him. "Get off me," he growled.

Othello didn't fight him and sat up, looking at him.

"What the hell do you mean you knew?" Des shouted.

"You can't get angry with me—not when I did as you asked," Othello said in an even tone. "You told me you didn't want to know what your father was into, and I'm a man of my word, Des."

"But something as important as my father having a lover and another child is something you could have warned me about," Des yelled. He got off the couch and stomped to the bedroom, grabbing his clothes and angrily pulling them on.

"What are you doing?" Othello asked.

"What does it look like? I'm leaving," he spat.

"Des, don't do this. You asked me not to tell you about your father's affairs."

"I get that, alright. But you go on about trust and being upfront with each other. The least you could have done was warn me. Do you know the doctor who assisted me with Emilia's birth is that woman's son? If I'd known who he was that night, I would have kicked his ass for breaking up my family."

"No, I didn't," Othello mumbled. "You're right, I should have warned you about your father's infidelity."

Des nodded, understanding where Othello was coming from, but his anger didn't diminish. He had asked not to be told about his father's dealings, but that was when he thought it was only business. Who knew his father was a philanderer? He felt betrayed by Othello, who knew for a while that his father was cheating on his mother.

"I have to go," he said, not looking at Othello as he walked to the door.

"Wait," Othello said, stopping and meeting him at the door, handing him a thumb drive.

"What's this?"

"Everything I've got on your father," he said.

"Thanks," he said, taking it, then walked out of the door, wondering if he had done the right thing by not smoothing things out with Othello.

Once I calm down, I'll talk to him.

Des didn't waste time and went to the cafe where he'd meet Erin. He'd just gotten to the cafe and was about to open the door when an annoying voice whispered in his ear.

"Des, I was hoping to bump into you," Cassio Ricci said.

How the fuck does he always show up where I am? I really need to find out if he has a bug on me or something.

Des turned to face the man and crossed his arms over his chest. "Why? I told you the painting will take some time to complete."

"You seem angry. What happened?" Ricci asked in a calm tone.

"It's none of your fucking business," Des snapped.

"Did you have a fight with your *boyfriend*?"

"Cut the shit, you know I'm with Othello."

"What did he do to piss you off?"

"Why do you care if Othello made me angry? Our relationship has nothing to do with you."

Cassio Ricci cupped Des's cheek. "Don't be like that. I thought we were becoming friends."

Des smacked his hand away. "Don't fucking touch me," he growled, stepping closer to Ricci and staring the man square in his eyes. "I'm not Phillip. So don't hold your breath waiting for me to spread my legs for you. I belong to one man, and that's Othello Romano-Moor."

"So he told you about Phillip?"

"Yes," Des said, stepping back, putting much-needed distance between them. "And since I know what you did, I no longer want to work with you. I will send you your deposit back with interest and give you the unfinished painting to do whatever the fuck you want with it."

"So he tells you one little story, and you believe him? How easily he fools you into thinking he's some good guy," Ricci snarled. "If I told you who he really is, you'd leave him in a heartbeat."

"And what?" Des cocked his head to the side, studying Ricci. "Run into your arms like a damsel in distress? Is that how you seduced his last lover? Look, I don't give a fuck what he has to do for the family; at least I know he'll protect everyone he loves. Now, get the fuck away from me."

Ricci didn't move but smiled as if Des had said something funny. "You really are a gem, Desmond Ellington. I can see why Moor is drawn to you." Before Des could fathom what was happening, Ricci grabbed him by the back of his neck and brought his lips down on his.

Des's eyes widened in realization. He pressed against Ricci's chest pushing him away as he struggled for breath. Opening his mouth, he bit down on Ricci's lip, drawing blood, and pushed him away.

"You asshole," he spat, dragging the back of his hand across his mouth.

"Delicious," Ricci said, licking his lips, chuckling. "We'll meet again, Des." He then walked off, leaving Des feeling disgusted.

"I told my brother you were a slut, and he should dump you before you break his heart, but he wouldn't listen to me."

Des looked over his shoulder as Iago Romano walked up to him.

"I didn't kiss him. He kissed me," Des said defensively.

"That's not how it looked. I'm sure my brother will see it my way. Unless..."

"Unless what?" Des quirked a brow.

"If you want this to remain between us, you will dump Othello. You're not good for him."

"I'll just tell Othello the truth," Des said.

"You really think Othello will believe you, especially after seeing this?" He held up his mobile phone, showing Des a video of what happened with Ricci, and he felt his world crumble. From the way Ricci held him possessively at the back of his neck and the tilt of his head, his palms on his chest, it appeared he was into the kiss when it couldn't have been further from the truth.

"It's really not what it looks like," Des mumbled.

Iago reached into his pocket and pulled out a business card, pushing it in front of Des, who didn't take it. "Call me when you're ready to break things off." He stuffed the card into Des's hand and walked away, leaving him unsure of what to do.

He wasn't sure how long he had been standing there when he heard Erin's question.

"Des, why are you standing out here in the cold?"

"Erin, I fucked up," he said and rushed into her arms, holding her.

"It's okay. Tell me what it is, and we'll deal with it," she said, wrapping her arms around him.

"I hope so," he said, holding her tightly. "Because if we can't, I will lose Othello."

* * *

LATER THAT NIGHT, Othello threw his phone down on the coffee table, frustrated for the fifth or maybe the hundredth time. He had been trying to call Des, but it went to voicemail. He wasn't sure when he had grown so attached that Des's voice would put him in a good mood.

He still can't be angry with me, right? I did what he asked me to do. Fuck!

He was about to reach for his phone again when someone knocked on his door. Othello quickly got up and opened it, hoping it was Des.

"Oh, it's you," he said, walking to the kitchen for a drink.

"Don't look so happy to see me, little brother," Iago said, letting himself in, following behind Othello.

"What are you doing here, Iago?"

"I came to see if we're cool about last night."

"As long as you stop thinking Des is going to fuck me over, then, yeah. Besides, we're brothers; we fight and argue, make up and move on."

"You're right, we are." Iago smiled.

"Good. Want a drink?" he asked, holding up the whiskey decanter.

"Sure," Iago said. "But you don't normally drink. What's going on? Are you worried about the commission?"

"No, I just feel like having a drink," he said, pouring them two glasses.

"I heard you were summoned," Iago said. Othello's glass stopped halfway to his lips, and his brows tightened in question, which Iago noticed. He hadn't informed anyone of Luca's message, and he was certain Des hadn't either. "I was informed that, as your consigliere, I needed to be there with you."

"Oh," he said, downing his drink in one gulp, ignoring the slight burn.

"You have to be careful, O. For what happened, they might take our properties or demote you to a capo."

"Enough! What's with you being so fucking negative lately? It's not my time to die yet. I plan on living a long fucking time."

"I'm just worried, okay? We've worked hard to get the family as far as we have..."

"And we're going to go to the top. Soon Ricci and Greco will be out of the way and we will be the only

powerful family in Verona Heights."

"Are you planning on telling Papa?"

Othello shook his head. "No, Alessandro and Maria don't need to be bothered on their vacation."

"But what if they..."

"Iago, stop. I'll be fine. We'll be fine. If they demote me, you'll be the don."

A gleam flashed in Iago's eyes but disappeared quickly at the mention of him becoming the don, and if Othello hadn't been paying attention, he would have missed it.

"I'm not don material," he said softly. "If I were, Papa would have picked me over you."

"There was more to Alessandro choosing me than you," Othello said.

"Yeah, what's that?"

"You're not a killer. You're strategic and tough; you can handle yourself in a fight, but killing is not your thing. Growing up, you were the one who came up with all the plans; I followed them. The night we were ambushed, you went and hid, Iago."

"I..." Iago started, but Othello stopped him.

"Don't try to defend it. I know that you did. I'm not mad at you for that. You did what you had to do."

"Then it proves I'm not cut out to be a don."

Othello smiled and placed a gentle hand on Iago's shoulder. "If I get demoted, I will have your back just as I know you will have mine."

Iago smiled and cupped the back of his neck, bringing their foreheads together. "Damn right, I will."

They chuckled and spent the next few hours discussing everything under the sun and moon. After a couple of drinks and a long talk, Iago finally went home. Othello felt it was too late to call Des and planned to see him in the morning to make up with his lover.

* * *

THE NEXT MORNING, Othello groaned, reaching for his phone when it vibrated. He hadn't slept well since he'd grown used to Des being next to him. He grabbed his phone and saw that it was Zoraki Law calling.

"You better have a good reason for waking me up."

The throaty laughter on the other end of the phone made him scowl.

"I'm in your neck of the woods, my friend," Zoraki said in perfect English.

"Why?"

Zoraki Law was born in Japan, but his parents moved to the States when he was five. They'd moved back a few years later.

It was then that he found out that Zoraki was part of the yakuza and had moved up in the ranks, becoming the leader, which was handed over to Zoraki after his death. When Othello set up the meeting with Kurohue's rival, he had no idea it was Zoraki since he had changed his name and persona after moving back to Japan.

"I'm meeting with an investor. I knew you'd be interested in it."

"Really?" That had Othello sitting up in bed. "Who?" "Cassio Ricci."

"When did he contact you?" Othello asked seriously. "And why am I just now hearing about it?"

"I'm telling you now. So, do you want to go with me or not?"

"Postpone it," Othello said. "Why? Is something going down?" "My execution," Othello joked.

"Ah, brother, who did you piss off?" Zoraki joked.

"Can I join in on the fun?"

Othello chuckled. "Sure. I'll send you the details later." "I'll be waiting. Until then, I'll enjoy your city."

They ended the call, and Othello put his cellphone back on the nightstand and flopped back on the bed, staring at the ceiling. He hadn't heard from Des since he left yesterday, and he couldn't shake the feeling that something was wrong. His cellphone vibrated, and he grabbed it, seeing that it was a message coming through from an unknown number. He was going to ignore it until he realized it was an image. The second he opened it, he saw red.

Des kissing Ricci.

"What the fuck," he snarled, pushing to blankets back and getting out of bed.

He called Des, and just like yesterday, it went right to voicemail. Othello growled in anger as all kinds of thoughts ran through his mind. He didn't want to think everything was a lie between him and that Iago was right, and there was something going on between Des and Cassio.

He didn't want to think he'd been wrong all this time about Des, and the argument was a ploy to throw him off, stopping him from asking about Cassio. Othello was about to call Des again but instead threw his phone at the wall, angrily smashing it. It felt like it was the fucking Phillip situation all over again.

Cassio seducing his lovers was an act of revenge for an act of the past. Cassio was a fucking prick on all levels, and his every action was to bring Othello down. He had been angry when Phillip cheated on him with Cassio, but not enough to kill.

Othello had figured that if Phillip loved him, he wouldn't

have cheated. Othello sat on the bed and dropped his face in his hands, trying to calm down. He wanted to believe that Phillip and Des weren't the same.

"I need to know the truth, even if it hurts." Getting up from the bed, he dressed, ignored the broken phone, and left his apartment. He headed straight to Des's apartment and banged on the door and wished he had his gun because, at that moment, he wanted to kill Cassio Ricci, who opened the door.

So he did the next best thing and used his hand and started slapping and punching Ricci before the man could open his mouth to utter a word. He heard a crack and someone yelling, but he suddenly went deaf, and his mind went blank because all he could see was red.

He could tell they were moving back as Ricci fell and Othello straddled his waist, not letting up. Othello didn't know how many times he'd hit Ricci, but he was pushed away just as he raised his fist again.

Othello growled and was about to lunge at the person who interrupted him, giving Ricci the beatdown he needed. He stopped when he saw Des standing between him and Ricci.

"Othello, what are you doing? What the fuck are you even doing? Why would you attack someone like that?"

"Is that all you have to say to me?" Othello shouted.

"What do you want me to say?" Des asked, looking away from him.

"What the fuck is he doing here?" Othello bellowed, pointing to a bloody-faced Ricci groaning as he got up off the floor. He waited for Des to respond, but his lover had not spoken. Othello scoffed and shook his head. "So, this is it."

"Othello, it's not what it looks like," Des whispered.

"Really? So you kissing him is not what I think it is?" Othello raged.

"How did you find out?" Des exclaimed, his eyes widened in shock.

"So you're not even going to deny it?" Othello shouted.

"Shut the fuck up, Moor! Can't you see you're scaring the little dove," Ricci said, standing next to Des. "I told you he was a beast and not good enough for you. He's been hiding this part of himself. Imagine what else he's hiding."

"Keep talking, Cassio, and I'll snap your fucking neck," Othello said, burning with anger.

Cassio went to retort, but Des spoke up, stopping him.

* * *

"Leave," Des said.

"Don't you hear him, Moor? He wants you to go."

"I meant you." Des turned his gaze to Ricci. "You got what you came for."

"Are you sure you want me to leave? Especially when he's like this? He might do something to you."

"I'm not the one he wants to hurt." Des looked at Othello. "It was a mistake to call you here, Mr. Ricci. I should have met you in a public place, but like yesterday, I'm sure it wouldn't have stopped him from doing what he did." Des sighed. "I will repeat this: you and I will have nothing to do with each other."

"Call me if you need me," Ricci said, ignoring Des's words and Othello's growl, purposely spurring on his anger. "Moor, count your days. You have one week to get your shit together. Be grateful that I might not add this

little incident to your list of crimes."

"Fuck you, Ricci," Othello spat. "I went too easy on you since you're able to fucking stand and talk. But I can fix that real quick."

"You're a fucking unmannered bull who's never been taught how to heel," Cassio sneered.

"Say that shit again, and I'll pull your fucking tongue out and shove it down your throat," Othello roared.

"Don't you dare say another word," Des cut in. He couldn't take Cassio insulting Othello, calling him names, and referring to him as an animal; it was degrading and disgusting. "Please, just go."

"You're right, I should go. After all, I have a trial to prepare for. Lots of evidence to collect. And Moor, I'd rather fuck the pretty dove instead."

With that last barb, Cassio left them alone. Des didn't want to look at Othello. He had been avoiding his lover's call since yesterday. After what happened, he'd spent most of the night at Erin's house, crying on her shoulder.

Erin had convinced Des to cut all ties with Cassio by giving him the unfinished painting and his deposit back with interest. She also suggested that Des tell Othello everything. He didn't expect Othello to show up at his front door and beat the shit out of Cassio, who deserved it in many ways.

Des had never seen Othello so angry before, but it didn't scare him as much as it should have. His only worry was how he would hide the evidence from Gray.

Fuck, I'm not even concerned if a man dies, but how to protect Othello.

If he was being honest, he had to force himself to stop Othello from kicking Cassio's ass. He couldn't deny that a tiny part of him was shaking in fear. The rage he saw in his lover's eyes should have made him want to run and never look back, but it aroused him. And now he might lose him over something as stupid as a kiss he didn't want.

He loved Othello too much. Othello was the man he wanted to have children and build his life with. A family of his own was something he yearned for but thought he couldn't have because he'd been so focused on living the life his parents set out for him. But now he had a chance. Othello knew and understood him far better than he did himself. Although it wasn't his fault, he knew their trust in each other was fractured but not unrepairable.

"I'm sorry," he mumbled.

"For what? For liking him touching you?" Othello hissed. "For ignoring all of my calls? Or could it be for

liking his lips on yours? For giving in to him?!"

"No!" Des shouted. "For not telling you the second it happened. We were arguing, and I told him we shouldn't work together anymore. Then he just hauled off and kissed me, and by the time I got my head on straight, Iago..."

"What the fuck does my brother have to do with you kissing another man?"

"He saw us, so I assumed he told you..."

"My brother would never keep something like this from me," Othello said, cutting him off. "I received an anonymous video this morning."

"Then he must have sent it," Des said.

"You're saying Iago would send me a video of you kissing Cassio? For what reason?" Othello shouted.

"I don't know," Des yelled back. "Yesterday, when everything happened, he told me to break up with you, or he'd tell you himself. I guess he jumped the gun and sent you the video," he explained, a bit calmer than he felt.

"You're lying to me, Des."

"I'm not, Othello. Please, listen, I'm telling you the truth," Des pleaded, hoping the man he loved would see he was telling the truth, but to his disappointment, Othello scoffed and shook his head.

"After every fucking thing I asked you not to do, you did it. I asked you never to cheat or lie to me, and you did both."

"Othello, I..."

"I saw Iago yesterday, and he mentioned nothing. And I know my brother. He would tell me, no matter how much it would hurt me."

"Well, I don't know what to tell you," Des screamed, not hiding his anger at Othello for doubting his word.

"How about the damn truth?" Othello exploded.

The tension between them was so hot that Des was sure his apartment was going to burn down.

"Why bother fighting when you don't believe me?" Des growled. "Is there so little trust between us that you can't even tell when I'm telling the truth?" Des shook his head, taking ragged breaths, trying not to cry that the illusion he had built of him and Othello was a mirage.

"Othello, please believe me. I'm not like Phillip or any other man who has trampled on your heart. What I feel for you is real. What happened yesterday wasn't my fault. I didn't ask to be kissed. He simply did it on his own. In fact, I told Ricci to go to hell, and then Iago threatened me..."

"Leave my brother out of this," Othello said furiously. "He warned me you would break my heart, and I refused to listen. I kept telling him you're not like Phillip."

Hearing that, tears slid down Des's cheeks, unable to stop them.

"Othello." He went to touch the other man, but Othello backed away, cutting Des deep. "Fine, if you don't believe me, ask Iago yourself."

"I will," Othello said. "But until then, I don't want to see you. I can't trust you right now, Des."

"Othello, don't do this, please. We need each other. I need you," he cried, wanting to hug his lover and feel his comforting arms around him, but Othello simply walked by him and out the door. Des let out a howling cry, falling to his knees as he felt his heart shatter into pieces.

* * *

OTHELLO STOOD outside Des's apartment, listening to him cry. It broke his heart even more. Part of him wanted to return inside, and the other refused to let him cave in. Othello couldn't believe Des lied to him.

Shaking his head, Othello walked away. He stopped by the Romanos' home to get an extra phone he had stashed away, before heading to Iago and Emilia's place. With so many things happening, he needed to contact his men, but he wasn't in the mood to talk with anyone.

No more than one hour later, Othello pulled up to Iago's home, still burning with anger. He could have had one of his guys get the phone for him, but he didn't want to deal with the hassle of explaining things. Getting out of his car, he noticed Roderigo's car sitting in the driveway and shook his head. Lately, it seemed that Roderigo was everywhere. Iago was like his little puppy, begging for scraps.

Othello thought he should turn around and leave because Roderigo was another person on his hit list, but he needed answers. Clenching his fists, he ignored the slight pain he felt as he took a deep breath. Othello had forgotten how hard Cassio's face was. He walked up to the house and knocked on the door, waiting for Emilia or Iago to open it. But he had to hold on to all his anger when Roderigo opened the door.

"Moor, what the fuck do you want?"

Othello grunted and pushed Roderigo out of the way, not saying a word, and entered the house just as Iago came out to meet him.

"I need to talk to you," Othello said.

Iago furrowed his brows. "You look upset. What's wrong?"

"Get rid of your friend so we can talk," Othello told him. He went to the living room, sat on the couch, and waited for Iago to get rid of his annoying guest. Othello looked around, seeing pictures of the twins spread out around the room. He smiled for the first time in hours. They were getting bigger, and it had only been a couple of months since they were born.

"Alright, talk to me," Iago said, walking into the room.

"Where's Emilia?" Othello asked, not answering immediately. It was unusual for him to be in Iago's home for more than five minutes, and Emilia hadn't come to greet him.

"She went to meet one of her friends." He smiled. "She said she wanted to show off the twins."

"Oh. Things getting better between you two?"

"Not even close," Iago tsked. "She keeps pulling away from me."

"I don't know how to help you."

Iago shook his head. "I'll get her back. I need to give her time to get over her anger. So," Iago said, sitting down and staring at Othello.

"Did you see Des yesterday before you came to my place?" Othello asked, getting right to the point.

"No," Iago told him. "I haven't seen him since the night the twins were born." He leaned forward. "Why, did something happen?"

"He lied to me," Othello whispered, his voice cracking. "He said you told him to break it off with me."

"What?" Iago said, his eyes widening in shock, sitting on the edge of his chair. "I know I have problems with him because he doesn't understand our world, but I've never even talked with him. Why would he say that? Is he trying to come between us?"

Othello stared at Iago for a few seconds before responding. "I found out he kissed Cassio Ricci."

"Fuck. What? Please tell me you broke things off with him?" Iago asked.

Othello didn't say anything.

"O," Iago growled. "You can't do this to yourself again!"

"I know, alright," Othello shouted. "It's just..."

"It's just what? You think it won't happen again. Isn't that what you said with Phillip?" Iago argued.

"Des is different, okay! And just because he made one mistake, I don't..."

"You know, for a smart man, I swear when you get a piece of ass, you become stupid," Iago shouted at him. "I kept telling you..."

"I'm not in the mood to hear I told you so, Iago."

"Well, too fucking bad," Iago snapped. "I warned you he would break your heart."

"It was only a kiss," Othello said, no anger in his voice.

"For now." Iago huffed. "What's to stop it from being more next time? And again, another of your lovers runs to Cassio Ricci. Are you sure he's not working with him?" "You know, I'm getting the feeling that you're enjoying my heartbreak," Othello said, looking at his brother.

Iago rolled his eyes. "Of course not. I want you to be happy. You know that, but with someone who never betrayed you."

"I don't think that will ever happen," Othello mumbled. "Look, I'm going to go. I need some time to myself right now."

"Are you sure you should be alone?"

"Yeah, I have work to do." Othello didn't forget that he still had to meet with Gratiano later that night. He thought about telling Iago about the meeting, but that would mean breaking a code between him and Gratiano.

No one, not even Iago and Alessandro, knew he was their agent on the police force. The Romano family and all the other families had their own people, but Gratiano was his alone. Othello stood and wobbled just a bit as his stomach growled loudly, reminding him that he hadn't eaten anything all day.

"You alright?" Iago asked, coming to stand next to him.

"Yeah, I gotta go," he said, brushing off Iago's worry.

But before he could take a step, Iago stopped him.

"You don't look so good; you should rest here a bit.

"I'm fine, Iago," he said, walking away before his brother could stop him again. He needed to be alone and think about what to do about his relationship with Des.

FINAL ACT

"O fool, fool, fool!"
Othello (Act 5, Scene 2)

OTHELLO

*O*thello arrived at the docks thirty minutes early, sat in his car, and waited for Gratiano and his guest to arrive. He had been ignoring Des's calls since he left Iago's house. Othello rubbed his chest, hoping the pain he'd been experiencing all day would disappear, but it only worsened.

He slumped in his seat and closed his eyes, suddenly feeling exhausted. His emotions had been in turmoil for the entire day—hell, for the past few months. He was just happy that he could close the door on who the rat in the family was.

Othello vowed to make the fucker suffer before he killed them. He was drifting off to sleep but snapped his eyes open when a light tap on his window woke him up, revealing

Gratiano standing there. What made him frown was the person standing next to him.

Emilia, what is she doing here?

Othello noticed that she also had the twins with her, which bothered him. He rolled down his window. "You two get in," he said. They nodded, and Gratiano helped Emilia settle the twins before getting on the passenger side. Othello drove off. Neither one asked where he was going, but during the entire drive, Othello kept looking in the rearview mirror at Emilia, who seemed nervous.

Thirty minutes later, Othello pulled off the road and stopped in a wooded area covered by many trees. He hadn't been in this area before but had driven by it many times, knowing that no one would suspect them to be there.

"Alright, someone tell me what's going on?" Othello said them both. "How do you two know each other?"

"It's not what you're thinking," Gratiano said quickly.

"Why don't you tell me what I'm thinking?" Othello said, looking at Gratiano.

"Emilia isn't the traitor, but she is connected to him.

You both are," Gratiano said.

"What are you talking about?"

"You're not the only one I know in the family, boss. Emilia and I have interacted on many occasions because of our jobs. Did you forget she does public relations for the police department? You asked me to investigate, and I did. I brought you the name of the traitor, along with the evidence, Othello."

Othello didn't respond. His brain felt muddled, and while it hadn't occurred to him earlier, it still didn't explain why Emilia was here. He also felt a sinking feeling in his gut that he wouldn't like what they told him.

"Othello," Emilia said in a shaky voice, trying to get his attention. "I'm leaving Verona Heights and taking the twins with me."

"What?" He turned in his seat and glared at her. "What nonsense are you talking about? What about Iago?"

"What about him? After all he's done to me and you, do you expect me to stay?" she argued.

Othello knew one day Iago would lose her with all the shit he'd been doing. "What do you mean what he's done to me?"

The car was silent for a few seconds before Emilia spoke. "I debated how to tell you this, gods. I can't believe this is happening."

"Just tell me," Othello told her.

"I can do better than that. I can show you," she said, pulling out her cellphone. "A few months ago, I stumbled on a conversation between Iago and Roderigo. I don't like him. There's something about how he fawns over Iago; I almost suspected they were sleeping together." She smiled wryly. "Anyway, I only heard the last part, and Roderigo said everything is set at the warehouse. I didn't know what that meant, but then you got shot, and at first, I didn't connect the dots. But after that, Roderigo kept visiting. Once, when Iago thought I was out, Roderigo came with

another man I'd seen before."

"Who?" Othello asked, as the pain in his chest intensified, and his stomach felt as if it were going to burst as his anger started to rise.

"Cassio Ricci," she said, and Othello closed his eyes, holding back his anger.

"What were they talking about?" Othello asked, his chest tightening.

"You," Emilia answered, then handed him her cellphone.

Othello did not reach for it right away, but he knew he would regret it if he didn't. It was a video, and on the screen, Iago, Cassio, and Roderigo sat in the living room as if they had been friends for years. Othello didn't know how long he stared at the screen before he pressed play, and that was when he heard the conversation.

"Falcon has everything ready. His men will ambush Moor at the docks," Roderigo said excitedly.

"How did you get his schedule?" Ricci asked.

"I'm his consigliere. It's nothing for me to ask for his assistant for those things," Iago responded.

"I thought they've been guarding his schedule since the shooting?" Roderigo asked.

"They are so fucking tight-lipped, I can't wait to get rid of them and him. Hell, I didn't even know he was fucking someone one until Cassio told me," Iago grumbled.

"Well, it won't be for long," Roderigo said giddily. "I can't wait to stomp on him for what he did to me."

"All you care about is your club," Iago said.

"It's more than that, and you know it," Roderigo huffed. "I couldn't move the gold bars and drugs before Moor took over the place. Building a secret compartment large enough to hold the goods in the storage room was a good idea, but I knew I couldn't keep them there for long. Moor is so stupid. I bet he still doesn't know it's there."

"Make sure once you get your club back, I get my fucking cut," Cassio said.

"We won't cheat you. Just do your part and give us the resources we need," Roderigo said.

"You need to teach your boy some manners. I should go," Cassio said and stood. "I await your word on Moor's capture."

"Wait, how are you doing with the other thing?" Iago said.

"It will take some time, but I will have the good little doctor in my bed soon. Once you get Moor out of the way, I will swoop in and comfort him. Hell, I might not even wait until he's dead."

Othello stopped the video and looked out the window. He couldn't believe what he'd just watched. He didn't want to believe the man he had called brother for most of his life was working with the enemy.

"There's more," Emilia whispered. Othello or Gratiano did not interrupt. "Since then, I've secretly recorded each time Iago and Roderigo meet. It was all Iago. He planned the ambush with Roderigo and Ricci to kill you, but each time you survived, he grew angrier. I don't know what they did, but Iago and Cassio plotted to break you and Des up. I'm not sure what they did, but they want it to appear as if he cheated on you, like Phillip."

At Emilia's words, Othello's heart broke. Othello recalled all the instances in which Iago tried to get him to see that Des was a cheater. But it was all a ploy. Othello didn't want to believe it, but his brother lied to him and wanted him dead.

"Why?" he asked, feeling choked up, but he held it together. He couldn't show how angry he was.

"I don't know. Maybe he's jealous," Emilia answered with a shrug. "It's one reason Iago won't give anyone whenever he's asked. They know he wants you gone from his life. And not just you."

"What do you mean?" Othello asked, even though he might know the answer.

"Alessandro and Maria. Once you're dead, he plans to send his men to kill them," Gratiano answered for her. "I suggest you send some more people to protect them."

"They've got Carlo, Vito, Marco, and Nico with them. Trust me, no one is getting close to them," he growled through gritted teeth. Othello gripped the steering wheel so tightly, he thought he might tear it out of its socket.

"What are you going to do?" Gratiano said.

"I don't know," Othello answered honestly. He was so confused, angry, and heartbroken. Part of him wanted to confront Iago, while another knew he needed to work things out with Des.

Fuck, Des. I accused him of lying to me. Will he ever forgive me?

Othello took deep, calming breaths, but he couldn't

explode, not yet. He didn't want to scare the twins. But he was ready to hurt someone for fucking with his life.

"Give me the rest of the evidence," he said to Emilia.

"It's all on the phone. You can keep it. After tonight, I want nothing more to do with Iago," she said.

"You understand what could happen if I decide to take revenge, right?" he asked, looking Emilia in her eyes.

"Othello, I knew the world I walked into when I agreed to be with Iago. I knew it was dangerous, and yes, it was exciting. I guess it's one of the reasons Des is attracted to you." She smiled. "But I'm tired of his cheating, I'm tired of feeling under-appreciated, and I'm tired of his lies. The only good thing that came from Iago is my twins, but I can't be with him any longer. I'm not asking you to take revenge for me; it only looks that way. I've spent enough time crying and dealing with what will happen."

"Is that why you didn't want him in the delivery room with you?" Othello asked.

Emilia nodded. She dashed away the tears that slipped down her cheeks. "Do you know how jealous I am of Des? Just one night, I saw how much you love him, and it made me realize that Iago didn't understand my love for him."

Othello felt like an asshole because hours ago, he had accused Des of lying to him.

"Don't let Iago and Cassio's game work, Othello. Hold on to Des, and build the family you've always wanted."

Othello nodded, her words sinking in. He had to apologize to Des, but first, he needed to get his shit together.

"When are you leaving?" Othello asked Emilia.

"Tonight, I'm driving out of town," she answered. "I hope to be hours away before he realizes I'm gone. Iago thinks I'm out with a friend." Emilia chuckled, but her eyes didn't sparkle. "But I doubt he even knows which friend since he's never taken an interest beyond his own needs." "Where are you going to go?" he asked her.

"I'd rather not tell you," Emilia said. But I'll send you updates on the twins. I don't want them to forget their uncle." She handed him a piece of paper. "This is my new number. No one else has it."

"I understand," Othello said, putting the paper in his front jacket pocket. I wish it hadn't come to this. If you need me, Emilia, call."

"I will, but make sure you survive for me to do that. Tell Alessandro and Maria I'm sorry. They were the parents I never had, and I hate to leave them."

Othello nodded, started the car, and drove her back to the docks. It was another silent drive, as all three were deep in their thoughts. Before Emilia exited the car, Othello reached into his pocket, pulled out a prepaid credit card with nearly twenty thousand dollars, and handed it to Emilia.

"I'll add money to it monthly," he told Emilia.

"You don't have to do that," she said, pushing the card toward him.

"They are my niece and nephew; I want to care for them."

"Thank you," Emilia smiled. "I will miss you, Othello. Now that I'm leaving, I can tell you that I had a serious crush on you when we first met. But Iago won my heart; too bad he abused it."

"I'm sorry," he whispered.

Emilia shook her head, leaned forward, and kissed him on his cheek. "Don't be. You've been the perfect gentleman. I know how angry you are right now, and I can tell you're doing everything not to show it. I'm sorry I didn't come to you earlier, but I needed evidence. I know how much you love and trust Iago. It hurts me to the core that I had to do this, but he forced my hand."

"What did he do?" Othello calmly demanded.

"It doesn't matter. It's in the past now," she told him, then cupped his face. "Don't let him win, Othello."

Seeing that he wouldn't get any answers from her, Othello nodded. They all got out of the car, and before she could get the twins out of the vehicle, Othello hugged her tightly.

"No matter what, thank you, and take care of yourself," he said softly. "I will."

"Drive safe," he told her.

They held each other a little longer before letting her go. Othello kissed the twins, saying his goodbyes. He had hoped he'd be able to see them grow up, but he understood why Emilia had to leave. Othello's heart was breaking as he watched Emilia's car disappear into the night, and he let loose all the anger he had been holding at bay.

He howled and rammed his fist through the back passenger window. He ignored the pain and shards of glass cutting into his skin. The pain in his chest intensified. He felt lightheaded and dizzy but didn't fall because Gratiano caught him and held him against the car.

"I got you," Gratiano said, holding him in a bear hug.

At Gratiano's words, tears rolled down his cheeks, and Othello didn't stop them. In all his life, he had never thought that the person who would try to kill him was his brother. They had been through thick and thin and had each other's back. Or maybe it was all in Othello's head.

Unlike the videos Iago showed him, Othello didn't need any more evidence that Iago had betrayed him. He wanted to know why but knew the only way he would get answers was to confront Iago, which he was not ready to do. His heart ached, and tears continued to fall as images of him and Iago laughing and talking played through his mind as if reminding him of a different time.

He recalled the first time they met, the mischief they got into, and the birthdays they celebrated when the house matron would forget. Othello never thought that he would have to worry about Iago being the one to smile in his face and stab the knife in his back.

Othello didn't know how long he had been leaning against the car, crying, but he was thankful that Gratiano hadn't spoken. He just stood by Othello's side and waited for him to collect himself. During his meltdown, Gratiano had also removed the glass shards and wrapped his hand in a hand-kerchief.

"I won't ask you about your plans yet," Gratiano said. "But I want in."

"What are you saying?" Othello asked, feeling muddled.

"I want to take my rightful place at your side, Othello. It's time. I've already turned in my resignation to the department. I'm tired of living a double life."

Othello sighed and looked up at the stars. "Clear things up with Des first."

"I planned to," Gratiano said.

Othello nodded. "Take care of him for me. Protect him, Gratiano. Iago and Cassio's plan almost worked," he told Gratiano. "I got a video of him kissing Cassio, and things esca-lated." Othello felt choked up, remembering that he had called Des a liar even after he had told him he loved him. "I fucked up, but before I make things right with him, I need to take care of Iago and the rest. So, I'm not sure when I'll see him again."

Othello sighed and shoved his hands in his pockets. "I don't care what you do with it, but get rid of the car."

"Why?" Gratiano asked. "It's a good car. We just need to get the window fixed."

"It was a gift from Iago," Othello said and continued walk-ing. Othello didn't have a plan for handling Iago, but he was certain he would make him pay.

* * *

"Des, tell me what's wrong," Bianca asked softly, brushing his hair from his face.

Des was sitting on the sofa with a blanket draped over his shoulder and his phone, his hand redialing Othello's number every five minutes and sending a text in between. All went unanswered. Sometime during the day, his mother had returned home and hadn't left his side, only to answer the door when Bianca showed up.

It was as if she knew he needed her. Des looked away from his cellphone when there was a knock at his front door. Ava got up from his side and went to answer it. Des's heart thundered in his chest, hoping that it would be Othello coming back.

"Desmond, you have a guest," his mother said, returning with Gratiano behind him.

"Gray, what are you doing here?" Des asked, his voice hoarse from crying.

Gray didn't answer but looked at his mother and Bianca. "Ladies, could you give us the apartment? I need to talk to Des about something."

When Gray said that, Des knew something had happened that involved his lover, and Gray had to arrest him. It was the only way he could explain why Othello hadn't come to see him after talking with Iago.

"Why do we have to leave?" Bianca argued, crossing her arms over her chest.

"Do you know why he's in this state?" his mother asked worryingly.

"I think I might know, but what I have to say is for Des's ears only," Gratiano responded.

"Very well," Ava said. "If it will pull him out of this funk, we will enjoy a cup of something warm at the nearby cafe. I realize I know nothing of my son's friends."

"I don't..."

"Bianca, please, not right now," Gratiano said tiredly, cutting her off before she could go on a rant.

"Fine," she huffed and left with his mother.

"Did you arrest him?" Des growled.

"No," Gratiano said and sat beside him. "But you won't be seeing him for a while."

"How do you know that?" Des asked.

"Because I was with him a couple of hours ago."

"Why were you with him? Did something happen?"

Des gasped in horror. "Don't tell me he killed Iago for lying about the kiss."

"What are you talking about?" Gratiano asked.

Des sighed and wrapped himself in his blanket, looking at his phone screen. "Cassio kissed me, and Iago caught it on video," Des explained everything that went down, not leaving out the argument between him and Othello.

"I love him so much. Why didn't he believe me?" Des cried, dropping his head on Gray's shoulder.

"It's complicated, Des," Gray said, getting Des's attention, and he lifted his head to look at his friend.

"How do you know that?"

Gray stood and took off his overcoat, then walked to the kitchen. He opened the freezer, rooted around the back, pulled out a bottle of vodka, and grabbed two glasses off the open shelf. Gray returned to the living room and put the items on the coffee table before sitting back down.

"What I'm about to tell you must stay between us," Gray said, pouring them both a shot and handing it to him.

"Does it require getting me drunk?" Des asked, taking the glass. "You know what happens when I get drunk off my ass?"

"I'm hoping for it." Gray smiled, clinking their glasses. "Here's to living your truth," he said, taking his drink in one go.

Des followed right behind him, then put his glass down for

more. "Did you know Othello attended the same college we did? He was years ahead of us, mind you."

Des didn't know that. They'd talked about many things, like his growing up and being adopted by the Romanos, not remembering his birth parents. What he wanted in the future, but funny enough, education was one topic they'd never broached.

"He's the reason I chose that school. He even paid my tuition with the stipulation that I work for him in the end." Des gasped at the horror that Othello could do that.

"Don't," Gray said. "Get that look off your face. I wanted to work for him. In fact, I begged him. But he told me I had to get an education first." Gray smiled as if recalling a moment in time. "I wanted to be useful to him, so I chose criminal justice. I figured if he had a guy on the inside, I'd be able to watch his back."

"You—you work for Othello?" Des asked, feeling the need for another drink. He hadn't expected that the man he'd known as his best friend for so many years was a double agent.

"Yes, but it was a secret between him and me. Now you, and until things are settled, it has to stay that way." "So the night I introduced you to each other...he lied to me," Des shouted, getting off the couch. "You lied to me!" "Yes," Gray answered. "But we had no other choice." "Why tell me now, then?" Des asked.

"Because things have changed for him and me," Gray responded.

"Wait, are you in love with Othello?" he asked in shock, pouring another drink.

"For fuck's sake," Gray grumbled. "Maybe you shouldn't drink anymore. I'm not in love with him. I admire Othello, and it's one reason I wanted to work for him."

Des smiled after downing his shot. "He has that effect on people."

"You know, I thought you'd be angry to find out I work for your lover," Gray said.

"Can I still call him my lover?"

"Of course you can, but you won't be seeing him for a while," Gray said.

"I don't know why I'm not mad, okay?" Des huffed and flopped back on the sofa. "Maybe it's because you plied me with alcohol before telling me everything. Hell, I'm not even mad at Othello for all the mean things he said to me today. I get how that kiss looked. If I were in his shoes, I wouldn't have trusted my words either. He's been burned by love before, making it hard for him to trust again." "He loves you, you know," Gray said.

"I love him too." Des stood. "I need to see him."

"You can't." Gray grabbed his arm and pulled him roughly back to the sofa.

"Why?" he growled angrily.

"Fuck, didn't you hear me? I said you can't see him yet. Things are hectic in his world right now, and as much as you and I want to be by his side, we can't."

Des stared at Gray, and for the first time, he saw worry etched in his friend's eyes. "What's going on, Gray? What's happening to Othello?"

"I wish I could tell you, Des, but it might put you in more danger. Othello is about to enter a dark place neither you nor I can reach. All we can do is stay out of it."

"I can't," Des said, standing again and heading to the door, but Gray got to him before he got far.

"Don't be stupid," he shouted at him. "Are you trying to get yourself killed?"

"Othello won't hurt me," Des argued.

"But they will use you to hurt him!" Gray yelled, releasing Des. "Fuck, fuck!" he cursed, dragging his fingers in his hair as he paced the length of the couch.

Des had never seen Gray so angry in all the years they had been friends.

"I told him to send you out of town before shit hit the fan, but he wouldn't listen. You two were so caught up in each other you didn't even know people were plotting against you both. And he thinks he's fucking invincible, but he's not!"

"How bad is it?" Des asked, his voice cracking in fear.

Gray stopped his pacing and looked at him. "Do you want truth or lies?"

Des swallowed. "Truth."

"They are plotting to kill him. Fuck, they've been trying to kill him for close to a year now. But this time, I think they might succeed. And the worst part is he knows he's walking into an ambush."

Des gasped and clutched his chest. He had been hurting all day, but it grew increasingly worse the second he heard Othello might die.

"I can't lose him, Gray," Des said, his voice shaking as he spoke.

"I know," he said, pulling Des into his arms and kissing him on the top of his head. "He'll figure something out. I know him."

"Are you sure?" Des buried his face in Gray's chest, allowing his tears to fall. The answer he was expecting didn't come. All he got was Gray's arms tightening around him.

SCENE II

OTHELLO

Othello walked into The Mirage, ignored the patrons and staff, and headed straight to the storage room, where high and low shelves were filled with supplies and boxes stacked neatly against the walls. He locked the double door to ensure no one would interrupt him. Othello stood at the front of the room and tried to get into Roderigo's head. After leaving the docks, he'd walked to clear his head for a while before taking a cab to the club.

During his walk, curiosity got the better of him, and he played more of the recordings Emilia had given him. Othello had to admit the three men went to great lengths to kill him.

When they couldn't get to him, they targeted his establishments, like the auction house.

Roderigo had given the cops information on the weapons
he had hidden there, but it was all Iago's plan to have the cops
raid the auction house. Ricci instructed the judge to sign off on
the documents, and it didn't help that Detective Oz was on
Greco's payroll. Othello had already suspected Ricci and Greco
were gunning for his head. He never in a million years thought
Iago was part of their pack.

He wasn't sure how Emilia got the recordings without Iago
catching her, but he was thankful she had. Iago, Roderigo, and
Ricci were so confident that they even outlined their plan to
kill Alessandro and Maria after finishing off Othello.

To be safe, Othello called the team assigned to his parents
and instructed them to tighten security and keep their location
confidential. If his parents asked, they were to say it was just a
precaution. Othello knew he would have to call Alessandro and
explain things, but he wasn't ready.

Othello knew why Roderigo and the commission despised
him but was at a loss about Iago. He loved Iago, the man he
called brother, so much that he knew he would die for him. He
scoffed and took a shaky breath to relieve his melancholy.

He couldn't afford to break down again; right now, he
needed to find the drugs and gold bars Roderigo bragged
about. Othello's emotions were all over the place. He was
missing Des, mad at himself for not noticing what was
happening around him, and confused and unsure what he
would do about Iago, but he was sure he would make the rest
of them suffer.

Othello walked around the storage room and banged on
the walls, wondering if he was losing his mind. However, he
didn't stop, moving boxes and shelves out of the way and
continuing to search. After moving at least twenty boxes, he
reached the far end of the room and noticed something off

about the wall. The room was painted gray, but this wall was a shade lighter.

He got the rest of the boxes out of the way, slid his fingers over the wall, and struck gold when he found a tiny button on the lower left side. Othello pressed it and watched as the wall slid open, where he encountered another door.

He almost gave Roderigo some credit for the ingenuity of the hidden switch, but he took it back when he saw the simple lock on the door. Othello scanned the storage room and smiled when he spotted a hammer.

"Someone is really looking out for me," Othello said to the empty room.

He grabbed the hammer, smashed the lock, and kicked the door in. Othello stepped inside, and the first thing he noticed was a pallet stacked with cash, making him wonder if it was counterfeit. He walked further inside and spotted the drugs on another pallet, with a few gold bars sitting on top of it.

A thought came to Othello, and he pulled out his cellphone and dialed Zoraki's number.

"What's up? Is it time for your execution?" Zoraki asked.

"Not for a couple more days," he answered. "Want to have some fun tonight?"

"What are you thinking?" Zoraki asked.

"I want to hire you and your men for a few jobs."

"I don't come cheap, my friend."

"I can match and triple your price," Othello said, looking at everything in the room.

"Alright, tell me what you want."

"First, I want you to pick someone up for me. I don't care what condition he's in; make sure he's alive when you get here. I'll send you the addresses." Othello hung up and texted Zoraki The Mirage's address, then cleared the club. Othello didn't care about the money he would lose and wanted the club empty when Zoraki and his crew arrived.

Iago, Roderigo, and the commission planned to kill him in a few days; however, Othello would make sure they never got the chance, and the first person he'd start with was Roderigo.

A couple of hours later, Zoraki and his men showed up with Roderigo slung over one of Zoraki's men's shoulders. Roderigo was knocked out and dressed in nothing but his underwear.

"Was he any trouble?" Othello asked Zoraki.

"No more than the usual," Zoraki responded. "Where do you want him?"

"Come this way." Othello directed them to the storage room.

"Want to tell me what's going on?" Zoraki asked.

"Your questions will be answered soon. Have your man tie him to the chair," Othello instructed.

Zoraki waved a hand, and his man did as he was told.

"Before I wake him up, have them bring everything out of the room." Othello pointed to the extra space, and Zoraki poked his head through the door and whistled. "It's all yours," he told Zoraki.

"Just for bringing a man to you? We should do business more often," Zoraki said.

"The job's not over yet," Othello said.

Zoraki stared at him for a few seconds before nodding, then instructed his men to empty the room. While Zoraki and his crew worked, Othello sat in front of the stillunconscious Roderigo and watched more videos. He replayed a few of them repeatedly, ignoring the dialogue and keeping his eyes fixed on Iago's face, searching for any signs that his brother was being forced into all of this. He still couldn't comprehend that this was entirely Iago's plan.

It was maybe one hour later when Zoraki told him everything was done. Othello nodded, stood, and, without warning, slapped Roderigo so hard it sounded like thunder cracking in the air.

"What the fuck?" Roderigo screamed, waking up.

"Nice of you to join us, Roderigo," Othello said, reclaiming his previous seat.

"Moor," Roderigo snarled. "What the fuck are you doing here?"

"Setting up your death the same way you have been planning for mine," Othello drawled.

"My death. What are you talking about?" Roderigo cackled, but his laughter died down as he looked around, noticing where he was and what was surrounding him. "H —how? How did you find my secret room?"

"I'm the one asking questions," Othello said, bringing Roderigo's focus back to him. "I've told Iago and your father you were an idiot, and every time I give you the benefit of the doubt, you crush my expectations."

"Do you think I live to please you?" Roderigo snarled.

"No, I suppose I'm not the one you're trying to impress, but I bet all you got to do was suck his dick," Othello said.

"I don't know what you're talking about?" Roderigo turned his gaze away, and Othello was sure he was close.

"My brother," he said. "How long have you been in love with him?"

"I'm..."

"Even when you're about to die, you deny it." Othello scoffed and took a shaky breath, trying to relieve the weight of his melancholy. "I guess I was an idiot to miss the signs. I knew he kept you around. Maybe your technique is that good, and he couldn't help himself." He gave a mocking smile. "We had the biggest argument when I came out of the closet. I thought the brotherhood we built from childhood was over. At least that would explain why he's trying to kill me, right? But to know that he's—"

"We never, I mean, he's never... We've only shared partners,"

Roderigo whispered. "He doesn't see me that way and never will."

"But you want him to?" Othello said sympathetically.

Roderigo was silent, and Othello thought he would not answer. "I wish just once he'd notice me. See all the things I've been doing for him," he growled. "I know he doesn't care for me like I do for him, but he hates you to the core. I bet you want to know why." Othello didn't respond.

"Look at you, all composed. Are you a man or a robot, Moor?" Roderigo snapped.

"How many of my people are loyal to Iago?" Othello asked, shutting down Roderigo's ramblings.

Roderigo didn't answer, and Othello looked at Zoraki, who got his message. Zoraki pointed to one of his men, who pulled out a gun with a silencer and shot Roderigo in the right leg, causing the man to scream bloody murder. No one moved to help him. Roderigo writhed and moaned in his chair as the scent of blood and burning flesh filled the room.

"I suggest you answer the question before you lose your other leg," Othello said. "How many of my men have gone over to Iago's side?"

Roderigo groaned in pain, and Othello grew impatient and annoyed the more time Roderigo took to answer.

"Why are you doing this?" Roderigo whimpered.

"You three sat around and plotted how to kill me, and you ask why?" Othello snarled.

"How did you find out?" Roderigo asked.

"Stop stalling and answer my question," Othello snapped.

"Are you going to kill me?" Roderigo panted, sweat coating his face.

"Stupid question," Othello said, rolling his eyes.

"Are you going to kill Iago?"

Roderigo asked the one thing he'd been wondering himself. It had been a couple of hours since Othello learned about Iago's deceit, and he was still trying to wrap his head and heart around it.

"I don't know," Othello whispered, then stood, staring at Roderigo. "I planned on burning this place down with you in it since I know how much you love this place. But it was the drugs and money you had hidden that you cared

about more. Too bad it's no longer yours."

"Moor, what are you planning? I'll tell you, none. Not one of your men would side with Iago. They don't trust him. Please don't kill me. I'll finally listen and stay away," Roderigo shouted, but Othello ignored him and looked at Zoraki.

"I don't care how you do it; just make sure it's nice and clean," he told Zoraki. "His father won't care that he's dead. His mother, on the other hand, is a different story."

Othello walked away, ignoring Rodrigo shouting his name. He then walked out of the storage room and over to the bar, pouring himself a glass of bourbon. He picked it up to drink it but growled angrily and threw his glass across the room just as Zoraki walked over to the bar. Othello was angry with himself. He wanted to feel some joy in torturing and killing Roderigo, but he felt unsatisfied and empty.

"It's hard when those closest to you betray you," Zoraki said. "What's harder is knowing that you can't let him live."

Othello knew what Zoraki said was the truth. He couldn't let Iago live. He was about to say something when his cell-phone vibrated. Pulling it from his jacket pocket, his brows furrowed when he saw Iago's name on the screen. He gasped, staring at the screen, unsure of what to do. His thumb trembled as he hesitated before he connected the call.

"Yeah," he answered, his throat scratchy and tight.

"O, I need your help," Iago said hurriedly.

"What's wrong?" he said.

"It's Emilia. She didn't come home. I called her phone, but it kept going to voicemail. Fuck, O, I think something might have happened to Emilia and the twins. I need you to help me find them."

Othello was a little shocked by the worry in Iago's voice. It was as if he really loved her.

"Didn't you say she went to see a friend?"

"Yeah, but that was hours ago. She should have been home already."

"Did you call the friend she went to see?"

"I—I don't know who she was with. I actually don't know any of her friends."

"Un-fucking-believable," Othello cursed, closing his eyes, not meaning to voice his thoughts. Emilia was right; the man knew nothing about the woman he had claimed to love for many years.

"Wait. I'll be there as soon as I can," Othello told him.

"Why can't you come now?" Iago asked.

"I'm tied up with something."

Iago was silent for a few seconds. "You're with him, aren't you?"

"What if I am?" Othello said.

"After what he did, you ran back to the fucking whore."

"Watch your fucking mouth, Iago!" Othello growled.

"Fuck, forget it. I don't need your fucking help. I'll call Roderigo. At least I know I can count on him."

Othello hung up, and a drink was pushed into his face. Othello took it, and this time, he didn't throw it and downed it in one clip, hissing at the burn.

"I don't think I can do it," Othello told Zoraki. "Even now, Iago calls me asking for help, and instead of telling him to fuck off, I can't stop myself from going to his aid."

"You don't have to kill him right away, but know the longer you wait, the more you will be looking over your shoulder. You're in a rough spot, Othello. One I wouldn't want to be in."

Tears threatened to fall, but Othello blinked them away.

Othello reached into his pocket and pulled out the keys to the club. "Lock up for me," he said, throwing them on the bar top and then walking out of The Mirage. He hailed a cab and gave him the address to the only place he knew he could feel normal. Thirty minutes later, he knocked on Des's door and pulled the man into his arms the second he opened it. He felt like he was home for the first time since finding everything out.

"I'm sorry," he whispered in Des's ear, holding him tightly.

"I know," Des said. "You came back to me, and that's all that matters."

* * *

DES SNUGGLED CLOSER TO OTHELLO, listening to his every breath. They hadn't said another word since Othello showed up on his doorstep. After his talk with Gray, Des had put it in his mind that he wouldn't see Othello because his lover would sink into a dark place, so he was surprised when the gentle knock came at his door well after midnight.

"You're going to leave me again, aren't you?" Des said, closing his eyes.

"I don't want to, but I need to."

Des sat up and looked at him. "Can't you tell me what happened?"

Othello cupped his face, staring into his eyes. "I want you to leave town for a while."

"N—"

Othello cut him off. "Don't argue with me right now, Des."

"I know you feel the need to help me, even though you know nothing about what's going on."

"I know some. Gray told me. I know he works for you. I'm still not sure how I feel about that, but I'll deal with it later. But you have to let me help you."

"You can do that by listening to me," Othello told him. "I don't know what will happen in the next couple of days, but it will take a load off my shoulders, knowing they can't get to me by using you."

"I want to cry and pout, but deep down, I know you're right. But I will do as you ask. It's the grown-up thing to

do, right? It's going to be a lonely trip."

"Why don't you take your mother?"

Des sighed. "My mom has decided to go back to work at the hospital. She said it was time for her to shake up the staff."

Des recalled the look of glee in Ava's eyes when she said those words, which he had to admit scared him a bit.

But he knew a certain doctor was about to be jobless.

"What about your friends?"

"Bianca had to leave for a trip. Erin's busy sifting through the information to take my father down and help my mom with her divorce. And I know Gray's going to be with you."

"I don't want anyone to know about Gray yet, so I'll send him to protect you," Othello said, getting out of bed.

"Are you sure?"

"Yeah." He leaned down and kissed Des deeply. "Everything I have now belongs to you, Tesoro."

Des wrapped his arms around Othello's neck and pulled him down on top of him. "I won't forgive you if you die."

Othello tightened his arms around Des, not responding. They stayed like that for a few more minutes before Othello kissed him again, leaving with more than just Des's heart.

* * *

OTHELLO OPENED the door to Iago's home. When he stepped inside, he didn't expect to see the house in disarray, as if there had been a home invasion, but his instincts told him it was Iago's doing. He closed the door and followed the trail of torn paper, broken furniture, thrown clothes, and other things to the twins' bedroom, where he found Iago sitting in a corner with a piece of paper between his fingers, staring out the window.

"You warned me, didn't you?" Iago said, not looking at him. "You told me to pay attention, to stop cheating, to get my shit together, or one day, Emilia would leave me. Why is it you're always fucking right? Why can't you be wrong for one damn time in your life?!"

"Don't blame me for your fuck-up," Othello growled.

"Do you know where she is?" Iago asked, glaring at him.

"No."

"Are you lying to me?" Iago asked.

"I can't believe you just fucking asked me that," Othello snapped.

"What's that supposed to mean?" Iago shouted.

"Do you hate me, Iago?" Othello blurted, getting right

to the point. Othello hadn't planned on bringing things up, but since he threw it out there, depending on Iago's answer, he knew what he would do.

"What the fuck are you asking me?" Iago said.

"Answer my damn question. Do you see me as your brother? Would you still take a bullet for me? Would you stay by my side and stand against the world that would want to tear us apart?"

"Are you fucking kidding me right now? My woman just took off with my children to god knows where, and you're asking me if I would die for you. I knew you were selfish, but this is too much, even for you."

Othello looked down and let Iago's words wash over him. Iago couldn't answer the question. Othello knew that if he were asked, the answer would be yes; there would be no hesitation. Othello mentally shook his head and realized he had been a fucking fool.

He'd put so much blind trust in Iago, for the man to use it against him. Othello knew that Iago could be calculating and sneaky, but that was always used against the ones they saw as rivals. Othello never thought Iago would count as one of the enemies, or maybe he did, and he pushed the thought down deep inside that he was easy to play with.

Taking a deep breath, he raised his head and looked at Iago. "Emilia's not coming back, Iago, and you must deal with what you've done. You didn't give a fuck about her when she was here, and now you want to wallow in your damn guilt."

"Fuck you, Othello," Iago roared and rushed toward him, but Othello blocked him with a hard kick to the stomach, pushing him back and to the ground.

Othello looked at Iago with disgust. "I'm meeting with the commission in two days. You can stand by my side as my brother or face me as my enemy. The choice is up to you, Iago." With that, Othello walked out of the house, stood at the front door, and noticed the sun was peeking through the horizon.

Othello was exhausted. Other than the time he spent with Des, he hadn't gotten any sleep, and he still wouldn't be able to until it was all over. His cellphone vibrated, and he looked at the screen, seeing a text from Zoraki telling him that Roderigo's body was taken care of and wouldn't be found for a few days. And that he was waiting for Othello's following instructions. He pocketed his phone and walked to his car. He had plans to make.

Two days later, at eight in the evening, Othello pulled his car up to the Black Anchor warehouse. He got out of the car, but before he could close the door, Tallen joined him on his left, along with a few others, leaving the right side where Iago usually stood empty.

"What are you all doing here?" he asked, having never told them what was going on.

"Boss, did you really think we would allow you to enter the lion's den alone?" Tallen said.

"How did you find out?" Othello asked.

"Consig Iago called us all together and told us what was happening," he explained. "Boss, why didn't you tell
us? Don't you trust us to protect you?"

"I didn't want to involve you," he said.

"We're a family," Tallen responded. "When one walks into the fire, we all jump in."

Othello chuckled and shook his head. Tallen's analogy was a bit suicidal, but he had a point.

"Whatever happens today, we're all a family," Othello said. "No matter what."

"He's right," a voice on his right said.

"You came." Othello looked at Iago.

Iago nodded. "Let's go. They're waiting."

The doors groaned on their hinges, slicing through the chatter like a blade. The sudden silence inside the warehouse hit hard, an unsettling lull that hung in the thick, dimly lit air as Othello and his crew stepped in. Every eye followed them, but the room was as still as prey holding its breath.

Tallen's voice shattered the quiet like glass. "Fuck, who beat the shit out of Underboss Ricci?" His words, sharp and unapologetically loud, echoed in the cavernous space. It should've been a whisper. It wasn't.

A few uneasy glances darted around, but the tension didn't crack. It only deepened.

Tito, young and far too reckless for his rank, snickered. "Yeah, didn't anyone teach him to duck?"

The suffocating tension in the room twisted tighter, but Othello allowed himself a rare grin. It was slow and challenging, spreading wide across his face for the first time in days. Ricci's icy glare locked onto him, only making him smile wider. Othello knew he irritated Ricci more. However, that momentary flash of amusement didn't dull the knife-edge of danger that lurked beneath it all.

Ricci's growl cut through the moment, pulling the focus back to him. "Let's get started," he snapped, forcing himself into his seat at the head of the table, flanked by Greco and the conspicuously empty chair meant for his ever-absent brother.

Othello didn't bother to sit. Instead, he tilted his head toward his men. The subtle gesture was enough. All except Iago moved to take positions around the room, standing as sentinels, backs straight, eyes sharp. The message was clear: We're ready for anything. It made Othello feel proud.

Ricci sneered. "I see where your people get their manners from, Moor."

Othello's lips twitched, but Greco's impatient voice cut through before he could reply. "Don't start," he muttered, his fingers drumming on the table. "I've got shit to do after this."

The air was thick with unspoken threats, barely restrained violence simmering just beneath the surface. Othello's grin faded, and the tension sharpened, poised to break at the slightest spark.

"Fine." Ricci gathered a stack of paper. "Moor, you have declined to invite Don Alessandro to this meeting; instead, you will have your consigliere to stand at your side. Is that correct?"

"Yes." Othello wasn't sure why Ricci was stating the obvious.

Othello wished they didn't need to be so formal, but he understood that this was Ricci's twisted form of payback. How utterly ridiculous.

"You are charged with the unsanctioned killing of Don Julian Falcon, an ally of the commission. How do you plead?" Ricci continued, his voice dripping with mock seriousness.

Othello clenched his fists. "Why don't you drop the theatrics and get to the heart of it? We all know you don't give a damn that Falcon is dead. This is your way of trying to humiliate me in front of my men."

Ricci merely smirked, the satisfaction in his eyes unmistakable. "Fine. As for your crimes, we are demoting you from your esteemed position as don to that of a footsoldier —where you will never rise in rank."

The moment Ricci said the words, shouts and sneers erupted in the warehouse, drowning out anything else he had to say. Othello's gaze darted to Iago, whose slight smile flickered and vanished, replaced with a mask of neutrality.

Hope had abandoned their relationship long ago. He turned to Greco, who was banging the gavel with increasing desperation, trying to restore order to the escalating chaos. Othello's men were restless, some brandishing their weapons, their anger palpable in the air.

"Quiet!" Othello commanded, his voice sharp enough to slice through the clamor. Instantly, the room fell into a tense silence, a fragile calm that only heightened the anticipation. He turned his eyes back to Ricci and Greco, who wore expressions of disbelief and irritation, unaware of the storm brewing for them by night's end.

"You may continue," Othello said, a hint of challenge in his tone.

"As of today, the new head of the Romano family is Iago Romano," Greco declared, his voice steady yet electrifying. "Do you accept the position, Iago Romano?"

"Does this make you happy, Iago?" Othello's heart raced as he looked at Iago. The looming question hung thick in the air, charged with unspoken stakes and impending betrayal.

"Why would you ask me that, O?" Iago asked, his eyes wide.

"You can cut the fucking act," Othello said as he looked at Greco and Ricci. "It would have been more

believable if you had ordered him to kill me."

"Who said they have to order me to do anything?" The clicking sound made Othello look at Iago, who had his gun aimed at Othello's head. At a quick glance around the room,

Othello saw his men outnumbered and outgunned by the Ricci and Greco family.

"So you decided to drop the act," Othello said, settling his gaze on Iago.

"I was getting tired of playing the good little sidekick," Iago replied.

"I see," Othello sighed, his voice heavy with sorrow. "You played me for a fool, Iago. I put my trust in you— above everyone else."

"When did you figure it out?" Iago's voice dripped with malice, eyes narrowing.

"Two days ago," Othello replied, each word edged with betrayal. "I had an unsettling conversation with someone just before they left town. You've not only burned bridges but shattered hearts. I warned you to treat her right. A woman scorned, Iago. You should know better."

Iago's fury erupted in a primal growl. In an instant, he threw his gun to the side and lunged, delivering a vicious punch to Othello's face. "You bastard!" he barked, gripping Othello by the jacket lapels, keeping him from collapsing. "Tell me where Emilia and my twins are!"

"No," Othello snapped back, his rage igniting as he shoved Iago away. "You don't deserve her! Just as you don't deserve to be the head of this family!"

"How dare you say that?" Iago shouted, his voice cracking with fury.

"You have some fucking nerve," Othello roared, not hiding his anger. "After everything Maria and Alessandro have done for you, after they've given you a home and love, you turn your back and join the enemy?"

"Love?" Iago spat, dark eyes blazing. "What love did I ever get from them? It was you. Always you! They never wanted me. No one wanted me. You've been the apple of everyone's eye since our days at Willow-Brook. Do you know what it's like to be compared to you? It made me feel less than human. Do you want to know when my hatred for you began, Othello? I overheard Maria and Alessandro deciding whether to adopt us or just you. But deep down, they knew you wouldn't go without me. Your little *tagalong*, right? I despise them just as much as I hate you."

Othello was surprised to hear that, but his expression was firm, masking the turmoil inside.

"I did everything I could to please Alessandro, to show him I could be a worthy heir, but it was a lost cause. He had already decided. You were the golden child, and I was left to stand by your side, bearing it all. It's fucking humiliating, and I refuse to be anyone's second choice."

A gasp echoed in the warehouse; Othello had forgotten that he and Iago weren't alone. Othello stared at Iago, wondering if he had ever truly known the man he'd called brother. Othello couldn't say that he hated Iago even now, with death looming over his head.

"I forgive you," Othello said, breaking one of his own codes.

"I don't want your fucking forgiveness," Iago sneered.

"Then what do you want?" he said, completely exhausted in mind, body and soul.

"To erase you from existence," Iago said.

"I can't let you kill me, Iago. Because, unlike you, I have someone who truly loves me and whom I love back."

"Oh, are you talking about your whore? Don't worry. He'll be joining you right after I put a bullet through your skull."

Othello furrowed his brows, hearing the threat against Des. "What did you do?"

"I'm glad you asked. You see, I wasn't sure how this was going to go, so I brought some insurance. To think, your own lover is fucking a cop right under your nose. Bring him in!"

A door opened in the far back of the warehouse, and a large man walked in, dragging a reluctant Des into the room. Des had tape covering his mouth, and his hands were tied behind his back. He looked scared but unharmed, which was a good thing, but Othello knew if he kept his lover here for too long, he might get hurt.

"Iago, what the fuck are you doing? Des isn't a part of our fight!" Othello growled.

"He became part of it when he got mixed up with you. I tell you he's fucking a cop, and you don't even flinch."

Othello ignored Iago and looked at Des, who was shaking his head vigorously, struggling to escape his captor, his eyes wide with fear glaring back at him. *Why is he here? Why didn't he get out of town like I told him to? Fuck, where the hell is Gratiano?*

"You have broken my heart, Iago! You've torn our relationship apart, and despite that, I was ready to forgive you. But dragging Des into this? That's something I will never let go! If one hair on his head is harmed, I will kill you all."

"You and what army?" Iago scoffed, then boasted.

"Look around, O, you're outgunned and outnumbered."

Othello quirked a brow. "Are you sure about that?"

A sharp whistle pierced the air, cutting through the tension like a blade. For a single, heart-stopping moment, everyone froze. Then nothing—silence, thick and suffocating. Relief washed over Iago's face, his lips curling into a smug grin.

"You had me there for a minute," Iago laughed, glancing at Cassio. "Cassio, the whore is yours, a token of thanks for your help in making today happen." His voice oozed with cruelty, the words sharp enough to sting. But before the moment could settle, the ceiling exploded into shards of glass.

Chaos detonated like a bomb in the warehouse. Armed men swarmed the room, gunfire erupting like a violent storm. The once-solid ground turned into a battlefield.

Othello was too far away to get to Des, and his breath caught in his chest. He relaxed somewhat when he spotted Zoraki's figure, who had landed next to Des and the man holding him hostage. "Zoraki, get Des out of here!" Othello shouted, his voice barely rising above the roar of bullets and fighting, but he was glad the man heard him. Zoraki took down Des's captor and got Des out of the chaotic warehouse.

While everyone else was distracted, Othello stepped forward, a growl tearing from his throat as he landed a vicious punch to Iago's face. Iago stumbled back, shocked by the sudden attack, but Othello didn't let up. Blow after blow, he drove Iago back, away from the bullets, away from everything. Each hit reverberated with rage and hurt from Iago's betrayal.

"Never call my lover a whore," Othello snarled, slamming his fist into Iago's ribs. Iago gasped, struggling to regain his footing.

"I call 'em like I see 'em," Iago countered, fighting back more fervently.

"You fucking caused this shit, Iago," Othello said, raw emotions building inside of him.

"You brought backup?" Iago spat, blood dripping from his split lip. They traded blows like old times, as if locked in some twisted memory. "What? Don't you trust your own men?"

Othello grinned, his face twisted in mockery. "Who said they're not my men? Your boy toy Roderigo paid for them without even knowing it. How could you use him like that? I might have hated the guy, but I wouldn't have given him false hope. You're fucking disgust me, Iago."

The jab hit Iago hard. His eyes flared with rage as he swung back, landing a punch square in Othello's stomach. "Did you kill him? I never used him. Anything he did for me was of his own will."

Before Othello could respond, an animalistic roar ripped through the chaos.

"Moor! You bastard, I'm going to kill you!" Cassio's voice ripped through the room, his eyes wild as he charged toward them, gun raised. Othello's blood turned to ice. "This is for my lover." Time seemed to slow as Cassio squeezed the trigger, the gun kicking back with each shot. Othello wanted to move—he needed to—but his legs felt rooted to the ground. A million scenarios flashed through his mind in that split second—if he could just dive for the gun at his feet, if he could just find cover —anything.

But none of that mattered.

Before Othello could react, Iago stepped in front of him. The bullet tore through Iago's chest, the impact sending both men crashing to the floor.

"No!" Othello's scream echoed in his ears as the world snapped back into harsh focus. He knelt beside Iago, panic clawing at his throat as blood bloomed through Iago's shirt, staining the white fabric with a dark, spreading circle.

"Why can't you just die already?!" Cassio's enraged shout barely registered as Othello grabbed the gun he'd seen moments before. In a blind fury, he fired round after round, the recoil jerking his arm back as the bullets found their mark. Cassio staggered, his body jerking with each hit before collapsing to his knees.

"Fuck," he gasped, and fell forward, lifeless.

The room fell eerily quiet except for Iago's faint gasps.

"Iago, stay with me!" Othello pleaded, his hands shaking as he pressed down on the wound. Blood seeped through his fingers, warm and terrifying. "Don't you dare die on me."

Iago's breath came in ragged, shallow gulps, his once confi-dent expression now contorted with pain. He coughed, blood staining his lips. "O, I… "

Othello's heart twisted, tears streaming down his cheeks, mixing with Iago's blood. "Save your breath," he said hoarsely, choked up with emotions. "You're not allowed to die. Do you hear me? I won't forgive you if you leave me."

"S-stubborn to the end," Iago panted, blood filling his

mouth as he tried to force a smile. "Tell S-sandro Ma— Maria, sorry."

"Tell them yourself, you bastard," but as he said the words, he could see Iago's eyes fading, his grip on life slipping. Othello did not want to admit it, but Iago wouldn't make it. "No," Othello cried.

"I love her," he panted. "Take care of them." Othello nodded as Iago struggled, lifting one of his hands. Othello caught it and brought it to his cheek. "I'm sorry." With those words, Iago closed his eyes and died.

Othello pulled Iago to his chest as a gut-wrenching cry erupted from deep within his soul. He didn't care who was watching. He felt more pain than the burning sting in his side. The only pain he could feel was the ache in his chest that felt as if it was going to explode. His brother was gone, and no one could bring him back. He held Iago, crying and letting out all of his pain until his world went dark.

SCENE III

Othello stood in front of the mirror, running his fingers over the tattoo that covered the gunshot wound on his side. It was another reminder of what had happened two years ago: the bullet that went through Iago and clipped Othello in his side, not damaging anything major but leaving a scar. He had woken up in the hospital, suffering not only from the bullet wound but mostly from dehydration and exhaustion.

"You're not ready yet?"

Othello smiled while buttoning his shirt and greeted Alessandro, who had entered the hotel suite. Alessandro was wearing a black tuxedo, matching shirt, and bloodred tie.

"Are you nervous?" Alessandro asked.

"A little," Othello admitted. "It is not every day a man marries the love of his life."

"I'm happy and proud of you, Othello. I don't know if I tell you that enough. I only wish Iago were here to see this. He'd be the one to take your nerves away by saying something outrageous."

Othello smiled, hoping to mask his pain. Since Iago's death, many things had changed. The Romano family now ran the underworld, and all the businesses thrived.

"I'm sure he would have," Othello said, turning away.

"I miss him."

"I miss him too. We all do," Alessandro said.

Othello couldn't look at his father at that moment. He had lied to his parents about the events and how things unfolded, keeping only one truth: that Cassio had pulled the trigger, killing Iago. He had kept Iago's dignity intact, not wanting Maria and Alessandro to know about the hateful words Iago had uttered.

They had been good parents to them both, and Othello took it upon himself to carry Iago's biting words. Even though, in the end, he was sorry. He had instructed his men not to say a word about what happened that day, and he was glad they were loyal to him and remained silent.

"You're still not ready?" Gratiano's voice came into the room, and Othello groaned.

"Don't start. We still have at least one hour before I need to be at the altar." Othello said, looking at the former cop.

"You realize Des is probably freaking out right now?" Gratiano said.

Alessandro said, "He has his mother, my wife, Bianca, Tallen, and Erin with him. I'm sure he's fine."

"Whose idea was it that he and I couldn't see each other before we walked down the aisle again?"

"Ava and Maria, now shut up and get dressed," Gratiano instructed.

Gray and Zoraki have become true friends in the past couple of years. In the days that followed, while Othello was in the hospital, Gratiano and Zoraki worked together to clean up the mess, keeping the cops, news reporters, and everyone else distracted and off their scent while they mourned their loss and buried their loved ones.

It had taken the family a while to accept that Gratiano had been one of them all along. Othello had been considering naming him the new consigliere. The position had been vacant for too long, and it was time he and everyone else moved on. Iago left a big hole and shoes to fill. It was too bad he didn't realize that he wasn't second but the best.

A gentle knock came at the door, and Gratiano went to answer it. "What are you doing here?" he asked softly. "Is everything alright with the boys?"

At the last question, Othello knew who had shown up. Emilia had returned for Iago's funeral but left again, stating she needed time. No one stopped her, but everyone encouraged her with a great understanding that she should keep in touch. Emilia returned six months ago with the twins.

At that time, she and Gratiano had grown close, and Othello was certain there would be wedding bells for another couple soon. He wasn't sure which one, since Zoraki had been trying to woo Bianca and Erin, and neither woman seemed to mind sharing his foreign friend. Zoraki had returned to Japan only long enough to check on his operations, then returned to the United States and integrated the two families operating under Otherllo's leadership.

Othello hadn't pictured his life turning out the way it had. He was committed to being alone, never marrying or having children. His only plan was to fulfill his promise to Alessandro of making the Romano family the most influential and successful in Verona Heights. As per the rules of the games, the Romano clan had accumulated all the major properties of the Greco and Ricci families.

Greco had an heir, but he wanted nothing to do with his father's business. He gave Othello everything without a fight and walked away with millions that would last him a lifetime. After learning of Cassio's death, Dominico Ricci died, leaving no heir, meaning all properties belonged to the Romano family. Othello wouldn't deny that the events had changed him. He had more than just the Romano properties to protect; he had to keep the people safe, especially those he held dear.

"You don't look nervous." Emilia handed Antonio to him. The twins came into their features daily, combining Emilia and Iago's appearance.

"It's lessened since everyone showed up," he answered, rubbing Antonio's back. They moved away from the others, taking time to talk. In the months since Emilia returned, they'd grown closer and become more like

brother and sister. "How are you doing?"

"I'm better," Emilia responded, looking in Gratiano's direction, who was holding and playing with Tybalt, making him giggle.

"He's good with the twins," Othello told her.

"He is." She nodded. "Do you think..."

"It's time, Emilia," he said, cutting her off. "You don't need to hold onto him anymore." "Gray feels guilty," Emilia whispered.

"For what?" Othello asked.

"He thinks if he hadn't convinced me to speak to you, things might not have turned out the way they did. Des might not have gotten kidnapped if he had stuck around."

"Nothing Gratiano said or did was his fault. Things were bound to happen. Iago kidnapping Des was on me for what I said to Iago the night you left."

Des had told Othello everything that had happened. Iago

had shown up at Des's apartment, ready for an argument. He saw the two best friends hugging afterward and assumed they had something going on. Gratiano left to collect a few things for their trip, allowing Iago to kidnap Des and get him to the warehouse as an insurance policy to make Othello behave. The only thing that made Othello angry was that the two hadn't left town when he told them to. After he instructed Gratiano to take Des out of the city, he cut off all communication with him to keep him safe. Othello could admit now that it was a stupid mistake.

"He's asked me out," Emilia said, breaking into his thoughts. Her eyes hadn't looked away from Gratiano.

"And?" Othello handed Antonio back to her.

"Maybe after the wedding," she responded.

"Why not as his plus-one?"

"This is your day with Des. You two have been waiting for this moment. Especially after all the trouble his mother gave you."

"We wouldn't be getting married if I hadn't won her over," Othello said.

"I swear even the big, bad, Don Othello RomanoMoor is afraid of his boyfriend's mother."

"She was a hard nut to crack." He smiled, turned, and finished getting dressed.

When he woke up, Des was sleeping next to him on the bed, practically draped over him, and Ava was on the chair not far from the bed, sternly staring at him.

"I'm glad you're awake, Mister Moor." "Othello, please," he responded.

"Very well."

"I take it you have something to say to me."

"I do," she said. "I don't like you. You put my son in danger, and I'm very displeased that you made him cry. But I also know you have helped him more than I could have. He's become stronger since he met

you. I have no right to anything that happens in his life, not after all the things I've done to him over the years.

"Do you love my son, Mister Moor?"

"With every ounce of my breath," Othello responded.

"Then earn my trust as I must earn his. I won't stand in your way if I deem you worthy of his love."

"What if I never win you over?" he asked.

"Then you just have to keep trying until you do. Don't waste time, Mister Moor. I know many suitors who can easily take your place. Oh, and don't make me a grandmother until you're married.

Despite my impending divorce, I'm a traditionalist, Mister Moor."

Othello knew she was bluffing; it was her way of having some say in Des's life. Of course, Othello indulged Ava. She wasn't so bad and got along well with Maria, who encouraged her to start dating. As for not making her a grandmother, Othello couldn't wait to see her face when they announced the good news. After Othello had gained Ava's approval, they found out Des was pregnant, and at Des's first art showing, Othello proposed.

Des had come into his own in the past couple of years. He opened his art studio, where he taught art and had showings for other up-and-coming artists. He entered a few art competitions, losing and winning a few of them, bringing recognition to his studio. Des welcomed students of all levels and no longer held onto the belief that he did not want to be famous. That thought went out the door when he won his first competition.

As for David Ellington, his life went down the shitter. It started when Ava publicly announced that she was filing for divorce due to infidelity and a love child. His ratings in the polls dropped, but not enough to put him out of the race. However, after all his crimes of bribery, embezzlement, and even murder that not even Ava knew about came to light, he lost his race and his dignity and was now spending life in prison without parole.

With one last look in the mirror, Othello walked out of the suite, ready to claim his man and show him off to the world. He couldn't wait for Des to be in the aisle; he needed to see him now. Taking a few short steps, Othello knocked on Des's room and gasped when he saw his lover dressed in a sparkling white suit and a long jacket that touched the floor with slits on the side. His long hair was cut, revealing his big, beautiful eyes and bright smile.

"You look gorgeous, Tesoro," Othello said in awe.

"So do you," he replied, going to his toes and kissing him on his lips.

"Are you ready to conquer the world with me, Tesoro?"

"We're bound, Othello. Anywhere you go, that is where we will be." He touched his stomach, and Othello placed a hand on top.

"Do you regret it?" Othello asked.

Des chuckled and shook his head. "I'd be a fool to regret a man who would burn the world down just for my love."

Othello leaned down and kissed him. "Then let's go."

Hand in hand, they walked to the altar, with respected dons and business tycoons watching as they took center stage, showing the strength of their love.

THANK YOU

Dear My Wonderful Readers,

Thank you for taking the time to support me. I hope you enjoyed reading Moor. I genuinely enjoyed stepping into the world of Shakespeare. I hope you will continue to read and share this book with the rest of the series.

With all of my thanks and appreciation,

Giovanna (Gia) Reaves

BOOKS BY GIOVANNA REAVES

Audiobooks Available on Audible

Jordan's Pryde

Ryland's Inferno

The Cowboy's Baby

Winter's Promise: Omegaverse Romance

The Drummer's Heartbeat: A Winter Romance

Protecting His Omega

ABOUT THE AUTHOR

Giovanna (Gia) Reaves is my alter ego, who is a dreamer. I spend my days and nights dreaming and thinking of the worlds I want to create with words. I started writing about three years ago, when I was introduced to the world of fan fiction.

I loved the idea of creating a new world around characters that people will fall in love with and come back for more. I am a mother, wife, and military veteran. I enjoy trying new things such as traveling, cooking, and reading. I try to incorporate some of the things I have experienced into my books.

I currently live in Newport, RI, with my two favorite men. If I am not hiding in my cave writing, I love to read and spend time with my hubby and son. I also love listening to R&B and neo-soul when I am writing.

When I'm not writing, I am trying to perfect my baking and decorating skills or learning something new. I love spending time with my husband and son playing video games and traveling.

I love hearing from you.
Email me at GotRomance@GiaReaves.com or sign up for my newsletter to receive updates on what I'm doing next.
Check out my website for more deals and more:
https://giareaves.com
Join my reader's group:
https://www.facebook.com/groups/GiovannasSecretOne-Nighters/

 facebook.com/GiovannasSecretOneNighters

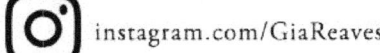 instagram.com/GiaReaves

 tiktok.com/@giarwrites

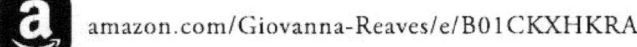 amazon.com/Giovanna-Reaves/e/B01CKXHKRA

 reamstories.com/giovannareaves

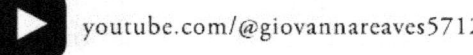 youtube.com/@giovannareaves5712